WATCH HOW
YOU GO

WATCH HOW YOU GO

Tim Hill

ATLANTIC PUBLISHING

Atlantic Publishing
38 Copthorne Road
Croxley Green
Hertfordshire
WD3 4AQ

First published by Atlantic Publishing in 2022

The author would like to thank Peter Lavery for his help.

This is a work of fiction. Names and characters are a product of the
author's imagination and any resemblance to actual persons,
living or dead, is entirely coincidental.

A catalogue record is available for this book from the British Library

ISBN: 978-1-915143-01-3

Printed and bound in Great Britain by
CPI Group (UK), Croydon CR0 4YY

In memory of Jacqueline Keenan

Prologue

She wonders if this will be the last time she'll pass through these double doors; wonders on how many more occasions will she catch June's eye, or Margaret's or Alison's and be buzzed in. She's become pally with them over the past two months, but it's a friendship born of circumstance, one that won't endure once the establishment's mission statement to *make every moment count* is fulfilled.

How does she feel about it if this is the time? Ambivalent, it must be said. Does that sound cold and uncaring? It's not meant to, it really isn't. She loves her grandad, and once he's gone she'll have no immediate family left. But that isn't him in there. Stretched out on a bed, oxygen mask clamped over his face, barely moving, eking out what remained of his time on earth. Bed-bathed. Incontinent. Stripped of dignity. A husk. When he slept, which was most of the time, he looked as if he were laid out on a mortuary slab already. The slight rise and fall of the chest, the odd guttural retch, the occasional lucid snatch of conversation; this was all that separated Graham Price from curtained-off incineration and an RIP notice in the local paper.

"I'm so sorry, Emily, he's gone. Slipped away not half an hour ago. It was all very peaceful."

Margaret, whose last name she doesn't know, squeezes her arm. Emily nods appreciatively at a gesture the woman must have made countless times yet still made it seem a crushing personal blow. Empathy both practised and heartfelt.

Emily is quite calm. The tears have all been shed. She is ready and willing to usher her grandad's cancer-riddled, organ-failing shell on the final leg of its journey. Seventy-six years meant he'd passed the old three-score-years-and-ten rule, yet in 2018 it felt like being short-changed. Still, he was the longest lived of her immediate family. What would her own span be? Had she inherited a genetic time bomb on the maternal side? On the other hand, her mother and sister hadn't died in a way that had implications for her. Or had they? It was difficult to know.

"Can I see him?"

"Of course."

There was no icy chill when she clasped his hand. And the lack of response when she poured out her tender valediction was no different to any number of one-way conversations she'd had with him in recent weeks. Had she not been told he'd gone, it could almost have been like any other visit.

She kissed his cheek, passing her palm up across his forehead, taking in the familiar contours of his skull one final time. She'd done the same when her mother went, glad then, as now, that she'd had the courage to capture that final skin-on-skin imprint. There had been no such goodbye with Chloe, though. She'd been judged too young to cope with seeing her sister's lifeless body. She bore no grudge about the decision. Her mum had lost one treasured daughter, and it was understandable that she should go into protective overdrive with the other.

Emily's eyes wandered. A few cards on the bedside table, a child's drawing Blu Tacked onto the wall. It was the work of *Oliver age 4*, no doubt dragooned by his dad – her cousin Richard – to provide some spiky-sun cheer for his poorly great-grandfather. There wasn't much to clear. Once the body had been removed, it wouldn't take long for the room to be made ready for its next doomed occupant.

She was making ready to leave when she saw it. A thick envelope bearing her name, written in her grandad's unmistakable hand. She'd have recognised it just by the letter y alone, for he always turned the downstroke into an underscore flourish of all five letters. It hadn't been there the day before, had it? Surely she would have noticed? But then, she'd been almost out of the door when she spotted it this time.

Emily waited until she was in her car before opening it. Oddly, she felt more apprehensive pulling open the gummed flap than she'd been when stroking his lifeless hand. She'd been steeling herself for the corporal leave-taking. But to receive a message from – well, not quite beyond the grave – was somehow disconcerting. She thought they'd said all that needed to be said, both on the personal and practical front, long ago. They'd articulated their love for each other. She'd been directed towards a whole sheaf of paperwork relating to the house: deeds, insurance policies, bank accounts, utilities – all the usual paraphernalia. And now this, a curve-ball missive to disturb her equilibrium.

It did that, all right. For this was no addendum to the bulging file already in her possession, no late-order emoting in keepsake cursive.

It was the work of a different dead hand.

1

Donna Kuzminski had made up her mind even before the taxi disgorged her and Zbiggy out into the night air. Before the two had undressed, with neatness levels reflecting her fastidiousness and his more laissez-faire attitude. Before the perfunctory foreplay. Before he lost his erection – which at least saved the bother of another pregnancy-testing rigmarole. Before she spooned into him in a tacit demonstration of an intimacy that went far beyond the sexual. Before she heard the familiar nasal purr that signalled he'd drifted off. And before she pulled away and pleasured herself, consciously clamping her mouth shut at the crucial moment so that the wave broke too inaudibly to disturb him.

She'd hoped it wouldn't come to this, but at 37 Donna had no time left for chance to be the determiner, no time for another false dawn; and no money in the kitty for another medical intervention. They'd tried placing their faith in high-tech equipment and polished professionals, who had taken their cash and advised that IUI and IVF had no guaranteed happy outcome. Wasn't that the truth! Now it was time to load the dice.

Even in a state of post-orgasmic contentedness, she was too aroused to sleep. Twenty minutes of iPad searching told her that what she had in mind was perfectly doable. A smile played on her lips as she swiped, a smile lit up in the device's conspiratorial glow. It was bright enough to have woken her if she'd been asleep, whereas Zbiggy, once gone, was dead to the world. And even if he had stirred, she could simply have brought forward by a few hours what she was proposing. Well, not exactly *everything*.

She tried not to think of it as deceit. It was such an ugly, loaded word, best suited to sordid acts of cheating. It might be stretching a point to describe her plan as noble or pure, but it was well-intentioned and born out of love. Zbiggy was already feeling fragile and emasculated, and she had a gut feeling that there was only so much more strain the marriage could take. Couples with as strong a bond as theirs had been broken by the issue – she'd read about that, too. So if he was to be given a partial truth, it was only because that's all he could cope with. She'd carry the burden, and if there was a child at the end of it, it was a load she was confident she could bear.

"Good night last night. Ben was on form."

There was a perceptible delay before Donna qualified her first remark with the second, not wanting her husband to dwell on how the evening had ended. She needn't have bothered, for Zbiggy's ostrich mentality kept his head well below the parapet of difficult conversations until they were forced upon him.

"Thought he was a bit subdued – by his standards."

Zbiggy dug into his fry-up with gusto, as if to suggest that lazy Sundays and leisurely cooked breakfasts provided some kind of counterbalance to low sperm count and sub-optimal motility. And in truth, though having "poor swimmers" was undoubtedly a blow to his ego, he would have baled out of the baby-making journey long ago if it had been up to him.

"Come to think of it, you're right. Definitely a bit quiet over dinner. Made up for it during *Pictionary*, though … *such* a show-off. Did he say anything to you?"

"Nope."

Zbiggy and Ben had known each other since primary school. They were opposites in many ways; Ben the extrovert, envied by Zbiggy for his easy ebullience, his gift of the gab, his uninhibited guffawing at his own jokes. Zbiggy had used the connection to his advantage in snaring Donna, a blonde beauty he'd thought way out of his league. She was best friends with Ben's wife, Zoe, giving Zbiggy a my-mate-fancies-your-mate conduit when he would never have risked a direct approach. He couldn't believe his luck when he and Donna hit it off. Maybe it helped that they were in their mid-20s, by which time Donna had had her fill of smooth, shallow types who spent longer in front of the mirror than she did, and was drawn to his kindly gaucheness, his steadfast dependability. But if she chose him out of some deep instinct that his qualities marked him out as good father material, that was a ship still firmly anchored in port.

"I've been thinking," Donna began. She'd already blotted Ben and Zoe from her thoughts. They already had the complete set in four-year-old Freddie and Tara, who had just turned two.

It was time to strike.

"Yeah? What about?"

With the last of the toast Zbiggy mopped up the remainder of his egg.

His question was redundant, for he had not the least doubt what it was about. Donna had that look about her, the look that announced they were going to have "a conversation". And "conversation" meant another round-the-houses dialogue about how to complete their family, how to give Donna the broken-night heaven that Zoe and Ben were all too familiar with and which Donna desperately craved.

"Well, I came across this info on Google. It's … oh, best if I just show you. Let me get my iPad."

Donna had the speech all ready, the redacted version, that is. The blacked-out parts were to be filled in later. But she never got the chance to deliver any of it. She padded back down the stairs to find Zbiggy frowning at his phone.

"What's the matter, love?"

"Problem with the Burton Road extension, apparently. Some of the blockwork's collapsed. Need to shoot over and have a gander."

He gave her a bearhug, kissed her cheek and bounded upstairs to get dressed.

"Can't Ben go?" she called after him.

"I'm meeting him there," came the floated reply.

The lie didn't come easily. Ben knew it wouldn't, which is why the text had been quite prescriptive.

Need to talk. Fucked up big time. Can you meet at pub in 30? Don't tell Donna. Say we have collapsed wall at Burton Rd. Thx mate.

2

"Do you remember Jasmine?"

"What, your babysitter?"

Ben nodded. "Was. She's gone off to university."

Zbiggy played with his pint glass, noting that Ben was already three-quarters down his. He was unshaven and unkempt – that was unusual in itself when they were away from the site – but it was the hangdog expression and hunched posture that was the real giveaway. He looked a shrunken version of the man who'd had them rolling around barely twelve hours earlier with his efforts to depict *Ride a Cock Horse to Banbury Cross*.

"Jesus! Don't tell me you've got the hots for her." Then came the inevitable corollary. "You didn't … did you?"

"Don't be a twat. 'Course I never."

Ben took another swig of beer. That was *something*, at least, that he couldn't be accused of, and he allowed the exculpatory declaration to linger before he went on.

"Zoe found this new girl. Carly. Another student."

"So what's the problem? What's wrong with her?"

A wry smile broke across Ben's face, the first time his lugubrious expression had altered. Maybe it was because he liked the use of the pronoun. What's wrong with *her*. Not him. That sat better, even though Zbiggy would see soon enough how the blame game played out.

"Funny thing is, it was me that raised doubts. Might seem an OK sort, I said to Zoe, but what can you tell in five minutes? She said if I'd seen the way Carly was with the kids when they got chatting in town, I wouldn't ask. But at the last minute she did waver a bit. Not second thoughts, just being cautious. We'd done the same for Jas when we first used her."

"Done what? You're freaking me out, mate."

Ben lowered his eyes. This was the bit where he knew Zbiggy would start disapproving. He was the undiluted doting husband, a guy who felt he'd hit the jackpot and had no interest in rolling the dice again. Ben was an opportunist. If temptation fell in his path, he had neither the inclination nor the willpower to deny himself. He was able to compartmentalise a one-off shag without a moment's guilt, all the while convincing himself that his marriage was every bit as rock-solid as Zbiggy's. More so, even. For he knew that for them the baby thing was a biggie, an issue that might one day drive them apart. Zbiggy had said as much. He and Zoe had nothing on that scale hanging over them. That is, until now.

Ben drained his glass and went to the bar for a refill. Zbiggy covered his glass with his hand, just as he'd done at half ten the evening before. Donna had chided him about keeping a lid on the booze to maximise their chances of conceiving naturally. Fat lot of good *that* had done last night.

"OK, this is where it gets messy," Ben continued. "When Jas sat for us the

13

first time, Zoe had me rig up a camera. Just to keep an eye on things, peace of mind and all that. It showed up nothing, that Jas was good as gold. What she reported back was exactly what we could see onscreen. 'Course, there was no camera next time. We trusted her. Now we had this Carly and we wanted to be sure. You'd do the same."

You'd do the same – if you had kids, mate. Ben didn't pussyfoot round the childlessness issue like others did. After a couple of drinks, he was more than likely to toss the firing-blanks grenade into the conversation, even in the presence of strangers. Just for the reaction, just for the craic. One time, after he'd played away, he told Zbiggy what a pisser it was to have to faff about with condoms. Wouldn't it be great to bang away bareback, not having to worry if they were really on the Pill? He might just as well have said *I envy you your lack of firepower.*

"So we decided to watch her, that first time. This was three weeks ago, our anniversary. We even spoke about her over dinner. Zoe asked if I thought Carly was attractive. 'Course, I made all the right noises. I wasn't falling for that one. Said when she got dolled up, how could I possibly notice anyone else? Trouble is, Zoe didn't see it. Said she was feeling frumpy: never quite shifted the last bit of baby weight after Tara was born. She had this sexy red dress she knew was my favourite. But that night she chose something plain and conservative. Said frocks like that were for the Carlys of this world, not her, not any more.

"What should have been a cracking night went tits up. All seemed OK at home. Carly said there hadn't been a peep from the kids. I paid for a taxi to drop her in town – she was meeting someone, she said. That didn't help when me and Zoe made it upstairs – Carly off to party at midnight and Zoe feeling all mumsy. *I had an arse like that once. And she doesn't need any bloody make-up!*

"She was wiping her slap off when she came out with that comment. The usual ritual. I think I slid my arms under hers and cupped her boobs. Wrong move. OK, I know you're thinking it wasn't the most tactful way to show I still fancied her, but I'm better with actions than words, you know that."

"Can't argue with you there, mate." Zbiggy surreptitiously glanced at his watch. He didn't want to be stuck in a pub with Ben on a Sunday lunchtime.

He was suddenly thinking even a "conversation" with Donna would be preferable to wherever this seedy-sounding story was leading. And if the destination involved him being asked to provide Ben with a cover story, that's when he would bail.

"Anyway, she slapped my hand away, and then I got arsey. Told her if she felt the need to compete with stick-thin 18-year-olds, she ought to do something about it. I regretted that straightaway. Apologised, but it made no difference. The damage was done.

"Needless to say, sex was off the menu. Sex wasn't actually *on* the menu that often. She flounced off to bed in her passion-killer pyjamas, and I said, in that case, I was off to watch telly.

"I'd almost forgotten about the recording. I watched that instead. Most of it was fast-forward material. She had her nose in a book. TV was on. She was drinking from a bottle of water. At one point she disappeared upstairs, gone for a minute or so. Couldn't hear any crying or anything, so assumed she'd just been checking on the kids, maybe went to the bog.

"Then she took a call on her iPad. I couldn't make out what was said, but it was obviously a boyfriend on FaceTime. There was some giggling. I heard her say "No way!" – that was a fair bit louder. It was like she was pretending to be shocked but you could tell she wasn't really.

"I soon found out what it was about. She undid her jeans, pushed them down and put her hand inside her knickers. She held the iPad with the other hand, angling it so the boyfriend could watch her masturbate. I don't think she came.

"I know I did."

3

Donna had considered Ben, of course she had. And dismissed the idea in a millisecond. Where to start in the list of reasons why he was all wrong? Yes, the smoking and overindulgence on booze and fast food were lifestyle choices, not genetic factors. Or were they? Maybe he had some predisposition for the immediate, pleasurable hit, without a thought for the long-term consequences. That certainly went for his attitude to sex. She knew Zoe had issued more than one final warning during their dating days. He was probably still at it; it was in his nature. The quickfire arrival of two kids played in his favour, for Ben knew – as did Donna – that the chances of Zoe breaking up the family on the back of an indiscretion were virtually nil. Zoe was a nester, someone who would forgive almost anything to save rocking the domestic boat.

But even if Ben were a perfect physical specimen with a full tick-box of admirable qualities, Donna would have steered well clear. It was too close to home. Ben and Zbiggy were like brothers, and for what she had in mind, a little more distance was required. Donna needed someone of their circle that fitted her template, someone she knew well enough to sell the idea to but not so well that it would be impossible to keep the spinning plates from crashing to the floor.

Rob.

Rob was perfect. He and Andrea had been there the previous evening, making up the usual six. To get the superficial out of the way, he was the handsomest of the three guys by any yardstick. Six-footer. Well-proportioned. Thick, wavy, collar-length brown hair framed his regular features. He stuck with designer stubble rather than go with the full-beard trend. It suited him, and, Donna reckoned, suggested someone who didn't just run with the fashionable herd. The two of them would surely make a beautiful child together. Donna tried not to focus only on the shallow stuff, but it was there nonetheless.

Not that she fancied him – that was important, too. Well, maybe he fell into the Snog category, without ever threatening to jump over into Marry. Donna had all she wanted in sweet-natured, ursine Zbiggy, even if his hands sometimes felt like sandpaper as they stroked her skin. Rob had long, elegant fingers; she'd noticed that. They were fingers that worked a keyboard for a living, not a lump hammer. They were fingers that played some nice guitar when he and Andrea were playing host to their get-togethers.

She and Zoe had got to know Andrea first. They'd been on a fitness kick three years back – in between Freddie and Tara – and bonded with Andrea over the reviled cross-trainer at the local gym. It wasn't long before the lycra was ditched in favour of coffee and shopping dates. The invitation wasn't far behind. *You must come for dinner, we're dying to meet Rob.*

He came across as diffident for a good-looking guy. Take the previous night. He'd done his turns at Pictionary, but would happily have given up his spot, the polar opposite of Ben, who would have grabbed the chance to hold court if anyone wanted to pass. Donna quite liked that. She also liked the fact that he and Andrea had nine-year-old Bethany. Of all the traits she was looking for, the ability to get a live, healthy sperm into one of her eggs was right at the top of the list.

4

"So you jerked off watching film of your babysitter playing with herself? Is that it? Is that *all*? Come on, mate, you've done a *lot* worse than that in your time."

Zbiggy checked his watch again, less surreptitiously this time. He wanted to get back, now welcoming another ear-bending about where they should go next in their efforts to conceive. "I thought it was something *serious*."

Ben gave a hollow laugh. His elbows straddled his pint glass, and as he massaged the thinning hair around his temples, unnoticed flecks were being deposited into the drink.

"Oh, it's fucking serious, all right. We're talking shit creek, mate. Wouldn't be sitting here if I'd stopped at having a crafty wank, would I?"

5

"Hiya, Rob."

"Donna? Yeah, hi. You want Andrea?"

It was a silly question. If she'd wanted Andrea, she'd have rung a different number. But Rob was thrown by the fact that they'd never had a phone conversation. He and Donna had swapped numbers when the socialising had begun, but Andrea was invariably the filter when it came to making arrangements. *Does the 17th work for you? Check with Rob and get back if it's a problem.*

Donna had her cover story all ready. If Andrea had been around and within earshot, she was calling to see if Rob had noticed anything odd in Ben's behaviour the previous evening. Bloke to bloke. Had Ben said anything?

She had Zbiggy to thank for that little nugget, but it was a card she didn't have to play. Unbidden, Rob immediately offered up the information that Andrea and Bethany had popped round to see Andrea's widower dad.

"It was you I wanted to catch, actually."

"Oh? Right."

"Bit delicate. Not really suitable for a phone convo. I was wondering, could we meet up for coffee? Tomorrow, maybe?"

"Tomorrow? Er, yes. I guess. Is there a problem?"

Nothing you can't fix, Rob.

"Like I say, it's a bit delicate. How about one o'clock at Starbucks? That's near your office, isn't it? Oh, and can we keep this between the two of us?"

She gave a hurried goodbye and broke the connection before he'd finished his mumbled assent. Her heart was racing. Any longer and her voice would have cracked. She felt grubby. Clandestine meetings. Betrayal. This wasn't who she was. But then, ten minutes later, all negative thoughts were swept away. They were replaced by euphoria and excitement, for she had started the hare running. It was to be an unclean race, but if there was a baby at the end of it, the ends justified the means. Zbiggy would see that.

Or rather, he would see only what Donna wanted him to. She was going to be the producer, director, scriptwriter, editor and projectionist. Zbiggy was the guy in the stalls, suspending disbelief and taking it all in at face value. A happy punter when the credits rolled, that's the part she had in mind for him.

6

"I should have come clean to Zoe. About what I'd caught on camera, I mean – not about knocking one out of the park while I was watching it. I did the opposite. By the time we were talking again the next day, I mentioned that I'd checked the footage and it was all routine, boring stuff. Also said we ought to make more time for ourselves, get out more. She agreed. Apologised for being grouchy, said she was just on a bit of a downer.

"So last Monday, we're going tenpin bowling with a mate of Zoe's and her new bloke. She books Carly again. And what did I do? Only went and set the camera up again. The spying was only meant to be a one-off, to make sure she was an OK sort. And, let's face it, just 'cos she had her hands down her pants for five minutes when the kids were asleep, it didn't mean she was unfit to look after them. If that was the case, I'd be bang to rights meself!

"Anyway, she wore these tight jeans – Zoe, this is – and while I was winding up for a spare, she mentioned she wasn't wearing any knickers. Fair put me off me stroke, it did. Ball straight in the gutter. Anyway, we had the best sex in ages that night. Went at it like a couple of newlyweds. Dunno if she'd had words with your Donna, or Andrea, or this other mate we were out with – Holly – but it looked like somebody had put her up to it, suggested she spice things up a bit, keep me on me toes.

"Talk about fucking timing. I swear if I'd known what I was in for a few hours earlier, I'd've pulled the plug on the recording. 'Course, by then it was too late. It was already in the fucking can, waiting for a dickhead like me to watch it. And I did. Could've deleted it, but couldn't stop meself from seeing what I'd got. It was a lot more than I bargained for, I can tell you."

Zbiggy's phone pinged.

"Donna. Asking if everything's OK and when I'll be back. I need to shoot, mate, or she'll know something's off."

Ben drained his glass and accepted Zbiggy's half-drunk beer when it was slid across the table. It was obvious that, whether Ben had company or not, his session wasn't over.

"No probs, mate. You get off. No point us both being in the shit. Laters."

7

Donna had smelt the beer on Zbiggy's breath but said nothing. The whole thing had Ben's stamp all over it. Who sends a text if their wall's fallen down? That's something worth yelling down the phone about. Zbiggy had made some lame comment about a bit of green blockwork being knocked over. Probably kids, he said. He was such a crap liar. Too loyal to Ben by half. But then, she could hardly complain about that when it was a quality she so admired when it came to how he was with her. Zbiggy was a rock, to friend and lover alike. Whereas Ben, for all his good points, all his charm and easy affability, came with a trust health warning.

Their fingers were intertwined as they walked. It was warm for late September, and Donna had suggested they enjoy what may well have been the last coatless day before the weather turned autumnal. The forecast was for it to get chillier. Not that that bothered Zbiggy. He seemed to have his own central-heating system going full blast at any time of the year, and was used to Donna warming her hands and feet on him.

She had another reason for suggesting a walk. With people around, Zbiggy was a lot less likely to sound off over what she was going to suggest. It was unlikely anyway, really. It was years since she'd seen him lose it, and that was provoked by a bloke mistreating a dog. They were circling the very park where that had happened, where the owner turned very sheepish and sloped off, probably to continue the abuse once he was out of sight.

They'd discussed getting a dog themselves after the incident. Zbiggy's see-through idea. It was around the time of the second attempt at IVF, and Donna had closed the subject down pretty quickly. A dog to enhance the family was fine; one acquired as a proxy in case they didn't conceive was a non-starter.

"I know we said we wouldn't throw any more money at it," she began.

"Oh, here we go." His words were heavy with weariness and resignation.

"No, listen! It's not what you think. Hear me out."

"It's not about the money, love. Haven't you had enough of the disappointment? I hate to see that look on your face when your hopes are dashed over and over again."

"*My* hopes!" Donna flashed. "Don't you put this all on me, Zbiggy. That's *not* fair."

"I didn't mean … You know what I meant."

He cast his eyes down like a schoolboy wrongfully scolded. He'd done nothing, but sometimes that didn't matter.

Donna squeezed his hand to make the peace, to reset. The effect was immediate, like the teacher who has not only wiped the slate after dispensing a punishment but has handed out a gold star for meritorious effort.

"What if we could stack the odds a lot more in our favour, at virtually no cost? How does that sound?"

"Eh? I don't see …"

She had her phone at the ready, primed to show the screen grab.

"There's a guy here reckons he's helped hundreds of women to conceive. Just fifty quid a time. Look."

Zbiggy had always struggled with reading, preferring to mouth the words of the online article as a kind of verbal comfort blanket. He read in monotone:

Is Michael Phillips Britain's most prolific sperm donor? He claims his "love juice", as he calls it, is as potent as it gets, with hundreds of grateful childless couples and individuals to prove it. Phillips, 44, has turned his "gift" into a thriving business, charging £50 a time for wares that he advertises on Facebook. He maintains his success rate compares very favourably with other interventions. "In any case," he adds, "think how many pots of my love juice you could buy for the cost of one procedure at a fertility clinic..."

"You mean you want to use this guy?"

"No. Not necessarily. Maybe. I'm talking about the principle. It's a measly fifty quid, for God's sake. It's a chance."

Whether it was fifty quid, a hundred, or even a hundred and fifty down the pan, it was well worth it.

"So … do you have to do it with him? 'Cos if that's the case …"

"Don't be daft! If you'd read on, you'll see he supplies a pot of semen and a syringe applicator thingy. You do the rest yourself."

"Oh. Right. No funny business, then?"

"No funny business."

Down the pan and right round the U-bend.

He was such a crap liar.

She was quickly finding out that she wasn't.

8

Ben Fuller was well over the limit when he drove home. He convinced himself he was fine, as he always did. It only applied when he was on his own, without Zoe to apply the handbrake. And if the kids were in the car, that was different. In chancing it when driving solo, it didn't occur to him that he might hit a vehicle containing somebody else's wife or child.

If he could have accepted a drink-driving offence in return for wiping out the last six days, he would have jumped at it. For that would have rewound to the bowling night, the night he'd set another visual trap for Carly. The night the trap snapped shut with him in its teeth.

He'd played it back on the Tuesday evening, when Zoe was bathing Freddie and Tara. There was no phone call this time. But she kept looking at her watch, as if she were waiting for something to happen. She went upstairs twice, the camera catching her lithe denim-clad legs through the balusters before she disappeared out of shot. Checking on the kids. Checking the coast was clear.

The telly was on low, so he'd heard the phone ping on the audio. Carly immediately went to the door; it was obviously a prearranged signal. That's when Ben had his first sighting of Danny Croft – not that he knew his name at that point. He was a gangly youth, with low-slung jeans and high-swept fair hair. Piercings and bumfluff.

He had a four-pack of lager with him and immediately cracked one open. Carly declined. He then started to roll a joint, stopping in his tracks when Carly batted his hand. They channel-hopped and chatted for while, the conversation too indistinct for Ben to make out. Then they began kissing. His hand soon slid down to her crotch. She had a boyish figure, like a model's, and he lingered only briefly over her underdeveloped breasts.

Carly feigned protest, but this time there was no slapping of the hand. Weed was off the agenda. Sex clearly wasn't.

She'd laid her coat on the sofa and they did it there. Or rather, she gave him a blowjob and got nothing in return. It didn't take long. Afterwards she seemed keen to usher him on his way. Maybe the thought of being caught out made her too worried to think about her own pleasure. Danny Croft looked like he'd got what he came for, and was more than happy to go. A blowjob without having to reciprocate. Result or what?

It was when she called him back to gather the remaining cans of beer that he noticed. "This fucking thing's on!" he said, pointing to the camera. His face was right up against the lens; the audio now loud and clear. He made a wanker gesture. Carly said, "Oh shit!" and told him to find the off switch, quick.

Fade to black.

9

Ben would gladly have broken off contact with Carly. There was embarrassment and wrongdoing on both sides, so a mutual tactical withdrawal had a lot to recommend it. But it had to come from Carly. How could Ben explain to Zoe that they should look elsewhere for a sitter? *Because I was filming her on the sly and caught her getting it on with her boyfriend – who wasn't even supposed to be there.* That wasn't going to fly.

Zoe made the next move. It was Friday morning, before work. "You'll need your dancing shoes tonight, husband, because we are going to a gig. Well, a local band playing at the Half Moon, so the mosh pit might be a bit tame. Let's see how your moves are these days. Carly's booked for half-seven."

Ben knew right then that he was screwed. If Zoe had phoned her up, all chatty, Carly knew who was doing the spying and who was out of the loop. It gave her the whip hand unless he came clean to Zoe. He couldn't do that, not as a first resort, anyway.

He'd insisted on giving Carly a lift home that night. Stuck to shandy, then soft drinks, so that he'd be OK to drive. *You have a few, though, love … enjoy yourself.* Pretending he was doing Zoe a good turn when the main objective was to extricate himself from deep shit.

Neither of them had wanted to blink first. Nothing much was said during the journey, just idle chat. Then, when she directed him to pull over, Carly had invited him in. There were things that needed discussing, she said. He nodded, almost relieved that it was out in the open.

She'd done what kids get up to all the time. Bang out of order to do it under somebody else's roof, but nothing to raise an eyebrow these days. A non-story. On the other side of the ledger, she knew if Ben was filming her and not telling Zoe, that was the kind of thing that could wreck a marriage. Imagine the field day the papers would have with it: *The Peeping Tom dad... Ben the Builder.* Can he film it? Yes, he can. He stood to lose a lot more than her, and they both knew it.

Ben wanted to apologise, tell her the recording had been deleted and it wouldn't happen again. He wanted her to say sorry in turn, for breaking a trust and bringing a stranger into their home. He wanted them to call it quits. There, we're even. That hope died a swift death at her overture.

She'd asked for money. Quite up front about it. Ben felt like saying the swish, white-walled flat was nothing like the mould-infested gaff he'd shared when he was nineteen. This was no student accommodation. Bank of mum and dad, he'd thought. On the other hand, if she had plenty in the bank, why was she bothering babysitting for pin money?

She'd laid it all at her boyfriend's door. It was all Danny Croft's doing. He was pressurising her, she said. Chance to make a quick buck. Nothing personal.

Ben didn't know what to believe. Then she'd showed him the bruises on her legs and abdomen. Sobbed her heart out. Said it'd go worse for her if Ben didn't come through. Said she'd tried to break with him, but it wasn't so easy, not when she was doing a college course and tied to a routine. He knew where to find her pretty much any time, day or night, and what buttons to press. He controlled her.

Ben had asked if she'd involved the police. She said she had no proof, they wouldn't be interested. And it would just make things worse. Was that true? Or was she one of those women who just seemed to be drawn into abusive relationships, a permanent victim?

He'd put his arm round her, offering comfort. She was in pieces, poor thing. Ben wasn't normally a sucker for waterworks, but blokes who used women for a punchbag, that was bang out of order.

Carly had buried her face in his shoulder for quite some time, sniffling and sobbing. There was an awkward moment as he angled his head down to try and catch her eye, just as she raised hers. Their lips had all but touched. For a fleeting moment he thought she'd wanted him to kiss her, but it passed in an instant.

She'd pulled herself together then, thanked him for his understanding and said she'd do her best to get Danny off his back.

"Yeah, you do that, love." That was his parting shot before haring back home to avoid arousing Zoe's suspicions.

On the Saturday, while Zoe was busy in the kitchen ahead of that evening's dinner party, Ben had texted, offering two hundred pounds. He and Zoe had a joint account, he told her, and it was all he could get without raising suspicion. She'd replied saying she wasn't sure it was enough but she'd do her best to persuade Danny. Had anyone noticed how edgy he was over dinner and during Pictionary, until the message came through? Had he put on a good enough front?

Carly seemed to be on board – that was a positive. But then the doubts crept in. What if this was just the opening gambit? That's when he'd texted Zbiggy. He needed a mate as a sounding board. Zbiggy knew him better than anyone, knew he'd sailed close to the wind many a time. He wanted Zbiggy to tell him it was just another scrape, that it would blow over like all the others.

But Donna had reeled Zbiggy in before he could finish the story, so it would have to wait until they were back on site the next morning. Maybe it would all be sorted by then. If the problem went away for two hundred quid, he reckoned he'd dodged a bullet.

Two hundred quid from his own bank account. It never paid to be too honest, in Ben's experience.

10

Donna played with her latte, creating pathways in the froth and watching them close up. She checked her watch for the umpteenth time. Seven minutes to one. She'd got to the coffee shop ridiculously early, which achieved nothing except allow time for her doubts and fears to be stoked anew. There was still time to cancel; all it would take was a text. No. She'd come this far, there was no backing out now.

She'd already messaged Michael Phillips and received a swift, cloyingly rehearsed response saying he would be happy to assist. Mostly copy-and-pasted, no doubt, with just a minor tweaking to give the impression of personal service. Terms were restated, success rates underlined. She learned nothing that hadn't been detailed in the article she'd shown Zbiggy, save for his location. The love juice merchant was an hour's drive away: sixty miles at a pound a mile, or thirty if agreement could be reached on a midway meet. Still cheap compared with the clinical services they'd tried. Too cheap, the white-coat brigade would say. She'd read of the risks, scanned a host of scare stories. Private arrangements meant no screening, no regulation and a murky legal situation, the Wild West of the conception landscape. On the other hand, warnings were irrelevant if there was no baby at the end of it. And the official, kitemarked, rubber-stamped, expensive channels had failed that key test.

Michael Phillips had spread his seed far and wide, of that there was no doubt. One of the many red flags about pursuing such a path concerned the possibility of half-siblings meeting up in later life, oblivious of their blood tie. She wouldn't be troubling Zbiggy with that particular detail. It was important that he believed Michael Phillips represented the best way forward for them.

Rob Allen arrived a couple of minutes past the hour. The place was rammed now, and it took a few moments for him to scan the room and pick out Donna's raised hand.

"Sorry I'm late. Had to take a call just as I was about to leave."

"Just got here myself," Donna lied, pointing to her still untouched latte to prove the point. It was tepid when she finally took a sip, watching Rob as he ordered himself a flat white and chicken wrap. He looked good in a suit, businesslike without any hint of stiffness or pomposity. If it was true that women are the decision makers when it comes to buying a house, she reckoned Rob Allen must do pretty well. *It's a cracking little buy. Good location, local schools performing well. Just needs a bit of TLC. The vendor is a keen seller and would consider an offer.* There were probably a fair few wives who wouldn't have minded if Rob himself had been included in the goods and chattels. But Donna was more interested in the businesslike aspect, for that was what this was about: trying to put their friendship in temporary abeyance in favour of a detached, formal relationship.

"Don't tell me. Let me guess. You've got itchy feet and Zbiggy's not keen. You want to find a property on the q.t. and sell him the idea as a done deal. Yes?"

"No, Rob, we don't want to move. We're perfectly happy where we are."

"Oh, right." He seemed taken aback that his guess had been wide of the mark.

"It's a personal thing, nothing to do with work. A favour."

"OK. Shoot."

He took a bite of his wrap, drawing a serviette across his mouth to prevent food particles becoming lodged in the stubble.

"We like our house, apart from the fact that the room we had marked out for the nursery still isn't occupied."

Rob stopped chewing momentarily. His eyebrows went up a slight notch. He was so convinced that Donna wanted to speak to him with his estate agent hat on that he hadn't considered an alternative reason for the meeting. But he was used to hearing domestic stories covering the entire relationship spectrum. *I know we only moved in last year, but we need a quick sale as Simon's been made redundant ... The wife's been diagnosed with MS so it's got to be a bungalow ... Too many memories now Pete's gone, I need a fresh start ...*

He quickly recovered his poise.

"How's all that going? Still attending a clinic?"

Donna shook her head. "We had our one free go at IVF, plus two more that we paid for. Zbiggy's ready to call it a day. I'm not."

So far, so factual. Merely stating what probably more people than she imagined already knew. Gossip travelled. She'd been told of a woman in the next street who ate nothing but crisps and Diet Coke. Donna didn't know the woman, much less know if there was any truth in the rumour. Maybe it was a Chinese whispers-style distortion, that she ploughed through a tub of Pringles and two-litre bottle of cola every day, on top of regular meals. But the story sounded much better given a touch of drama and dietary exclusivity. For all she knew, people she'd never met were being fed all manner of misinformed twaddle about her and Zbiggy's situation. *I heard it's her tubes … she aborted one without telling him, apparently … he's already got kids, just not with her … there's a dodgy hereditary history, that's why they're steering well clear …*

"Ah! I see," said Rob.

She doubted that very much.

"He's incredibly sensitive about it, as you can imagine. You know what it's like, men and their manhood."

"Mmm. Hard-wired that way. We're simple creatures."

She returned his smile with a wry version.

"The thing is, Rob, I've been looking into finding a donor. A sperm donor. We found this guy on the internet who does it, with a good success rate, apparently."

She waited as he polished off the last of the wrap. She could see he still hadn't guessed. There was no flicker. If he had worked out what was coming next, he ought to have packed in the estate agency business and joined the million-dollar poker circuit.

"Go for it. Sounds like a good idea as long as you do all the checks. Not really my area …"

"I'd like you to be part of it," she cut in. In the end, blurting it out was easiest. "We want to use this internet guy, but I'd like to use yours too."

Did he notice the change of pronoun, she wondered?

"Blimey. Jesus. Phew."

"It wasn't a problem for Jesus's parents, as I recall. If immaculate conception was on offer, I'd take it."

It was her turn to smile now, his to give the wry reaction.

"Look, Rob, I know it's a biggie, but let me give you my reasons, and if it's a no-go I don't want it to affect our friendship."

Donna paused in case he wanted to pull the plug without hearing any more. But she could see he was struggling to field the ultimate curve ball, so ploughed on to fill the void.

"The way I see it, having two donors is a big plus. Obviously it doubles the chance of success. But it also creates anonymity. I wouldn't want to know who the father was, and it goes without saying that Zbiggy would be on the birth certificate, the dad in all respects except biologically. We could just find two random internet sellers, but I'm nervous enough about going that route as it is. Plus it would add to the costs …"

She knew that was a weak point in the argument and deliberately added it as an addendum to the prepared spiel. Would Rob know that sperm changed hands privately for so little?

She continued. "I remember learning in history at school about how one person in a firing squad was given a blank cartridge in their rifle." She was filling now, winging it as there was still no response forthcoming. "So no one knew for sure who fired the fatal bullet. That's kind of what I'm getting at. Preserve the doubt. Could be the internet bloke's, could be yours. No questions asked."

Actually, Rob, that's a teensy bit of bullshit. If you go along with this, the one that made it to the egg would indeed be yours. The bloke who has semen incontinence at fifty quid a pop will have that batch of his famous love juice lost to the drainage system, I can guarantee that. So when he reaches the magic figure of one thousand that he's so proudly hankering after, he'll in fact still be one short of the mark.

"So. What do you say?"

11

Ben hadn't flirted with Mrs Hennessey that morning. There was none of the usual banter, no comments suggesting she must have had a string of admirers back in the day, and that even pushing pensionable age she was still hot to trot. *Fifty-five? Never. I don't believe it. Come on, I want to see the birth certificate.* There was none of that today. He just accepted the proffered tea and biccies when they appeared, and focused on getting the extension up to the wall plate.

There was no Mr Hennessey. She'd said her crematorium goodbyes to him two years before. Indeed, it was with the proceeds of the various policies and payouts that she'd decided to splash out on an orangery. Ben, naturally, chose not to point out that she was extending a property when the number of occupants had reduced by half. *You indulge yourself, love. Gotta have the odd treat. What's the point of living if you don't enjoy yourself?*

He could have fucked her. They both knew it. And she really was fit for her age. OK, not commensurate with the buttering up he gave her, but not bad. He'd done pity fucks before, maybe not quite Julia Hennessey's age but on the flip side, with meatier and less attractive women. Maybe he still would have her, when the project was just about over. A golden goodbye to reciprocate the last stage payment.

But he wasn't thinking about that today. He couldn't focus on anything until the mess with Carly had been resolved.

Zbiggy was now up to speed, for all the good that did. He could lug large timbers around in ways that would have made a Health and Safety inspector have a clipboard meltdown, but he was not a natural problem solver, not an ideas man. He hadn't even heard of an orangery when Ben told him that was their next job. *Just a posh conservatory, mate, no sweat.*

In this case, though, it was unfair to expect Zbiggy to uncover a loophole, spot a get-out clause, when there clearly wasn't one. The ball was in Carly's court, hers and that toe-rag of a boyfriend. *Scrawny little fucker dips his bread on my sofa and now he tries to screw me over for two hundred quid.*

He'd already withdrawn the money. He'd swung by a cashpoint on the way to work, hoping that Carly would come through before the end of the day; that he could hand over the money and draw a line under the whole thing. All that would then remain was for her to tell Zoe her circumstances had changed the next time she was asked to babysit. Nothing to bat an eyelid about. Sitters came and went. No explanation needed. First Jasmine. Now Carly.

He was put out of his misery at three o'clock. *Danny says he'll take the 200 but he wants it today. Where can we meet?*

Ben exhaled loudly, the pent-up worry released in one lung-emptying breath.

Where r u now?

In town. Finished college for the day. How about Starbucks?

OK. 20 mins.

The jauntiness wasn't quite fully restored as he took the dirty mugs to the threshold of the kitchen door and called out to Mrs Hennessey. Another hour and he could put it all behind him.

"Mrs H? Are you there?" he called.

She appeared within seconds, waving her hands around in a way he'd seen Zoe do after putting on nail varnish. "Trying out a new colour," she said, brandishing a set of fuchsia pink talons. "What do you think?"

"Depends where you're digging them in, love."

"Cheeky! You and Zbiggy ready for another brew?"

"He might, but let your nails dry first. I've got a bit of an emergency to sort and gotta dash. Don't suppose you've got a spare envelope by any chance?"

She rummaged in a dresser on the opposite wall, while he stood, muddy-booted and shirt-sleeved, in the doorway. Was that bit of bending over in the too-short skirt for his benefit, he wondered? Probably. And he probably would fuck her before the job was out, turkey neck and all.

He never learned.

12

Ben had no idea that he'd missed Donna and Rob by a couple of hours in the same coffee shop. That awkward stand-off was thus avoided, none of the three having to fumble for a reason why they were having their respective *tête-à-têtes*. It was left to conjecture as to who would have waved away their cosy-looking afternoon assignation best.

Just bumped into the teenage babysitter and thought we'd pop in for a brew, chew the fat, hang out.

What, idle the afternoon away with a teenage college girl you barely know when you're supposed to be at work? Leaving Zbiggy to crack on with the extension? How would Zoe feel about that?

Rob wanted some birthday gift ideas for Andrea.

Really? Why not just call or text? Isn't a lunch date just a *little bit* OTT for suggesting a spa day or what kind of bangle to buy?

Fortune had favoured them equally. No explanations were needed. Donna and Rob were long gone by the time Ben slipped the envelope into Carly's lap. He assured her again that the videos had been deleted. Videos, plural. For Ben decided it wouldn't have passed the smell test if he'd claimed that he'd recorded her the second time but not the first. It was left unsaid as to what he'd seen. She didn't ask whether he'd masturbated while watching her, either her solo performance in Act One or the duet with Danny Croft in Act Two.

"I'm not a bad sort, you know," said Ben. "Bit of a knob at times and, OK, a bit of a letch. What red-blooded 35-year-old bloke isn't?"

"And I shouldn't have let Danny come round to your place."

Both knew this was no let's-put-it-all-behind-us-and-start-afresh moment. There was no airbrushing of the record to be done. It was the parting of the ways.

"Can I leave it to you to tell Zoe you can't babysit any more – I mean, to come up with some excuse?

"I guess."

"Zoe's the kind to take stuff at face value, so she'll believe whatever you tell her." He'd profited from that gullibility enough over the years. "And if I were you, I'd ditch that dickhead of a fella soon as. You're an attractive girl, you could do a lot better for yourself. Obviously brainy, a lot smarter than me. Look at these hands; I bet yours will never look like this."

He showed them, palms up and palms down, rough and calloused, grime permanently embedded under the fingernails.

"I'll try. To break it off, I mean."

With that, Carly jumped up, gave him the kind of hug that a dad and daughter might share, and left.

Ben allowed himself a satisfied smile. Job done. He'd fleetingly considered offering to sort this Danny Croft kid out. The little prick had got his end away on their sofa and rinsed him for two hundred notes. Part of Ben wanted to see if he was as handy with his fists when he wasn't facing an eight-stone girl. But it was too risky. He didn't want the little fucker turning up on his doorstep black and blue, spouting off to Zoe about the footage. *Check your bank account, yeah? You'll see your nutter husband withdrew two hundred quid at the beginning of the month to pay me off. Ask yourself why he'd do that?*

No. Best left. Not his problem. If she wanted to play the victim, why should he care?

He decided it wasn't worth going back to the job site, choosing instead to

32

linger over the remains of his cappuccino. He noticed Carly had left some of hers so he tried that, too.

"Jeez, that's disgusting. What is it?" The question was aimed at one of the table clearers, a girl of about Carly's age, taller, with a curtain fringe and overload of eye make-up.

"That's one of the nitro range. Don't you like it?"

"Not my cuppa tea, love. More of a Tetley man, meself. Each to their own, eh? Wouldn't do for us all to be the same."

On another day he might have pursued it. But his wedding ring was in plain view and anyway, it was a bit too close to home, especially after having only just extricated himself from one tight spot. It wouldn't be long, though. Julia Hennessey, or A. N. Other. He couldn't resist the chase or the danger – just maybe not the next babysitter. He was stupid, but not a complete idiot.

13

In the end it was Zbiggy who insisted on The George. Donna had said the Travelodge near the motorway roundabout would do just fine, but he wouldn't hear of it. It was almost as though he was thinking, *I may not be able to give you a baby, but I'll bloody make sure no missus of mine has to try and impregnate herself in a Travelodge bog.*

They'd settled with Michael Phillips on £150, for The George was just a short hop for them, a 115-mile round trip for him. Bit of discount, to show good faith, said the love-juice purveyor. It was still dirt cheap compared with what Donna and Zbiggy had shelled out already over the years.

They ordered tea and cake for want of something to do to oil the wheels of the transaction. Phillips said it really wasn't necessary, that he was happy for a quick turnaround once the exchange had been made. That was the norm, he explained. But he deferred when he saw that an extra bit of hand-holding was required. It was nothing new. Everyone who used his service was well aware of his track record – after all, he trumpeted it loudly enough himself. When all was said and done, that was the main attraction, his USP.

Some of the couples or singletons he'd dealt with didn't just want a firm handshake and a sealed deal. Some wanted a feeling that they weren't one of a large herd, to know a little more about the person whose genes they were potentially piping aboard into their familial line.

Phillips was nothing if not a pragmatist. At forty-four he was long in the tooth for the official donor list. Not that he would have wanted any part of that, thanks very much. Why on earth would he? You couldn't sell even the most potent love juice for a profit, and they limited you to ten kids. Ten! That wasn't a business model. No, far better to strike out on his own, make direct contact with the cash-strapped, desperate childless, cut out the expensive middleman.

These two, Donna and Zbiggy, seemed perfect customers. He got a bit edgy when unattached, broody women contacted him, saying they wanted a baby, which they'd raise alone if there were no co-parenting takers. None of those had come back to bite him ... paternity suits, claims for child support. But he knew it could happen. There was no getting away from it these days. Anonymity had been swept away in 2005, which sent most sperm donors running for the hills. The accredited facilities took a massive hit after that. Blokes who'd been used to earning an easy thirty quid – *no questions asked, on your way, mate* – decided in their droves it was no longer worth the candle. Even the altruistic brigade were scared off. But Michael Phillips ploughed on in true entrepreneurial fashion. He had no other real marketable skill, anyway.

Donna and Zbiggy were his favourite kind of customers, a devoted couple who just needed him to light the touch-paper and then fuck off. Which he was more than happy to do. And who knows, the extra twenty minutes he'd spent chatting with them might end in a rebooking if the first go didn't work. That was good business. Plus the traffic would be lighter if he left it a bit before heading off.

"Right. All done."

Donna looked exactly the same as she had before she'd gone to the loo twenty minutes earlier. Zbiggy couldn't stop himself from clamping an arm round her shoulder, as though she needed comforting after a distressing ordeal; like she was in the recovery room following a life-threatening operation. It was all he could bring to the party.

"Good. Well, I'll be on my way, then. It was great to meet you, and, you know, if the need arises to do this again …"

"Let's hope not, eh?" Zbiggy replied brusquely, thrusting out a hand to close proceedings. "How do you feel, love?" he said, after Phillips had gone.

"I'm fine. Don't fuss, Zbiggy."

It was sharp and wholly undeserved, and she instantly regretted it. "Come on, love, let's go home."

Inside her handbag lay the plastic pot and syringe, the former sluiced out, the latter unused. Michael Phillips' love juice was somewhere in the underground pipe network, presumably on its way to a sewage treatment plant. She'd considered putting a little of the stuff in the syringe for effect, but Zbiggy wouldn't have rumbled even if it was left under his nose in its pristine state. She'd bin it and the plastic pot as soon as they got home. Donna had already ordered her own multi-pack insemination kit off Amazon. Ten sets for twenty quid.

That ought to be more than enough to keep Rob busy, she thought.

14

Wednesday saw Ben and Zbiggy make speedy progress on the orangery. The roof timbers were going up well, the bird's mouth joints fitting snugly at the eaves. They took turns with the circular saw and nail gun. Their skills were pretty much on a par, except that Zbiggy could wield an eight-by-four sheet of plasterboard or plywood on his own, if needed, while Ben was the salesman, the one with the smooth patter, invariably able to talk a customer into a lucrative upgrade somewhere along the line. *These bathroom suites might look good in the catalogue but, trust me, I've installed them before and they're a bit on the flimsy side. Now the Orion suite, that's a beauty. Bit more expensive, but it'll last. You know what they say: buy cheap, buy twice.*

Julia Hennessey plied them with tea and chocolate biscuits. "I have to be careful with sweet things," she said, "I don't work the calories off like you boys, not any more. Now, in my dancing days I could eat what I wanted. Had my own school for a long while, you know."

Ben mentally stripped twenty-five years off her and pictured her in a leotard. Yes, he could see it: a dancer's body and poise. The vestiges were still there.

"Bet you love all that *Strictly* stuff, Mrs H. My missus is the same. Me, I'm more of a freestyle man on the dance floor. Can't be doing with learning all those rules. But I can throw some shapes when I'm in the mood, I can tell you. I've got all the moves, love."

Yeah, especially between the sheets, Mrs H. As you'll see if you play your cards right.

He doubted whether mentioning his marital status would alter anything. She might even prefer it: a roll in the hay with no strings. An uncomplicated way of getting back in the saddle. Reading between the lines, he didn't think there'd been much going on between her and the departed Mr Hennessey during the latter years of their marriage. She spoke of him only in matter-of-fact terms. *We married young … I was a mother to two kids by the time I was twenty-five, that was my dreams of joining Ballet Rambert down the drain … David worked in insurance, always made sure we had good cover … had some nice holidays in the south of France, used to drive down in our camper van …* It sounded like a functional, working relationship, all a bit passionless to Ben. Maybe there was an inner minx that had been lying dormant for years. He'd now pretty much decided to have a crack at her. Opposite end of the age scale to Carly and that twat of a boyfriend. Post-menopausal, so safe as well as grateful. Just what he needed.

After lunch, Mrs Hennessey announced that she had a hair appointment. No, not a bleach blonde crop or cornrows, she'd replied to Ben when he teased her about what she was having done.

"Bit of colour – auburn, I think – but I'm not one for battling nature. Well, maybe just give it a poke in the eye, eh?"

"Spot-on, Mrs H. Gotta be done." He'd tell her it looked great, whatever the result. He wondered if she shaved downstairs.

"You boys help yourself to the kettle and whatever else you need. Don't worry about the muddy boots; I'll be mopping the floor later."

"Living the dream, eh!"

"Haha, precisely."

She told them if they packed up and finished before she was back, just to lock the back door and post the key. Not many were so trusting these days, not with all the TV and newspaper reports about rogue traders. *We was just working in the next road and got this load of tarmac left over from a job if you want your drive done cheap. No? Well now I'm here, how about I have a butchers at yer roof. You've got a loose tile up there. I'll do you a special deal.*

Ben had told Zbiggy that he'd squared things with the babysitter. "I'm well out of fucking pocket, but I'll find a way of squeezing an extra couple of hundred out of this job. If not on the extension, summat else."

"Oy, she's a decent sort, Mrs Hennessey. No funny business."

Zbiggy held back over the dealings with Michael Phillips and what had taken place at The George. Donna hadn't specifically forbidden him, but that might have been more out of pragmatic acceptance that he wouldn't be able to keep his mouth shut anyway when he spent all day around his best mate. It was playing on his mind, though. He'd messed up the roofing batten layout, which Ben ripped into him about. He claimed it was just down to a bad night's sleep, but later, when they were tidying up, he found a way of broaching the subject that was unusually subtle for him.

"Does Freddie look like you did at his age? Who do people think your Tara takes after?"

"Well … Freddie's a handsome little man, so naturally, he takes after me. Tara is very cute, so, yep, that'll be me again." He guffawed loud and long at his vainglorious joke, which he thought had more than a kernel of truth.

Zbiggy hadn't given any thought to a child that might already be forming in Donna's womb looking like a miniature version of Michael Phillips. He was already struggling to recall Phillips' features. Wiry frame. Receding hairline. Bulbous nose. Sticky-out ears. Those were the bullet points. He wasn't sure how he felt about that side of things. Donna presumably was OK with it, as she hadn't mentioned Phillips' physical appearance after the meeting. Not a word. But then, he figured, she was so desperate for a baby that she was obviously only interested in the outcome.

He brightened. Maybe it would be a girl: a beautiful daughter the image of her beautiful mother. With any luck, there would be absolutely nothing outwardly to connect their future, longed-for baby with Michael Phillips. Nothing at all.

15

"I'm not gonna lie; this feels a bit weird."

"Not exactly part of my everyday routine, either."

"It was part of your routine yesterday, so you've got me beat when it comes to how this all works."

Donna smiled. She'd told Rob about the meeting with Michael Phillips, accurate in every respect save for where the famous love juice ended up. Both he and Phillips were left to imagine the cramped cubicle scene, the insemination money-shot. Let them.

They'd decided on the out-of-town M&S cafeteria as the venue. The loos were spotless and spacious – much better than The George. Not that that had been an issue when she sat on the toilet, lid down, counting the minutes until she could reasonably return to the hotel lounge without raising suspicion.

No one would have taken a blind bit of notice of the bloke and woman in the corner, chatting over coffee. So what if they were both married to other people? Who in their right mind would come to Marks and Sparks in broad daylight to carry on a clandestine tryst? The small package he'd just passed her could have been a pot of home-made jam or chutney, for all any casual observer knew.

Rob had said he could run a house viewing into his lunch break, which gave him a window to pop home. Andrea was at work, Beth at school. All was quiet on the domestic front.

"You, er, managed OK, then?"

Rob waved his hand in the direction of the scrunched-up bag he'd just passed her. "Probably best to leave out the details. Let's just say an internet search was involved."

Donna spluttered and had to cover her mouth. "I see. Yes, let's gloss over that. Well, I suppose I'd better go and … you know. Fresher the better, and all that."

She went into the disabled toilet, which made it even easier to complete the task. Not as comfortable or convenient as if she were laid out on her own bed, where she could maintain the horizontal position many online advice forums recommended. But no great hardship. It was a trade-off:

if she took the pot home, it would add to the post-ejaculation time. She casually wondered how old Michael Phillips' sample was when he handed it over – not that it mattered. Assuming he hadn't pulled into a lay-by en route – imagine *that* being caught on CCTV! – it had to be a minimum 90 minutes old when he handed it over, maybe longer. Were his little tadpoles already starting to die off before the rest got flushed away?

That was by the by. For this first go with the sainted Rob's seed, the serious business, she decided to sacrifice optimal body position for a specimen warm off the press.

Turkey basting, it was colloquially called. Donna carefully made sure there was no air in the syringe, like she'd seen nurses do on countless episodes of *Casualty*. Then it was just a matter of drawing the sample from the pot and pressing the plunger once the syringe was in place. As straightforward as inserting a tampon.

She stretched out on the floor, her legs raised high against the panelled wall. It was important to raise the hips so she stuffed her handbag under the small of her back. She'd expected that; it made sense to let gravity do its stuff. What she hadn't anticipated was some of the online conception cognoscenti advocating an immediate orgasm to help the process along. Apparently, the convulsions helped to hoover up the spunk already knocking at the door. She'd have to pass on that, this time at least. There was no way she was going to bring herself off at the spiritual home of St Michael.

It wasn't comfortable; she could only stand the spreadeagled body position on a tiled mattress for ten minutes, not nearly as long as the experts recommended. Even had she been able to hold out for another half hour, she felt she couldn't very well linger in the cubicle that long. Someone might need it, and she could do without disgruntled tutting from a wheelchair user when she went out. Plus Rob said he had to be back in the office by two. It wouldn't do to piss him off first time out, in case a repeat performance were needed. And she herself had a work appointment, dammit. Next time – if there needed to be a next time – she'd plan things better. To call this a dry run was a clear misnomer; she could feel the oozing back of the semen into her knickers even now. But as a practice go, she already felt confident, that it had been a success.

"Sorry to leave you hanging. You're meant to, you know, let it seep in."

"That's OK. But I really need to push off."

"Yes, of course. Sorry. Hope I haven't made you late for an appointment. I have to be somewhere myself, actually. Bloody work, eh?"

"I'll be jacking it in if the Euromillions comes up, no sweat. Not that I ever buy a ticket, which might be a slight flaw in the master plan."

Donna laughed. "You know how grateful I am about this, Rob. And Zbiggy would be, too. But hey, you never know, I might already be pregnant by Mr Supersperm." *Very good. Make him think he's the long-shot candidate, the rank outsider in the Gamete Stakes.* "I bet Andrea would understand as well, but, like I said, I'd rather keep this between the two of us."

Rob nodded. "This really is weird, you know. Wouldn't be surprised if we end up on Jeremy Kyle."

16

Donna made it to Superdrug by two-thirty. The time wasn't overly critical; she was just given a window in which to carry out the task. This one involved checking the range of female depilatory products, from creams to sprays to razors. How much they cost. How they were displayed. What kind of promotions were being offered. It was mostly a tick-sheet exercise, quite prescriptive. This one didn't involve a Q and A with the counter staff. She was glad of that. She just wanted to get done, get home and do the admin. It probably wouldn't help by then to lie down with a pillow underneath her bum, but she'd do it anyway. Then she'd take a shower and ditch the skanky knickers. She wanted Rob's semen inside her, not on her skin.

Donna had been doing market research work for three years. It was varied and easy enough. Not very lucrative, but she and Zbiggy got the occasional free meal out of it when she was tasked with mystery-shopping at an eatery. She'd been a nursery assistant before that, and she'd go back to her real passion one day. Some might have thought being around kids when you had none of your own was a decent substitute. *Goodbye Mrs Chips* and all that. Hundreds of little darlings under your care without the full-time responsibility. Do your bit and pass them back. But in the end, she'd found it all too much. She had a craving, and the last thing she wanted was to have to face up to the gaping hole in her life on *Groundhog Day* repeat. Kids being scooped up by their mums at the end of a session, the latter maybe delighting in a painting proudly presented. Parents squeezing their little ones tight if an upset had occurred, or scolding if a child was being recalcitrant and they'd had had a bad day.

She'd decided she couldn't hack that any more. Donna wanted a job she could just pick up and put down, one without emotional investment. One she could jack in without a backward glance. Her dream scenario would be to have two kids, one of each, be a stay-at-home mum in their pre-school years, like Zoe – they could just about afford that – and then dovetail motherhood with another nursery job once they were in full-time education. It would be fine second time round, when she wasn't confronted by the emptiness she used to feel every second of her working day.

17

Andrea Allen was just coming off shift when Donna pushed the syringe plunger, expelling Andrea's husband's semen into her vagina. Andrea was thirty-nine, three years older than Rob. Most would have put the gap even wider, for while he'd retained his youthful looks – even with the stubble – Andrea was finding it a lot harder to stave off the march of time. Her round face had got a little fuller since giving up the gym where she'd first got to know Donna and Zoe. *Shall we go for a drink instead? It's not like you two need the workout; I'm the one struggling to shift the pounds.* The bond had been forged over playing hookey from the treadmill.

The Sainsbury's staff discount and yellow-ticket items put constant temptation in her way. She was carrying a bag of cut-price stuff as she made her way to her car. If Jamie Oliver had carried out a stop-and-search, only the bananas would have survived the cull.

There were days, like at Zoe and Ben's the previous Saturday, when she made an effort to beat the size 14 rap and get back to a 12. She'd starved herself since breakfast just to accommodate two tiny new potatoes with Zoe's divinely creamy salmon dish. *Just a sliver*, she'd instructed when the baked cheesecake came out. But such occasions were in the minority compared with the cheat days and the fuck-it weekends.

Would she have worried more about her appearance if she feared losing Rob? Probably. People watchers who couldn't resist assessing couples – which of the pair might have done a lot better for themselves, who was batting well above their average – would have spoken with one voice. Andrea, like Zbiggy, was firmly in the latter camp. *She's let herself go a bit … lucky cow to have bagged him … can't think what he sees in her …*

Any comparison with Zbiggy ended there. While he doted on Donna, would have been lost without her, terrified of losing her, Andrea and Rob merely rubbed along. It wasn't so much that she could imagine a life without Rob, more a case of actively willing it, anticipating that eventuality. They would have gone their separate ways already had it not been for Beth. Both agreed that since they got along fine and could still make each other laugh; since neither had anyone else in mind that they wanted to marry, that there were worse things in life than playing happy families while their daughter got through puberty. At some unspecified future date, when they decided that Beth would cope just fine, or when one or other of them fell in love, they'd pull the plug. Until then, they divided their time between parenting, united-front coupledom and solo downtime, when both were free to do their own thing.

Andrea's phone sparked into life with the familiar tri-tone text alert. She reached into her bag, half-expecting what she'd find.

I'm looking at you right now
No, round to your right
You got me
I was wondering
If youve got time
Id really like to lick you out

18

"Daddy's home, everybody!"

"Thank God! Kids are driving me up the wall."

"What? These two? Never!"

Freddie got to him first, Tara thundering into his leg a second later. He stooped to his haunches to envelop them, as he always did, disregarding the work grime he was transferring. Nothing wrong with good old dirt; it was the muck that put a roof over their head and food on the table. It was nearly bathtime anyway. He'd jump in after them, have a long soak with a beer if he could get away with it.

"We had shepherd's pie."

"And 'nana and custard."

"I spilled my drink. Mummy told me off."

"Calum was sick at school. He had to go home."

"Can we play football?"

"I want to do a jigsaw!"

"Welcome to my world," said Zoe. She was already pouring herself a glass of wine, the acknowledged cut-off point for Ben to take over holding the parental fort. Maybe it would have to be a quick shower tonight, he thought.

It was the usual chaos for the next hour. They both wanted to play with the same water wheel in the bath, then the same plastic frog, which squirted stagnant water from assorted openings when squeezed. Freddie got Tara in the eye with it, which brought forth tears. Andrea and Rob had probably forgotten what it was like, and in any case they'd only had one to deal with. Donna and Zbiggy hadn't given up on trying to join the club. Well, Donna, anyway, by all accounts.

The final battle was at story time. In the end, without consensus, Ben gave up and rattled through both *The Jolly Postman* and *Not Now, Bernard*. He usually did all the voices and acted the key scenes out with manic gusto, but this was the express version. Freddie even pulled him up when he tried to skimp on the postman's visit to Cinderella.

Then they both wilted, like flicking a switch.

"All quiet. I'm off for a shower," Ben called out in a loud whisper, hanging over the landing bannister.

"Hurry up. Stirfry's nearly ready."

Having missed out on a bathtime beer, Ben soon made up for it with the white wine. He didn't have the willpower to cut down. On a rare visit to the GP a few months earlier, he declared he'd halved his weekly unit intake.

What about smoking?

Trying to cut down, Doc.

It was an acute case of hedonism. No known cure in Ben's case.

"Oh, there's a letter for you. Brown envelope. Looks ominous."

He topped up his glass before picking it up off the hall table. No plastic window, which was always a good sign. Handwritten, not printed. He tore it open and took out four sheets of A4, stapled neatly together. The first was a still ripped from the video of Carly and her boyfriend having sex. He was standing less than twenty feet from the sofa where she'd laid out her coat and they'd gone at it. He felt sick.

The wave of nausea increased as Ben flipped over to the second sheet. It was a shot of him and Carly at her white-walled flat. Of all the things that took place that night, this was the moment that left him the least wriggle room. His arm was around her, their lips almost touching.

He scarcely dared turn to the next. It was a picture of Carly embracing him in the coffee shop after he'd handed over the money. In flat two-dimension it looked far from a fatherly embrace.

The final page, written in the same hand as the envelope, was almost superfluous. What other reason could there have been? It read: *You had your fun watching. Now you're the star. See how you like it.*

19

They were ready to fit the orangery's centrepiece, a two-metre-long roof lantern that would flood the extension with overhead natural light. It had been Julia Hennessey's non-negotiable feature when they were discussing the job: something with a bit of wow factor, she said. Ben had initially tried to talk her out of it. *I've fitted loads of these, Mrs H, and they're nothing but trouble in my experience. Prone to leaking, make the room too hot in the summer and too cold in winter. How about a nice Velux instead?*

In truth, Ben and Zbiggy had no experience with roof lanterns whatsoever. Ben simply couldn't be arsed to get up to speed with a new product, not if he could sell her on the idea of something he could fit in his sleep. He thought the piece of kit she'd set her heart on would be fiddly for the uninitiated, that they'd spend too much time faffing about trying to get it right. He had his bottom line to think of when he was working to a price.

But she wouldn't budge, and as it turned out, the two of them were pleasantly surprised at how easily the lantern went up. Julia Hennessey was clapping her hands in delight just at the sight of the spider frame rising above the roofline, even before the glazing panels were slotted in. Ben was convinced they should now make every effort to flog more of them, for they were a doddle to erect and attracted a premium price. *Yeah, I've fitted loads of these. Big fan. Expensive, but give your house a nice bit of ta-da. Think of it as an investment …*

He'd gone through the complimentary motions when Mrs Hennessey appeared with the day's first tea tray. "That haircut's taken years off you, Mrs H … you could pass for thirty-five any day. That Gok bloke off the telly wouldn't be able to knock any more off if he tried."

She patted her bob, wondering aloud if it wasn't a bit too short, or the style a bit too young for her.

"It's very nice,"said Zbiggy.

Ben looked askance at him, as if to say: *Very nice? Very nice? Haven't you learned anything from watching the master at work all these years?*

"Bobby Dazzler, love. Move over, Tess Daly and Darcey Whatshername, that's all I'm saying. Any more of that flapjack going, by the way?"

They got through to lunch, both men managing to keep their private preoccupations in check. Ben had tried ringing Carly several times, getting voicemail on each occasion. He'd used the first of those opportunities to launch a torrent of F-word-littered abuse, then immediately regretted it. A message was a digital footprint, just like a video recording or photograph, and he'd put his size tens in it quite enough already in that regard. He sent a bunch of texts instead, just asking what was going on and telling her to contact him *asap*. Nothing back so far.

"I'll have to shoot off a bit early, mate. Fucking babysitter's back playing silly buggers. I've had enough of being reasonable. Need to nip it in the bud good and proper now."

"No problem. I can finish the shingles off. I'll get Donna to pick me up."

Zbiggy would never have Ben's spark. Then again, he would never dig a great messy hole for himself with extra-curricular activities crazily close to home. But Ben detected that even by his mate's lumpen, taciturn standards, something wasn't quite right. He could do nothing about his own situation until either the two-faced little bitch responded to his messages or he had it out with her face to face, so he prodded and poked Zbiggy until it all came out. About him being reduced to the role of chauffeur and minder as Donna sluiced herself with another man's seed in a hotel toilet.

"Fuck me, mate, I'd've done it for a tenner."

He realised straightaway that the joke was misjudged. The two were backslappers and fist-bumpers by default, not huggers, but Ben clamped an arm round Zbiggy's powerful shoulders and gave a squeeze of manly support. "Must take some gettin' used to, mate. Strugglin' to get me head round it meself. But, you know, needs must."

"I guess. Thought we'd be giving adoption a go, but s'pose I gotta see it from Donna's point of view. Why should she bring up someone else's kid when she can have one herself? She's all in working order. What can I do other than back her decision?"

Ben left the question hanging. No way could he contemplate taking Zoe to get a seeing-to by another bloke, even if there was no shagging involved. On the other hand, he could well see himself giving this Mickey Sperm fella a run for his money. He'd only looked at Zoe twice after she came off the Pill and that was enough to get Freddie and Tara started. He was a prize fucking bull, no doubt about that. He'd put it about often enough over the years, both in his single days and – when the chance presented itself – after he'd got wed. Fancy being able to do it and get paid for the privilege. Now that's what he called combining business with pleasure.

20

Ben pulled up at the apartment block just after four. The communal door presented the first hurdle, but he didn't have long to wait until a woman emerged and he was able to catch it before it clicked shut. He wasn't expecting an answer even if Carly was in, but he tried her door anyway. Then he rang her mobile again, listening for a muffled ring-tone. Nothing.

She was out there somewhere, looking at the screen, laughing at him. Ben calling. *Decline. Your call can't be taken right now.*

He retraced his steps to the van, trying to put himself in her shoes. Would Carly anticipate him coming to confront her, scuttle off to some friend's place after college to lie low? Every chance. She held all the cards at the moment. He had one: that she had to come back sooner or later.

An hour passed. There was more coming and going but no sign of her. He was tucked away down a side road, the van sticking out just enough to afford him a good view of the entrance. He was pretty sure Carly wouldn't spot him when she approached the building, even if she was on the alert.

He raised his eyes up the five-storey edifice, counting the floors and establishing a mental fix of which windows were hers. It was easy enough, for he recognised the pot plant from her kitchen sill. Even at this distance, the splayed fronds were clear as day. No other road-facing third-floor window had any greenery. That was the place where he'd tried to make amends, put an arm round her after she'd showed him the bruises. But all the photograph captured was an embrace, lips so close to each other that a frame either side would surely have caught the kiss.

His gaze was just descending back to street level when a hint of movement caught his eye: a shadowy presence in the frame. It was the same window, wasn't it? Yes! There it was again. A figure keeping well back, trying to avoid observation. The fucking bitch. Either she'd been there all along and had her phone on silent … or she'd been in one of the other flats, having a nice cuppa and chat with a neighbour. Or maybe she'd slipped in via a back entrance; there must have been one. Now that he'd clocked her, the possibilities piled up as to how she'd managed to get there. It also gave him another card to play.

He considered a second direct approach, this one more persistent. He thought about banging on the door, letting her know he knew she was inside and telling her he wouldn't stop or go away until she opened up. Create the mother of all scenes. But he checked himself. Blundering in without any thought to the consequences had landed him in enough hot water over the years. It had got him into fights, it had got him laid. This was a time for being smart. He definitely didn't want to be picked up on a security camera, marching aggressively up to the flat's entrance, yelling obscenities, hammering to be let in.

This time he ignored Carly's door and knocked on her immediate neighbour's. No reply. He tried the flat on the other side, the one that had Carly's place piggy-in-the-middle. This time, footsteps. *Is this where she'd been skulking?*

"Yes?"

He recognised the man as one of those who'd entered the building in the previous half-hour. Forty-something. Wire-framed glasses. Though nothing else had registered, it was definitely the same bloke.

"Yeah, hiya, mate. I've got something for Carly next door and was wondering if I could leave it with you?"

He brandished the package, which had been sloppily lashed together from stuff lying around in the back of the van. Inside was a bottle trap, the cheapest bit of kit that came readily to hand. He couldn't remember her surname, so he'd just written Carly and the address, ripping the paper packaging just where her last name would have been written. He knew it wouldn't fool anyone, banking on the fact that when you were giving stuff rather than taking, people's suspicions were more likely to be allayed, their judgment more likely to desert them.

"No one by that name living there, pal. That's Sue's place. Susan Loxton. What address have you got?"

Ben stared at the badly wrapped bottle trap. He didn't have to check the address.

"That's funny. Does she live alone?"

"You've knocked, I take it?"

"Yeah, no answer."

"She's usually in at this time, I'm always scrounging stuff off her."

The neighbour slid past Ben, clearly intending to prove to himself that no one was home. Before he could knock, with the kind of timing that principals in a well rehearsed play would have been proud of, the door swung open.

21

Grace Newman was already beginning to wonder if she'd been stood up. He was only five minutes late, but even so, it wasn't an auspicious sign. Arriving behind schedule was all very well for A-listers attending a post-red carpet party, or even for Joe Public if he was meeting a friend or family member. For a bloke on a first date it was a big no-no.

She'd got there ridiculously early. And that was even factoring in a change of blouse and shoes in the work loos, plus a lengthy make-up reapplication and, quite literally, letting down of her hair. He'd probably roll up – if he came at all – in his office gear. Not that that was a bad thing. One of his profile pictures had been tagged "at work", and he was obviously one of those blokes who looked effortlessly good either in formal wear or throw-on casual. Grace thought he was out of her league, that he'd go for the kind of pneumatic, pouty blondes that were everywhere on social media. She wouldn't have contacted him at all if Phoebe hadn't egged her on. *Go on, what have you got to lose? I would if I wasn't spoken for. Look at him, he's a hunk.*

Her younger sister had had the better of the genetic dividend: prettier, slinkier curves, more vivacious. She'd married a handsome high-flyer and was already installed in a house many rungs above their parents' modest semi. Grace had had only one serious relationship in her thirty-two years, an engagement that had receded into the distance every year since their late teens. Once that had been broken off, her confidence dropped through the floor. Phoebe had set up the Tinder account, presenting it as a fait accompli. *Get out there and have fun, Gracie. If you don't meet the man of your dreams, at least get some action.*

Phoebe had also monopolised the swiping, providing a running commentary as she added the men to the possibles pile or consigned them to the no-chance bin. *He's got nice eyes … OMG, look at that shitty jumper … at least this one can spell … I think we can guess what 'cuddly' means …*

"What about him? Yes, now we're talking."

"Oo, I don't know."

"Done!"

"Pheebs!"

"Now we just need to start the ball rolling with a message, something between mysteriously unapproachable and total slut. Let's reel him in."

Phoebe, on Grace's behalf, had angled for a dinner date. *Thurs eve works for me. If that isn't any good, it might have to be the next weekend but one.* She didn't want him to think her sister's diary for the following ten days had nothing more exciting in it than a check-up at the dentist. He'd taken the bait, but Grace had got cold feet and sent a follow-up message asking if they could do a quick after-work drink at Wetherspoons instead. Phoebe was initially miffed at the change, but eventually conceded that it was probably for the best. Any self-respecting, non-desperate woman would want a quick initial meeting so you weren't lumbered for an entire evening if there was no spark. Privately, she feared he might be the one looking to bail. Much as she loved her sister, Phoebe had to concede that she lacked oomph, almost wilfully refusing to make the most of her assets. She'd never be a beauty, but she had a trim figure and great legs, and with judiciously applied make-up, her angular features could look quite striking.

Grace had had precisely two tea-time starts at Wetherspoons in the previous year: one at Christmas, the other for a workmate's birthday in April. It was between those two visits that she'd become single, Gavin deciding that he needed some "space" in February. His Christmas present had been still outstanding on her credit card. Instead of a Valentine's Day weekend away, she'd spent it with a box of tissues, bottle of Aldi plonk and a DVD of *He's Just Not That Into You*.

This new bloke might have been a catch, but she decided she was off as soon as she'd finished her spritzer. She had her pride to consider. If he'd had a better offer, she didn't want to have her nose rubbed in it. The thought struck her that he'd already been and gone, clocked her and decided to bail. Maybe she'd tell Phoebe it went OK but that she didn't think he was her cup of tea.

And then there he was, standing over her, breathless.

"Grace. Hi. Sorry I'm late. Got held up. Phone died so couldn't let you know."

"Don't worry about it," she smiled. "Only got here five minutes ago myself."

"Let me grab a drink and get you a top-up."

She studied him in profile while he ordered. The photos didn't flatter him, and they certainly weren't years old, which Phoebe had warned was always a possibility when casting a net in the virtual pool. His thick, wavy hair contrasted with Gavin's number two and widow's peak. She'd never kissed anyone with designer stubble, and was already rather hoping that unimpressive osculatory record might be about to change.

"So, Rob," she enquired when he'd returned from the bar, "what kind of properties are selling well and have you got any bargains on the books? Just in case I was thinking of moving."

22

Susan Loxton could reasonably have been Carly's mother. There was no readily discernible resemblance, but her age made it entire feasible. She would have been a youngish mum, Ben thought, for the woman who stood before him looked to be in her early forties. She was taller than Carly, with somewhat pinched features and uniformly dark hair that smacked of covering up early-onset greying. Susan Loxton could have been Carly's mother, but Ben had the unnerving feeling that she wasn't.

Their conversation was brief. She was on her way out and gave no indication that she was about to alter her plans for more than the bare minimum to deal with this door-stepper. Ben glanced at the neighbour with the wire-framed specs, who showed a similar level of disinclination to withdraw, forcing a triangular face-off.

"Sue, this bloke's got a package for someone called Carly with your address on it. Any ideas?"

"I don't know anyone of that name. Sorry, must be a mistake."

Ben didn't bother showing her his lame effort with the handwritten address torn to conceal a forgotten surname. There was a simpler way to bring it to a head.

"Fact is, Mrs Loxton …"

"Miss."

Her marital status did nothing to allay the existing doubts. Unmarried mother? He somehow doubted it.

"I was here on Monday night. This Monday just gone, here in your flat. I gave Carly a lift home and she invited me in."

Susan Loxton's demeanour altered, slightly but noticeably. The change was clearly down to a combination of penny-dropping and indignation. In one respect it was no business of hers what the girl had got up to. She'd paid the asking price, and the money was there in her PayPal account. The place had been left in good enough order. Even so, the image of seedy goings-on in her home presented itself, and the girl definitely hadn't mentioned there would be another occupant for any part of the stay. Maybe she ought to do a more thorough check, make sure there were no unwanted stains anywhere.

"She's our babysitter," said Ben, reading the disapproving signals and hoping that the revelation might defuse the obvious tension. Just as quickly, he realised that it wouldn't. *Had to see the babysitter right to her door, did you? Worried she might be attacked on the staircase? Did you ask if there was any coffee going?*

"The young lady in question," said Sue Loxton, "the one who stayed here on Monday night, was a paying guest. She said she was attending an interview and required overnight accommodation. It was booked through Airbnb. That's all I know."

"What name did she give?"

"I don't see that that's any business of yours, and I wouldn't divulge confidential information anyway. Now, if you don't mind."

She shut the door behind her, closing down the conversation as well as cutting off the glimpse Ben had of the hallway he'd passed through three days earlier. One by one, he lost sight of the construction workers having lunch on that famous skyscraper girder. Their legs were dangling above the vertiginous void; one slip and it was a one-way ride. Ben was queasily beginning to know how that poster troupe felt.

The neighbour, seeing that the show was over, soon followed suit. He knew Sue spent the occasional night with her parents to make some money letting out her property. He'd thought about doing likewise, for he'd done a search and knew what she charged. But he'd also read a few horror stories, and whatever had gone on next door on Monday evening was another mark in the debit column. Maybe it just wasn't worth the hassle.

23

Grace checked her watch. It was quarter past eight. They'd long passed the quick-drink threshold, and Rob had shown no inclination to escape. The conversation had flowed, from jobs to dating disasters to movies to books to desert-island must-have records – plus the permitted luxury – to bucket lists and pet hates. He'd scoffed at her putting *Sleepless in Seattle* in her all-time top five (*That is SUCH a girly choice*). She'd articulated her astonishment that he could rank Nirvana above Whitney Houston, but they'd found common ground in pitying the latter's sad downward spiral.

"Just goes to show," she said, "all that money and it didn't bring her happiness."

"In that case, cheer yourself up and lend me a tenner."

She laughed at that.

On the question of being marooned, she'd said her luxury was probably between hair and make-up products and an electric blanket. Rob said surely it had to be the blanket because what good would the preening and pampering stuff do you if you were there alone? That prompted a lengthy detour on whether the sexes dressed to please or impress others, or whether it was enough just to feel good about yourself.

"I bet you anything Joan Collins puts on the full slap even if she's not going off the doorstep. Whereas blokes would just slob around all day scratching their nuts."

"Pistachios or Brazils?"

It was his turn to laugh.

Grace was not a natural social butterfly, but she was warming to the occasion on the strength of his easy manner.

"Anyway, my luxury would be a jet ski. I'd give you a lift if you asked nicely – and if the lippy was perfectly applied, of course."

She'd wormed relationship history into the conversation. There was a banding mark on his wedding-ring finger, which tied in with his account of being recently separated. An amicable split, he'd claimed. Grace would have preferred there not to be a primary-school-age daughter on the scene, but knew that few blokes in her age bracket would come totally unencumbered.

Like herself. By the time she ducked into the toilet cubicle, she was already wondering if Rob was going to be her second-ever lover.

Going well (I THINK!!!), she texted Phoebe.

Trust you're playing hard to get, came the immediate reply. *No bump 'n' grind till at least half nine.*

I think not!!!

OMG!!! Hope your not wearing your Bridget Jones pants!!

Laters

Rob was also busy on his phone.

Hey love all OK at home?

All good. Beth already gone up … shes reading. Home soon or dirty stopout!!??

Not sure. Cd go either way

Grace decided she'd leave him wanting more. Better to make a tactical withdrawal while it was going well rather than hang on and run the risk of the first awkward pause.

She declined his offer of a lift. "You can chaperone me to the bus stop if you like, though. I never got round to learning, as Gavin used to do all the driving."

It was a good feeling to be able to mention her ex's name without feeling a pang. It came out as matter-of-factly as if reporting that she'd once had a bout of shingles, or been to Alton Towers.

"Ten-minute wait by the look of it," she said, consulting the timetable and her watch. "Listen, you get off, why don't you?"

Yes, I'd quite like to get off, now you mention it. If you're offering.

"Can't possibly leave a lady unattended. Though I have to say, I don't think I've done this since I was sixteen."

They both giggled at the thought. Grace had been eighteen when she met Gavin, and had celebrated another birthday before losing her virginity. She wouldn't be sharing that information, certainly not yet.

"I suppose, in the circumstances, a teenage snog would be appropriate. What do you think?"

She didn't need to answer. He took her arm and drew her over to the fence bordering the pavement. Just a few weeks earlier, it would still have been bright daylight at this hour and she would have demurred. Under the cloak of dusk, though, and seven gaping, hollow months on from being dumped, she allowed herself to be enfolded. The kiss began as a tender exploration, then he pushed his tongue into her mouth with an urgency she mirrored. It was a submission, she was a willing participant.

But only so far and no more. Of course, it wouldn't be a wait counted in months this time. But neither would it be counted in hours, never mind what Phoebe said. She wanted courtship as an *hors d'oeuvre* to passion. She wanted to be wooed and pursued, in a Tom Hanks kind of way. She accepted the fact that his hand slid round the front, inside her coat. Phoebe would consider it a badge of honour that he couldn't resist the urge to caress her breasts through her clothing. *Be patient and you could soon be fondling the real thing.*

Just as quickly, the hand was withdrawn. Good. He'd played the game, not tried get inside her blouse.

Too late did she realise he was playing by a different set of rules. The hands dropped down to her bottom and he pulled her into him. Now it was her turn to force her arms between them, but in her case to push him off, using her elbows as levers. Their groins had been forced together only momentarily, but long enough for her to feel the distinct, unmistakable outline of his erection.

24

Sunday was the first morning Ben had been able to relax. Just a little. He was no churchgoer, but the rest day brought a merciful respite from the potential tyranny of the postal service, the clatter of the letterbox that might deliver a straw to break the camel's back for Zoe. A few more hours with no incriminating pictures dropping onto the doormat, copies of the ones he'd been sent but this time addressed to her. They might land tomorrow, though. Or the next day. Or at any time if they were hand-delivered. It wouldn't be difficult for one of the little shits to wait for an empty house and make a risk-free delivery.

If – no, when – the photos came, there was little prospect of Zoe seeing them and not doubting he'd had sex with Carly. *The babysitter,* for God's sake! Talk about shitting on your own doorstep. The truth, for once, wouldn't save him. She knew him too well, there was too much history. Even if he managed to convince her that it was a blackmail scam, she'd say it only worked because he was thinking with his dick in the first place.

Another working week loomed. Surely it was coming, it was only a matter of time. The fuckers were letting him stew.

Stewing but not idle, for he'd casually managed to get Carly's surname out of Zoe.

"Met a fella down the pub who might want a bathroom refurb. Mike Benson. Wonder if he's related to the babysitter?"

"Carly *Fitzroy*, love. You've got a head like a sieve."

Fitzroy. Yes, he remembered now. Not that it helped when he went on the college website or phoned them up. The brick wall he expected was every bit as unbreachable as the one Miss Susan Loxton had put up. *That's confidential, I'm afraid. Data protection and all that. Sorry.*

Facebook was another dead end. None of the Carly Fitzroys matched; at least, none of those with a picture attached. There were a few phantom entries: just a name and nothing else. Was she one of those ghosts? The bitch was haunting him, for sure.

"Oh, by the way, speaking of Carly, we've been invited round to Holly's next Friday. Luke's all but moved in. She thinks he's the one."

They'd only met Luke the once, on the bowling night. The night of the tight jeans. The night of *I'm not wearing any knickers.* The night when their sex life had been reinvigorated. The night when he'd been caught out recording two kids going at it like rabbits on his sofa.

"I've texted her to see if she's free. Waiting to hear back."

Waiting. Stewing.

Having ignored all his messages, how would Carly react to one from Zoe, asking her to babysit as if nothing had happened? It told her that he still hadn't come clean to Zoe. That remained her ace. All Ben had to do was fess up and the problem went away. *She knows, Carly. I've told her everything. We're still strong. You and your streak-of-piss boyfriend can't hurt us, so you can whistle for your money. Now fuck off and bother someone else.* It might come to that, he reckoned. But not yet.

"Damn. She can't do Friday."

Freddie and Tara were in bed by now. The little cow had left it hanging for four hours before replying. Ben imagined her chortling away with lover boy. *Make 'em sweat a bit longer.* Or maybe he'd told her to leave it that long, or else she'd feel his fists again. Either way, Ben didn't care.

"Donna would probably do it if she and Zbiggy haven't got anything on. I'll try her."

Ben didn't answer. He was staring at his own phone. A picture of Carly, her arm extended in the corner of the frame to show that it was a selfie. But not one she would have posted to garner likes or temperature-related comments. Not *Wow, hot hun!!!* Unless such a comment referred to the heat of the red welt stretching from her temple to her cheek; a livid wound that ran next to the purple disc encircling a half-closed eye. Not the alluring vixen, not the aggressive tiger, but the passive, put-upon, sad-face panda.

"I'm sorry," ran the attached message.

25

Rob left it until Monday to text Grace Newman. He'd misread that one, all right. She'd been flirty enough in the pub, gagging for it, he thought. *Pistachios or Brazils?* A cheeky smile, a glint in the eye. If that wasn't an open invitation … But obviously not, considering the way she reacted. Overreacted, more like. Yes, that was probably it. Grace was doubtless cringing with embarrassment now, not daring to tell her workmates what happened for fear of ridicule. *So you snogged and felt his stiff cock? Par for the course in a slow dance, in my experience. I'd take it as a compliment. Don't get me wrong, he shouldn't have pounced. His timing might have been a bit off, deserved a slap on the wrist, the naughty boy. But ask yourself this: would you rather have met a limp dick? Would you rather have had zero effect in his downstairs department? I know I wouldn't. The day that happens to me, I'm gonna buy a beige twin-set and give it up as a bad job.*

Rob thought pretty much along the same lines. He didn't say any of that, of course. He kept it quite simple and let her join the dots.

Enjoyed the other night. Sorry about how it ended. Youre just too sexy I guess! Hope we can do it again sometime.

He really did hope they could do it again, as otherwise all that spadework had been for nothing. "Oh dear, you didn't strike out, did you?" Andrea had said when he got home. "Losing your touch, darling!" It was all right for her, she was settled. Andrea knew who she was spending her away days and away nights with. Those two might even get hitched one day. With every passing month, Beth was maturing. She could probably handle the split now, to be honest. But there were no guarantees. And they'd agreed to wait, that was the deal.

Meanwhile, Rob was back in the sweetshop and not inclined to make any rash decisions, with so much delicious confectionery on offer. Try before you buy. He intended to try as many as he could, as often as he could manage.

He was office-bound for the next two hours. There was paperwork to catch up on, and a phone call to the Worthingtons to tell them he'd had an offer of £245,000 for their bungalow. *I appreciate it's well below the asking price … OK, well below our valuation … but are we really that far apart? How about if I can squeeze another five out of them? There's a lot of market talk about a correction, which could more than wipe out any gains you make if you hold out … It's your call entirely, but I know what I'd do. OK, have a think and get back to me.*

Tinder had been open throughout the conversation. There was fresh meat to consider. He went mostly for a scattergun approach, 25–49 age range, discarding only the plainest, the plumpest, the highest maintenance and those who made no bones about being husband hunting. His own *separated* status was obviously a slight misnomer, but everybody massaged the facts to suit on these apps, didn't they? There would be a lot less candy for the candid. *Technically, we're still living under the same roof. Yes, and sharing a bed. But it's over between us. Just a convenient arrangement until we can get things on a proper footing. Just trying to make things easier for our daughter. No, we haven't exactly put a date on when we're going to split up.*

Cue stampede for the exit. His good looks and boyish charm wouldn't help him one little bit if he presented the whole picture. Everyone was economical with the truth.

Still nothing from Grace.

His mind wandered to Donna Kuzminski. Sexy, blonde Donna. If she'd been available, he could imagine closing his Tinder account for her. Not for Grace but definitely for her. She looked a bit like a girl he'd once worked with in the Bristol office. He and Andrea were solid then, and Beth was pre-school, so it was never going anywhere. But he flirted with Becky terribly, and she always flirted right back. It went no further than a one-off drunken snog at a Christmas do, which obviously didn't count. Things might be different if he met her now.

Becky wasn't around, though. Left the company, the last he'd heard. Sexy, blonde Donna was here, though, slap bang in the midst of his circle. Wife of steady old Zbiggy. The nice guy who came first for once. Zbiggy and Ben's friendship went back too far for him to get much of a foothold. It was all matey enough when the six of them got together, but that had been driven by Andrea's connection with the two women. Zoe and Donna were close too, but they didn't go way back to primary school, so it was easier for Andrea. Those three might get together on a girly whim, whereas neither Ben nor Zbiggy included him in anything in between the couples nights.

He wondered if Donna would want a repeat performance of the Marks & Sparks meeting: a straight shoot-out between him and the internet guy for whose live rounds would hit the bullseye first. Not that he was allowed to bring that up in front of steady old Zbiggy.

He came off Tinder and Googled artificial insemination. There were a string of sub-categories. *Process. Definition. At home. In humans. Kit. Success rate.* He clicked on the last of that list. One source reckoned that even after six goes, the chances of a pregnancy were still less than fifty per cent. Another suggested the odds were better when insemination was natural. He liked the sound of that. It would only be a short-term thing, but risk-free, guilt-free sex with Donna Kuzminski for a few weeks was undoubtedly an attractive proposition.

Some positions are more liable to lead to pregnancy than others, one advice site stated. Those where the woman is horizontally orientated, such as the missionary or doggy positions, are preferable to a more vertical stance, as these give the sperm more chance to reach the egg.

If Donna wasn't aware of this, he really thought he ought to bring it to her attention. *Best if you get on all fours, Donna – that's what they recommend.*

59

"Hi there. I'm looking to buy, up to 200k. Already sold so a cash deal. Just wondering what you had on the books?"

Rob smiled professionally and was soon pulling sheafs of property details from the filing cabinet. This has just come on the market ... this one needs a bit of tlc ... *this semi's in a lovely little cul de sac ... open views, with a chance of squeezing in a third bedroom ...*

Still nothing from Grace Newman.

Fuck her.

26

"What time did you say you were meeting him?"

Even muffled by the half-closed bathroom door, Donna could hear how heavily the question weighed on Zbiggy. If only she could tell him she carried the more onerous burden, the load increased with every untruth.

"Two."

Zbiggy asked yet again if she wanted him to come with her. She kept the answer as light possible, as if his concern, well intentioned as it was, was also unnecessary. "Don't be silly. It's a waste of your time. Pointless for you to take the afternoon off work when I can drive myself."

Still in her towelling robe, Donna pushed open the bathroom door and threw her arms round his shirtless midriff as he shaved. The fingers then became featherlight tentacles playing over his ticklish skin, both waiting to see how long he could stand it.

"Oy, I'll nick meself!" he said, wriggling out of her grasp, laughing. He scooped up a nob of foam and planted it on her nose.

Theirs was a house that would be filled with joy when the family was complete. Joy! If it was a girl, she would definitely throw that name into the mix. It was far too premature to be discussing such things, though. The important thing was to keep her eyes on the prize and hope the dagger of her deception remained sheathed.

She'd picked the time of the non-appointment specifically to put him off. Now that he'd seen Michael Phillips in the flesh and knew the transaction was about as routine as flogging his old chop saw on Gumtree

– firm handshake and away you go – she guessed he wouldn't take much persuading to absent himself from round two. It was tantamount to playing cuckold, the husband having to witness his wife being served by another man. Non-sexual it might have been, but no less demeaning to witness.

There was no guarantee, though. That desire not to be forced to confront his own inadequacy might have been overruled by Zbiggy's default protectiveness towards her. He might have swallowed his pride, insisted on accompanying her, eyeballing the man bearing the potent seed. Had he been immovable, Donna would have told him of the last-minute email from Michael Phillips, apologising for having to cancel and reschedule. She was thankful that a further layer of duplicity hadn't been necessary. Zbiggy was glad to be off the hook.

"Well, if you're sure you'll be all right ..."

Donna told him she'd agreed to meet Phillips at a hotel near him this time, one that he'd used before for the same purpose. It was silly, she said, to pay Phillips a hundred quid for that short hop down the motorway. It was money that could go towards the million and one things they'd need when the baby arrived.

Or, rather, it meant she didn't have to make a cash withdrawal to tally with the supposed payment to Phillips. Zbiggy was the one who assiduously checked the bank statements against all the receipts they accumulated. Fifty quid was a slush-fund amount that would slip through the net. A hundred and fifty might raise an awkward question, necessitating yet another lie.

"I filled up yesterday and checked the oil, water and tyres, so you're good to go."

"Thanks, love. Fingers crossed this'll be the last time."

She waited until he'd left for work before messaging Rob. A few days' discrepancy wouldn't matter, but better if there was a reasonably close alignment between her supposed meetings with Michael Phillips and the assignations with Rob.

How r u fixed for a repeat performance!? In next 24 hrs if poss ... cycle and all that. Sooo grateful

Donna hadn't carried out a pregnancy test since the unedifying experience of being laid out in an M&S toilet cubicle. She just knew it would be a waste of time and money. Whether or not that was down to the fact that she hadn't maintained the recommended body position long enough, she'd make sure to address that issue this time.

Her phone pinged.

Happy to oblige. Just need time, place, plastic pot and suitable stimulation!!!
Will buy u a mag if the internets down
Drat! Was afraid youd say that, spoilsport!!

27

Zoe hadn't slept well. Tara was teething, and there was an ongoing battle with Freddie to persuade him that there were no monsters in his room, and that he wasn't to trot through to mummy and daddy's bed just because he'd woken up. Zoe belatedly realised she'd made a rod for her own back in staying with him until he fell asleep, both at normal bedtime and in the middle of the night. Mumsnet informed her that this was a bad idea, but the habit was already ingrained by the time she read up on it.

Ben was usually in a state of blissful ignorance over any such nocturnal shenanigans. It wasn't until over breakfast – maybe even dinner if it was a rushed morning – that he learned about the wardrobe being emptied at 2am, or that Zoe had been on all fours shining a torch under Freddie's bed to prove he was the room's sole occupant. Last night had been different, though. When she heard him cry out and was steeling herself for another battle, Ben had laid his hand on her shoulder.

"I'll go, love, I'm wide awake."

In the end, she might as well have gone herself. For though she was dog-tired, she just lay there, ears pricked, picking out the odd soothing word, unable to think about closing her eyes until Ben returned to bed.

"He's gone off. He's fine."

"Magic touch. You've got the job," she mumbled, drawing the duvet tight up against her chin. Unless he'd had too much beer and needed to pee, Ben was usually a sound sleeper. Even if he needed the loo, he had a way of completing the task while semi-conscious at best. She once found him weeing in the bath when his radar went awry after a boozy night out. But being wide awake in the small hours was certainly out of character. Was he worried about anything? He and Zbiggy were as busy as ever workwise, so she doubted it was anything to do with money. She'd ask him. Just not now, not when she needed to sleep.

Not in the morning, either. That was as manic as ever: Tara with more yogurt in her hair than in her mouth; Freddie spilling Ribena down a clean-on T-shirt; Ben chasing his tail with a piece of toast clamped between his teeth.

Calm had descended by nine-thirty. One at work, one at nursery, one happily squidging Play-Doh through her fingers. Zoe reached for her phone.

"Hey, Donna, just wondering what you had on this morning. Fancy a coffee in town? Or lunch?"

"Bum! Would have loved to but a bit pushed on the work front today, sorry."

There was a brief exchange of pleasantries. Zoe was mindful never to flaunt any heart-melting moment involving the children; sparing her the details of the latest cute painting Freddie had done, or of Tara telling her not to be sad when she was chopping onions. Equally, she didn't sound off about what was driving her mad about them, the petty squabbles, the mini-rebellions, the dinner-table battles, her sleep-deprived tetchiness. She didn't want to appear ungrateful for a gift she knew Donna would do anything to receive.

She scrolled further down her Recent Calls list.

"Hey Andrea, how's things? You working today? Just fancied a scoot into town and wondered if you were up for coffee and cake?"

"Sounds good. I'm on lates today. Where and when?"

Two hours later, they were studying the Pret-A-Manger menu. Tara was zonked out in her pram, and Zoe said it was too good an opportunity to miss.

"Oo, I think I'm going savoury. That coconut chicken curry soup sounds good."

"Go on, then. I'll have a brie and tomato baguette – just to be sociable, obviously."

"This is nice and civilised," said Zoe when the food arrived. "Makes a change from eating on the hoof or round what the kids are doing. It's all right for you, Beth's way past the hard-work phase."

"Yeah, right. Puberty, secondary school and teens round the corner. Calm before the storm."

"And boys! Yeah, forget I said that. It's the lack of sleep talking."

The guard Zoe felt the need to put up when Donna was around didn't apply with Andrea. Donna was an older friend, but motherhood did make a difference. Not only was she able to discourse with Andrea on all aspects of childcare, but the latter was ahead of her on the parenting curve, someone who could give her a steer about what lay down the developmental road.

"Did you decide early on that you only wanted one?"

"Decision was taken out of our hands. I suffered a bad bout of endometriosis, ended up having a hysterectomy. That was me out of the game."

"Oh! I didn't know that. Ah, well, at least you and Rob already had Beth by then."

Andrea paused before taking a bite of her baguette.

"It happened before I met Rob, Zoe. Didn't I tell you?"

28

The work commitment Donna had spoken of when she declined Zoe's invitation was a lot more modest than she had made out. It consisted of a visit to the local Toyota dealership, where she was to pose as a prospective purchaser. She had a lot to assess. How welcoming and attentive the sales staff were; how long she was kept kicking her heels, suggesting she might be on the receiving end of gender prejudice: pegged as a browsing time-waster until the husband showed up to give the green light, even though statistics suggested the opposite was the case; if they were overly pushy; how well they knew their stuff about the product range; what kind of finance deals were explained and offered.

It was dull, untaxing stuff, a notch above office-bound clerical work but not what she wanted to do. She wanted her old nursery job back: interaction with bright, young, eager, smiling – sometimes sobbing – faces; singing and clapping and reading and painting and cooking and playing and toilet accidents; the whole works. Indeed, the garage visit just brought home the difference between the two jobs. The oily artifice of the salesman, who feigned interest in your day, your family – your very existence; who sought to put into practice everything he'd learned on the training courses while trying to make it sound genuine and unscripted; who just wanted to close a deal and bump up his monthly figures. Set that against the open-book spontaneity of being around nursery-age kids, where it didn't get much slyer than a pinch under the table, where minor transgressions were soon rumbled, dealt with and forgotten.

Before setting off to see whether she'd be steered in the direction of an Aygo or Yaris, Donna had called into Barker & Samuel Estate Agents. Rob was at his desk, and she was glad to see the only other negotiator in the office was deep in conversation, dealing with an enquiry.

"About that deposit, madam ..." he grinned as she approached.

"I think you'll find this all in order."

She handed him the small package extracted from her handbag. He peered inside.

"Yes, this all looks fine. I'll make sure it gets priority attention. In fact, I'll handle it myself."

Donna sniggered. Then she lowered her voice. "Are you sure it's OK? To use your house?"

He'd sent her a message suggesting it made sense all round. Better than a public loo at any rate.

"I've got to go back anyway to, er ... do the necessary. I'll text you when I've gone and then you've got the place to yourself. Andrea's working two till ten, so will have left by half one at the latest. Beth's going to a friend's house straight from school, and I won't be back till six. So from, say, two-thirty you've got at least a three-hour window. Easier than me handing the pot over and you having to go back to yours."

She thought of the traffic, of more sperm dying off with every red light and set of roadworks. Yet still she hesitated; it just didn't feel right.

"Spare key." He dangled it in front of her. "Go for it."

Donna fished in her bag, selecting a Yale from her own bunch. "Snap. We're on your security team, remember?"

"Oh, yes, I'd forgotten. There you go, then. Breeze in under your own steam. If the Rembrandt's gone when I get in, I'll know who to come looking for."

She laughed. Another time, another place, another life, who knows, maybe she and he might have … But not now. She'd got her Marry. Rob was definitely Snog material, and who in their right mind would choose Avoid?

"If we do ever get a real alarm call-out at your place, I think it'd be better all round if I send Zbiggy. Can't see any burglar being put off by me."

Yeah … send sweet, loveable Zbiggy round if we're being robbed. But if it involves lying down half naked, with legs in the air, I'd much rather it be you, Donna …

"What about the internet spunk fella, what's happening with him?"

"Rob! Don't be so …" She couldn't think of the word she wanted so just said she was meeting him that afternoon. "Better to do both on the same day … you know, keep the timings aligned."

The lying was definitely getting easier. And it was always better to stick to one story, that's what they said, wasn't it? She was almost feeling smug at how she was playing it. Shame it wasn't the kind of cleverness she could flaunt.

29

Ben was on his third fag break. The orangery walls were now battened out, ready to take the cedar cladding. Apart from the detailing at the corners and around the windows, it was a job that didn't require too much concentration. The mitre saw was set up for repeat full-length cuts. The new wood smelt wonderful. "Cop a lungful of that, Mrs H," he'd said. "This is the business."

It smelt even more fragrant to Ben, who'd managed to get a job lot off eBay for twenty quid a square metre. *Left over from a Grand Designs* project.

Few dings and scuffs, otherwise perfect. Dry stored. Grab yourself a bargain.

Western red cedar was soft and light, seemed superficially delicate yet was very hardy. Durable. Could take pretty much whatever was thrown at it. Had strong natural defences. Ben didn't see the parallel between the timber he was working with and Carly Fitzroy, but had it been pointed out, he would have conceded the common characteristics.

There was still no word from her, from either of them. Maybe she was too busy tending her wounds and feeling sorry for herself. Maybe she was dead? The thought had crossed his mind. If it got him off the hook, he wasn't going to lose any sleep over it – he'd done enough of that already. One of them out of the picture wasn't enough, though. If she was lying in a ditch somewhere, or even if she'd suddenly got cold feet, the boyfriend wasn't going to walk away. No chance. If that little fucker was happy to use her as a punchbag, he wasn't going to get a sudden attack of conscience about a spot of blackmail. Especially when the risks were so low. He knew plenty about Ben and his family, while Ben knew nothing about him bar his name. A search for Danny Croft on Facebook had drawn a blank, too.

Ben realised that his best bet lay in the handover. Follow the money. He'd been caught out when he gave Carly the two hundred quid, fooled by the piffling amount demanded. The next demand would raise the stakes for sure. He'd be ready.

"Donna's meeting him again today. That bloke off the internet."

"You knocking off early then?"

"Nah. Giving it a miss. No point me going, is there? Might as well crack on here where I'm more use."

"Suppose."

Ben tried to imagine what it would be like to bring up someone else's kid. If you got hitched to someone who already had them, that was one thing. But when it was right under your nose …

"At least it's just fifty quid and not a grand, mate."

It was the only crumb of comfort he could think of.

30

Donna called their eight-year-old Clio Rosie, for no other reason than it was white and she liked the name. Zbiggy, on the quiet, had a less chummy, more sweary relationship with the vehicle. He didn't so much get into the car as lever himself into position. The seat alignment only had to be slightly out, either in height, rake or distance from the wheel, for the whole thing to be unworkable. When he drove it after Donna, he made the adjustments with a practised hand, and if he knew she would be driving it next, he went through the entire rigmarole in reverse to set it up ready for her.

He grudgingly conceded that at least it was easy to park and cheap to run. *Averaged 48.3mpg on the last tankful. Not bad.* Donna would pat the dashboard when he worked out the figures. Good girl, Rosie. But she still looked forward to the day when she could list the car on *AutoTrader*. As soon as a baby arrived, dinky, three-door Rosie would be immediately sacrificed in favour of a four-wheel-drive, mobile safe house. She'd join all the other mums, with their Britaxes and bike-swallowing boots. For now, Zbiggy left her to it as often as he could, grabbing lifts in Ben's van with its cavernous footwell and room to stretch out.

Rosie pulled up outside Rob and Andrea's place at two-fifteen. There was no vehicle on the drive, neither his works Astra nor their blue Golf, which Andrea used most of the time. Donna still rang the bell, though, and as the key turned in the lock and the door swung open, she called out to ask if anyone was home in a sing-song voice that belied her nervousness.

All clear. Forty minutes earlier, she'd received a text: *Bedside table spare bedroom.* And there it was. Good old Rob. He'd even been thoughtful enough to put a fresh towel out on the duvet.

She found it a lot easier this time, being more relaxed probably having as much to do with that as the fact that it was a second go. She'd brought her own hand towel with her, making Rob's considerate act redundant. She laid it out on the floor such that her bottom could rest on it, with her stockinged feet propped up on the edge of the bed. She had no cushion; bringing one of those from home would have been an obtrusive step too far. So she grabbed one of the pillows off the bed, placing it so that her pelvis was raised. She hoped the towel would absorb any seepage, otherwise she'd have to tell Rob to find a way to add the spare-room pillowcase to the next wash.

This time she gave the procedure a full thirty minutes. It still wasn't exactly a comfortable experience, but certainly a sight better than the tiled floor of a department-store cubicle. Inspecting the pillowcase afterwards, she was relieved to find it had survived intact. Once that was replaced and the towel scrunched up in her bag, there was nothing to suggest that anyone had been there. She smoothed over the towel Rob had laid out, for her heels had rested on it. Is that what he wanted, for her to leave it as she found it? Or should she put it in the bathroom? Or the laundry bin, even though it was still fluffily clean? Andrea might seize upon any of those choices if she arrived home first and noticed it. She didn't want to leave Rob fielding awkward questions, so she quickly texted him. *All done. Just leaving. Didn't use towel … brought my own … have left it where it was. Hope thats ok. Thx again. x*

On the landing, she caught an oblique view of a Justin Bieber poster in Beth's room. It was Take That and the Backstreet Boys back in her day. If a seedling was already taking root, what pop star might adorn her child's bedroom wall in a decade's time? Then, later, he or she might be a Goth, mother and child sharing eyeliner but not a love of funereal garb.

Listen to this track by The Cure, Mum.

It's all right, I suppose, but not a patch on Shania Twain.

How long would it be before he or she would demand that the cutesy nameplate on the bedroom door be removed in favour of a forbidding Keep Out sign?

31

"What do you think? Does he sound genuine to you? Do you think I should reply?"

Ben studied the screen and read.

Hi Julia. I'm not in the Fred Astaire category – thank god cos hes dead lol – but i can jive a bit when ive had a few lol. I see u also like scrabble. Cant say Ive ever played but if u want to teach me ill take u fishing.

cant say fairer than that! hope to hear from you soon. Great pic btw. Cheers, Stu

"You're a dark horse, Mrs H. Never had you pegged for this kind of thing."

Had she really pulled him aside to offer dating tips? Or was it her way of telling him she was available?

"This geezer's 61 … not sure his ticker would hold out. When you were jiving, I mean."

He winked and brushed his elbow against hers.

"Maybe he is a bit long in the tooth for me. And I can't think of anything worse than going fishing."

"He might wanna keep his maggots in yer new conservatory."

"Orangery."

"Yeah, that's what I meant."

Julia Hennessey had clearly had all the confirmation she needed to pass on Stu, 61, without feeling the need to let him down gently.

"It's my own fault, I did put 60 as my upper limit, and he was only just the wrong side. Hope this doesn't sound vain but he looks a lot more than six years older than me, don't you think? I mean, never mind the maggots and bad English, he just looks far too old for me."

"Maybe he's telling porkies, Mrs H. Might be seventy for all you know. Definitely too old, anyway. People would think you were taking yer dad out to give the care home staff a few hours off."

She laughed, grabbing his arm and squeezing it. It was a notch up the intimacy scale from his own gesture, one that he'd registered.

"So how long have you been dabbling in this Tinder lark? Leave the fruity details out, I'm not sure I'm old enough for all that stuff."

"Chance would be a fine thing!"

Duly noted, Mrs H. Thanks for the steer.

"Not long. Just dipping the toe, you know, seeing who's out there. But you hear about all these scammers targeting older women with property and a bit in the bank."

Ben thought fleetingly of the cut-price cedar, which he could see Zbiggy pressing on with apace while he was inside, chewing the fat with the boss. Not a scam, just enterprising.

"So, let's have a gander at what you've put about yerself."

She yanked back the phone, but the coquettish laugh told Ben she was surprised and slightly disappointed it had taken him this long to ask.

"It's not the most flattering photo."

She brought up her profile page and turned the screen to show him.

"Forty-eight! Mrs H, you naughty old thing."

"Well …" she replied, as if to begin an explanation but realising it was fairly pointless. "It's how I feel, so there!"

"There's me slagging poor old Stu off, and all the while he was fishing in a different pool to the one he thought! Not that he'd've suspected a thing – that is, if you'd decided to hook up with him and his tin of maggots."

Ben drained his cup of tea and said he needed to get on or the staff would start to complain. So, Julia Hennessey was officially on the market, was she? Or was it simply a ploy to push him into making a move? *You have your fun, Mrs H … and as soon as I've sorted out this little domestic problem I've got, I'll do you the turn of your life.*

He wasn't so very wide of the mark. Julia Hennessey did like his muscles and his cheeky banter. She could easily imagine allowing him to seduce her. He'd then toddle back to his wife and family, with her blessing, for they weren't cut from the same cloth. "Who's this Bally Ram-bet geezer, then?" he'd enquired during one of their earlier exchanges. "Never heard of him."

So, short-term at best. It might suit both of them. But she wasn't going to wait around to see if that flirtation went anywhere. There were plenty of distractions just a click away. Not poor old Stu. Much, much younger men, with better hair and teeth and skin; men who could converse about the arts and knew their way around a wine list; men with vigour and drive; men who knew how to treat an attractive woman – a woman who could easily pass for 48 – both in and out of the bedroom.

Right on cue, her phone provided corroboration that her wish list wasn't just a hopeless pipe dream.

Rob, thirty-six and very good looking, had added her as a favourite.

32

Sharp eyes would have been needed to pick Donna Kuzminski out as she glided effortlessly through the water. All but the odd strand of her head-turning blonde hair had been cajoled into her swim cap. Goggles hid her striking, almond-shaped green eyes. Her celestial nose – a shape that many a plastic surgeon would have been asked to recreate for an enormous fee – was pinched with a proprietary clip. And if an observer's gaze penetrated all those props, Donna's long, languid breaststroke meant that her face was submerged as often as it rose above the waterline.

It had been a last-minute decision to go to the leisure centre. This was the time window when she should have been fifty miles up the motorway, supposedly injecting Michael Phillips' semen into her vagina. A low profile made sense, and as her fitness regime had slipped recently, this seemed like as good a way as any to spend a leisurely hour unnoticed. It was quiet enough here, too. There were a few mothers and toddlers, a couple of older kids who looked like they should have been at school and a handful who, like her, were happy just bashing out the lengths at a metronomic pace, uninterrupted. She recognised no one, and apart from exchanging a smile and nod with an older man when they happened to pause simultaneously at the end of a length, she kept to herself.

Donna had read up on washed sperm. It was when the clinics put the donor semen through a separation process, extracting only the best material to go straight into the uterine area. They extracted a lot from your bank account at the same time. But, for coating the neck of the womb, the natural stuff was fine and dandy. Why wouldn't it be? Why medicalise the issue and impoverish yourself into the bargain, when you can do what Mother Nature intended?

Five more lengths, she decided. It was good to set a target. Rob's own swimmers had no conscious goal, but if they could express an opinion and were still vacillating, they surely would have preferred to go onwards and upwards rather than take the downward path to a cool, chlorinated end. Just one of them, that would do. Only one tiny tadpole had to finish the course.

Out in the car park, none of those factors that hampered recognition applied. The freshly washed hair was damply glossy. The nose that could have been on the cover of a rhinoplasty catalogue had just the faintest indentations where the clip had pinched. And the ungoggled visage restored the almond eyes, which could have matched Elizabeth Taylor's Cleopatra, given ten minutes with her make-up bag.

Those same eyes were checking her phone as she ambled towards Rosie. One from Zbiggy: *Hope all well. C u at home. Do u want me to pick anything up? x*

He'd never wooed her with words, never possessed the kind of poetic turn of phrase that could make a woman's heart skip a beat. His birthday and Valentine card messages were interchangeably generic. Flipping between *All my love, Zbiggy* and *Lots of love, Zbiggy* was about as ambitious as it got. If she wanted anything other than flowers or chocolates for a present, she shepherded him in the required direction. *It's called J'Adore, love. Just the 30 millilitre spray, that's enough to spend. Ask one of the assistants if you can't see it. Or I can pick it up and you can wrap it if you like?*

She typed: *All done. Just about to head back. Was going to make spag bol – got everything in for that. Love you. x*

He didn't deserve this. Not the lies, not the lousy trick nature had played on him. He'd make a wonderful father: besotted, doting, probably overindulgent. She'd end up playing bad cop, for she couldn't see him being good at setting boundaries or acting the disciplinarian. Wait till your mother gets home.

The ends justified the means, she kept telling herself. He didn't deserve it, but neither did she. Consider all those women who popped out kids at the drop of a hat, only to lose interest in them other than as a ticket to Child Benefit. Or, even worse than inflicting the pain of neglect, carried out the most terrible abuses. That was the greater crime, far more heinous than what she was doing. All she had to do was stay strong, stay calm. Focus on the outcome, not the process.

If only it were that simple. Process matters. Process can trip you up before you reach the goal that's meant to render it irrelevant.

Donna had already made one miscalculation that day. And now, unknown to her, a second was occurring. She didn't hear the car horn. She didn't see the frantic wave. She didn't see Zoe at all as she got into her Clio, throwing her kitbag on the passenger seat, wondering if the magical transformation had already started to occur within her body, if Rosie's days were numbered.

33

"So Beth isn't his?"

"Andrea was quite open about it, as if it was common knowledge. She thought we already knew."

"Fancy."

It was just turned nine. Freddie and Tara had finally gone down, but not before encroaching on the window of peace and quiet Ben and Zoe enjoyed before they hit the sack. A smear of Bonjela and yet another dose of Calpol eventually eased Tara's tender gums enough to be able to get her off to sleep. Freddie insisted on his bedroom door being left open so that the glow from the landing would bolster that from his rocket-shaped night light.

Ben took a swig from his bottle of Grolsch. It was his second, Zoe noted. She was still worried about him. He'd always drunk a fair bit, but two on a midweek night in was becoming the norm rather than the exception these days. Even the way he was flipping the TV remote into the air and catching it suggested an edginess – or was she just shaping the facts to suit a flawed theory? She'd even rummaged through the recycling bin to see if the contents of that A4-sized brown envelope were as innocent as Ben suggested. That proved a fruitless task, a small detail that, once again, could be read two ways. He might have taken it to work, dealt with it and binned it. Or had it been buried because it contained something he wanted to keep from her?

Before she could frame a suitable question to broach the subject, Ben beat her to the punch.

"Andrea and Zbiggy make a right pair between 'em. He's got no live ammo, and it wouldn't matter in any case with her if she's had her bits removed."

The utterance threw Zoe off her stride. But it also provided an opening for her to offer him comfort, a little soothing balm if there really was anything bothering him.

"See? I know it's hard going at times, but we ought to be thankful for our two."

Zoe swung her legs up onto the sofa and kneaded his thigh with the balls of her feet to press home the point. She'd already showered and was wearing a robe. She could let it fall open, a well-trodden route to dissipating any tension he might be feeling. Definitely for recreation, not procreation. Two kids was quite enough. They were at least on the same page about that, although it was agreement that always faltered when the subject of vasectomy arose.

What about if you ran off with another bloke and I wanted to start over again? Look at Rod Stewart, how many sprogs has he had past the age of 50?

Maybe I'll run off with Rod and see if wants to add to his tally.

If you do, I'll take his missus in part-ex any day.

"You OK, love? It's just you don't seem to have been yourself lately. If you're worried about anything …"

"Me? Nothing wrong with me, love. Todger still working like a good 'un."

"I didn't mean that. Wondered if it was work or money or …?"

"Nah. We're doing OK. Plenty on. I'm turning jobs down, we're so busy."

He ran his hand up her leg, far enough to make the robe fall open. But the expected follow-up didn't come, and she realised it was nothing more than a gesture of reassurance. He took another gulp of beer, seemingly oblivious to the fact that she was fully on show. His passing up the chance of school-night sex did nothing to allay her doubts, another tiny fragment of evidence that something was awry. Taken individually, those small things didn't amount to much. Collectively they left Zoe with a nagging feeling that wouldn't go away.

"You do know Zbiggy ain't feeling too chipper about this internet thing. He let Donna go on her own today, poor bugger. Can't say I blame him."

Nice one. She's getting suspicious. She knows something's up. Good idea to shift the convo to another couple's difficulties.

"What internet thing? I've no idea what you're on about. Where's Donna gone?"

"The internet fella, the one they're buying the spunk off. She must've told you?"

34

Price is 10k. I won't be negotiating so don't bother. Cheap for keeping the missus in the dark Idve thought. 10k and you get your life back. No 10k and our Zoe finds out shes married to a scumbag.

Almost immediately a second text arrived: *Get the money and wait for instructions.*

And then a third: *Any luck searching for Danny Croft??* It was followed by the crying-laughing emoji.

Ben breathed hard and swore, flinging the phone on to the passenger seat. He'd almost driven into the back of someone as he read the trio of messages, and got a blast from a horn as he cut someone up to make a turn he almost missed. As the offended party fleetingly drew level, he just had time to give her the finger before speeding away.

Ten grand was a non-starter. It might as well have been a hundred. But he'd spin the little fucker along. Remember: *follow the money.* He tried to work out how thick a wad of newspaper would have to be to pass for ten grand. Not much with twenty-pound notes, even less with fifties. *Come and get it, Danny boy, or whatever your fucking name is. Then we'll see what's what.*

Zbiggy was already hard at work when he pulled up. Ben had texted to say he was running late, and as Donna said she didn't need the car that day, Zbiggy had squeezed himself into the Clio.

"If something crops up during the day and you need transport, I can easily nip home," he'd told her. "I'd need a lift back to the site, but I can get Ben to drop me home."

"Thanks, love, but I don't think it'll be necessary. Got a bit of paperwork to do so won't be going far."

Not necessary, but thoughtful nonetheless. Typically considerate. She hoped all the deceit would soon be over.

They were working inside now, ready to fit the internal timber sills and plasterboard. The orangery walls mostly consisted of glazing, so infilling the exposed blockwork with plasterboard wasn't going to take long.

"David was never a fan of plasterboard," Julia Hennessey had said. "He always thought it sounded hollow and cheap."

Well David's pushing up the fucking daisies, so who cares what he thinks?

"Lot of amateurs make that mistake, Mrs H. Fact is, wet plaster on blocks is a shocking thermal bridge. Be like a fridge in here in winter."

The truth was that he and Zbiggy were average at best when it came to wielding a plasterer's float. He brought a specialist subbie in when he had to, whenever he couldn't talk the customer out of it. Today was not one of those days.

"Oh, I see," she'd said. "Yes, I never thought of that."

"Tricks of the trade, Mrs H, tricks of the trade." He tapped his nose.

Apart from what he'd seen on the telly, Ben didn't know any tricks of the blackmail trade. But he was a fast learner. And handy with his fists.

Follow the money.

35

It was one of those conversations where the smiley facial expression and sing-song voice were for the benefit of the child being dandled on the knee, while the words were for adult ears only.

"I was going to tell you – yes, I was, wasn't I, Tara? – but it's all been sooooo hectic …. sooooo hectic. It has, you know! Auntie Donna's been a really busy little bee."

Donna made a buzzing sound, swaying her head erratically before planting a kiss on the child's cheek.

"Again!" cooed Tara.

"Crafty little B, you mean, Auntie Donna," Zoe chipped in tartly.

"Bzzzzzzz …. mwah!"

"I had no idea these groups existed," Zoe continued as she scrolled down on the iPad. "Get this: *Lesbian couple based in Leeds looking for genuine donor, travel expenses paid … My husband and I are desperate after two failed IVF cycles. Must be STI free, strictly AI only, Leicester area …. Can you help us complete our family? Pref dark hair and blue eyes but not essential …* Not essential? Well, that's all right, then, I thought for a minute we were sending the blond ones back."

"Zoe, don't be so … *judgmental.* You don't know what it's like."

She'd slipped out of character now, aeroplaning Tara back into her mother's arms.

"It just seems so … tacky. And risky. I mean, listen to this dickhead …"

"Zoe!"

"Yes, all right, I promise I'll rein it in – when she's older. But get this: *Hi all, I'm Jack, 32 years old, well educated and available as a sperm doner. Loads of successes. NI only. can travel or accommodate. pm me.* That's doner spelt with an ER. All things considered, I think I'd rather order a kebab, thanks anyway, Jack."

"I'm not asking for approval, Zoe, but a bit of support would be nice."

"You've probably got that already from the world and his wife who already know what you've been up to."

"Oh, now we're getting to it. You're …" – she checked herself before the expletive slipped out – "… peed off that I didn't tell you first up, not about the choice we made."

"OK, yes. Both. I don't know. It was just weird hearing it from Ben through Zbiggy instead of straight from my best mate."

"I get that, and I'm sorry."

"You had the opportunity right there when I suggested we meet for lunch. But you just lied and said you were tied up at work all day."

"I know. I'm sorry. How many more times do you want me to apologise?"

It was tantamount to a penance to have to go through it all again. Donna felt she'd let her friend down, and had more than enough guilt on her plate already. This wrong was more easily righted, though. All it took was a comprehensive account, from the germination of the idea to the most recent interaction. It was littered with questions and interjections. Was it legal? Was it safe? Did Michael Phillips have a wife and kids? Did he suggest full sex? In the bog of The George! Really!?

Had Zoe noticed that the details of the previous day's assignation were far more sketchy than those Donna provided for the first? *I met him just off the motorway junction and followed his car from there. It was a small hotel a few minutes away … can't even remember its name.* Vagueness born of anxiety, that's what she hoped she was channelling.

And then she got carried away, adding an unnecessary detail, garnishing the story when Zoe already seemed quite content with what she'd already heard. An embellishment she had no reason to expect would raise an eyebrow. "It was all quick and easy. I was back by half four."

36

Shelf dressing was up there with Andrea Allen's least favourite jobs. Bringing stock to the front, giving the wares a user-friendly look and, in the case of the date-sensitive chiller aisle, pulling goods off it and marking them down, was a chore not designed to make the shift fly by. She preferred a busy till, more customer interaction, a chance to chat. That was a dwindling role as far as she could see. It wasn't too bad yet, but automation was casting a large shadow over the retail sector. The self-checkout area was on a creeping mission. She'd read of a superstore where shoppers just loaded goods into a trolley and exited without any human intervention, the whole transaction registered electronically. Trolley sensors picked up your purchases, the appropriate amount deducted from your account in a seamless exchange.

She did worry about the future, and she'd certainly steer Beth towards a career path with better prospects, one that robots couldn't make redundant. Medicine, maybe, or journalism. Andrea regretted that she hadn't been more goal-orientated in her teens. It wasn't entirely her fault. Her parents had been too strait-laced, too restrictive, and she'd spent more time rebelling than studying. Exams were flunked. Home was left early. A disastrous relationship had only Beth to recommend it. Then Rob came along, a lifeline she grabbed as a young, single mother; one that enabled bridges to be built with her parents. He brought security, gave her the stability that was lacking, became the proxy dad. She'd done well for herself – she knew that's what people thought. Turned it round nicely. *She did well to bag him, especially with a kid in tow.*

She'd played the lucky cow role for a good while. Was still playing it outwardly. But she'd known from the start that this wasn't how things were meant to be. Had it not been for Beth, she'd have made the change already, happily added a failed marriage to the lousy liaison with Beth's father. Taken another dose of parental disapproval. Andrea had struggled to walk the line between what she owed her daughter and owed herself.

"When are you finishing, Andrea?"

"Four. Can't come soon enough. You?"

"Six. Be glad when I'm till-trained, just for the variety."

"And the better money."

"That too!"

She wondered if the new girl working alongside her would be Rob's type. Certainly pretty enough. Right age. She knew Amy was single, not long out of a relationship and currently back living with her parents so she could boost her savings. *They've been good as gold. Don't charge me a penny.* Andrea had never wanted to return to her own family nest. No fatted calf there, just an uneasy stand-off so that her parents weren't denied contact with their granddaughter. After her mother was killed in a car crash, her relationship with her dad had improved. Dutiful visits were paid, but the feeling that she'd disappointed them had never gone away.

She had no intention of playing matchmaker for Rob, or Amy. That was just an idle thought to pass the time. Rob was more than capable of getting a date without any help from her. Andrea was glad he was so open about the ones he met. *She was called Melanie. Nice enough but no real connection ... Sarah works at the Nationwide; I thought she looked familiar ... Grace gave out mixed messages; don't think I'll be seeing her again ...*

Of course he was looking for sex. It was only natural. She couldn't very well expect him to live like a monk when she was far from taking a nun's vows. If he had fun and stayed safe, he went looking with her blessing. The acid test would come when he met someone he was serious about. As serious as she was about Drew. Then it would be decision time.

37

"Final knockings, Mrs H. Not much left to do now."

"It looks great, Ben, exactly like I hoped. I'll be glad to see it finished – of course I will – but it'll be strange not having you and Zbiggy around."

"Bet you say that to all the boys."

He glanced at Zbiggy, who was finishing off the taping and jointing of the plasterboard. They'd get the first coat of paint on before the end of the day.

"Make me a half-decent offer and I'll leave him here," said Ben, nodding in the direction of his partner. "Barely got a word out of the miserable git today. Bear with a sore bleeding head. Trouble at home, you know …"

There was another of those conspiratorial brushes of the elbow. It was no different to the others, thus it didn't up the intimacy ante. Had things been different, he'd have been a bit more suggestive by now; commented on her legs, thrown in the odd rude joke to test the water; made it clear that he was game for a roll in the hay. But the timing was shit. Better to leave well alone with the blackmail threat hanging over his head. There'd be other Julia Hennesseys. It wasn't a great loss.

"Oh, dear. I'll make him a cuppa, cheer him up. I've got chocolate digestives in."

Having slept on it, Ben was feeling better about the situation today. The punk kid had laid his cards on the table, made his pitch. Smug little bastard thought he was holding all the aces. But there'd be a mistake somewhere along the line. It was hardly going to be a case of *deposit ten grand in this Swiss bank account. Once the money's there, you'll get the photos.* No. This kid looked like he hadn't long jacked in a paper round. He thought this would be a soft touch. Big mistake. Little twat would be lucky to come out of it with all his teeth, never mind a penny more of Ben's money.

They were tidying up, ready to call it a day, when Ben noticed her hovering. He could tell she was trying to catch his attention, and that it had nothing to do with the extension. Mrs Hennessey had floated in and out, sometimes with a tea tray, sometimes not, since day one, running her hand over materials, asking technical questions, why things were done one way rather than another. More to the point, if she wanted to raise an issue, she didn't tend to do it when they were packing up.

Zbiggy didn't pick up on such things at the best of times, and had been even more of a head-down merchant that day. Something was bothering him, but he'd dead-batted all approaches that weren't work related. Ben assumed the whole thing with Donna and the guy off the internet was hitting his mate even harder than he was letting on.

"Right. I think we're about done."

"Yeah, you get off, mate. Just gonna nip to the toilet. Am I picking you up in the morning?"

"That would be great. Donna might need the car."

He waited till he heard the Clio's engine fire up. It suddenly crossed his mind that she might be about to proposition him, knowing that the job was nearly finished and opportunities were running out.

"I don't really need a wazz, Mrs H. You looked like you wanted a word in private, like."

She smiled. "You don't miss much, do you?"

"Need to get by on me wits, love. Didn't leave school with nothing, that's for sure."

"Oh, I think you're a lot sharper than people I've met with a whole wad of paper qualifications."

He turned his palms outward. "What can I say? It's a gift."

If you want to suck my cock, love, you've only got to ask nicely.

"It's a bit more advice I was after, just so I don't make an idiot of myself."

"Don't tell me you've fallen for the maggot fella!"

"Goodness, no! That's definitely a closed book. But I've had a couple of new messages, and wondered if …?"

"Go on, give it 'ere, let's have a butcher's."

Slight dent in the ego, Mrs H. Are you sure you don't want to sample the goods in front of you instead? Last chance …

She handed him the phone, stationing herself by his shoulder as he read. "This is Pete."

"This is a bloke who calls *himself* Pete, Mrs H. There's a world of difference. Not saying he's not legit, but you gotta be careful with this lark. Trust me. There's blokes out there preying on …" He nearly said vulnerable old ladies. "… attractive widows such as yourself."

Scare her off the competition and blow some smoke up her ass at the same time. It was almost too easy.

"Our friend Pete, or whatever his name is, ain't exactly Mr Universe, is he? Likes astronomy and military history. He's got an *allotment* – that should've been all the info you needed to bin him. And it must be true 'cos, trust me, no one on the pull would make that up."

"I don't think that's such a bad …"

"Mrs H, between friends, if you want a pound of carrots, get yourself down to Lidl and save yourself a whole load of bother."

"He sent me quite a sweet message. Look."

She leaned across him to call up the page. He felt her breasts against his upper arm. *That's it, girl. You rub those wherever you like. It might not have done much for dear departed David but it works for me.*

"He sounds a bit of a wet lettuce, Mrs H. Probably grew it himself!" Ben laughed, smugly pleased with his joke. *"I'm looking for my last first date. Could it be with you?* Jeez, did he get that one out of a cracker?"

"I just thought he sounded … nice."

"You'd have no trouble getting off to sleep if Pete was telling you how his greens were coming along, love. What about the other fella, show us that one."

More leaning over. Those breasts again. Maybe it was the bra doing all the work, or maybe they really were able to stand up loud and proud of their own accord.

"This is Rob. He's far too young for me, I know that. But a girl can't help being flattered."

Ben stared at the screen. *I'm an estate agent, but I've got some good points too, honest!!! … Are you a fan of Cats? The musical, I mean, not moggies!! I saw it on a school trip, Stephanie Lawrence was in it … You don't look anything like 48 … If you fancy a coffee sometime, or a drink …*

38

It was no good. It had been nagging away at her for twenty-four hours, an itch that showed no sign of going away. As soon as she'd got back from taking Freddie to nursery and cleared away the breakfast things, Zoe punched a message into her phone.

U working today? Fancy meeting up?

Andrea's reply was swift.

Off today thank god. Sounds good … rescue me from housework!!!

An hour later, they were taking it in turns pushing Tara on the swings. She squealed with delight as Zoe delivered a peekaboo in her ear at the top of every backswing. She kicked her legs wildly as Andrea jumped into her path, pulled a funny face, then hopped aside at the last second to avoid a collision. From there it was on to the slide and a game of peepo up the ramp and along the perforated walkway before Tara chose whether to come down on her bottom or tummy, forwards or backwards.

Zoe said nothing till they were seated in the café. Tara was on her lap tucking into Pom Bears and juice, occasionally offering them to the wild-haired troll she was clutching. Her gums seemed to be bothering her less today.

"Did you know that Donna's getting sperm off the internet?"

Andrea's face provided the answer. At least she wasn't the last to know, Zoe realised.

She told Andrea what she knew, about the meet-up at The George, about the iPad search, about dickhead Jack who couldn't spell but was insistent on *NI only*.

Andrea shrugged. "It's their business, but it does all sound a bit … yucky."

"That's what I said. Not to mention risky. She doesn't know the guy from Adam. Think of all the b …" – she remembered Donna's admonition about swearing in Tara's earshot – "… all the rubbish people write about themselves on dating sites."

Andrea nodded. She thought about Rob's Tinder profile and her own complicity in the massaging of the facts it contained.

"You or I mightn't fancy it, Zoe, but it's their call. If you've said your piece I think you need to back off."

"You're right, I should. But there's something not right, and I'm worried about her, about both of them."

She described how she'd seen Donna in the leisure centre car park at around three o'clock on the afternoon she said she met her donor. It couldn't have been later because she was on the way to collect Freddie from nursery. She described Donna's reaction when she told her she'd bibbed her horn at her. *Flustered, that's the only word for it. She recalled Donna's response after she'd regained her composure. Really? I must have got back earlier than I thought. Completely lost track of time. Come to think of it, the motorway was clear, I fair flew back.*

"I'm not buying it, Andrea. I didn't say anything to her, but there was a bad smash on the M5 that day. There were massive hold-ups – our neighbour got caught up in the jam. She lied in the morning, when I asked if she wanted to meet for lunch. And I'm convinced she was lying again about what she was doing that afternoon."

39

"The thing to remember," said Rob, "is that you can't add oranges and lemons. You can only add oranges to oranges and lemons to lemons. Get it? So, if you've got two oranges, and then add two more oranges, what have you got?"

"Nearly all your five a day covered?" Beth offered.

"A potential vitamin C overdose?" suggested Andrea, who happened to be passing the kitchen table carrying the laundry basket. Mother and daughter high-fived in mutual appreciation.

"Oh, I see," said Rob. "It's gonna be one of those ganging-up days, is it?"

"Dad, what's with the fruit? It's supposed to be maths."

She pushed her hair behind her ears and exhaled. All her friends would be on Facebook now, or Instagram.

"The point is," Rob ploughed on, "you can't add a quarter to an eighth, just like you can't add an orange to a lemon."

Andrea was about to point out that in a St Clement's cocktail you did exactly that, but thought better of it. They'd teased him enough, and Rob was much better with homework than she was. He'd obviously been more attentive than her in their own classroom days, made a better fist of jumping through the academic hoops, not wasted too much time trying to buck the system.

He was a good father, no question about it. He was the one who'd taught Beth to ride a bike, clapped thunderously when she did a solo spot in a school show, paced the corridors of the hospital when she fell and broke her wrist. He was the one she called Dad. Beth knew she had a real father out there somewhere; someone who "left" when she was little. She seemed to assimilate the information in a matter-of-fact way, perhaps because she had no pre-Rob memory. He'd always been around. They wondered if she'd one day get the urge to revisit the issue, to find out who else's genes she was carrying. By then the domestic picture would almost certainly be much altered, even more complicated. They would both be with different partners, Beth shuttling between them and having a fresh step-parental layer imposed upon her. Not now, though. Not yet. She needed to be shielded a little longer before her world was again turned upside down.

"So first we have to turn the quarter into eighths, then Bob's your uncle."

"I don't have an Uncle Bob. Will Auntie Josie do?"

He tweaked her snub nose. "You, young lady, are one smart cookie, do you know that?"

The fractions were finally cracked. At least, Beth got it while there was a hand to guide her. Whether she'd internalised the method and fully understood the reasoning was another matter. A smart cookie, but more likely to show it in the performing arts than in number-crunching.

Aware that the clock was running on her screen time – *one hour, that's it* – Beth took herself off to her room to see what the latest group chat was about, under the smokey-eyed gaze of a bare-torsoed Justin Bieber. With her ear-buds in, she was completely cocooned, sealed off from the conversation going on downstairs; a conversation that would have much deeper implications for her than would her friend Kelly's latest crush.

"So, what do you make of it all?"

Rob shrugged. He had little trouble showing a mixture of surprise and bewilderment as Andrea related the conversation she'd had earlier with Zoe. "I dunno. Maybe the internet guy cancelled at the last minute."

Andrea shook her head. "If that was the case, why didn't she just say so?" *Why indeed, thought Rob.*

40

Six miles away, Ben was taking a more collegiate view than Zoe regarding sharing of newly acquired information; collegiate in the sense of not dropping a mate playing the extracurricular circuit in it. *You sly old dog, Rob, you kept that quiet.* He wouldn't dream of following Rob's route – far too open, too dangerous – but he was quibbling only with the means, not the end goal. He was hardly one to judge any husband dipping his bread away from home. Pot and kettle.

Rob wouldn't be dipping anything into Julia Hennessey, though; he'd made sure of that. For the moment, Ben wanted to keep that door ajar exclusively for himself. There was a limit to what you did for a mate, and it wouldn't have felt right going there after Rob had done the dirty.

I know this fella from somewhere, Mrs H. I think he's a scammer. I'd steer well clear if I were you. Trust me.

And she did.

Sorry about that, Rob, mate. Find an old slapper of your own. This one's mine.

She'd been grateful for the advice. It's such a minefield these days. I could have walked right into a whole heap of trouble if you hadn't been here. He still hoped to cash in those gratitude chips.

"So you don't think I should tackle her about it?"

Ben had lost count how many times Zoe had returned to the subject. If she was like this on a vague assumption, on circumstantial evidence, it didn't take much imagination to work out what she would be like with unshakeable facts – like Rob's Tinder account, or compromising photos of him and Carly.

"Like I say, she'll have her reasons, love. I'd leave well alone."

"Hmmm," came the unconvinced-sounding reply.

He had *The Great British Bake-Off* to thank for some welcome respite. Ben was more interested in whatever was on his plate than watching programmes about people cooking it. Give him a Ginsters pasty and he was more than happy; he didn't need to see the filling being prepared or how the pastry was crimped. When he and Zoe had celebrated their third anniversary at a restaurant specialising in nouvelle cuisine, Ben had bought chips on the way home.

"Might go for a quick pint, love."

Zoe waved a hand at him, like the regal dismissal of a lackey. He didn't mind. Whether she was salivating over the grub, or Paul Hollywood, or a bit of both – which was closer to the truth – it gave him a bit of breathing space. He wondered what excuse Rob used when he went out shagging – assuming he'd been at it for some time.

He'd barely made it out of the door when the text alert sounded. The screen – which had needed shielding during the dog days of summer, heat-haze days that had extended well into September – now glowed bright and clear in the chill autumnal air.

Im getting out. Taking yr advice. Going to a friend a long way away. Fresh start. Ill be ditching this phone after sending this so he can't get to me. Sorry again for everything. Be careful.

Ben rang the number immediately. Not to put her off but to get any last fragments of information about the boyfriend, anything that might help or give him an edge.

The line was already dead.

41

On the Friday evening, it was Donna who suggested going for a drink. She'd agreed to babysit for Zoe if they were stuck, relieved to receive a message saying one of the neighbours had offered.

"What, just you and me?" said Zbiggy.

"Just you and me."

They went out far less than many of their friends who had kids. While others shelled out for sitters or dragooned grandparents into hosting weekend sleepovers so they could nurse their hangovers in peace, Donna and Zbiggy were more likely to be found in some kind of intertwined state on the sofa watching *Strictly* or a Scandi thriller box-set. If the dialogue of the subtitled crime shows was a bit too rat-a-tat, she was used to him needing a recap. *I missed that. What did she say? Can you rewind it?* She sometimes showed mock-annoyance at the break in flow, but secretly loved his ponderous ways: the tortoise who would keep going and get there in the end, not the hare who would streak off and get sidetracked.

He thought nothing of it when she refused her usual white wine spritzer. *Just a tomato juice, love.* That was Zbiggy all over. He took everything at face value. He didn't dig for hidden meaning unless he was led. And she wasn't going to lead him tonight. She wanted to do another test, to be sure. And even then, she'd leave it just a little while, long enough not to tempt fate. Get through the early weeks, she decided, when the danger of miscarriage was greatest. If the worst happened, she would have no choice but to deal with it. Zbiggy could be cushioned, though. She couldn't bear the thought of seeing him crushed, the disappointment etched on his big open face. Or the thought of him saying they'd put themselves through enough, that now they should seriously consider adoption or fostering. Or accept their childless state.

"Fancy another episode of *The Bridge* when we get back?"

Donna had had to agree when Zbiggy commented that she and the show's detective star could have been sisters. *Yeah, but she's a cold fish, and none too fussy who she sleeps with.*

That observation was made before all this business with Rob started. But the difference between her and Saga Noren still held true. She had bucketloads of empathy, a quality in short supply in the detective's character. And she was not sleeping with Rob. Still, she'd be glad when the pregnancy was well along, when Rob's walk-on part was over, when the smell of newborn skin and dirty nappies was in the air.

"If you like, love," replied Zbiggy. "I'm a bit lost, though, to be honest. Think I need a recap."

If the worst happened, she'd have no choice but to deal with it.

The trouble was, Donna had no yardstick for measuring what the worst entailed.

42

Freddie Fuller's Manchester United shirt buried him. There was enough growing room in it to last him a couple of seasons, and by the end of its life, it would fit in the skintight way the pros wore them. For now, the excess material billowed and flapped as he dribbled in and out of the cones.

The soccer school coaches wished more parents were like Ben. He stuck to the sidelines, gave the odd whoop and clap, and didn't interfere. He wasn't one of those dads who hurled obscenities or issued threats if he thought his darling child wasn't getting a fair crack of the whip, or wasn't being touted as the next Harry Kane.

"Great stuff, Freddie," said one of the coaches, ruffling his hair. "Try and use both feet next time, but that was excellent!"

The boy beamed beatifically.

"Go, Freddie!" yelled Ben.

Ben had played rugby at school, which partially accounted for the model parent tag the organisers labelled him with. He didn't really understand football beyond the basics. Had it been the oval ball, his outbursts might have been rather less generic and he would probably have been less well regarded. Ben would have been impatient for tag rugby to be replaced by the real thing. *What, you have to grab a handkerchief? Call that a tackle? It's more like a cuddle.*

Ben had been a stick-thin, slippery centre back in the day. He liked the hits, the collisions, the bruises, the bloody noses and split lips. Zbiggy had played number eight in all those school teams, the monster of the pack who could carry on running with a couple of tacklers on his back. He was the hulking, unsung forward laying the foundation for the glory-grabbing, quicksilver showboaters in the backs. The two were prime examples of the cavaliers and roundheads the game embraced – roles that had spilled over into adulthood.

The Saturday morning ritual offered plenty of touchline wriggle room: time to thumb through a newspaper, to nod and chat to other watching parents, the ones who hadn't just dropped their darlings off and disappeared for an hour. A couple of the mums were real lookers. There was no such distraction on this occasion, though; nothing except for his phone.

The session was almost over when the message came through. It was just a number; he hadn't assigned a name to it. But he recognised it all the same.

Leave the money here at exactly 2pm tomorrow. ill be watching. dont think im gonna dissapear like her. dont fuck up.

The picture attachment made it obvious where "here" meant. It was the local park, on the opposite side to where the children's play area was situated. In the background was the path and the fenced-off skate zone, where a number of indistinct figures were frozen in time as they tackled the ramps. Filling the foreground was a dark grey, municipal waste bin.

43

Donna had loaded the car and was about to return the trolley to the Aldi bay. Her shopping didn't include any fate-tempting baby products, but she'd lingered over those shelves all the same, taking in the range of own-brand goods on offer. She imagined her own child fast asleep on her shoulder, just like in the cutesy picture on the *Mamia* nappy packs. She'd scanned the food and drink selection, with their Stage One and Stage Two markings as if it was describing widgets on a production line or a rocket launch. Organic they might be, but she would be using those for occasional back-up or when she was out on the go. This child was not going to be fed on anything mass produced; at least, not as the default option. Why take their puréed butternut squash and blueberry when you could buy them fresh and blend to taste?

The prices were good, though. She could see herself stocking up on their wet wipes and baby bath and cotton wool pads when the time came. The Sainsbury's where Andrea worked was just down the road, but even she was a regular here, for her staff discount was often not enough to beat Aldi prices. The bosses wouldn't have been best pleased to see a still-uniformed staff member patronising the competition.

Though money wasn't especially tight, it still made sense to boost their savings. That wasn't difficult to do, for she and Zbiggy indulged in few extravagances. The odd pub visit like the previous night: two rounds of drinks and back for another hour of Nordic noir; a cinema trip; the odd takeaway. Their get-togethers with Zoe and Ben and Andrea and Rob added to the shopping bill, but that only came round three or four times a year for each couple. Conversely, when it was one of the others' turn to host, it was a cheap night out: a bottle of supermarket plonk, four-pack of beer and a taxi fare.

Rob. What to do about Rob? Crystal ball-gazing for baby toiletries and foodstuffs was one thing, but how would those social evenings work when they were playing host after the birth? Imagine a bleary-eyed child appearing in a doorway holding a favourite teddy.

The noise woke me up. Can daddy tuck me in?

Do you want to go, Zbiggy, or shall I?

"I'll have the trolley, Donna. Here's your quid."

It was positively spooky. Rob, with one hand on her trolley and proffering recompense with the other, appearing as if from nowhere at the very moment when she was wondering whether a clean break might be the best thing after the baby was born. How to cut the ties with the Allens while keeping Zoe and Ben onside, she didn't have an answer to that.

"Hi. Where did you spring from?"

"Regular haunt. You looked like you were miles away."

"Caribbean island would do." She smiled weakly.

"Actually, I'm glad I've caught you. I take it all went OK the other day?"

"All fine. I hope Andrea didn't notice anything untoward? I think I left everything …"

"No, I didn't mean then, at our place. I meant later. The meeting with the other guy."

Donna flushed. She knew her cheeks were betraying her, or, if not them, then her eyes. Fooling Zbiggy was one thing. Other gazes were more penetrating, and Rob's piercing eyes certainly fell into that category.

"Yes. Good. It went well."

"Really? Was the helicopter flight smooth? Or maybe you went by magic carpet?"

"What – ?"

"You're suddenly looking very *flustered*, Donna. Apparently, that's the very word Zoe used when she said how she'd seen you at the leisure centre that same afternoon. She told Andrea and …" He left the final link in the chain hanging. "Nice relaxing swim, was it? Better than being caught up in all that motorway traffic, I should think."

"Rob, I told Zoe I must have got …"

"… the timing wrong. Sure. Funny how I can't seem to get rid of the smell of bullshit ever since I heard that line. Must see what kind of air freshener they sell here."

With that, he pressed the pound coin into her hand and took possession of the trolley. Donna hadn't agreed to the deal. He'd dictated terms and she'd dumbly accepted the exchange.

44

Ben strained his eyes to see if he could allocate all the adults present to each of the children. Was the guy in the grey hoodie looking after anyone? Yes, a little girl just raced over to the bench where he was sitting to hand him something – a hairband? – then was back on the tyre swing before anyone else bagged it.

The play park was almost a hundred yards away. Would he really choose that as a lookout spot? Ben had been here countless times with the kids, but only now did he cast his eyes around in a 360-degree sweep to assess the possible vantage points. Countless windows looked on to the green space, from the properties across the main road skirting the park to low-rise apartments recently built on the site of the old bowling green, to flats above the swathe of retail outlets backing on to it. Sunlight played on hundreds of window panes. The blackmailing gobshite could have been standing at any one of them right now, unseen.

Then again, would he really go to the trouble of arranging temporary occupation of one of these properties just to watch Ben deposit a bag in a waste bin, to make sure the coast was clear before retrieving it? It was unlikely. Carly had done exactly that and shafted him, but that was different. The flat had been used to screw him over, not to observe.

Unless, of course, it wasn't temporary accommodation. What if he lived in one of these houses or flats and chose the park *for that very reason?*

So many variables, too many imponderables.

He looked at his watch. Five past one. Coming to the spot early wasn't much of a wrongfooting move – zero advantage if he was being watched – but it was all he could think of. There was an outside chance he could turn the tables, a chance he felt he had to take.

Getting away from home had not been as tricky as he'd imagined. As usual, work was the failsafe excuse. *This couple have had a bit of a flood, the whole bathroom will need replacing. Insurance job, could be a good wedge in it. Early bird gets the worm and all that.* Zoe knew that if a sales spiel was required, it was no good sending Zbiggy. He'd most likely help them clean up and tell them it was all salvageable. Nevertheless, he'd expected a bit more grief than he'd got. In fact, Zoe seemed to be worried that there was enough work in the pipeline.

We are OK, aren't we? Moneywise?

Course, love. Still, can't look a gift horse and all that. You and the kids have dinner without me if I'm not back when it's ready to dish up.

Easy-peasy.

"Oy, son," Ben called out. "Come here a sec, will ya?"

"Talkin' to me?"

The boy was in his early teens. Razor tracks visible in his hair beneath a backwards baseball cap. A T-shirt sporting the legend *All I need is wifi, food and bed.*

"Wanna make an easy tenner, son?"

"You a peedo?"

"What? No, I'm not a friggin' peedo, you cheeky … It's an easy job, you don't even have to leave the skate park. But you do have to keep your eyes skinned."

"What for?"

They were now eyeballing each other through the wire netting. Ben briefly flashed a ten-pound note, realising he needed to make it quick. It would have looked fishy to a casual observer, and if the little fucker was watching, it wouldn't take much to put two and two together.

"You just need to watch that bin over there." He jabbed a thumb in its direction. "Between two and three o'clock. Anyone goes near it, anyone drop anything in it, you take their photo and ring me pronto. You've got a phone, right?"

The boy whisked a high-end Samsung from his jeans pocket, a better-specced phone than Ben's.

"Is that it? Watch that bin for an hour?"

"That's it. That's all."

Ben figured that an hour would be enough. Would anyone risk leaving it longer? A tramp might raid the bin. It might be emptying day. Whatever. Once the little fucker was sure Ben was well away from the area, he'd surely want to get his hands on the money quickly and get away.

"OK, deal."

He held out his hand for payment. Ben dug into his pocket

and pulled out a five-pound note. "Half now, the other half at three o'clock."

The money was passed through the netting. No one shouted. No one approached to ask what he was doing. But that didn't mean there weren't prying eyes wondering what that bloke was doing near those kids. *Is he a pimp? Did he just pass drugs through the fence?*

It couldn't be helped; it was a risk worth taking. Ben gave the boy his number and sloped off at a sharp pace.

There was still over half an hour to kill before he was supposed to make the drop so he went for coffee, choosing an outdoor table so he could have a smoke. He laid the Boots carrier bag on the table as he drank his flat white. It looked like it might have contained a pack of socks or pair of thick gloves. The contents were actually far less valuable. He'd spent no more than five minutes tearing up pages from an old Argos catalogue into rough, note-sized pieces. Poor man's shredder, but the result looked the part, that's what mattered.

A distant church bell confirmed that Ben had got his timing right. Two strokes. The bin was around three-quarters full when he tossed in the Boots bag. Close up, it was clearly visible through the side slots, resting on top of a foil takeaway dish. Hidden enough so that it wouldn't attract attention unless someone was singling it out. Far enough down so that anyone depositing rubbish wouldn't come anywhere near touching it.

He took the same path alongside the skate zone. There was the kid hovering on the other side of the fence, board under one arm, phone in the other hand.

"An hour starting now?"

"That's it," replied Ben, without averting his gaze.

Surely the little fucker couldn't be a lip reader too.

45

Keep it light. Play it cool. Grace Newman could feel her heart rate rise as she called up her messages. Technology took the embarrassment out of these interactions. Gone were the days of plucking up courage to gauge someone's interest face to face, of beating a retreat with burning cheeks if the answer wasn't the one you wanted. Withdrawing with dignity dented. Now you could brush someone aside – or be brushed – with a quick swipe. Block messages from this person. Delete contact. Unfriend.

Had her next couple of dating experiences not been so bad, Grace wouldn't have contemplated the reassessment. But they'd been cringingly awful, and she began to think Rob deserved a second chance. Take away that last twenty seconds and she'd had a great time. The same couldn't be said of the meet-up with Nigel. He was a sallow-complexioned, overweight gaming nut who bored her rigid with talk of *Call of Duty* and *Minecraft*. Worse than that, he'd banged on about blokes he followed on YouTube, blokes who gave themselves weird names and shared the same passion. Men with stunted growth watching other men with stunted growth playing video games. *You can laugh but they make millions, the top players.* She'd laughed just the same, and pulled the plug on the evening very early. Nigel had almost seemed relieved, able to hurry back to his bedroom, back in front of a screen with tea and snacks provided by his indulgent mother.

Then there was Kevin. He was decent looking, said he had a job that regularly took him overseas, and wrote a neat profile full of self-deprecating humour. *My ex left me for a sous chef. He poached her, you could say. It rubbed salt in the wound, but at least it was probably good-quality rock salt.* Grace had found him dully inarticulate when they met up in a wine bar, an anomaly that was explained when she forced out of him that he'd cut-and-pasted his profile and got a teacher mate from his darts team to pull it all together. Kevin had grinned when he said the job that regularly took him overseas was that of long-haul lorry driver. *I thought of that bit, that was my idea, not Will's. Good, eh, admit it.* For Grace that was the icing on another disappointing cake; icing that Kevin's ex's new boyfriend would no doubt have been able to whip up in short order. Except he was actually an insurance broker who, Will and Kevin decided, needed to change jobs for poetic licence reasons.

The reappraisal of her date with Rob thus began. If he'd been a bit handsy with her, maybe it was because she was so hot he couldn't restrain himself. That was what Phoebe and a couple of other mates she'd confided in had said. And she had to admit that if he'd acted in the way he had on the third or fourth date, she'd have happily gone along with it.

So it wasn't the action *per se*, just the timing, that had scared her off. She'd been with Gavin so long that maybe the rules of engagement had changed. They'd met on Tinder, after all, not at a church social. Rob might have thought she was in it for a one-night stand, that a grope and a hard-on was the least expected of him. If she clarified the point with him, he might even be relieved to find she wanted a more traditional type of courtship.

She reread his last message. *Enjoyed the other night. Sorry about how it ended. Youre just too sexy I guess! Hope we can do it again.* She'd let six days slip by, and it was more than a week since they'd met. It was too long a gap. That rule surely hadn't changed from her teenage years. But she had the benefit of that all-important face-saving anonymity. It was just a question fired into the ether, and if he blanked her the way she had him, then at least she could move on without wondering what if, and with her head held high. No one would know.

Hey Rob, how's things? Sorry not to have got back to you sooner – manic week. Apologies for scooting off like that, it was just a bit too soon. Trust issues after Gavin, I guess. Not crazy or a prude, just need a bit more time. Anyway, if you haven't forgotten me and want to give it another go, let me know. x

She vacillated over the kiss. In the end she thought: sod it, it's the least Pheebs would have done. Phoebe had grown up during the swipe-left-swipe-right explosion, and had the body confidence and love of shocking people to send the odd risqué pictures not long into the getting-to-know-you stage. She'd admitted there must have been a few ex-boyfriends out there with raunchy photos of her still in their possession. *In the next one I might lose the bra – depends what you've got to bargain with.* She was lucky that none had come back to haunt her, now she was an old married woman.

Grace read the message over after hitting the send button. Manic week. Yeah, right. No one was going to buy that. You could have been the head honcho in the thick of Brexit negotiations and still found time to dash off a one-line reply. *Bit pushed this week, country going down the pan. Will be in touch.* It was all very well for Phoebe to give the impression that her work and social diary were both rammed, but Grace was the one who'd have to account for all those days and hours if he enquired. As a 9–5.30 legal secretary with regimented breaks and long evenings, that wasn't going to be easy.

Less than three minutes after she fired off the message, Grace Newman learned that she would not have to field any such tricky questions. Nor would she have to decide whether she was happy for him to press his stiff dick into her on date three or if she should hold out until the fourth meeting. The promise suggested by the swift response evaporated in three short sentences.

You missed the boat love. Ive moved on to a hot blonde wholl be a lot more willing. Your loss.

46

The boy rang just once in the allotted time window. Ben answered as he stared at the image the kid had sent: an image of a woman in half-profile; mid-forties at least, wearing a three-quarter-length waxed coat and carrying one of those plastic contraptions that launched tennis balls for dogs to fetch. The waste bin was in the left of the frame, the photo clearly snapped a second after she'd passed it.

Ben broke into a run, his phone clamped to his ear. He'd stationed himself just round the corner from the exit near the play park, well out of sight.

"What happened? What did she do?" he asked, wheezing the questions through exhaled breath. The fags always hit home when he tried to go through the gears.

"I can't be sure but I think she chucked a bag of dog shit in the bin."

"Did she put her hand through the slot or just throw it in from a distance? Did her hand go down inside the bin at any point?"

"No, she just chucked it in as she passed, I'm pretty sure. Little plastic bag, it was."

"Can you still see her?"

"Yeah. Her dog's sniffing another one's arse and she's calling it, trying to get it to come. Dog ain't havin' any of it."

Ben stopped. He'd reached the far side of the play park now, and peered through the rope climbing frame. He took in the squared scene the boy was describing: a woman agitatedly trying to bring to heel a dog that had found a new playmate. The other animal didn't seem to have an owner, and it was left to her alone to try and restore order. The boy slouched inconspicuously against the fence, looking on.

What to do? Ben was pretty sure it was a false alarm, that this wasn't some accomplice doing the little fucker's dirty work. He could go and check the bin to make absolutely sure, but that risked being seen, probably for nothing. He might have been spotted already, but the game was definitely up if he went any further. If he backed off, there was still a chance of the pick-up being made.

"OK, son, well done. There's still twenty minutes left. Let me know if you see anything else. Same drill."

He turned his collar up and retraced his steps.

Twenty-one minutes later, Ben's phone rang again. This time there was no accompanying photo, it was just the boy saying the hour was up and there was nothing else to report. By the time Ben had walked back to the skate zone, the woman had clearly reclaimed her dog and gone. He passed another five-pound note through the netting, and the boy pocketed his prize with an air of someone who had got the better end of a negotiation.

As the kid returned to the ramps happily enriched, Ben decided he might as well check the bin. Yes, there it was, exactly as he'd left it, save for what looked like a dog's poo bag now resting in the foil tray. He cast his eyes around. *Are you watching, you little twat? You'll make a mistake, and when I catch up with you, you'll be sorry you fucked with me.*

47

Donna's Weetabix had come up and she was now retching clear stomach juice. She was holding the side of of the toilet bowl with one hand, keeping most of her hair back with the other. It was starting. Only a professional knew as much as she did about what the next forty weeks held; forty weeks minus the days since conception. Donna had become a book-learned expert on every aspect of pregnancy, theories she had witnessed in practice in Zoe and other friends. Now it was her turn.

She'd expected it to be the most joyous moment of her life, nature's miracle occurring inside her at long last. She'd envisaged producing the Clear Blue kit like a magician's rabbit, waving it in front of Zbiggy's face and waiting for the joyous news to sink in, for his beaming smile to match hers. A triumphant *we did it* moment, maybe taking a goofy selfie for dissemination once the uncertain period had passed. Parcel it with the 12-week scan image and wait for the congratulations to roll in. Instead, her overriding emotions were trepidation and doubt. No matter how well she hid those, an array of tell-tale signs was waiting in the wings. On this occasion, the nausea hadn't come on until after Zbiggy had left, but it was only a matter of time before the penny dropped.

She could have done a million and one other things instead of going for a swim; or she could have emerged from the leisure centre two minutes earlier or two minutes later. Zoe would never have seen her, and the trail of deception wouldn't have led back to Rob. It was her sliding doors moment: the thin line between triumph and disaster.

How much of a disaster depended on him. He was pissed off at being conned, and rightly so. But having slept on it, he would surely see things in a better light. After all, it was a huge compliment. *I only wanted your sperm, Rob, not some Jack-the-lad's off the internet.* That was the bigger picture. Hold on to that.

She showered and changed, feeling a lot more positive. The nausea had worn off, and she convinced herself that she was being unduly anxious. Forty-eight hours had passed since the car park exchange, and he was probably now feeling sheepish about his sharp-tongued reaction. Still, the first wrong – the greater wrong – was hers, and it was up to her to hold out the olive branch. He deserved an apology, an explanation. *We'd be thrilled to have a little boy with your attributes, or a beautiful little girl like Beth.*

She was ravenous now. Popping two slices of bread in the toaster, she made herself a cup of camomile tea. The latter went down the sink untouched after some idle googling suggested herbal teas might not be a good idea during pregnancy. Who knew? Clearly there were still plenty of gaps in her knowledge, even more to mug up on during the coming weeks and months. She and Zbiggy were not exactly the kind to frequent sushi bars, but caffeine, soft cheese and wine spritzers were common enough over a week's consumption. The less time she had to dodge those situations, without Zbiggy knowing why, the better.

She decided it was bull-by-the-horns time. She had a job to do at Wetherspoons, routine stuff involving how long it took to be served over the busy lunchtime period, seeing if a drink was supplied in its branded glass and giving feedback on one of the menu options. The pub wasn't far from Rob's office, but she decided a frontal approach wasn't the way to go. She did opt for the office landline rather than his mobile, though. Better not to give him a Donna calling forewarning, the chance to decide whether he was available or not.

"Yes, he's here. Who shall I say's calling?"

She would have liked to gauge his facial expression when he was told who was on the line. At least he couldn't sidestep her.

"Hi, Rob. Sorry to bother you at work. If it's a bad time …?"

"No. It's fine. Pretty quiet."

"About Saturday. You were obviously angry. I don't blame you. I just thought we ought to, you know, clear the air."

"I'd be lying if I said I hadn't given it any thought."

"Right. Yes, of course. And where have these thoughts led? I mean, have you come to any conclusions?"

She realised she was skirting round the issue, not owning the error by owning up to it.

"Before you say anything," she pressed on, "this was all my doing. It was wrong, but for good reasons. I hope you can see that."

The line went silent for several seconds. Donna had half-expected a tirade commensurate with the entrapment. Having nothing to feed off was unnerving. His voice was lower when he finally spoke, more like an animated whisper. She guessed it was so he wouldn't be overheard.

"Tell me, was the first meeting with the guy off the internet a sham too? A big fat lie?"

"Yes."

She'd anticipated that question being asked at some point and had decided to come straight out with it. The alternative would simply mean digging another hole for herself.

"So right from the start you only intended to use my …"

"Yes." Even whisper-quiet, she didn't want him to say the word. Not now.

"And just carry on until you fell pregnant, was that the idea? Having phantom appointments with whatshisname on the same day?"

"Yes."

He knows everything now. Almost everything.

"Obviously we have to stop," she said. "It was a mistake before. It certainly wouldn't be right now."

There was the small matter of what do when the blueberry turned into a plum, then an aubergine, then a watermelon. The pregnancy was the only issue she'd decided was for another day. That was too much to handle for both of them at this moment.

"Oh, I don't know," said Rob. "Now I think about it, I don't see why it changes anything."

"You can't be serious? It changes everything."

"It was 50-50 before, now it's all down to me."

"No, Rob. It's down to me."

Oh, God, please let it not have to come to that, not after waiting so long.

"OK, Donna. But that's an awful lot to lay on Zbiggy. All those lies. Big lies. Provable lies."

"Zbiggy isn't going to know anything."

I refuse to book an appointment. This is my baby, not tissue waste.

"If it were just up to me … but Zoe already knows you were lying. All it would take is a quick phone call to the internet guy to see what he was doing the afternoon you went for a nice swim at the leisure centre."

"Now you listen to me – "

"Then there's all that kit you bought. Has it appeared on a statement yet?"

"What the hell are you playing at, Rob?"

"I have a client. Must go."

48

It was a bit like that children's memory game. *I can see a Boots bag, a takeaway foil dish, a dog poo sack … and a banana skin.* The last of those had been added by the time Ben swung by the park early on Monday morning, before picking Zbiggy up. There were a couple of dog walkers on the green and headphone-sporting jogger, but not the woman with the wayward animal from the previous day. There were no takers yet for the skate zone. The same windows looked out on him as he examined the bin, a bin with its single new addition. Theoretically, dozens of pairs of eyes trained on him. More likely, none.

It had elements of a different children's memory game, too. Not just repeating a list and adding one on. Spot the difference in a scene where something had been moved. The Boots bag was partly obscuring one of the banana skin's flaps. That couldn't have happened by random settlement. Someone had disturbed the pile, rummaged through the detritus. The question was, had it been a search for a morsel of discarded food, a drinks bottle containing dregs, an item that could be repurposed or sold? Or had it been a targeted search? A plastic bag examined and thrown back in disgust on discovering the hacked-up pages of an Argos catalogue, not a wad of crisp twenty-pound notes?

"Morning, mate. Good weekend?"

Zbiggy climbed into the cab, clutching his usual Tupperware container. Ben knew, without looking, that Donna would have packed it with two doorstep cheese and pickle sandwiches, a four-finger KitKat and an apple.

"We had a quiet one," Zbiggy grunted.

There was something bothering him, he hadn't been his usual self these past few days. Ben put it down to his missus going off to baste herself with another man's jizz, the blow to his masculinity, the cuckolding with consent. *Here's fifty quid, Mikey Boy, see if you can get her pregnant.* Ben was better at fronting up, putting on a show even when he had shit to deal with.

"Morning, Mrs H. Looking more glam than ever this morning, if that were possible."

They were pretty much done on the orangery. There was some siliconing to do, the sill needed staining and varnishing, and there were snagging checks to be carried out. The floor was still bare concrete, but they were going to leave that a little longer to make sure it had completely cured. Then it was a case of coming back, once Mrs Hennessey had finally decided between sheet vinyl or ceramic tiles. They'd agreed that was a separate arrangement; she'd pay the balance for the work to date.

"I'm thrilled to bits with it," said Mrs Hennessey as she handed over the cheque.

"Just needs a woman's touch now, Mrs H. If you choose curtains or blinds, we can whack them up when we come back to do the flooring, if you like. Then you'll just need a few pot plants, comfy chair or two. Be like Kew Gardens. Lady of the flipping manor."

"My neighbours are all going to want one."

"Tell 'em we'll do 'em a good deal. Always happy to oblige." He added, winking, "Yours was the first, though, eh? Proper trendsetter, that's what you are."

49

By abandoning most of her burger and chips, Donna was passing up one of the job's main attractions. Assignments that involved dining meant a free meal, often worth at least as much as the fee for doing the job. The lucky few market researchers bagged gigs that were, quite literally, a lot further up the food chain. Fine dining, buckshee. Who cared about being paid on top? Wetherspoons was more in the fill-a-gap value sector: decent quality and portion size for the money. Not a free lunch, of course; there was a detailed report to write. She had to assess the brioche bun, the new red wine-infused beefburger, the fries and side salad. Confirmation was needed that the Peroni had been served in the correct glass. A tickbox exercise for the service at point of sale, and whether a staff member had checked back with her. *Everything all right for you?*

Donna consumed just enough to complete the task. It was a terrible waste, really. She thought of asking for a doggy bag so that at least one doorway down-and-out might benefit. Just the food, obviously. The lager would be left untouched. She'd already bought herself a sparkling mineral water with a slice of lemon. No booze. No caffeine. Whatever happened now, it wasn't the baby's fault.

She sat in her booth, waiting for the queue to die down. A young couple had installed themselves opposite her and were huddled over a single menu. It made her even keener to leave.

"Excuse me, would you mind watching my stuff while I go to the bar? Don't let anyone clear it away, will you?"

"No probs," said the girl.

"Oh, and have that lager if you want it. It hasn't been touched."

"You sure? OK, cheers." The boy swooped on that.

Donna swung her legs out, but stopped dead. There he was. Grinning from ear to ear as he breezed through the pub's swing doors. She couldn't hear what he was saying above the hubbub, and didn't need to. For the woman on whose back his hand was placed was laughing, so it was obviously some well told joke or witty observation. He was gesticulating now, a sweeping arc covering the whole room rather than indicating a particular location. *Why don't you go and grab us a seat?* was the obvious translation.

Donna ducked back into her own. The booth's bench had shaped and polished wooden cheeks, which shielded her from lateral view. She placed her bag on the vacant inside seat and began rooting around in it, feigning a search. Out of the corner of her eye, she could see that the young couple were too wrapped up in their own food selection conversation to be interested in her behaviour.

When she risked another look, she was relieved to see his back view as he waited his turn at the bar. Blue-suited, broad-shouldered, wavy-haired. A stubbled cheek briefly displayed as as he glanced to his left and nodded. Donna followed the sight line and traced it to the woman. She looked around 30. Petite. Tousled dark hair that had a managed unruliness. It had probably taken no small amount of effort to create that just-out-of-bed look. Donna took in her swan neck and oversized glasses. The woman was staring at her phone, obviously using it as a mirror, for she was running her tongue over her teeth.

Donna kept her eye on Rob's back as she made for the door. He was being served now, so she was safe. She wouldn't be getting a doggy bag after all, and some homeless unfortunate was going to miss out on a square meal.

There was a Caffè Nero directly opposite. Ordering an unwanted soft drink, Donna waited for a window armchair to become vacant and pounced. There were a few pavement tables and chairs for the hardier souls and smokers, but she now had prime position for taking in a long stretch of the high street, seeing while remaining unseen.

The woman with Rob could have been a colleague or friend. But there was something about that hand planted on the small of her back that suggested otherwise. Something about the way she was checking her appearance. Donna smelt a spark already lit. She smelt foreplay, never mind that it was in a public space. What was completely absent, as far as she could tell, was the unpleasant undertone of her and Rob's phone conversation a few hours earlier. *All it would take is a quick phone call to the internet guy …*

The wait lasted forty-five minutes. Donna still had half her juice left, and behind her back, there were doubtless customers – maybe staff, too – wondering how long she planned to eke out that beverage at a busy time. There had been no takers for the leather armchair on the other side of the table, so presumably no singleton customers during that time. One man had coldly asked if he could have the newspaper that lay folded on the table, either the establishment's copy or left by the couple Donna had supplanted. What he really wanted was for her to go so that he and his partner could make full use of a window table for two. *We've got cake, you know. It came to over a tenner. Finish that juice and bugger off, for Christ's sake.* Donna remained oblivious and kept her station.

At last. Hoo-frigging-ray. That was the unspoken verdict of Newspaper Man as she suddenly collected her bag and work file and left, leaving him and his partner to claim their prize. Donna tracked Rob and the woman from across the road, keeping some twenty yards behind. They were in animated conversation. At first she thought they were making for Rob's office, for that lay a hundred yards ahead. Maybe she was a colleague after all? The deputy manager taking a new staff member out to lunch? That idea faded as they turned into a side road leading to the pay-and-display. Donna dropped further back, for there were fewer people along here than on the main drag. She quickened her step once they passed the barrier, since the parked vehicles provided plenty of cover. She watched them stop beside a red Mini. She watched the woman take out a key fob and open the door. She watched as Rob kissed her on the cheek. She watched him pull back. She watched the consensual tango being played out. She watched him plunge forward again, this time mouth to open mouth.

She captured it all, a scene that could be played back wholesale or in still frames ripped from the video.

Fuck you, Rob. Fuck you.

50

Mr Worthington rang – they'll take 247.5k. Said you'd call him back.

Rob screwed the Post-it note into a ball and pinged it into the bin, giving a truncated goalscorer's raised-arm salute. A right result. He'd told the purchasers the bungalow was an excellent buy at two-five-five, but he'd do his best to get it under the quarter-million stamp-duty threshold. He'd actually merely sat on his hands, waiting for someone to blink. The Worthingtons, who hadn't had any new viewings in a while, had duly obliged. Now he just needed to reassure them they were doing the right thing in a tightening market. *Brexit's casting a cloud of uncertainty over the property market. Cash is king, Mr Worthington.* Then it would be a straightforward deal-sealer to nudge the buyer up to the new asking price. *It's a steal for that money, you're meeting them well south of halfway.*

He was feeling pleased with himself. Smug, even. The day had already been looking up, and now it was just a hop and skip to another Sale Agreed.

Esther Greaves. Well, well. Fancy. When was it he'd hooked up with her? May? Early June? They'd only been out twice, he knew that for sure, because on the second meeting they'd had a ride out to a country pub and she'd let him finger her in the car before the drive home. That was the kind of detail you didn't forget. If they'd had access to a room that night, she wouldn't have needed much persuading. But she'd not long moved back in with her parents, and he and Andrea had agreed that nothing was to come back to their door.

The third date would have been better organised, a bed factored into the equation. But it never happened. Instead, he received a phone call to say she was off to the Vendée. Having not long split from a long-term partner and moved out of their rented flat, Esther had decided it was the perfect moment to jack in her call-centre job and spread her wings. A friend running a gîte with her husband had invited her to come down to France, help with the running of the place, accommodation included. The bloke was a potter, and having largely abandoned his kiln while getting the letting business established, it now made financial sense for him to get back to making his brightly-coloured, Clarice Cliff-style wares and employ someone to help out with keeping the holidaymakers happy.

And she had kept most of them happy. Except for a brash Australian woman who all but accused her of stealing a bracelet. *Who else could it have been, tell me that?* A shouting match had ensued, and even when the missing piece had turned up, the owner's mea culpa admission paled in comparison to her renewed tirade over how the chambermaid had spoken to her.

"That was me done," Esther had reported to Rob over lunch. "The owners apologised for the false accusation – them, not the Aussie bitch. She just said she was sorry it had happened, didn't say sorry to me. What a cow! So I packed it in. It wasn't just that. I'd had enough after three months anyway. The place was too remote. Fine for them and their kids, great for cycling, making pots and all that bollocks. But not for me. It was dead. So here I am. Back with the folks again – temporarily, I hope, otherwise blood may well be spilt. Looking around jobwise, see what's going. Happened to be looking through my contacts this morning, see if I could pull in any favours. And there you were. So I thought, why not? That's it. You're bang up to date. What about you? What's been the story of your summer?"

Rob had kept his recent history low key. Work. A family holiday in Majorca where he and Andrea had put on the usual united front. He told her about Grace Newman. *She wanted to see me again but she wasn't really my type.* Nothing about Donna Kuzminski.

Donna. How would that phone conversation have gone if it had taken place after Esther Greaves had called? Maybe he'd have let her off the hook. Esther wasn't just a dead cert, she was an unattached dead cert. Not half bad looking, either. Plus he'd be shitting a long way from his own doorstep. Logic said it was the way to go.

And yet. And yet …

51

Donna didn't bother calling ahead to check. She knew it was slap-bang in the middle of Zoe's afternoon me-time. Another hour till Freddie needed picking up from nursery; Tara having a daytime nap you could almost set your watch by.

"Hey! I was just passing and could've sworn I heard the kettle."

"You heard right. Come on in."

She let Zoe go first with any news. Tara's gums weren't playing her up as much now. Freddie was sleeping better after being allowed to decide exactly how far ajar his bedroom door should be.

"I'm a bit worried about Ben, though. Hasn't been himself lately. I wondered if it was to do with work. Has Zbiggy said anything?"

Donna shook her head. "Not about work, no."

Zoe was about to bite into a chocolate digestive, but checked herself. "Oh, I'm sorry, banging on about all my … What's happening with … you know, what's the latest?"

"Nothing to report on that score."

What else could she have said? Best friend or not, Donna couldn't go any further. At some point before the new little life growing inside her was plum-sized, she'd have to make a decision. Not now.

"Early days, eh?"

"Mmm. I guess."

They were on opposite sides of the kitchen table, their hands inches apart. But Zoe suddenly decided a supportive squeeze wasn't enough. Without speaking, she walked round and gave her friend a hug. For now she saw it. *Mmm. I guess* wasn't about disappointment. It was second thoughts. Donna had begun to doubt this route was for her after all; that's why she'd lied the day Zoe saw her at the leisure centre.

"What's that for?" said Donna as they broke the embrace.

"You do know we're with you whatever you decide, whatever happens?"

What, even if you find out I lied to everyone about having Rob Allen's baby, then chose to abort it?

"I know that."

"Top up?"

"Just water, thanks. I think my hydration levels are up the spout. My wee's a funny colour at the moment."

"Thanks for sharing that."

They laughed.

One cup of tea can't have done any harm. Think of all the women who stuck with booze, cigarettes and poor diets and still delivered healthy babies. She'd do all the right things, right up until decision time.

"Look," said Donna as Zoe swished her tea bag round to speed up the infusion. "I don't want to speak out of turn, but I saw something a bit odd today. In town, just before I came here."

"Gossip! Do tell."

Definitely tell. Not show. Showing would make her look creepy. Like someone compiling evidence in a seedy divorce case. Her phone remained firmly in her bag.

"I saw Rob. From a distance – he didn't see me. He was with a woman, someone I didn't recognise. I don't think it was a work colleague, and I'm sure it wasn't a client."

"Go on. What happened?"

"They had lunch, or at least a drink, together – they were coming out of Wetherspoons when I saw them. I was over the other side of the road. I shouted hello, but he couldn't hear me…"

An unnecessary lie, but one that can't be disproved. That's fine.

"The woman's car was in that little car park just off the high street. Mine was there too …"

Ditto, unless anyone goes to the trouble of wading through the CCTV recordings to find that Rosie was in fact in the multi-storey at that time.

"I wasn't that far behind them now. They stopped by a Mini – that must have been hers – and basically went in for a full-on snog."

"No! Get away!"

"Andrea hasn't said anything to you, has she? About the marriage being in trouble, I mean?"

Zoe shook her head. The last time she'd seen Andrea, the main topic of conversation had been Donna's own laxity with the truth regarding her motorway trip. "You wouldn't call them the most touchy-feely, lovey-dovey couple, would you? But no, she hasn't said anything to me."

"Poor Andrea," said Donna.

"And poor Beth. It'll break her heart if they split up. He must realise the kid loves him every bit as much as if he were her real dad."

52

Andrea hammered on the horn barely a second after the filter had turned green. She knew it was hypocritical. She'd been daydreaming and missed that same arrow on more than one occasion. When she was the guilty party, a conciliatory hand would be raised, not a middle-finger *you-impatient-twat* salute. She'd then blast away to make up for the lapse in concentration, rather than crawl tortoise-like to show what she thought of the inconsiderate, tin-box mentality. But this evening she was in a foul mood, and it was coming out in her driving.

She wasn't sure if the person in front gave her a rude hand signal, wasn't even sure if it was a man or woman. Their paths soon diverged, the incident forgotten. If only the episode at home could have been wiped so easily.

Rob had tried to browbeat her in that old familiar way, sought to get what he wanted while making you think he was doing you a favour. No wonder he'd succeeded so well in his chosen career. But she wasn't buying or selling, and she knew him too well to be swayed.

Yes, I know it's your night.

Good!

I was just hoping you might fancy switching?

Thanks, but no thanks.

You can have Friday, that's a lot better night.

No it isn't. I'm on an early shift on Saturday.

It's just that this mate isn't in town long, whereas you and Drew …

What's she like, this "mate"? Anyone I know?

She'd said it jokingly, of course, but it made him think, not of sealing the deal with Esther Greaves if he could wangle a pass, but of Donna.

No. No one you know.

Well I'm not changing my plans, and that's it.

And so it had gone on, until even he could see she wasn't going to budge.

A couple of babysitting possibilities were tried. He'd even had the nerve to suggest she call her dad. That really pissed her off.

I could pick him up and drop him back. Bet he'd be glad to do it, to see Beth.

He'd flounced off when she told him that was a non-starter. She was being unreasonable, he'd said, already jabbing at his phone as he ensconced himself in the downstairs loo. Probably telling his "mate" what a cow his wife was, and that he couldn't make it tonight after all. Tough. They had a deal, no one tied his arm behind his back. He'd be the loser if he forced the issue. He was a good stepdad, but a stepdad all the same. Set that against motherhood and there was only one winner.

Not that it would be plain sailing if Rob did decide to blow the thing open. Who knows how Beth would react? She was at a funny age: old enough to be aware of sexuality, too immature to deal with it. Yes, there were divorced parents in her peer group, and if that was all it involved, Andrea wouldn't hesitate to bring matters to a head. Beth couldn't remember her real dad, so it wasn't like this would be a second domestic upheaval in a short life. She'd be on a par with a fair few others in her school. But this bombshell would have marked her out for special attention. The teasing to her face. The vile comments on social media. The bullying.

Is it true your mum shags other women?

No, it wasn't true. She just makes love to one woman.

Yuk, that is gross.

No, it wasn't. It was beautiful. It was how it was meant to be.

Are you going to be a dyke too? That's what my dad says it's called when women prefer other women.

Probably not. But it didn't matter a jot either way.

The front door opened before she reached it. Drew had heard the car engine, watched her get out. They'd exchanged a wave as Andrea walked up the drive. They embraced as soon as the door closed on the outside world.

If only her life had been as uncomplicated as Drew's. Her lover had come out early, not gone through that turbulent, wasted period of trying to conform to the expectations of others. Drew hadn't got herself knocked up. Drew hadn't had a crash-and-burn relationship with the child's father, then jumped straight into marriage with another bloke. Drew had parents who were completely accepting. Drew wasn't living a lie. It was like Andrea's life had suffered a false start, a deferral that had nothing to recommend it apart from bringing Beth into the world.

"Sorry I'm late. Rob was being a pain."

"You're here now, that's the main thing. I've made chilli con carne and there's a bottle of Sauvignon already open."

53

Ben was practised enough to look suitably surprised when Zoe told him. He could have thrown his own tuppenceworth into the mix, about knowing Rob was on Tinder, but he could see that was an avenue best left closed. Standing by a mate was no longer the issue. If the cat was out of the bag, it was every man for himself. It was all about self-preservation. He'd have had to explain about Julia Hennessey showing him pictures on her phone, conjuring up a cosy scene of the two of them vetting a list of dating possibles.

Why on earth would a customer – pushing sixty, I think you said? – be discussing such things with you?

Why indeed.

Rob, my old son, you're on your own. I did me best.

"What an arsehole," said Zoe. "If Donna doesn't tell Andrea about it, I will."

"Steady on, love. Don't go wading in. There might be an … explanation."

He nearly said "innocent", but knew that wouldn't wash. Rob and he were obviously out of the same mould, except he wouldn't have been so stupid to flaunt it in a town-centre car park. What a prize idiot.

"An explanation? He had his tongue down her throat, Donna says. That's good enough for me."

Ben said he was going to check on the kids and put the kettle on. Zoe said she didn't want a hot drink, and neither did he, not really. It was just a way of breaking the thread, changing the subject. He hadn't seen her so incensed for a long while. As Ben looked in on the two sleeping children, making sure not to disturb the angle of door opening Freddie had insisted on, he couldn't help wondering what would happen if he was pegged as the arsehole in question. An extended period in the doghouse, for sure, and a concerted charm offensive would be required. He had previous in that area. Not since the kids came along, though. Zoe wouldn't do anything rash, would she? Not break up the family?

"All quiet. You sure you don't want anything?"

"No, ta."

He dropped a tea bag into a mug. Late-evening caffeine never bothered him; he was a sound sleeper no matter what chemicals were coursing through his body. The daily physical exertions saw to that, along with a handy lack of conscience. If there was a bump in the road, he defaulted to a Micawberesque belief that something would turn up to make everything right. And still it might. But there had been bile in Zoe's condemnation of Rob, venom that could be coming his way, if he couldn't get Carly Fitzroy's ex off his back. Lack of conscience was no help if there was a rogue fucker out there waiting to drop incriminating photos on to their doormat.

Ben had still heard nothing from him.

What was he waiting for?

54

"I could see us living there."

"Where? America?"

Zbiggy raised a large paw off her leg and pointed to the screen. "Not just anywhere. There."

It was *Autumnwatch*, Chris Packham waxing lyrical about the spectacular changes in the New England flora at this time of year. Donna had been letting it wash over her, like a televisual jacuzzi, rather than taking in the details.

"Look at those colours. And all that space, love. I could knock us up a cosy log cabin."

"Yeah, and what about the ten-foot snowdrifts in winter? You know I can't stand the cold."

"We could learn to ski. Or get one of those jet thingies."

"That's a great idea!"

"You think so?"

"Yes. But instead of a jet thingy, maybe a pack of animals to pull it. You know, Dancer, Prancer, Rudolf …"

"Oh, ha flipping ha."

"Donna and Blitzen! My own personalised sleigh!"

"It was just a thought. You don't have to be so …"

He couldn't think of the word, so he let it hang. Donna slid her arm up from his shoulder and curled a lock of his hair round her finger. Poor offended Zbiggy. Sometimes she wished he did irony, played jokes, was quicker witted, more impulsive, more romantic, a bit less strait-laced. But if it came at the cost of a tiny fraction of his heart, she wouldn't have traded.

Crazy as it sounded, maybe emigration wasn't such a bad idea, she thought. Not Vermont or Maine, but a fresh start in a place with a more temperate climate had a dreamy appeal. One of her old school friends had settled Down Under, and though regular contact had been lost, she saw Facebook posts showing a seemingly never-ending round of outdoorsy fun. Or was that just the image she wanted to project? No mention of 45-degree broiling heat or spiders the size of frisbees.

Donna was barely in the foothills of social media, and Zbiggy's Facebook posts were mostly photos of completed jobs for advertising purposes. That domain was so much a vehicle for familial ostentation. *Hey, everybody, check out how great our life is.* The new competitive sport on the block. Without children – children to parade, to flaunt, to praise publicly for accomplishments; children whose major rites of passage and humdrum actions were publicised alike – she felt consigned to the substitutes' bench. So there'd be no selfie of the two of them, his head in her lap, posted with the tagline: *Me and Zbiggy chilling watching a fascinating nature prog. My legs gone to sleep though haha.* But even if she joined in with the vacuous mundanity, it would be a false domestic snapshot. The reality was, *Eek! Zbiggy's head must be about six inches from the baby growing in my womb. It's not his!!!!* Add the emoji that looks like a terrified alien, and wait for the likes and responses to roll in.

"Do you think we'd score highly if we tried to emigrate?" she asked.

"What do you mean?"

"You know, countries look at jobs and skills, don't they, to see who they want to let in?"

Donna recalled that her Aussie friend's husband had been an IT wiz. She herself was a nurse.

"No idea, love."

"You've got all that construction experience. And I assume my nursery nursing qualification would count for more than the market-research work."

He rolled onto his back to make eye contact. "You serious?"

She shrugged. "Dunno. Just thinking out loud."

Who was she kidding? Emigrating was a long-drawn-out process, something that might take months, even years. She was seduced by the thought of a clean slate, whether or not it was in another country. If only she could be pregnant by Zbiggy, or by a donor with Zbiggy's blessing. Or not pregnant at all. Anything but this limbo. Anything but living with this ticking time bomb.

The credits rolled. Chris Packham signed off, the lush kaleidoscope giving way to an edgy drama. Reality bit. She could have kicked herself for telling Zoe about what she'd seen in the car park. In doing so, she'd undermined her chance of using it as a bargaining chip. *Don't rock the boat about me using your sperm, Rob, and I'll quietly forget your own little indiscretion in the pay-and-display.* She couldn't barter now, not when Zoe might splurge it out. She shuddered mentally at the thought of what Rob might do if the two of them came to an understanding, then Zoe let rip and blew the lid off the deal.

The afternoon conversation had told her something she didn't know, though: that Rob wasn't Beth's father. That only made her even more uneasy. She'd chosen Rob for a host of reasons, and one by one, she'd been shown to be misguided. Not a steady husband. Not an existing paid-up biological father. Not altruistically minded. The only thing that hadn't been misrepresented was his looks; the superficial cake-icing. She'd have been better off taking her chance as one of Michael Phillips' online army. At least he was upfront about it, offering a deal with strict parameters. She could have taken that route and not worried about the minuscule chance of the child meeting one of its horde of half-siblings.

Zbiggy hauled himself into a sitting position, allowing her to stretch out her legs and get the circulation going. "Come on," he said, patting his lap. "Your turn."

She knew it would give but temporary respite, but just at that moment it was a fleeting escape she was happy to take.

"Or we could just go up?" she suggested.

55

Rob was five minutes early for the viewing. On a nice spring or summer's day he might have formed his one-man reception committee; but the temperature had dropped considerably, a chill blast that was like a winter outrider. He'd wait until Mr and Mrs Evans appeared, then go through the motions perfunctorily as he knew they'd only just put their own house on the market.

He'd texted Esther the previous night to tell her he couldn't get away. *No worries, she'd replied. If you've got family stuff to do …* He'd asked her if any other night would suit. *Friday works for me,* he'd written, failing to add, *because Andrea's on early shift on Saturday so it's fine with her.* Esther hadn't responded to that yet. Maybe, a few months on from their first meeting, she was having second thoughts about getting involved with a man still living under the same roof as his wife. Was he reading too much into Esther's "family stuff" comment? Was it purely prosaic or a little dig? His and Andrea's marital arrangement rendered the idea of "a bit on the side" redundant, yet to her it could have seemed that way. And with no prospect of any change in the foreseeable future, maybe she'd decided to dabble in less complicated waters.

One thing was for sure: Esther Greaves was not enough to stop him from shopping around.

He hit the call button. No texting, with its scope for thinking time and calculated comment. He wanted to hear her voice, gauge the reaction.

"Hello, Donna."

"What do you want? I'm busy."

The tone of that opening was clear enough, whether vocalised or written down. Frosty.

"I just thought we ought to clear the air after the way we left it yesterday."

"I told you. It was a mistake. Please forget all about it."

"Forget it? Not the kind you forget easily, is it, passing someone your semen – twice – putting yourself in the frame to father their child?

"Do your best, Rob. Try really hard."

"Look, I meant it when I said it doesn't have to change anything. I've done my own bit of research on the subject. Plenty of people reckon the natural method's best. Certain positions better than others. I just wanted to let you know I'm game if you want to give it a try."

The briefest of pauses afforded Rob a glimmer of hope. With no visual cue, he couldn't tell that the hiatus was born of incredulous fury, not a weighing of the pros and cons of the offer.

"What! What did you say, you slimy bastard? That is not going to happen."

"Why not? You've already as good as cheated on Zbiggy. You might as well have something to show for it."

"You've got a nerve. Talk about cheating? Yeah, I saw you yesterday, with your tongue down that woman's throat, your hands all over her in the car park."

Another pause, this time Donna's turn to experience a momentary anticipation of getting the upper hand in the conversation. She, too, was quickly disabused of that notion, but where Rob's suggestion had prompted outrage, Donna's *gotcha* revelation provoked the flattest of responses.

"Ah. Her."

"Yes, *her*. So maybe it would be a good idea if you backed off. Don't get me wrong, I'd like Andrea to know what a cheating scumbag she's married to. But she won't hear it from me, not as long as you keep your mouth shut."

There, she'd said it. It wasn't planned, it just came out. Heat of the moment. She'd laid down the terms of the bargain, a *quid pro quo* she couldn't guarantee sustaining now that Zoe was in the loop.

Rob smiled at Mr and Mrs Evans as their car pulled up facing his, bonnet to bonnet. It was unlikely there would be an early return on the time invested.

"You really don't know, do you? You think that's a threat? Telling Andrea? Be my guest. Let's see who's got most to lose."

The unctuous smile never left his lips as he broke the connection and got out to greet the Evanses.

"So, as you can see, the front's been paved to give off-road parking, a very useful feature. It can lower your insurance premiums, you know? Shall we go in?"

56

"Canada? What's Canada got, for fuck's sake? Mounties, maple syrup, crap rugby team – that's about it, isn't it?"

"We were only talking."

"Oh, just remembered, I think Bryan Adams is Canadian – but he probably fucked off as soon as he got famous."

"It was only because it was on the telly."

"So's *Neighbours* but you don't hear me say I'm fucking off to Australia."

Zbiggy heaved another shovelful of sand into the cement mixer, wishing he hadn't mentioned it. Ben was tidying up the sides of the auger holes, ready for the concrete. The posts were propped up against the back fence. They'd been lying around in Ben's garage for months, left over from another job. They hadn't bought the rest of the decking kit yet; there'd be a window for that while waiting for the concrete to go off.

It was a retired couple's bungalow, and looked it. The monotony of the rendered cream walls was broken only by a large multi-coloured metal butterfly screwed on to it, and a wagon wheel propped against it. The lawn was sculpted to within an inch of its life. Mr and Mrs Jacobs already had a full-width patio; the new deck was to be their bottom-of-the-garden haven, a place to sit out and catch the last of the sun's rays with a glass of something, before it disappeared over the rooftops.

"She ain't gonna win any prizes for brewing up, that's for sure. She forgotten where the sodding kettle is?"

Zbiggy looked up to make sure the comment hadn't been overheard. "Jeez, Ben!"

Ben pointed to the empty mugs on the grass. "Well over an hour ago, that was."

They covered the bases of the holes with a mixture of loose gravel and broken house bricks, Ben doing the pouring, Zbiggy following on and tamping it down with a timber offcut. Then they began setting the posts, checking the alignment and bracing them with a joist temporarily affixed as the concrete went in. Ben struck off the top of the mix so that the posts sat slightly proud, avoiding hollows where standing water might have accelerated any rotting process. They'd go eventually, even with preservative treatment. Zbiggy had once suggested they switch to one of the foundation methods where all the timber stayed above ground. "Why build summat that'll last twenty-five years when you can knock it out cheaply, so it'll need redoing in ten? Use yer noggin, mate."

They were just finishing the setting-out when Mrs Jacobs appeared. She was sprightly for her age, which she'd taken no steps at the hairdresser's to mask. The ash-grey pageboy suited her. She was wearing a floral gilet and charcoal, narrow-leg slacks. "I wondered if you'd like a fresh cup?"

"Bin so busy I never even thought about it, Mrs J. But since you ask. Very kind. Smidge more sugar if you can manage it. Sweet tooth, see."

Zbiggy swooped to pick up the mugs, even though Ben was nearer. "Same again would be lovely, thanks," he said as he handed them over.

Mrs Jacobs made to turn away, then paused. "Are those posts not meant to be level?"

'These?" said Ben. "Nah. We just set them like that while they're being cemented in, then trim 'em to length after."

"Oh. I see."

"We've bin doing this a long time, Mrs J; don't you worry."

When he'd booked the job in, Ben had talked her into non-slip deck boards. *Bit more expensive than regular, but well worth it. Ordinary timber's like an ice rink when it gets wet, trust me. I've seen some very nasty accidents.*

It was true as far as it went. He made no mention of the nice mark-up on the premium boards, which he could get at a decent discount.

Zbiggy chucked some leftover gravel into the cement mixer, running the motor to scour the drum. Ben started laying out the weed-control matting, cutting it loosely and making sure they had enough. The tea tray came and went. *Lincoln Fucking Biscuits. I mean, who likes those? Old people with no teeth and under-fives, that's who. Fall to bits if you dunk 'em. Like fucking cardboard, they are.*

They'd already made out a list ready to take to the suppliers. There wasn't much else to be done after picking up the materials, not until the following morning. There was a kitchen refurb job to be priced up, and Ben thought he might as well drop Zbiggy home for an early finish and do the estimate solo.

That was turned on its head in three short words. Three words that meant Zbiggy would be the one doing the supplier run. Zbiggy would be the one doing the dropping off for an early finish. Zbiggy would be the one pricing up the kitchen refurb solo.

Message from Zoe: *Get home. Now.*

57

The sign said there was a strict four-hour parking limit. Who could possibly need more time than that for a supermarket run? Maybe if you added in a visit to Boots, Next and the retail park's handful of other shops you might have been flirting with a fine. But Donna didn't have those outlets in her sights. Only Sainsbury's.

Hey mate, you working today?

Yeah worse luck. Finish at four. Why?

Might swing by, maybe catch you on a break.

OK. Not sure when thatll be. Wanna msg me when your here? Will see what I can do.

Donna still hadn't made up her mind. She'd used an hour up already, a quarter of the allotted time spent sitting in her car turning the options over.

It wasn't going to be possible to avoid seeing Rob for long. Any time now there would be phone calls or texts criss-crossing between the three couples to see when they might next get together, a date to be pencilled on the wall planner. A convenient last-minute illness might get her out of that one. Her and Zbiggy. *Oh, poor you, what a shame. You get yourself better, we'll reschedule when you're up and about.* But then the festive party season was on the near horizon: even more boozy, with sillier games and fancy dress. It didn't bear thinking about. Last year, which happened to be at Rob and Andrea's, she'd had to pass him a balloon wedged between her knees, then an apple lodged under the chin. She dressed as a pixie in a tight-fitting mini-dress and pigtails, he in a hired Batman costume with plasticky pumped pecs and ripped abs. She couldn't go through anything like that again, not knowing he was looking at her in that way, and prepared to blackmail her to get what he wanted.

What was the alternative? Sit on her hands and watch her belly grow? Pretend to Zbiggy that he must have fired a miracle bullet, knowing that Rob could bring the house of cards down at any time for her refusing to play sexual ball? *We can soon decide who's telling the truth and who's lying, Zbiggy. Get her to have a blood test.* Canada wouldn't be far enough away in those circumstances.

The other option – the ugly, horrific option – was to wait it out but without the ticking clock and tell-tale bodily changes. She'd done a google search and found scores of women who'd chosen to keep babies conceived in an act of violation. Stories of supportive husbands who were still happy to call it a "gift". Stories that just confirmed her own view: the child was the innocent at the heart of it, the joyous fruit of a wrongful act. If rape victims could get through it – no, not just get through it but find healing in the resulting birth – then she ought to be able to. She'd suffered no violent trauma, just the insidiousness of a sword of Damocles waiting to fall.

Then there was Zoe. What if she decided to tell Andrea Rob was cheating on her? That could cause a major rift leading back to Donna's door, and he might pull the pin from the grenade to get his own back.

She got out and slammed Rosie's door shut. Decision made. If the sword was coming, better for it to fall on her terms. Call his bluff. Get her retaliation in first.

Zbiggy would understand.

58

"Dunno, mate. Zoe's in a flap. It'll be something and nothing."

That's as much as Ben offered on the van ride home. As casual as he tried to make it sound, Ben knew it was very much in the *something* category. Not a plea to *come* home; an order to get home. So not a burst pipe or an accident involving one of the kids. He'd tried to ring, but Zoe wasn't picking up.

"Any problems, give me a buzz," he said as he hopped down from the cab."

"Will do."

Tara, at least, looked pleased to see him. "Daddy!" she beamed, banging on her high-chair table and sending bits of her lunch flying.

"Hello, princess," said Ben. "Oh no, look over there!"

Tara followed his finger, and he stole a Quaver, which he munched noisily in front of her face. She squealed with a mixture of indignation and delight at a trick played for the umpteenth time.

"Eat up now, it'll make you big and strong like daddy."

He'd already seen the pictures. They were laid out like in a TV detective show, except flat on the dining table instead of plastered on a pin-board. Without the scribbled notes or arrow connections, but every bit as incriminating.

"Look what I got in the post."

There was redness in her face, and he could tell it was from anger, not tears.

"I need to explain. But shall we, you know …" he jerked his head in Tara's direction.

"No, we'll do it now. There'll be no raised voices, so she'll be fine. And it doesn't look from these that you gave Tara a whole lot of thought when you –"

"It's not what it looks, love!" It was he who cranked up the volume."

"Don't!" hissed Zoe through clenched teeth.

"It's the God's honest truth."

"Never been your strong suit, that, Ben. Honesty. The *babysitter*, for Christ's sake. I've tried ringing her, you know, that slut. Dead as a doornail. Now there's a surprise."

She swept her hand across the sheets of A4, sending all but one floating to the floor. The remaining image landed directly in front of him, a grainy, poor-quality but perfectly clear image of him and Carly Fitzroy in the white-walled flat he'd thought was hers, their lips almost touching.

"Finished, mummy!"

"OK, sweetie. Out you come, you clever girl. As you've been so good, would you like to watch some Paw Patrol?"

"Yes, mummy, yes!"

One of the photos lay halfway between the dining table and the high chair. Zoe scooped it up and slammed it in front of Ben. "I don't even like to think what's happening in this one."

Ben stared at a picture of himself handing a note through the wire fencing of the skate zone to a pubescent boy.

"I can explain everything. It's not what you think."

She'd already turned her back on him, showering more praise on her daughter and asking if she'd like some chocolate buttons. A question, unlike the ones she had for Ben, with a simple, straightforward answer.

"You can have three. Now which Paw Patrol story would you like?"

The programme was cued up, Tara savouring her sweet treat as she became glued to a cartoon with comforting familiarity.

"I know how this looks," said Ben when she sat down across the table from him again, "and I know you're angry. But you have to believe me, nothing happened."

Zoe laughed scornfully. "Nothing happened?" Gingerly, using the tip of her thumb and forefinger, she picked up a scrap of blue material lying at her elbow. Ben hadn't noticed it. He'd expected the pictures and focused on them. This could have been a dishcloth, maybe a favourite scrap of fabric that Tara liked to bury her face in if she needed comforting. But, as Zoe unfurled it, Ben could see it was neither of those things.

"Not my size, unfortunately. Before I had your children, yes, I could definitely have worn these. Maybe not this colour, though."

Ben shook his head as Zoe dangled the thong at arm's length. "Zoe, I've never seen those before," he said pleadingly.

"No? Did she slip them off herself before you got down to it? Didn't you notice the style or colour?"

"We didn't —"

"Only," she continued, ignoring the intervention, "she must've slipped them back on pretty soon afterwards. Maybe you'd gone by then?"

"No, it wasn't —"

"Because they reek. They honk. It's the smell of stale fanny and dried semen. All crusty where the spunk's seeped back out of her hole. Isn't that a nice cocktail for a wife to be served when she's looking after a two-year-old?"

"Do I get my say now?"

"No, Ben. No you don't. Right now I'd just like you to get out of my sight."

59

Another agonising twenty minutes had passed, this time in Sainsbury's cafeteria. Donna had sent Andrea a text when she arrived, a neutral *Just landed, having a coffee.* The dregs of that decaff latte lay before her. If she went through with this, that cup, with its scummy bottom and stained sides, might be replicated in two marriages: relationships drained and grubby, but with no rinse aid to bring the sparkle back.

There was still time to back out, she hadn't signalled any intent. There'd been a brief wave ten minutes earlier when Andrea scurried by. She'd tapped her watch and pulled a face with a palms-out gesture, as if to say, *Trying to get away but irritating stuff keeps cropping up. Donna could easily have fired back a quick Sorry, had to dash, another time, yeah?* and Andrea wouldn't have been any the wiser. But no. Too late now. Here she was, looking flustered. Donna had to decide whether to talk about the weather or render whatever was irking her friend supremely irrelevant.

"New supervisor. Just been promoted. Need I say more?"

"Oh dear. Let me grab you a coffee."

"I'll go. Staff discount and all that. What was yours?"

Donna said she was fine, the irony of which didn't escape her. Three more torturous minutes passed. And then it really was time. Andrea began bitching about a difficult customer, and the pressure just told in the end.

"Look, Andrea," she cut in, "I need to tell you something. This isn't really the time or place, and I shouldn't be laying this on you at work. But the truth is, if I'd waited till later I might not have been able to say it."

Andrea's face darkened. "Say what? Gosh, all sounds very ominous. Come on, Donna, out with it, it can't be that bad."

Donna tried to hold her friend's gaze but faltered, instead staring down into the dirty coffee cup.

"It's about Rob."

"Rob?"

"Hope you don't think I'm telling tales …"

Andrea sat back in her chair and exhaled, like a student who's just finished an exam. Simply glad it was all over. "You've seen him with another woman, haven't you?"

The flat tone – the same part of the scale that Rob had used when confronted about his lunchtime tryst – took Donna by surprise. The fact that, regardless of the question tag, Andrea was making a bald, matter-of-fact statement about her husband.

"You *know* about it? Is he having an affair?"

"Affairs, Donna. Plural. Or one-off dates. I don't enquire much. He tells me about them sometimes. You know. Snippets."

Donna lurched forward in her chair to close the gap Andrea had opened up. Her elbow rattled the coffee cup in its saucer. Her uncomprehending eyes were trying to read her friend's face.

"Am I missing something here? It almost sounds as if he's cheating with your approval, your *blessing*."

Andrea gave a thin smile. "I suppose he is."

She poured it all out. A whistle-stop tour of her confused teenage years, her difficulties with her parents, the disastrous relationship that brought Beth into the world. Hasty marriage to Rob when she was still trying to conform to the expectations of others. And, finally, about Drew, when it all finally clicked into place, when she knew who she was meant to be.

"Is that a problem?" she asked.

"Problem? No. No, of course not. Just a bit gobsmacked, that's all."

"I didn't think for a minute it would be but, well … not everyone is accepting, even in the twenty-first century."

Donna reached over and gave her wrist a light squeeze. What to do? The revelation had thrown her, but did it change anything? No, of course it didn't.

"As for Rob," Andrea went on, "he was quite understanding, considering. It must be hard for him. Anyway, we decided to carry on playing happy families for Beth's sake, at least for now. We rub along well enough for that. I still love him, in a way, and I know he does me. I mean, we must've put up a pretty good front because you and Zoe never guessed, did you?"

"No. No, we didn't."

"There you are, then."

"It's a lot to take in. I only found out yesterday that Rob isn't Beth's dad. Zoe told me." Andrea nodded. "News travels fast! He is in every way that matters – Beth's dad, that is. He's a good dad, too. Which is why we're happy with the status quo for the time being. Drew's OK with it – ish. Rob gets his time off the leash, I can't deny him that. All I asked was that he'd be discreet about it. Where did you see him anyway?"

"Snogging someone in the car park just off the high street."

"Oh, my days!"

She sniggered in spite of herself. Donna joined in, more out of a copycat response, like matching someone's yawn, than as a source of amusement.

"Seriously, though," said Andrea, "we weren't deliberately trying to hide anything. More like a sin of omission, if you like. There were times when I wanted to tell you both – you and Zoe – and of course it was going to come out sooner or later. But, you know, it was somehow easier to put it off. Please don't think badly of us."

Donna wanted to hug her, but as she was on uniformed show in her workplace, she stuck to another gentle squeeze of the arm and a nod of solidarity.

"Listen, I must be getting back," said Andrea, looking at her watch and getting up. "Misery guts will be on the warpath otherwise. See you soon, yeah?"

"Yes. Soon," said Donna, adding under her breath as Andrea strode off: "I don't think badly of you."

60

Ben couldn't remember the last time he took a bus. He'd been desperate to drive from as long as he could remember, and bought his first set of wheels just after passing his test, on the road almost before his mum had taken the seventeenth birthday cards down. Progression from that beaten-up Fiesta hadn't quite gone to plan. He never got the Caterham he'd lusted after; that became a bucket-list purchase once he got hitched and acquired kids and a mortgage. It was squeezed out by the need for a workhorse van and people carrier.

Right now he had neither, just a seat on the No. 36. Taking off in the Tiguan wouldn't have gone down well, not with Zoe already on the warpath. A phone call to Zbiggy confirmed he was at the suppliers on the other side of town. *Ring me when you're done and I'll tell you where to pick me up … No, I'm not at home.*

Zbiggy was in the firing line and got the sharp tongue of anger meant for Danny Croft, or whatever the hell his name was. And Zoe. She'd gone off on one without giving him a chance to put his side of the story. That was plain unfair. *If you hadn't forgotten my needs once the kids came along, none of this would have happened. You have to take a share of the blame.* That's what needed saying. That's what he would say, when she'd calmed down a bit.

As for Danny fucking Croft, that kid was going to cop it. He was in the shadows for now, but that would be an advantage down the track. There was nothing to connect Ben with the scrawny little bastard. If Danny Croft had a nasty accident, the police weren't going to be looking at the couple one of his ex-girlfriends used to babysit for.

The bastard still hadn't made contact. Why hadn't he sent the photo of him talking to the kid in the skate park straight to him? *Nice try, but did you really think I'd fall for that?* Up the price for Ben trying to double-cross him? This way he didn't get a penny.

Then there were those knickers. He didn't know whose they were or whose spunk was on them, except that it wasn't his. You could get tests done to prove that. How did you go about that, he wondered? How much did it cost? It would shut Zoe up, at a price.

He hadn't been taking in the surroundings. Not the strangers he was being herded together with, nor the houses, shops and gardens of the window's rolling vista. But suddenly, reality displaced reverie and he jumped to his feet. The bus ticket, with its unused portion, was tossed into the gutter as he stepped on to the pavement. Four stops from town, he'd had a better idea.

* * *

"Oh, hello Ben. I wasn't expecting you today."

"No, well, I was in the area and thought I'd just stick me head in on the off chance, make sure everything's up to scratch and hunky-dory. Any tea going, Mrs H?"

If I'm in the fucking dock, I might as well do the crime.

"Of course. Come on in."

He made a show of inspecting the orangery, telling her how jealous he was of her swish new sun trap. "Bit parky out today but warm as toast through all this glass."

"Do you think it'll be too warm in summer?" she called from the kitchen.

"Depends how hot you like it, love."

The inference was clear enough.

They had tea and chocolate digestives. Julia Hennessey had already brought a couple of kitchen chairs into her new extension. "Seemed silly to get the new furniture before the flooring's down. These old things will do *pro tem*."

"Pro what?"

"For the meantime."

"Yeah, right."

They danced round the subject of what kind of flooring to put down. Was she a traditionalist, did she want quarry tiles or the like? They looked the business but were cold underfoot, mind, in the chillier months. Vinyls had come a long way in recent years, not like the old lino from the dark ages. No problem for stockinged feet, and easier to swap if you fancied a change of decor in a few years.

"Easier to lay, too."

Come on, Julia. The penny must've dropped by now.

"That's the way I'd go, nice bit of Karndean."

"Do you know," said Mrs Hennessey, "I rather think you've convinced me."

He let his eyes travel down her body. The hair gathered up in a scrunchy, the smear of pink lipstick, the white figure-hugging T-shirt overlaid with a loose-fitting grey angora cardigan, the skinny jeans that plenty of teenagers would have been delighted to pour themselves into. He made no attempt to hide his gluttonous appreciation of her body. She made no show of discomfort at it.

"'Course," he said, in a neat change of tack, "you could always hang on and see what your new bloke thinks. If you move someone in, I mean. He might have strong views on orangery flooring."

She laughed. "I don't anticipate *that* happening for a long time, if ever. I'm still getting used to being single again, and must say I'm quite enjoying the freedom."

"Just playing the field, eh? With your dating app thingy? How's that all going?"

"Nothing to write home about so far. The only one who wasn't too old, too dreary or too far away was that one you warned me about."

"Ah, him. You dodged a bullet there, love. Trust me."

He was talking to her breasts, unashamedly. They weren't large, and the neckline of the T-shirt was well above the cleavage area. The gentle rise and fall, movement more pronounced when she laughed, held him transfixed. It might have been down to a very nifty bra, but he knew he wanted to find out.

"It's all right for you," said Julia Hennessey. "Happily married, young family. You've got it all in front of you."

So have you, Mrs H. And I plan to see what's holding it all up.

"Wouldn't exactly call it a bed of roses, Mrs H. Fact is, me and the missus are going through a rough patch."

"Oh? Sorry to hear that."

"Yeah," he said. It was on the fly but he had a way of making extemporised lies sound genuine. "I'm pretty sure she's having an affair. We just had another ding-dong about it, that's why I had to get out for a bit. She ain't owned up or anything, but you just know, don't you?"

"Poor you. I sympathise. My husband didn't stray – at least, I don't think he did – but we drifted apart and hadn't been close for a long time before he died. Bad marriages are poisonous, I see that now. We should have divorced but for some reason never got round to it. Stuck it out when we could have each found somebody else. What are you going to do?"

Ben grinned. "I'm gonna have that last choccy biccy, if it's going."

61

Donna wasn't counting the lengths. She might have done twenty; it could have been thirty. The pool was quiet that afternoon, and she relished the monotony of the stroke and anonymity she had in the cathedral-like surroundings. Not that it mattered, this time, if she bumped into anyone she knew or was spotted from afar. It was a free afternoon, her time was her own. She wasn't in one place when she'd claimed to be in another.

She replayed the conversation with Andrea as she pulled through the water. It made sense now, what Rob had said: *Be my guest. Let's see who's got most to lose.* The clandestine French kissing and handsy groping she'd witnessed counted for nothing. Andrea was simply miffed about where it had taken place. She wanted Rob to be as discreet with his bits on the side as she and her lover were. No boat-rocking, for Beth's sake.

So. One card laid and trumped. There was only one left to play.

She towelled herself down, and even before she dressed, she messaged Zbiggy. *Any idea when you'll be home?*

The reply was swift. *Home now. Got the van here. Got to pick Ben up sometime but waiting to hear. Where r u?*

She told him she'd been for a swim and would be home in twenty minutes. She had two grenades to drop. As long as the first one was survived, the second couldn't hurt them. As long as Zbiggy understood, they'd get through it. Before the day was out she would know if her husband was the man she thought he was; if she was going to go ahead with the pregnancy with his blessing. Or without it.

"Do you fancy a cuppa, love? Kettle's on. Still haven't heard from Ben so no idea when …"

"No. No, thanks. Come and sit down."

It had to be now. She was psyched up for it, ready to watch the pain wash over the face of the man she loved; ready to see the hurt she'd caused reflected in those big brown eyes.

She led him to the sofa, keeping hold of his hand as they sat down, not in the relaxed, intertwined way they sprawled out for an *Autumnwatch* episode, but perched on the front edge, their knees angled towards each other.

"I have to tell you something," she began. "Please let me finish before you say anything."

The way he blinked at her and nodded his assent could have reduced her to tears even then.

"It's about Michael Phillips. Or rather, it's about trying to get pregnant, us trying to become parents. Which we'd be great at, by the way." She gave a pained laugh, unable to prevent a tear from forming. "Don't you think?"

"I thought I had to wait till you were finished? You haven't finished, have you?" The words were softly spoken and heartfelt, not a sharp, clever comeback on her request. She spluttered another laugh at his prosaic response, one of the many things she loved about him.

"I didn't want Michael Phillips' baby," she went on. "I never wanted him to be the father of our child. If I couldn't have yours, I wanted it to be someone I had ... I don't know, more of a *connection* with. Not someone doing it for money for the umpteenth time. I didn't like the look of him. I didn't like to think where he'd been, what he might be carrying. And I didn't want our child to have God knows how many half-brothers and sisters around the country. People he or she might meet in later life and not know they were biologically related. That just freaked me out. So I lied. I lied about him, about using his sperm."

"Yes," said Zbiggy, squeezing her hand tighter. "I know you did."

62

"Do I get a discount on my vinyl now? Or just marks out of ten?"

Julia Hennessey lay on her side, propped up on an elbow anchored in her down and feather pillow. With her free hand she was tracing shapes on Ben's chest. She was glad she'd done it. There'd been too much lost time. She wanted to be wanted again. Desired. Lusted after. He was a perfect choice to put an end to the long abstinence. He'd go back to his wife now – a wife who may or may not have been unfaithful, for all she knew. Ben was a storyteller, after all. Cheeky and fun, though, and that was all she wanted. It was a one-off. Nothing was said but it was there all along, hanging in the air. From the moment he'd laid his hand on her thigh; from the moment she'd parted her legs to help him explore; from the moment he'd planted his mouth on hers and she'd sucked biscuit crumbs off his tongue; from the moment she'd taken him by the hand and led him to her bedroom. Yes, he could go back to his wife and she could begin her search for someone more suitable for a proper relationship, someone with whom she was more *simpatico*. Probably someone who, unlike Ben, would have known what that word meant. When she found that person, and when the right moment came after a few dates, she could undress in front of him, feel sexually confident after what had transpired in the past hour.

"I'll nudge you up to a solid seven if I can have a fag."

She pinched him, laughing. "You can smoke outside – with the rest of the tradesmen."

"Blimey, I never knew there was a queue?"

"Oh, yes. My four o'clock's due soon. He's a welder. So if you don't mind …"

"Welder, eh?" said Ben, swinging his legs off the bed. "Sparks should fly, in that case."

He laughed heartily at his quip. She could see he was looking for his boxers, and produced them with a flourish from under the duvet, where she'd slipped them off before taking him in her mouth. She was inexperienced in giving oral sex, but knew from movies, TV dramas and general discourse that it was more a part of a staple diet than occasional treat these days. It was as well to practise. He'd seemed to enjoy it but didn't offer to reciprocate. Never mind. Others would. She noted that for all his greater experience – certainly in recent years – he had thrust his way to a climax before she was ready. It wasn't a surprise to find that Ben's primary objective was to satisfy himself. All in all, though, she was rather pleased with how it had gone.

"You can leave a tip if you thought the service was up to scratch."

"My tip would be for your dear departed old man. Mr H, you should've filled your boots more often, mate."

63

Donna stared at him. "What do you mean, you know I did?"

"I knew it wasn't true, about you going off to see Michael Phillips. The second time."

She scanned his face but it was completely impassive. "Who told you? Was it Zoe? Andrea?" Not Rob. He'd been holding on to that information like a precious jewel, and wouldn't have offered it up for free.

"No one told me. Remember I filled up with petrol just before you were meant to go and meet him? The clock had just ticked over to 67,000. When I took it to work the next day, there was only another eleven miles on it."

Shit. Shit. SHIT!

"But why didn't you say anything?"

Zbiggy shrugged. "Dunno. Didn't know what to think. I was waiting for you to tell me, I suppose." And then, after a pause: "Is there someone else? Are we breaking up?"

"What! No! No, of course not. Come here, you great …"

If there was a noun to end the sentence, it died as she buried her face in his shoulder. She began to sob uncontrollably. She'd manipulated and deceived, yet here he was, all but apologising for her misdemeanours.

"OK," she said, suddenly pulling away so she could look him in the eyes, eyes that were also watering now. "No more lies. I didn't want to use Michael Phillips' sperm. Never. That day at *The George*, I flushed it away. I never used it. It was all a sham. The other time, when I said I was meeting him alone, I didn't go. I don't mean I cancelled. I mean there was never any such arrangement in the first place. I just said it because … because I thought it would be easier for you to handle. It was a terrible mistake, I know that now. But please believe me, I did it with you in mind."

He pulled her towards him, clamping round her neck, shushing away the tears. "It's OK. We're good. Don't cry."

"You don't understand. I didn't use Michael Phillips' sperm … I used somebody else's. Somebody I knew, somebody I thought I could trust. I thought he'd want to give me – give us – a family like he had. And now …"

He lifted her head gently. Their faces were almost touching. It could have been a tender prelude to a kiss. But Donna was struggling to make eye contact. She couldn't say it and hold his gaze. One of those two things had to be sacrificed, and as there was no turning back regarding telling him, she closed her eyes. It was a leap into the unknown.

"It was Rob. I used his sperm. Twice. I asked him and he said yes. Like an idiot I thought it could remain a secret. I told him about Phillips, but said I wanted to use his sperm as well. To double the chances of getting pregnant and so that we wouldn't know which of them was the father. That was a lie. And he found out, like you did. And … and …"

Emotionally spent, she reburied her face in his shoulder. His hands were still on her, but static now. They were holding her mechanically, not sympathetically. She didn't blame him. But nor could she pour soothing balm on the wound. Not yet. There were more blows for him to face. Only one for now, though. Just one more for him to endure today.

"It's all so *fucked up*, Zbiggy."

She hardly ever swore, and it visibly shook him.

"I chose Rob because I thought he was a straight-up guy, a friend, a father himself and in a marriage as solid as ours. But none of those things are true. None of them. I just found out that he isn't Beth's real dad and their marriage is a joke. Andrea's got a girlfriend – yes, that's right, a girlfriend. They're leading separate lives. She doesn't want to come out to protect Beth and … Oh, God, it's so *fucked up*!"

Zbiggy capitulated. He was struggling to take in what she was saying. But he could never hold out long when she was upset, no matter that it was self-inflicted and he was the innocent victim. A plate-sized hand stroked her back.

"Shush. It'll be all right, love. I'm here."

The pent-up anxiety broke like a burst dam, manifesting itself in laughter and tears. A snot bubble appeared from her nose and laughter got the upper hand. Zbiggy joined in.

"I need to tell you one more thing," she said. "He got angry when he found out the truth. Rob, I mean. I don't blame him for that. But he did get … quite aggressive."

Zbiggy stiffened. "What do you mean, aggressive?"

"Not violent. Not physically, at least. Threatening to use it, trying to get me to do stuff or else he'd tell."

Such was the release of the confessional that only now did it dawn on her: Rob had, at a stroke, lost any hold over her. *Be my guest. Tell my husband what happened, see how far it gets you. Because he knows. I told him. You can't hurt me. We're strong. Unbreakable. Our marriage isn't a sham like yours.*

No one could blame her for not seeing it coming. You couldn't call it a miscalculation. How could she have known that Rob Allen had one last bargaining tool in his armoury? The nuclear option. And as Zbiggy, grim-faced, slipped free of her and put on his coat, how could she have known that they were about to provoke that tool's deployment, an escalation that brought mutually assured destruction into play?

64

It didn't occur to Ben to try Donna's phone. He just kept speed-dialling Zbiggy, getting angrier with every failed attempt. Unaware that, at that very moment, the two were sitting right next to each other; unaware that Zbiggy had glanced at the screen and ignored it; unaware that Donna had offered to pick up and had the suggestion waved away, Ben turned his collar up against the chill air and stomped off to the bus stop. All those years of never being forced onto public transport, and now having to put up with it twice in the same day. Zbiggy was going to need a bloody good explanation when he finally caught up with him.

It was gone five when he walked up the drive, past the Tiguan. The squeeze between it and the partition fence felt the same as when he'd left, suggesting Zoe hadn't used it in the intervening time. Freddie's school was only a ten-minute walk, so unless it was pouring down, she usually did the pick-up on foot, with Tara in her buggy. So he could have taken the VW after all. On the other hand, she might have brought it up when the row got going. *And another thing … what if I'd needed the car? Selfish twat!* When she was in full flow, Zoe picked up any ammo that was lying around.

"Daddy, I did a picture. It's a rocket. Whoosh!"

"Wow, look at that! I could get to the moon and back in that."

Freddie had rushed to meet him as soon as the key was in the door. Ben swept him up and aeroplaned him through the air.

"Me go! Me go!"

Tara kicked her legs in her high chair as she demanded her turn, interest in dinner suddenly waning. Zoe, who was sitting next to her, overseeing and prompting as Tara fed herself fish fingers, waffle and beans, cast an icy look in his direction. *Not content with shagging around, you shit, you wind the kids up when they're having their tea.*

He took the unspoken cue, ruffling Tara's hair and pretending to pinch some of her food as he sat down at the table. The damning photos and soiled knickers had been spirited away, and it looked like a cosy domestic scene. The stand-off would last until the kids were in bed. Then it would come. Their arguments had always followed a similar pattern, blazing white hot until they burned themselves out. The last time it had been about him going to a lap-dancing club on a stag do, Zoe finding a card in a jacket she was sending to the dry cleaner's. *It was just a bit of fun, blame the best man, not me. No different to a hen do going to see the Chippendales.* Failing to mention that he'd stumped up for extras.

It had been the same even before they got married, rows about seeing other women even after they'd got engaged. Ben steeled himself for another reaping of the whirlwind, content in the knowledge that once Zoe had given him dog's abuse, they usually had vigorous, adventurous sex to usher in the reconciliation. Julia Hennessey had taken a fair bit out of him, the game old girl, but there was always a bit left in the tank.

He had no regrets. Conscience was for wimps and losers. It had been a very satisfying one-off. He'd meant it when he said her deceased husband should have paid her more attention in the sack. Especially as she was sure Mr Hennessey hadn't been dipping his bread elsewhere. Fancy choosing celibacy over *that!* What a prize dick!

65

When Zbiggy's mobile rang for the fourth time, Donna didn't even bother to ask if he wanted her to answer.

"It's just Ben wanting a lift. It's fine. I'll square it with him later."

She stared at the phone lying on his lap as it returned to its dormant state. Her husband did the same, even more taciturn than usual as he sat hunched over the Clio's steering wheel. Donna had set the hare running; it was out of her control now, and she could have no complaints about how it would play out.

It was Andrea she felt sorry for. There weren't any scenarios that didn't leave the facade she'd created shattered. She just hoped that her friend would look beyond her and Zbiggy when it came to apportioning blame for that broken illusion.

"You're not going to do anything silly, are you?"

"'Course I won't."

I'm just going to show him that he can't mess with my missus and get away with it. Nothing silly about that.

They fell silent. For Zbiggy it was a simple matter of cause and effect; there was nothing more to discuss, which suited him down to the ground. He wasn't equipped for deep analysis, much less articulating his thoughts on the subject. Donna, meanwhile, was filled with a sense of foreboding, yet could see no way to prevent the impact and resigned herself to bearing witness and picking up the pieces afterwards.

"Hey," said Andrea as she opened the door. "This is a surprise. Twice in one day!"

"Hope it's not a bad time," said Donna, knowing that tea-time social calls were a pain, and that Andrea would claim it wasn't the slightest inconvenience.

"Is Rob home?" asked Zbiggy.

"No, it's fine, always good to see you," said Andrea, backing away to let them through. "Rob's not back yet but shouldn't be long. Do you fancy a cuppa?"

"No thanks," muttered Zbiggy, terseness evident in the muted reply.

"We're not staying," added Donna. Just a flying visit. You'll be getting tea ready."

It was a redundant observation, for Andrea had shepherded them into the kitchen-diner, where the illuminated oven was humming and two different-sized pans were simmering on the hob.

"Beth's got a friend round," said Andrea as a muffled laugh descended from upstairs. Then, *sotto voce*, added: "Not a sleepover, thank God. Can't be doing with that on a school night."

Andrea smiled weakly, and there was an awkward silence as that thread fizzled out. Zbiggy would have struggled to continue it at the best of times. Making small talk about nine-year-old daughters was even further out of his comfort zone on this occasion. In other circumstances, Donna would have taken up the baton, maybe even stuck her head round Beth's door to say hi and see what the girls were up to. Maybe joined in if they were playing with make-up, or offered suggestions if they were dressing up. But not today.

"Sit down, at least. Is it too early for a glass of wine?"

Donna accepted the former invitation. Zbiggy ignored both.

"Zbiggy knows about … the situation. Yours and Rob's."

Andrea stiffened, glancing at the half-open door even though the faint laughter from upstairs told her the two girls were well out of earshot. She got up and closed it anyway. "OK. But if you don't mind, I'd like for it not to go …"

"I know, and I'm sorry about it, Andrea. We wouldn't dream of spreading gossip, would we, Zbiggy?"

Zbiggy grunted his assent.

"Who you love won't affect our friendship. At least, I hope not. I hope we can meet your … partner, one day." She paused, taking a deep breath before continuing. "Today's been a day for secrets coming out. Right after you told me yours, I told Zbiggy mine. About me and Rob."

Andrea looked at her uncomprehendingly. "You and Rob? What do you mean?"

"I mean I decided to use a sperm donor, my last realistic hope of getting pregnant, becoming a mother. And I asked Rob to help."

"*What!*"

"I pretended I was getting it off some guy selling online. That's what Zbiggy thought." He was standing just behind her, and she reached back and took his hand.

"That's what I thought, too. I don't understand."

"I told Rob I wanted to use his sperm as well as the internet guy's. Double the chances and keep the father of any baby anonymous. But he found out that I was only using his. He got … difficult about it when I said it had been a terrible mistake and to forget it had ever happened. He …"

She broke off, her courage failing her. The unspoken words would sting her husband and one of her closest friends. She'd put her own marriage in the balance, and even threatening to explode a union of convenience made her feel sick.

"What do you mean, 'he got difficult'?" said Andrea. "Rob's said nothing to me. You're not making any sense."

"I'm sorry, Andrea. I feel like I've let you down, too. You and Zbiggy. I shouldn't have gone behind your back. But I was so desperate."

The tears were flowing now, and Zbiggy placed a consoling hand on her shoulder. One of Donna's rested across her stomach. *You didn't deserve any of this, little man or little lady.*

"By the time I realised what an idiot I'd been, and told Rob I didn't want to carry on with it, he … he … suggested … No, not suggested. He tried to blackmail me." She hadn't thought of using the word until that moment, but suddenly saw that there was no alternative to describe the grubby bargain Rob had tried to strike. "Into carrying on the arrangement. Having sex. Or he'd tell Zbiggy everything. That I'd been lying to him."

Right on cue, as if bidden by a theatrical production's prompt, a key ground in the lock. It took two steps across the threshold before Rob gained an oblique view of Andrea through the half-glazed door. Those steps had been furtive, for the sight of the Clio had given him the demeanour of a burglar: one who'd gained entry to a property but was still unsure if any threat lay within. The look on Andrea's face, pained and knowing, told him his fears were about to be realised.

But all was not lost yet. By the time his hand was on the door handle, his bearing changed into one of practised, breezy insouciance.

"Hello, you two," he said as he took up station behind Andrea's chair. He placed his hands on her shoulders and stooped to kiss her cheek. She remained inert.

"They both know, Rob. I've made a clean breast of it, so we don't need to pretend."

"Know? Know what?"

Rob's hands fell from Andrea's shoulders. He turned his back on all three as he filled the kettle. "Beth's upstairs, I take it. Tea, anyone?"

"Donna's been telling me about your little arrangement," said Andrea coldly.

"Ah. I see. What did she tell you? Exactly?" He'd spun round to face them as the low hum of the kettle became audible. Having turned his back on his adversary to reset, he marched into front-foot battle.

"That she asked you to be a sperm donor, and when she had second thoughts, you tried to blackmail her into bed."

Rob nodded. "She said that? Really?"

Even Zbiggy couldn't have explained why he chose that moment. He never doubted Donna for a second, and could easily have lunged as soon as Rob appeared, wiping that smug expression of his face. Something held him back for those few seconds. Perhaps it was to prove to her he could show restraint. Perhaps he just wanted to hear it from Rob's own mouth. And now he was suggesting Donna was a liar, which was too much for him.

The two men were a similar height, but the brute power was all on Zbiggy's side. To that he added momentum, for he launched himself at Rob, throwing a haymaker punch as he did so. The small of Rob's back was tight against the edge of the worktop, so there was no riding the blow. His head snapped back and cracked against the cabinet door, then he slid down on to the floor, his hand clamped to his jaw.

"What the fuck!" The utterance was low and laboured. He rolled onto his front and drew up his knees, like a defence-minded animal. But there was no follow-up. Zbiggy just stood there, fists clenched but now clearly at a loss.

"Zbiggy! You promised you wouldn't!"

Donna grabbed his arm and pulled him back towards the table. Andrea rushed past him, squatting down next to her husband to see if he was all right. She rested an arm across his shoulder in a mirror of his gesture towards her moments earlier. This time it was his turn to ignore it. There was no kiss, though, for his head was buried in the crook of his arm, no stubbled cheek available even if she'd wanted to plant her lips on it.

The violence acted as a countervailing factor to the alleged misdeed. And, unlike that supposed crime, this one left no room for doubt, was more immediate, more brutal, more shocking."You need to leave," Andrea hissed over her shoulder as she cradled him; words that bore a clear implication. *No matter what he's done, he didn't deserve that.*

In the second that her attention was distracted, Rob rolled over on to his back. One hand was still covering whatever wound had been inflicted. The other he used to shuffle into a sitting position, his back propped against one of the cabinet doors.

"Wait!" he said. "Why would I blackmail her into having sex when she offered it willingly? On a plate? Ask yourself that."

Andrea's eyes shot straight to Donna, who was almost through the threshold and into the hallway when the grenade was hurled. She spun round to meet her friend's gaze, and her accuser's. And then her husband's, for Zbiggy, a step behind her, was also looking at her, seeking a response.

"I did no such thing, you ..."

Where others might have surrendered to the urge to deliver a torrent of affronted, expletive-filled abuse, Donna hesitated. How could anyone judge whether it was down to her antipathy to vitriol, her default conciliatory nature; or because there was a grain of truth in what Rob was saying?

"That's a lie," she said simply. Then, realising it was the other two she needed to convince, she locked on to each of their gazes in turn. "He gave it me in a plastic pot. I did the rest myself. Twice. Once in the toilets at Marks & Spencer. And once ... here."

The last word hung in the air, reverberating loudly even though it had died on her lips.

"Yep. Here. Upstairs. In the main bedroom." *Your bed, Andrea. Yours and mine.*

"You weren't here!" she flashed. Then, again addressing the two-person jury: "I let myself in and did it here. It was ... convenient. He offered and it just seemed to make sense."

"I'm struggling to make sense of any of this, to be honest," said Andrea, shaking her head. "The only thing I know for sure is my husband might have a broken jaw."

"Good!" said Zbiggy.

"We can settle this," said Rob. The wound was still covered up, but his voice was more animated now. "If I wasn't here, and I wasn't in the M&S

bog ... if you hadn't asked me to help you – the natural way – then answer me this: how would I know you have this delicate little butterfly tattoo on your upper thigh? Your right leg."

He tapped his own, just below the hip bone, to indicate the spot. "Just about here."

Donna's mouth dropped open. She could feel all three pairs of eyes trained upon her.

"You do have a tattoo there," said Andrea. "Remember I asked you about it on that spa day we went on? You told me you had it done when you were half drunk. You were in your teens and had to hide it from your mum."

Donna looked anxious for a moment, then snorted derisively. "There you go, then. That tattoo's no secret. I've told lots of people that story. *You* probably told him yourself, Andrea, that's how he knows."

"No, Donna. I wouldn't have. I'm positive."

"Someone else, then."

She looked at Zbiggy's imploring face. *No, not you, my love.* I know it wouldn't have been you.

"Wait! We're missing the obvious. There was that day the six of us went to Seaton. Remember? The summer before last. We had swimsuits on. The tattoo would have been on full view, everyone would have seen it."

"Yes," Zbiggy confirmed. "Everyone." He was struggling. All he'd wanted was to punch the wrongdoer and go home with Donna. This was all too much. The facts were starting to get messed up.

"Do you know what?" said Rob. "I think you may be right. We did do that, and we did go swimming. Except I don't remember it from then. I saw that tattoo a lot more recently, from a lot closer up. When I did what I was asked."

"I don't know why you're doing this, Rob, or what you hope to gain. Is it to get back at me because I rejected you? Or just to cause trouble for the fun of it? Tell them the truth, for God's sake, and then we can get out of here."

"The truth? That's rich coming from you. OK. Try this for size. Maybe you think I heard about that tattoo from somewhere, or noticed it on a beach. Believe that if you like. But explain this: what about the clit ring, Donna? Did you show that off at Seaton too?"

The colour drained from Donna's face. Zbiggy made as if to launch another attack, then checked himself. Andrea fixed her eyes on Donna and saw that confirmation was unnecessary.

"I've never seen the appeal of them myself," said Rob. "I certainly wouldn't fancy the male equivalent. Ugh! No thanks. Still, takes all sorts, I guess."

Nothing more was said. Donna grabbed Zbiggy's sleeve and pulled him after her. Her face was still ashen, her steps short, unsteady and deliberate, like a drunk trying to fake sobriety. Rob finally allowed himself to be helped to his feet. Andrea gently moved aside the hand that covered the spot where the blow had landed, checking the damage to his face.

"It doesn't look like the skin's broken. How does the jaw feel?"

Before he could answer, the two girls came bounding down the stairs. As they burst into the kitchen they presented two sets of hands, wiggling twenty fingers embellished with glittery nail varnish. "Is tea nearly ready? Me and Katie are starving."

66

Ben turned back on to his side, cursing both what lay beneath him and on top. The futon mattress had about as much give in it as a slab of chipboard. Worse than that, it was horribly uneven, lumps like malign pustules sticking out of the wadding. The top layer of the offending sandwich was the duvet, a sweat-inducing polyester with an old, scratchy cover. The floral pattern was faded beyond recognition.

He'd been boiling hot one minute, throwing back the duvet to allow the rivulets of sweat on his chest to evaporate, or just drip on to the futon and soak in. Then he was too cold, forced to pull the thing up under his chin.

There had been no steamy make-up sex. No screaming row that burned itself out. There hadn't even been raised voices to speak of. Zoe had been quite calm, taking herself off to bed early, telling him that he was sleeping in the spare room.

"If the kids ask, tell them it was because you were snoring."

Being kicked out of bed; that hadn't happened for a long time.

Naturally, he'd protested his innocence. Told Zoe he was being blackmailed by Carly Fitzroy and her boyfriend. Maybe just him. "See?

That's why you couldn't get hold of her when you tried. She's stitched me up and done a runner."

All he'd done was get caught out filming Carly, and kept it to himself instead of telling Zoe. Then made it worse by going into her flat. No, not her flat. The rented flat. Then trying to pay them off. "They fucking played me, Zoe, surely you can see that?"

But Zoe couldn't see past the photos and dirty knickers. Whenever Ben sloped off down a side alley, she brought him back to that central point. She didn't care about the blackmail, wasn't interested in his efforts to shift the blame. If he hadn't done anything wrong, there'd have been no leverage, nothing to be blackmailed about.

Her final words before she closed the door on him and went upstairs rang in his ears. "I can't believe you've brought this to our door again. To our marriage. To our children." No attempt to slap him or throw anything. Just a chillingly flat delivery and calm exit. She'd never done that before.

Ben punched the pillow, trying to beat it into a more comfortable shape. He checked his phone: two-thirty. Four more hours of this fucking torture. It irked him that he was in the doghouse for no good reason. He felt like telling her about Julia Hennessey, the afternoon's entertainment. *She's almost a pensioner but went like the clappers. And she gave me a blowjob. If you'd showed a bit more interest, put out a bit more, maybe I wouldn't have to look elsewhere. Have you thought of that!*

And here was his chance. For the door swung open and there she was, backlit by the landing nightlight. She stood there momentarily, arms folded across her towelling robe, staring at him, unsure if he was conscious or not as her eyes tried to adjust.

"You awake?"

He wouldn't tell her about Julia Hennessey, of course, or any of the others. He wouldn't complain that some of them were better in the sack than her. Because she was here now and they weren't. Because she was the mother of his kids. And because, every once in a while, usually after a few gin and tonics, she let herself go and they had very hot sex. There was no booze tonight, but he'd take whatever reconciliatory shag was on offer. A sweet quickie, followed by a few hours of pocket-sprung kip. Bliss.

"Yep, I am. You try sleeping on this bloody thing. We should chuck it out."

"I take it you'll want me to have it, then. When we divide stuff up."

She hadn't moved. The arms were still folded, a forbidding barrier against him, not a defence against the chill night air.

"Come on, don't be daft, Zoe. You don't mean that."

"What would be daft," she hissed, "would be to think there aren't plenty more Carly Fitzroys that I don't know about. I'll be taking the kids to mum's tomorrow. Give you a few days to find somewhere to stay while we get the ball rolling."

He swung his legs off the futon, the cold air assailing his clammy skin.

"Let's just talk. You know? Work it through. We're good together, you and me. You know we are."

"I'm tired, Ben," she said, the double meaning clear in a voice drained of fight. "I'm going back to bed."

67

Andrea was also wide awake. She lay on her back, blinking up at the ceiling even though it was too dark to focus. The image of Donna stretched out in that very position, on that very bed, kept coming back. Her legs wrapped round Rob's, her body doing all it could to extract every drop of semen he could give.

After Donna and Zbiggy had gone, after Katie's dad had picked her up, after they had the house to themselves, she'd asked him to flesh out the details. Demanded to know everything. How and when Donna had approached him. What happened in Marks & Spencer's. Chapter and verse on what took place on that very bed. On that score, they'd arrived separately, Rob told her. Donna used the key she and Zbiggy had in case of emergencies. They'd had sex on top of the bed, he said. It had been her call. She'd felt the chances of conception were better with the natural method, and he'd deferred.

The duvet cover hadn't been washed since, and Andrea had run her hand across it for any telltale residue. She found no trace, yet it did nothing to dim the mental picture of heaving bodies a few inches from where she slept, a few feet from Beth's room.

This wasn't part of the arrangement. He was supposed to be discreet, like her. Snogging someone at a town-centre car park was bad enough. Almost comical as no real harm came of it. But this?

She wasn't best pleased with Donna, either. That trust was broken now. That friendship couldn't be repaired. She'd admitted to propositioning Rob on the sly, long before she knew the truth about the state of her and Rob's marriage. That was out of order, tantamount to propositioning her husband when for all she knew they might have had a normal relationship. And now she was trying to make out it wasn't penetrative sex, forgetting that her fanny jewellery would find her out. She had no idea what baubles Donna wore down there, so there was no way Rob could have known. Unless he'd been there. Up close and personal.

Then there was Zbiggy, launching himself with fists flying. Beth could have witnessed that assault if she'd popped her head round the door a few minutes earlier. He'd say he was provoked, but it wasn't fair to throw punches when the person he should have been angry with was Donna. Taking his outrage out on the guy who'd merely been acting on his wife's wishes. It was a proxy punch.

Thankfully, the injuries seemed to be slight. A small cut on the back of Rob's head where it had thwacked against the cupboard door, and apparently just bruising to the jaw, discolouration masked by the stubble. Nothing that needed explaining to Beth, to his work colleagues, clients or friends. But it was too close a call. Maybe the act of cutting themselves off from Donna and Zbiggy ought to be a spur to further action, she thought.

Rob had his back turned to her, his breathing snuffly and regular. If his conscience had been pricked, it wasn't keeping him awake. Andrea wasn't superstitious, no believer in star signs or omens, but she began to wonder if this was the right time. Why should she lie here next to Rob when Drew was waiting with open arms?

She prodded him, then shook his shoulder when that failed to rouse him. Finally, he rolled over onto his back.

"What's up? What time is it?" he said groggily.

"I don't want to do this any more, Rob. That … scene tonight, I don't care who initiated it between you and Donna …"

"It was her, you know it was. She admitted it."

"OK, so it was her. It doesn't matter. This is no good, what we're doing. We need to think about a clean break. We've protected Beth too long. Kids younger than her have dealt with a lot worse. She'll be fine. She knows she's loved."

Rob rubbed his eyes. "Jeez, you pick your moments. Do we have to talk about this now?"

"No. But I was lying here and it suddenly became clear as day. We both need to move on. I want to move in with Drew and start over, not keep her hidden like a dirty secret. It'll be better for you, too. You can be a proper single bloke, find a new partner. Maybe get married again."

"Whoa! You're marrying me off when we haven't even started divorce proceedings. I know last night spooked you, but don't rush into anything because of it."

"Come on, Rob, you know I'm right. It was always going to happen sometime. It feels right now. And it's not because of last night. Not only that, anyway."

He took her hand, rubbing his thumb across her palm.

"It'll be weird for her at first. Beth, I mean. But she'll get used to it. It's not news any more for a kid to be living with two mums. Or two dads."

Rob's grip tightened, then he withdrew his hand. He'd been thinking about this day for a long time. It was hardly a surprise, yet it still stung. Having to sit back and watch the child he'd parented since she was a toddler thrust into the care of another woman. A fucking lesbian. Who knew what effect that might have, how it might mess his precious Beth up?

Andrea sensed the vulnerability and insecurity encapsulated in the withdrawing of his hand. "You'll still be her dad, you know that? See Beth as often as you like. No one's talking about having a timetable, Rob. We don't want any of that 'every other weekend and dinner with you one school night' nonsense. We're bigger than that. It'll be fine all round, you'll see."

She laid her hand on his shoulder as he turned away from her. Rob chewed his lip. All he could see was a role as a bit-part dad, marginalised, less relevant with every passing month. Puberty and periods would push her even more towards her mother and, by association, her mother's lover. The ones who were there 24-7. Beth would eventually find excuses to skip a bowling night with him, or a trip to TGI Fridays. Was it even guaranteed that he'd get to walk her down the aisle?

He was screwed. Over the years, he and Andrea had talked about him legally adopting Beth, but never quite got round to it. Once they walked, he was just a guy with no blood tie to the child, just her mum's ex. Birth mother against nominal stepdad; only one winner there, unless she was a lousy parent. Or maybe if Beth kicked up a fuss. Neither of those was going to apply.

This was all Donna's fault. If she'd kept her trap shut, this wouldn't have happened. Not now, anyway.

His hand went to his aching jaw. Slipping his little finger into his mouth, he prodded the two rows of teeth in the area where the blow landed, checking again if any were loose.

He wasn't going to stand by and let all this shit happen. He couldn't fight – certainly couldn't take on someone like Zbiggy. But he was smart. He could think on his feet. He'd enjoyed the reaction on those three faces when he'd played his ace: Donna's downstairs furniture. Andrea and Zbiggy had believed her until that moment. Then it all turned on its head.

I'm too quick for you. And I will be again. Just you watch.

68

Donna would have liked a midnight conversation with Zbiggy. But she instinctively knew she had to back off. The car journey home had set the template, Donna urging him to believe she was telling the truth, at a loss to explain how that squared with Rob's knowledge of her vaginal area. *I know I lied about Michael Phillips and about using Rob as a donor, but I'm not lying now. You have to believe me.*

Zbiggy had cut a forlorn figure all evening. He'd had an extra-long soak in the bath, given one-word utterances about what they might have for dinner, which he'd eaten in silence. He'd gone to bed first, giving her the option of whether to sleep together or separately. She'd slipped under the covers half an hour later, leaving her pyjama bottoms off. She hoped the intimacy of the bedroom might add weight to her denials. If only it could lead to a cuddle – it didn't have to be sex – then, when Zbiggy was back on her side, she could try and fathom out what was going on. How could she concentrate on what Rob's game was when there was a rift between them?

She couldn't initiate contact again. She'd been trying all evening and been shut down. So she lay there, hoping he'd turn round, stretch out his hand, envelop her in those tree-trunk arms, tell her everything was going to be OK. But he didn't. He was hurting and needed time and space; she knew that.

Her hand slipped down to her naked thighs. She wasn't in the mood, not in the least bit aroused. When her fingers ran across the labial stud, it was not for pleasure. Rather, it was a means to focus her thoughts on how something she'd had done as a self-dare ten years before could have come back to haunt her so.

She'd been with Jez at the time. He was a university dropout obsessed with base jumping. An early YouTube adopter who posted GoPro videos of himself leaping off bridges, buildings, masts, the lower – and the more illegal – the better, it seemed. He'd been killed on one of his first attempts using a wingsuit, unable to resist following the contours of the mountain face too closely, sucked into oblivion on a snow-kissed rock in the French Alps.

They'd split up by then, though she did go to the funeral. She didn't know many at the wake, sloping off as soon as she decently could. But she overheard many like-themed conversations, about how Jez always lived for the moment, always needing a rush, how he was never going to make it to be a grandad pottering around in a shed. The nearest she'd got to responding to his devil-may-care attitude was having her clitoris pierced. Far *ballsier than another tattoo*, she'd said, trying to impress him when he'd teased her about playing everything too safe; after he'd pretended to use a magnifying glass on the microscopic butterfly on her upper thigh that wouldn't have depleted the world's ink supply by much. *I don't see any metal bar sticking through your dick, Jez.* In fact, she'd been far too queasy about getting a more prominent tattoo, preferring the reversibility of the piercing. Jez had been right: she had indeed played it safe while appearing to match his breezy, fuck-you attitude to life.

She'd kept the jewellery as a kind of memento him, and maybe as a reminder to herself of her one real wild-child moment. It was even a struggle to recall if Zoe knew about it. Yes, she must have told her bestie. No one else, though, of that she was sure.

No one except Zbiggy. She'd met him around six months after the funeral, Zoe and Ben playing matchmaker. She wasn't blown away on that first date – the funfair wasn't that much fun. But she found it sweet that he kept going at the rifle range until he won her a fluffy toy. And he grew on her, this gauche, not-very-handsome bloke. Someone who made no attempt to paw her at the first opportunity, who she had to give a not-so-subtle signal to when she was ready to move things on. When she decided she'd had her fill of peacocks and adventurers. This was the straight-up guy she wanted to settle down and have kids with.

So. Jez (deceased). Zoe (probably). And Zbiggy. That was the short list of people who knew, or might have known, about her piercing. None of them a conduit to Rob.

Her fingers brushed across it again. It was meant to make sex more pleasurable, give a more intense orgasm. She'd never found it so. It was there just because it had become part of the vaginal furniture. She had the sudden urge to go to the bathroom right then and take it out. It was part of her distant past, and any sentimental value instantly evaporated with Rob's utterance. It was tainted now. Not only that, she remembered reading somewhere that they were frowned on on the labour ward. She needed to check on that, for she didn't want to reach the point where she was asked to remove it by some supercilious clinician. *That will have to come out, I'm afraid.*

Then again, would she even make it to the delivery suite? And if so, would she have a husband by her side?

No, she couldn't take it out now. It would smack too much of a guilty reaction. Getting rid of the evidence. There was no rush. It would remain there for the time being, and she'd focus her attention on working out how the hell that smug, sleazy, lying prick found out what was between her legs.

69

"Where the fuck were you yesterday? I was calling on fucking speed dial for a lift."

"Yeah, sorry about that. We had some shit to deal with, me and Donna."

Ben had no intention of mentioning his dalliance with Julia Hennessey. In the circumstances, the fewer people that knew about that, the better. It meant nothing anyway, just a bit of score-settling when he was at a loose end. Plus he now had bigger fish to fry.

They were unloading the decking gear from the van, walking it through the side gate of the Jacobs' house and down the garden to where the posts they'd concreted in stood like soldiers on parade. The tanalised joists, the premium non-slip boards with their high mark-up and the fixings were all carried to the site, then the mitre saw was wheeled to the rear patio and rigged up with power.

"What kind of shit?"

Zbiggy related what had happened. About Donna admitting she'd lied about using the internet bloke's sperm. About her asking Rob to be a donor. About Donna saying he'd tried to blackmail her into having sex. About the face-off. About the punch. About Rob trying to twist things round, saying it was Donna who'd suggested they do it. And about how he'd backed up his version of events, the revelation that was like a hammer blow to his own solar plexus.

"Dunno what to believe, mate," he said as he clamped a joist in position and Ben marked the posts ready for trimming.

"Jeez, what a fucking mess," said Ben. "Me, I'd never doubt Donna. Not for a second. She ain't the kind to mess around. Loves ya to bits, for fuck's sake, though I can't think why."

"'cept she admitted going behind me back, didn't she?"

Having no answer to that, Ben changed tack. "So our Andrea's a muff muncher, is she? Who'd've thought it." *That explains why Rob's sniffing around on Tinder, then,* he left unsaid.

"I was wondering if Zoe might, you know, speak to her. I need to find out what's happening, one way or another."

"That might be a bit tricky just this minute," said Ben.

Zoe had not mollified as he'd expected. He'd risen early, a relief to escape from that god-awful futon. He'd got the kids up and taken her a cuppa, expecting her to have reconsidered in the light of a new day. But, as soon as she was up, she'd started loading the Tiguan, telling the kids they were going to granny's as a special treat. Tara had clapped and danced, then decided she'd draw granny a picture. Freddie had asked if his friend Arthur could come, too. If he was going to miss nursery, why couldn't Arthur? Maybe next time, Zoe had said, when she'd spoken to Arthur's mummy.

"So you're going, then?" Ben had said as she piled clothes into a wheelie case. "Called your mother, have you?"

"Yes. Did it first thing."

"She must've been over the moon."

The note of derision had signalled that Pam Lester never thought him good enough for her daughter. *His charm cuts no ice with me. Too full of himself by half. He'll break your heart, that one, you mark my words.*

"She just said it would be a nice surprise. She never mentioned you."

"No. I bet she didn't. How long you staying for?"

She'd shrugged. "Not sure. I'll let you know."

"Come on, love," he'd said in a final attempt to stop her from leaving. "Let's take Freddie to school. Zbiggy can crack on with the job we're doing on his own. We can talk things through."

"What you need to do," she'd said, pulling away from him, "is look for somewhere to stay while I'm gone. Maybe Donna and Zbiggy will take you in."

He gave Zbiggy the bullet points of the exchange, told him about the photographs and soiled underwear that prompted it. He added that he might need somewhere to kip in a day or two. "I could act as ref between you two," he suggested, trying to make light of the situation. "Earn me keep."

"Dunno about that, mate. Normally, I'd say no problem. But this has shook me up, I can tell you."

Mrs Jacobs appeared with a tea tray. "That one's got the extra sugar in it. See, I remembered."

"Lovely job, Mrs J." There was a side plate with more Lincoln biscuits on it, but this time there were two KitKats added to the mix. Ben swooped on one immediately.

"How's it going?" Mrs Jacobs enquired, casting her eye on the handiwork.

"Soon have the rest of these joists up, love, then the deck will appear as if by magic. Job's a good 'un."

"Righto. I'll leave you to it, then."

Ben sat astride the joist already bolted in place, savouring the chocolate biscuit and sweet tea. Zbiggy remained standing, waiving his claim to the other KitKat.

"What a fucking pair we are," said Ben, spraying crumbs from his mouth. "Should be well set up, got a nice little business going. And bang, I've bin shafted by a pair of snotty-nosed kids and got to find somewhere to doss down. Kicked out of me own house for summat I never did. And there's you, stitched up by Rob fucking Allen. We're the victims here, you know. Me and you. Innocent as the day is long, that's us. Them that have stiffed us, they need a good slap."

"I tried that, and look what good it did."

"Yeah, but you went about it the wrong way, mate. You can't do it in front of the women, and with kids upstairs. You gotta box clever, mate." He jabbed a finger at his temple to drive home the point.

Stung by the rebuke, Zbiggy fired back with a rare lack of deference. "You ain't boxing at all. The girl's disappeared and you don't know jack about the other kid."

"True, mate, true. Seems to me we need to find stuff out before we decide how we're gonna play this. You need to work out how Rob could've known about Donna's ... you know ... downstairs department. And I need to find out where these little shits are lying low. And whose spunk is on those knickers, 'cos it fucking well ain't mine.

70

Zoe was in a foul mood. Under her breath, expletives issued forth like geysers: a slow build-up followed by a hot, swift release, only for the cycle to begin all over again. The M5 was crawling, thanks to an overturned lorry near Tiverton according to the radio travel news. The red line on her traffic map was thick and long, showing that the fifty miles to her mother's was going to feel like a trek to the Midlands. She'd just passed the Cullompton exit, so exhortations to find an alternative route were redundant for a good stretch. All they achieved was to bring an early spouting of her next flash of hot temper.

"Mummy! Tara hit me!"

"Minnie! Minnie mine!"

The stop-start progress at least enabled her to keep half an eye in the mirror. The children had been squabbling from the off, none of the toys stacked up between them worth as much as when they were in the other's possession.

"I saw that! Freddie, don't snatch Minnie Mouse!"

"But you said we have to share. It's my turn with Minnie Mouse."

"Sharing doesn't apply to Minnie Mouse. And Tara, we don't hit people, you know that. Even if they take Minnie Mouse off you. It's naughty. Now play nicely, you two, or we're turning around and going home. You won't see Granny."

They weren't going to do a U-turn, of course. She tried not to issue empty threats, but this was undoubtedly one. The thought of crawling to Tiverton and looping back was even more depressing than staying the miserable course. There was the faff of cancelling with her mother. She'd let slip that she and Ben had had "a row", for she knew her mother would guess as much anyway. Zoe never woke up midweek in term-time and arranged an impromptu day trip. Not to her mother's, anyway. Turning back would avoid hearing the *told-you-so* sideswipes, though it wouldn't prevent them from being articulated, either to her mother's gossipy friends at her precious book club and pilates class, or to Zoe herself at some point in the future. But much worse than suffering any maternal gloating was the thought of allowing Ben to feel he'd been let off the hook. That she'd threatened to leave but couldn't carry it through. That he didn't have to pack his bags after all. *Take this as a final warning, Ben. If there's a next time, I swear …*

No. He'd see it for what it was. Weakness. Lack of resolve. An invitation to flash his smile when another bit of skirt showed an interest. *Carry on shagging around, don't mind me.* She'd had her suspicions over the years, always with circumstantial rather than hard evidence. If she was being honest with herself, maybe if she'd dug a little deeper when her suspicions had been roused, she might have found that concrete proof. This time she hadn't needed to hunt for it; it had been thrown in her face. She couldn't overlook cradle-snatching pictures and dirty pants. It was a matter of self-respect as much as anything.

She knew she couldn't stay away more than a day or two. What then? Return to the empty house she'd demanded? Whether he'd complied or not, then what? Hold crisis talks? Insist they go to Relate? Go for full separation? She wasn't sure. Probably not. The thought of starting over with two young kids, asset-splitting, sharing parental duties, finding someone else; it was all too much to contemplate. She'd make him squirm, though. Grovel. Make him believe that it was a card she was willing to play if pushed too far.

Her screen lit up with an incoming call. Not Ben asking her to reconsider, or even to see if she'd arrived safely. Donna.

"Hey, what are you up to? I could do with a chat. Are you driving?"

"Yes. Doing battle with the M5. Taking the kids up to mum's."

"Oh. Right. Just for the day? You back later?"

Seconds passed. What to say? Everything, of course. She valued Donna's advice above anyone's. Just not now, not stuck on a motorway on a dodgy phone line with warring kids sitting right behind her.

"Hello? You still there?"

"Yes. Yes, I'm here. Might be home later. Or maybe tomorrow. Bit tricky. Can't really … you know. Kids driving me up the wall. Was it anything in particular?"

This time it was her turn to wait for an answer, to enquire whether they still had a connection.

"Not to worry, it'll keep. You have a good trip. Say hi to Pam for me."

"I will. She always asks after you, anyway. I often think she's fonder of you than me." Zoe forced a laugh at a throwaway line that she thought contained more than a grain of truth. She and her mum had always clashed. She'd been closer to her dad, her gentle, kindly, indulgent dad, who kept his counsel until it was asked for, who let her make her mistakes, who'd always been there to pick up the pieces when she messed up. Helping, never judging. But he was gone now, carried off by a heart attack at fifty-eight. Zoe tried to suppress the thought that she'd rather have lost her mother. Seemingly her sole redeeming feature in her mother's eyes was that she'd produced two grandchildren. If Donna ever had kids, even that advantage would be lost.

"I said I often think she's fonder of you than me ... Hello?"

"Yes, I'm still here."

The words were lifeless, a flat statement like sat-nav intonation. No picking up on her provocative tease. *I see your mum once in a blue moon. She might take a different view if she'd had to raise me.*

"You OK, Donna?"

"No. Not really. Not at all, in fact."

71

You may also want to speak to your partner, friends or family, but you don't need to discuss it with anyone else and they don't have a say in the final decision.

Donna didn't learn anything new from the NHS website. It just confirmed the routes and the risks, information she'd never actively sought out but which she'd somehow acquired. Maybe through episodes of *Casualty*. She'd been more used to poring over web pages to do with getting pregnant than scanning those dealing with termination procedures. Now she was reading matter-of-fact prose about how you go about ending a life. Take a pill or go for the surgical option. Clear the decks.

Then came the blithe punchline: *Having an abortion won't affect your chances of becoming pregnant again and having normal pregnancies in the future.*

Who were they kidding?

You may be able to get pregnant immediately afterwards, and should use contraception if you want to avoid this.

No Pill or condom required, thanks; not with her and Zbiggy.

The only crumb of comfort lay in the 24-week cut-off point. There was still time to bring him round. But not while he thought she'd lied about having sex with Rob. If she could find a way round that, there was still a chance. That was only half the battle, though. Even if Zbiggy could be convinced as to how the conception came about, would he be able to be a dad to Rob's child? How would she feel, pushing a pram down the road and risking bumping into him? She shuddered at the thought. No. They'd have to move, far away, for it to stand any chance at all. That effectively meant cutting ties with Zoe and Ben, too. Losing their best friends as well as Zbiggy's source of income. Fresh start. Wiped slate. If they did, what about Rob? How would he react if they upped sticks to the other end of the country?

She punched in a new Google search: *sperm donor legal rights.* The results offered some encouragement. *If you conceive using a donor sperm and do not put the donor's name on the birth certificate, they are not the legal parent and do not have parental responsibility.* Hooray for that.

If you are married or in a civil partnership, your spouse can be the legal parent. If they are named on the birth certificate, they will have parental responsibility. That was it, then. Get Zbiggy's name on the birth certificate and they were untouchable. Home and dry.

Or were they? She read on, something about the donor having the option to apply for a child arrangements order. Things got foggy, all down to Children Act legislation. That order, if successful, could grant the donor access. *Access!* But the chances were slim. It would probably be thrown out if the donor had played no role in the child's upbringing. Or if finding in favour risked *disrupting the child's life to such an extent that it would be detrimental.*

If!!??

The rest of it didn't apply, for it was all about what she should have done to cover herself at the outset. Even down to having a document drawn up beforehand. Apparently, it would have helped if she'd marched Rob down to a solicitors' office and got some co-signed agreement about the undertaking. It wasn't legally binding, but it would have weakened Rob's case still further – that is, if he wanted to rock the boat. Too late for that now. A suggestion to be filed under unlocked gates and bolted horses.

Donna shut her iPad. It was all stacked in her and Zbiggy's favour, as long as it was his name on the birth certificate. And yet. She was still queasy. What about that legal loophole, or any others she didn't know about? What if Rob chose to make trouble without going down the legal route? And what if Rob backed off completely but the child wanted to find out about his or her biological roots when they were old enough?

She wished Zoe had been able to talk. After the previous night's bombshell, there was no point holding back. Everything was out in the open now. Everything except the miraculous cell division taking place in her womb.

72

"First things first," said Andrea, "I need to bring Drew up to speed. I'll go and see her straight from work. I mean, if she turns me down, then there's not much point telling Beth, is there?"

Her animated words tumbled over each other as she paced the kitchen. Though they contained a caveat, it was delivered in jocular style. There was no hint of apprehension in them. For she knew it was what Drew wanted, what she'd hung in for all this time. The subject hadn't been raised for a while, but only because Drew hadn't wanted to ramp up the pressure on her lover, or build her own hopes on shifting sand.

Rob remained seated, staring into his coffee. So this was what she'd called him back for. He'd left for work while Beth was still readying herself for school, Andrea confining herself to mouthing her intention to call him later. It had come just after ten. Was there any chance he could pop back before she began her afternoon shift? He had a viewing at eleven, and told her he could call in en route for fifteen minutes.

"Isn't it all a bit sudden? Don't you think you're overreacting to what happened yesterday? We shouldn't be making decisions because of that little episode. Beth's a day older than she was yesterday, and you didn't think it was a good idea to blow everything wide open yesterday morning. Did you?"

His intonation was the opposite of hers. Cautionary. Portentous, even.

She blinked at him. "I thought we'd agreed? When we spoke last night?"

He gave a derisive laugh. "Come on, Andrea. That was a half-baked idea when we were both half asleep. This is the cold light of day."

"Well I haven't changed my mind," she fired back brusquely. "Even if *you* have."

He slammed his hand down on the table, causing concentric ripples to form in his coffee cup. "Come on, love, this isn't like waking up and deciding to go off on a picnic because the sun's out. There are all sorts of implications. Where were you thinking of living, for one thing?"

She blinked at him uncomprehendingly. "We'd move in with Drew. She's got plenty of room. I thought we'd agreed on that?"

"We've talked hypotheticals for ages. This is reality. So you want to tell Beth we're splitting up, tell her you've got a new partner, tell her that partner happens to be a woman and tell her she's being uprooted from the only home she's known. All in one go. Priceless."

Deflated, Andrea sank into the chair at the opposite end of the table. Put like that, it sounded more like inflicting a grievous punishment than an act of liberation. "At least it would get it over and done with, so she could start adjusting without having another big change round every corner. Surely that's better than a long drawn-out affair?" The words rang hollow even to her. How much could Beth take in one go? How much was too much? Falteringly, she batted it back across the table.

"OK, so what's the alternative?"

"Well," said Rob, "for a start, it would be better not to take away her familiar surroundings. Her comfort zone." His hand described a wide arc.

"Right. I can see there's an argument for that. So you mean for Drew to move in here, and you ..."

She left it hanging, wanting him to bring the sentence to its natural conclusion. A conclusion that was unexpectedly usurped.

"I meant for Beth to stay here. With me. You move in with Drew, then let her get used to ..."

"No way! No fucking way, Rob. That isn't gonna happen. You can forget that. She's my daughter."

"And mine!"

"Your non-legally adopted daughter." The words were out of her mouth before she could weigh them.

"Thanks. Thanks for that."

"I'm sorry. I didn't mean that. I don't want this to be about point-scoring. I want what's best for all of us."

Rob leaned forward. "Then give up the crazy idea that the three of you can play happy families at Drew's place. There's secondary school round the corner. Periods. She could end up in therapy, under some fucking shrink on Valium. That what you want?"

With that, he got up, looking irritatedly at his watch. Throwing the barely touched coffee down the sink, he told her he was late for his appointment and had to go.

Andrea suddenly recovered her confidence and poise. "You know what?" she said, stopping him before he reached the door. "At least at Drew's, Beth would be part of a stable, loving relationship. Compare that to you groping some woman in a car park the other day in broad daylight, then admitting shagging one of my best friends under our own roof. All in all, I don't think you should be at the front of the queue when it comes to giving out advice."

73

Hi Donna.

Just a quick catch-up, to see how everything's going. As I haven't heard back from you since our meeting, can I assume it was yet another one-hit wonder??!!! I do hope so. If you're expecting a happy event perhaps you would let me know. I like to keep my info up to date for future clients. For the record, if you've had good news it would make 161 first-time successes!!! 873 in total!!! If not, don't hesitate to get in touch for another booking – the old love juice is still as potent and plentiful as ever!!

Cheers,
Michael

She deleted it immediately. Too late for that now. But she couldn't help wondering what might have been. If she'd just gone ahead and used his sperm and had done with it. Either without telling Zbiggy – the miracle baby – or even with his blessing. Not flushed that 50-quid pot down the toilet at The George. If she'd ignored the thought of all the other women Phillips had serviced, all the half-siblings running around the country. Focused on nurture rather than nature, what they as parents could bring to the table, not whether their child was one of many to have Michael Phillips' nose or ear lobes.

All academic now.

All she could do was deal with the here and now. That meant phoning her ShopWatch supervisor to tell her she couldn't make today's assignment. It was a trip to the bookies, a dull, low-reward job she'd done before. She said she had a throbbing migraine and had to go to bed. Someone else could inherit the few measly quid for placing a small bet and filing a report on the shop's customer service and ambience. Or she could do it herself tomorrow, if that was any good? Yes, she told her supervisor, she was sure she'd feel much better by then.

She almost felt bad at how solicitous the boss had been. *You look after yourself, Donna. Hope you feel better soon.* This was the first time she'd cried off after accepting an assignment, so she knew her credit with the company was good. It was gig-economy work anyway, and low grade at that. Flexibility was its main attraction, and she was making use of that advantage for once.

Rosie fired up first time, as usual. Donna often gave the dashboard a little pat of thanks, like a jockey rubbing a horse's neck. Zbiggy would roll his eyes if they were driving somewhere together and she gave the car tactile feedback.

It's a pile of metal, love – just nuts and bolts and plastic.

Shhh, she'll hear you!

Not today, though. Zbiggy wasn't there, and Donna was too preoccupied anyway.

She'd considered phoning or texting Andrea, but in the end decided to take a chance that she was in. Andrea's shift patterns varied a lot, so it was pot luck, she knew that. But better a wasted journey than give her the opportunity to fob her off; to cut short a phone call or ignore a text. Tackle her face to face, that was the only way. She wanted to gauge how Andrea was feeling, try and convince her that nothing intimate had happened between her and Rob. To say her piece without him chipping away on the sidelines.

Neither her nor Rob's car was in sight when she pulled up. Damn. All psyched up for nothing. She parked up and tried the door anyway. Nothing. She immediately dismissed the idea of tracking her down at work

– assuming that's where Andrea was. If she was still angry – and she would be, given what she believed had happened – then a scene at the workplace was more likely to fan the flames than douse them.

But Rob? That was a different matter. Causing a stir at Barker & Samuel didn't bother her in the least. Yes, catch him at work, hopefully with plenty of staff and public around. WHY ARE YOU SPREADING LIES ABOUT ME, ROB ALLEN? WHY ARE YOU TELLING PEOPLE WE SLEPT TOGETHER WHEN WE MOST CERTAINLY DID NOT? Nice and loud. More uncomfortable for him than her. His head office wouldn't care about the rights and wrongs of it, just that it had happened at the workplace. Dirty linen aired in public. Not in keeping with the brand they'd spent decades building up.

She didn't know what made her pull over. Not second thoughts or lack of stomach for that confrontation. More of a gut thing. What it would achieve she had no idea. Nothing, probably. And there'd still be time to make him squirm publicly afterwards.

Three left turns and a right brought her back out on to the same road, this time heading back the way she came, back towards the Allens' house. Fifteen minutes earlier, she'd parked right out in front and marched up to the door. Now she brought Rosie to a stop a hundred yards from the house. There was no logic to it. It was no different to the day she'd let herself in and syringed Rob's sperm into her. Except for permission and intent. That day Rob had given the former, and the latter was transparent. This time there was no permission, and her intent was to find something, anything, that might help the situation. It wasn't breaking and entering, for she had a key. Just entering.

She called out as the door swung open, just as she had done that day. "Hello? Anyone home?" It was a knee-jerk check for she knew instinctively the place was empty. She went into the kitchen, tracing a finger across the table top as she circumnavigated it. She spotted a lone cup in the washing-up bowl, still containing coffee dregs, waiting to be put in the dishwasher. She placed her hand on the cabinet door that Rob's head had smacked against.

Further along the hallway was the door to the lounge. She hadn't been in this room since the last time the six of them had got together here. They'd played *Twister*, laughing like drains as arms and legs got tangled up. She remembered Zbiggy collapsing in a heap and rolling off the mat when he was given a stretch too far. Had Rob straddled her at some point? Rubbed himself up against her? Or was that a false memory, taking root in the light of recent revelations?

She went upstairs. Justin Bieber caught her eye almost immediately. She surveyed the bathroom from the threshold. The pedal bin was so full that the lid didn't sit properly. A piece of unidentifiable cellophane wrapping and couple of cotton buds had spilled on to the floor. She took in the toilet, the aquamarine of the fish-themed seat standing out against the white pottery. *The toilet!* She must have used the cloakroom downstairs dozens of times, and this one, too, on a fair few occasions. Where else would her naked nether regions be on display? Jeans tugged down, skirt hitched up, knickers dropped.

She sat on the seat and studied the wall opposite. An edifice of glossy cream tiles laid in brick bond. She got up and swept her hand across the cool surface. Her eyes ran right up, Donna craning her neck to examine the ceiling, an unbroken plane of matt white except for the nickel-finish downlighters. She was being silly, she told herself. The wall backed on to the landing, and a pinhole camera fed through from the loft was too outlandish to contemplate. She didn't even bother traipsing back downstairs to run the rule over the hallway cloakroom. Two of its walls were external, one was the divide between it and the kitchen, while the front pretty much consisted of the door and nothing else. Had there been one of those fisheye viewing lenses, the ones often fixed into external doors to let you see who was on your doorstep, that might have afforded Rob a ringside view of her genitalia. But of course there was no such monitoring device, and in any case, it would have meant standing with your face glued to the toilet door in the hallway. Silly. Too nonsensical for words.

That just left the spare bedroom, the one where she'd injected his seed. Had she left that till last on purpose, putting off returning to the scene of a terrible decision? She sat on the edge of the bed, the spot where he'd left a towel out for her. There was no towel now, just a swirly-patterned duvet cover taking the imprint of her bottom. Nor was there anything on the bedside table, where he'd left the plastic pot out for her.

Only then did she begin to see it as a stage setting. Minimalist theatre.

Just the two props. But that was all that was needed to shape the action. She didn't need to check her phone to recall the text he'd sent. *Bedside table spare bedroom.* Of course she'd use the stuff where she found it. Why wouldn't she? It was the obvious place. She wouldn't have carried it through to the main bedroom, that would have felt wrong, as would doing the deed in front of Justin. Nor would she have used the bathroom; the whole point of the exercise was to make it a more comfortable experience than using the M&S loos. No. This was the obvious place, the one she'd been guided to, the one she'd approved. *Good old Rob.* She'd given him a virtual pat on the back for shepherding her where he wanted her.

If this was the stage, if the bed was the centrepiece of the proscenium arch, where was the audience? Before her stood a tired old five-door wardrobe, the middle one of those a mirrored finish. Donna looked at her reflection, her gaze lowering to her groin area. She'd sat facing that mirror when she wriggled out of her jeans, slipped off her knickers. Yes, she'd turned her back for the next half-hour, facing upstage to allow the semen to seep in. But then she'd turned round once more to get dressed, checking her full-length appearance before exiting stage right.

She took the two steps that placed her on the edge of the stage's apron. Close enough to see her skin's individual pores. Then she opened the door to reveal the central stalls. The rail of overspill clothing might have been more in keeping with backstage, where the actors costumed up for their roles. It was sparsely filled. Maybe out-of-season stuff, or clothes that no longer fitted but it seemed a shame to throw out.

Donna was more interested in the space. Hardly capacious but plenty big enough. Even with a top shelf and rail, she had no trouble ensconcing herself. It would have been a tighter squeeze for Rob, maybe forcing him to hunch over a bit. But doable.

And then the acid test. Closing the door on herself, enveloping herself in the gloom. Except it wasn't fully dark. Shafts of light penetrated the ill-fitting doors. A sliver of a gap offered a glimpse of the bed. Stepping back out, she noticed the key in the lock. Had that been inserted when she was here before? Removing it, she ensconced herself inside once more, putting her eye to the keyhole. It was a narrow field of view but one, if she was not mistaken, that had the spot where Rob had placed the towel at its centre.

74

Rob was hammering the keyboard so hard that Karen on the adjacent desk was moved to ask what it had done to upset him.

"Not the computer, love. Just bloody people! This job would be great without them."

"Yeah, know what you mean. Wouldn't stay open long, though, would we? Without 'em?"

The office door opened at that moment and she fielded an enquiry. Rob returned to the task in hand, typing up some details of a property they'd just taken on to the books. The asking price was totally unrealistic, but the vendors were adamant they wanted to try it at that figure. They'd soon be giving it him in the neck over the lack of interest, and he'd have to smile through it all, even though he wanted to yell, *lower the asking, you stupid wankers!*

Then there was the couple he'd shown round this morning, the appointment he'd rushed to keep after having words with Andrea. That had looked promising, for on the phone they'd said they were cash buyers and this fixer-upper – a damp, dilapidated, structurally unsound house that had been for sale for ages – was just the kind of project they were looking for. Only it turned out that what they really meant was that they'd be cash buyers once their bungalow was sold, and their agent had assured them it would be snapped up in a week.

Fuckers. Fuckers. FUCKERS!

The real source of his ill humour wasn't the clientele. It was Andrea. All this talk about moving in with Drew had spooked him. Despite his kite-flying exercise, he knew he had about as much chance of having Beth live with him as he did landing a property on Sandbanks for a tenner. He was the latecomer, both in terms of taking on parental responsibility for Beth, and in being added to the deeds of their house a couple of years after moving in. He'd gained joint-ownership of the house Andrea had bought with her first husband – part of the wedding celebration. They'd spoken about making a fresh start with a place the two of them chose, but once Andrea had "found herself", embraced her repressed sexuality, the subject dropped off the agenda. What was the point? They'd decided instead to muddle along, see how things went. Once Drew arrived on the scene, there was no way back. It had been a state of limbo ever since. Not that it hadn't had its attractions: the pluses of home life and fatherhood along with off-the-leash encounters, a single bloke on the pull who didn't have to worry about the wife finding out he'd taken off his wedding ring before a night out.

If Andrea did take Beth and move in with Drew, where would that leave him regarding a roof over his head? Their place would fetch two-forty tops, the mortgage standing at half of that. Selling up would give them sixty apiece, assuming an even split. Not bad if it was going in the back pocket. Or a nice chunk paid off Drew's own borrowings – if there were any; if Andrea bought into Drew's property the way he'd done with Andrea's. But sixty grand wasn't a lot to slap down on a new place, even using insider knowledge to bag himself a good deal.

It was all Donna's fault. She'd set it in motion. Without her sticking her oar in, Andrea might have waited years, time for him to make better plans for his own future, time to savour being a hands-on dad and not a walk-on figure.

And without Donna, his jaw wouldn't be clicking as he moved it from side to side. It wasn't doing that before Zbiggy lashed out at him. And there was definitely bruising coming out now, masked by his beard. It was worth it, though. Just to see their faces when he told them. Him thinking his missus had been having it away with someone firing live ammo. She was far too glam for him anyway, that was plain as a pikestaff. He couldn't have been shocked. Then there was her, gobsmacked and embarrassed at having her pussy decoration revealed to the world. *Enjoyed the strip show, thanks very much. Would've been better if you'd got your tits out, but I suppose that was too much to expect. Another time, maybe. Oh, and it must go down as the closest I've been to anyone sending me a text.*

Just leaving. Didn't use towel … brought my own … have left it where it was. Hope thats ok. Thx again. x

I watched you type and send it, Donna. Of course, I didn't know it was for me until my phone lit up. Yes, I did remember to put it on silent. What else would you expect? I always think ahead. I'd read it before you even left the room. You were dressed by then, so I thought I might as well. The floor show was over. For the record, the towel was back in the airing cupboard before you'd reached your car. You didn't see mine, did you? No, it was parked down a side road well out of view. Had a quick brew, just to leave a nice little gap in case of curtain-twitchers. It's all about the planning, love. Keeping one step ahead. I'm pretty nifty at that, you've got to admit.

75

Zoe was happy to leave them to it. When her mother suggested that they make flapjack, she knew it meant a bit of peace and quiet for her. While she flicked desultorily through the pages of a *Hello* magazine lying under the coffee table, Zoe could hear the shrill "helping" noises emanating from the kitchen, Pam's voice occasionally rising above the cacophony to maintain order. "This is *cooking* chocolate, Freddie, it's not really for eating … golden syrup's *meant* to be gooey, Tara – try a little bit on your finger. You did wash your hands, didn't you?"

If there was a cooking gene, it hadn't been passed down the maternal line. To Zoe it all seemed such a faff when you could get the same thing from the supermarket, stuff that tasted better too. Better than she could make, anyway.

By the time you've bought all the ingredients, Mum, I can't see how it's any cheaper, either.

You should batch-cook, Zoe. That's what I did when you and Mattie were little.

They'd tacitly agreed to call a truce on that line of conversation. Pam held her tongue over the amount of processed food Zoe gave her grandchildren. Zoe accepted that she was never going to be a domestic goddess, and wasn't prepared to sacrifice takeaway pizza and curry, in any case.

Eleanor, of course, could do no wrong in the culinary department. Mattie's wife had endeared herself to Pam long before she assumed official daughter-in-law status. Passionate about the Mediterranean diet and cooking from scratch. Fruit and veg intake that made five-a-day look underwhelming. She was also a law graduate, adding high-flyer to her long list of accomplishments. Throw in Mattie's civil engineering qualification, and a son, Tom, who arrived between Freddie and Tara, and it added up to a golden package.

Zoe bore her brother and sister-in-law no resentment. She was close to Mattie and got on well with Eleanor, who was a good laugh when you got her down the pub and always had a filthy joke to hand. They were always embarrassed whenever Pam sang their praises in company, quick to defend Zoe and Ben's achievements and choices, to even up the scales.

The undisguised favouritism Pam showed regarding her children played no part in Mattie and Eleanor's decision to start a new life in Australia. They were outdoorsy, outward-looking go-getters, and no one was surprised when, in the gloom following the Brexit vote, they'd decided to leave. Pam had visited them once in the eighteen months since they'd gone. She'd had to make do with FaceTime and Skype apart from those three precious weeks. Her hopes that they might pay an early return visit suffered a blow when Eleanor fell pregnant. They were loving life in the Melbourne suburbs, couldn't contemplate a trip to England, *not with a fair dinkum Aussie kid in the oven*. Pam, of course, was welcome to come over again. And Zoe, Ben and the kids; they had plenty of room. The more, the merrier. But making an offer and accepting it were two different things when it involved travelling halfway round the world.

All of which left Pam rather better disposed towards Zoe, who at least had the attraction of living an hour's drive away. And if she came with the grandchildren and minus her son-in-law, so much the better.

It had been all pleasantries and small talk so far. Zoe knew that when Freddie and Tara were in bed and fast asleep, her mother would take her to task about the state of her marriage. There was no other feasible explanation for the impromptu visit. Plus there was history: the only other time she'd returned to the family nest at such short notice had been during their engagement, when she'd found texts from another woman on his phone. Her dad had been alive then, offering a shoulder to cry on, telling her not to worry about the costs already incurred, cancellations that would have to be made and awkward conversations with friends that would have to be had if she wanted to call the wedding off. Her mother had just expressed smug vindication that she'd been right about him all along. *A wrong 'un, you mark my words*. Maybe that was in part why Zoe had forgiven him.

They'd started singing now, Pam and the kids. *Pat-a-cake, pat-a-cake baker's man, bake me a cake as fast as you can.* They couldn't hear her phone ring. Pam couldn't suck her teeth at the words Ben calling on the screen.

She slipped out of the front door anyway, into the large glazed vestibule where she was buffered both from those inside and the street traffic.

"Yeah?"

"Just wanted to make sure you got there OK."

"We're here. Shitty journey. The usual."

"Still not sure how long you're stopping?"

"Till you find somewhere, I suppose. And hurry up about it 'cos it won't be long before me and her come to blows."

Ben laughed, misreading the signal. He thought Zoe's strained relationship with her mother might work in his favour, that the two of them could unite behind their shared antipathy for Pam. He was swiftly disabused of the notion.

"You spoken to Zbiggy yet?"

"No. Not about that. Him and Donna have got enough on their plate. You obviously ain't heard what happened last night."

"I haven't heard anything. I've been here, haven't I? Slogging up the M5 because of you."

She wasn't going to let him change the subject. But then she replayed the brief conversation she'd had with Donna on her way up. Donna had wanted to tell her something and she'd cut her off.

"So what's happened?"

"All kicked off round at Rob and Andrea's. It's a right royal mess."

He related what Zbiggy had told him. It boiled down to the same tactic as with Pam. Instead of: *I know you're pissed off with me but your mother's a bloody nightmare,* it was: *now I know we've got our problems, but look what's happening with them four. Better the devil you know, eh?*

"I have to go. The kids are calling," she lied. "And I need to speak to Donna."

Ben felt the door was slightly ajar and wedged his foot in it.

"There's nothing going on between me and that babysitter, you know. I was set up, I keep telling you. I've done some googling and found this lab place that'll prove it. All I've gotta do is send them the stained material and a swab from my cheek and they'll be able to tell you it doesn't match. Takes a week or two, mind. Where are they? Those knickers?"

"In the bin. Where they belong," said Zoe icily.

"Bollocks! Right, I need to shoot home and fish 'em out. They said it was important for the stuff not to get contaminated 'cos the test might not work."

"Don't bother. It's bin day. As you well know. And they didn't go in the recycling box, that's for sure."

"What! Shit! *Shit!*"

"You almost had me going there, Ben. Very convincing. Very convenient. You saw me put the bin out last night, and now you want to play your get-out-of-jail card, when you know it counts for nothing."

"Zoe, I swear …"

"No, Ben. It's my turn to swear. Fuck off."

76

Ben screwed up the chip paper, dragged it across his mouth and stuffed it into the bin. He hadn't even bothered to decant the food on to a plate, just grabbed a fork and scooped the pot of mushy peas over the battered cod and fries, then slathered ketchup over the lot.

The bin, he noticed, had a new liner. All the accumulated detritus of the past week had gone, cardboard and plastics off on their recycling journey, the rest – including the soiled knickers – presumably to landfill. He cursed himself for not thinking of it sooner, bagging up the article when he had the chance. But when that scrap of material had lain accusingly on the kitchen table, the last thing he'd wanted to do was take possession. Only now did he realise he'd missed a trick. An innocent party would have been happy to pick the article up, weigh it between thumb and forefinger, toss it aside like a well-used dishcloth. *Nope. Never seen these before in me life. Whose are they?* Whereas his reluctance to go anywhere near them smacked of guilt. *They've got my spunk on, for Christ's sake … I'm not putting me fingerprints all over them too.*

He opened a bottle of Budweiser and plonked himself down on the sofa.

If Zoe had been there, she'd have badgered him to take a bath or shower before eating. He sometimes jumped in the bath with the kids, if he wasn't too grubby and he was home in time. He liked to sink under the water and rise like a sea monster, making them squeal with delight by wiggling his fingers tentacle-fashion and bellowing ghoulishly.

The house felt empty without the three of them. One night was fine, the place to himself, able to slob about, drink beer and channel-hop. But the phone call hadn't gone the way he'd hoped, and if he didn't at least make the effort to find somewhere to stay for a few days, it would just antagonise Zoe even more. He could imagine her returning home from her mother's in a foul mood, ready to pick a fresh fight and having him firmly in her sights.

Ben scrolled down his contacts and stopped at Donna. He rarely rang her, calls between the two families usually going husband to husband and wife to wife. She was his go-to person for advice on birthday and Christmas presents, though, and if she got a call from him in the days before those occasions, Donna knew she was going to be quizzed about what kind of perfume or jewellery Zoe would like; what kind of gift would bring him brownie points. Neither of those occasions was on the near horizon.

"Hey, Donna," he opened. "How's tricks?"

"Ben?" came the quizzical reply. "Zbiggy's right here if you want me to put him on?"

"No, it was you I was after. He told me about the … about what happened yesterday. Just wanted to make sure he gave you my take on it. Told him at work today, I did. Trust your missus, mate, I told him. Whatever she says happened, that's good enough for me."

"Thanks. Thanks for that. I appreciate it. Nice to be believed."

There was an altered tone for the latter comment. Ben could tell it was for Zbiggy's benefit. He could picture them sitting together, Donna holding the phone between them to make it a three-way communication. *Did you hear that? Your best mate trusts me more than you do.*

"And no, he didn't tell me."

"The dick!"

"Oy! I can hear this, you know," Zbiggy chimed in.

"I know. And you're still a dick."

"Zbiggy did tell me about you not being in Zoe's best books at the moment. I spoke to her briefly when she was on her way to her mum's, but obviously we couldn't talk properly with the children around."

"I didn't do it, Donna. It was the babysitter and her boyfriend trying to make it look like I was guilty. It was a set-up. A sting. They were out to blackmail me, the little bastards. I believed you, no questions. You gotta believe me, love."

There was a long pause as Donna wrestled with his attempt at equivalence.

"I'd like to," she settled on. Not *I do*.

I know I've got to find a way to prove it 'cos Zoe sure as shit doesn't believe a word I say. I thought I'd cracked it but the bin men have been and …"

"Bin men? What's that got to do with anything?"

"Oh, it's … never mind. Let's just say I'm working on it. Proving to Zoe the whole thing's a scam. But she wants me out of the way for a day or two, and I was wondering if I could crash at yours? I did mention it to Zbiggy."

Another pause. This time Ben could hear whispering, too indistinct to make out.

"Can we talk about it tomorrow, Ben? We want to help, obviously. We're just in the middle of something here, so it's a bit awkward."

"'Course. I didn't mean now, tonight."

"No, I know you didn't. Don't worry, we won't see you out on the street. Let's sleep on it and see how the land lies tomorrow, OK? Maybe Zoe will come back and the two of you will talk it through so it won't be needed."

"Thanks, Donna. AND YOU, ZBIGGY, MATE. YOU'RE STILL A DICK, THOUGH!"

He took a self-satisfied swig after ending the call. He knew Donna was too soft-hearted to turn her back, no matter what she had on her own plate. And once she gave the green light, Zbiggy would always fall into line.

He'd secured a bed; that was something. Longer term, there were just two possibilities. Either keep out of Zoe's way and let her cool off, come round in her own time. Or find the proof he'd blithely mentioned to Donna. Something other than a lab test on knickers that were now buried somewhere in a mountain of discarded crap.

What did he have to go on? Two phone numbers, both flatlining corpses. A dead-end rented apartment. A brief meeting in a coffee shop. A park waste-bin that could be observed from a million and one vantage points. And some grainy video of two kids going at it.

He hadn't deleted the footage. When he'd tried to buy off Carly Fitzroy for two hundred quid, insisting that it had been wiped, it had been an easy lie. Even if he'd done so, there was probably some techie nerd who could have recovered it, so it was a moot point. He didn't need an expert, though; just a port for the memory card. He'd chucked it in his toolbox, in one of the plastic-lidded compartments containing lightweight Rawlplugs. The back of the works van was an area of mystery to Zoe, an Aladdin's cave of construction paraphernalia, a grimy paradise for bacteria and bugs. What was embedded in the fibres of the manky carpet covering the floor was anyone's guess. If Ben needed a hiding place after buying Zoe a Donna-approved gift, this was it, as long as it was well sealed against the filth and smell.

He watched it all again, including the bits he'd fast-forwarded through first time round. Even static shots of Carly reading and slugging water from a bottle. Just in case he'd missed something; something to give him an edge.

The FaceTime call that had made him hot and horny on first viewing left him unmoved this time. There was no jerking off to the low-rent porn scene. He watched her masturbate, and moved on when it told him nothing he didn't already know.

It was eleven-thirty by the time he reached the second recording. He studied Carly as she looked repeatedly at her watch, as if waiting for a signal. He watched her go upstairs to check on the kids. He watched those shapely legs through the balusters. He watched as Danny Croft breezed into their fucking house like he owned the place. Him and his four-pack of cheap lager. Him and his joint, which Carly stopped him from rolling.

Ben let it run while they watched telly, flicking through the channels, settling on nothing. Even on maximum volume and with his ear cupped, he still couldn't quite make out their chat.

And so to the action. Snogging first, then a hand sliding down over those tiny breasts to the crotch of her jeans. Carly laying her coat on the sofa like some ceremonial blanket and giving him a blowjob. Ecstasy written on his face as he clamped his hand on the back of her neck to set the tempo. A voluble *Jesus!* as he climaxed; that came across loud and clear.

Then the clearing up, with no reciprocal offer from him and no complaint from her.

On second viewing her keenness to usher him out was even starker, as was his readiness to oblige. He had the demeanour Ben would have displayed at his age and in his shoes with a casual girlfriend: he'd had his oats, why hang about?

And so to the final frames, the truncated finish. Danny Croft summoned back to collect his beers. Him noticing the camera was recording. *This fucking thing's on!* His face up against the lens. A wanker gesture.

Ben stopped it just before the picture blacked out. He put it into slow rewind, freezing it as the kid approached. Now he saw it. It was probably nothing, but what else did he have? There, on his grey hoodie, which he hadn't bother removing while being sucked off, there was a logo. Not *Superdry*, not *Adidas* or any other well-known manufacturer.

It was a badge.

77

"You don't believe me, do you?"

Zbiggy shifted uncomfortably in his seat, struggling to make eye contact. "I want to …"

It didn't occur to him that he'd used the same words that Donna had just used to Ben on the phone: a halfway house in the credit stakes. Thus he couldn't use that as part of his argument. *Why should I believe this far-fetched story when there's a more obvious one staring me in the face? I'm not convinced by your theory, just like you're not convinced by Ben's version of events. What's the difference?*

"It all makes perfect sense, Zbiggy, when you think about it. He wanted me to undress there so he could watch. Get off on it. He's a letchy single bloke; if you'd seen him with that woman in the car park, and if you'd heard the way he tried to blackmail me into sleeping with him, you'd see it was true."

Zbiggy wiped a large paw across his brow, as if trying to massage perspicacity into his brain.

"But, according to you, you made the first move. You approached him, yes?"

"I did, I've admitted that. I don't think that changes anything. He's an opportunist. With me he just saw an opening and … and … took it."

Zbiggy clammed up, as he always did when he felt unable to cope. He didn't want to throw the lies back in her face. She'd not been straight with him about that internet seller bloke, and she'd made the arrangement with Rob Allen behind his back. He couldn't dislodge the obvious from his mind. That she was desperate for a baby and chose a good-looking, fertile friend to do the necessary. Cuckolded him to suit herself. It was what he'd feared the whole time they'd been together; a fear made worse when his infertility was diagnosed. That one day she'd get a better offer. Have her head turned by someone handsome, funnier, cleverer. Or just someone with good-quality sperm.

"I'm struggling to get my head round the idea of him hiding in the wardrobe. I mean, we've been round theirs loads of times. The whole thing's too crazy for words." By which he meant too crazy for any words in his limited lexicon.

"But it's the only explanation that fits the facts. The only way he could know what he said about me is if he spied in secret. So it was either in their spare bedroom, where he suggested, remember, where he knew he could get a good view. Or else he must have followed me into the ladies' loos in Marks & Sparks in broad daylight, and had a gander over or under the door – without me or anyone else spotting him. Now *that's* what I call too crazy for words."

78

Ben took a screenshot of the badge. It got a lot fuzzier as he zoomed in, but he could make out a prancing horse – he knew that one well enough because he was a Formula One fan. It was just like the Ferrari logo. That was only one of a cluster of images, though. There was a spiky sun, the kind a child might draw. Some kind of fish. A sailing boat. A castle. He tried putting them all in a Google search and drew a blank. Up came all manner of images and information, but nothing that resembled this badge. He tried adding colour references. The five images adorned a shield; a shield with a red cross on a white background. Still nothing.

The only other detail was an inscription at the bottom. Straining his eyes, he wrote down the letters he could make out. Some foreign language, definitely not English. N I S I D O M I. That was the top line. There were more letters underneath, but they were a real struggle. He typed the eight he had into the search box: *nisidomi badge*.

The results offered him a choice. *Did you mean nisi domi badge?*

It didn't matter whether it was one word or two, for numerous versions of the exact badge confronted him. One with crossed hockey sticks through it. One advertising a synchronised swimming club, the badge's white quadrants containing water and symmetrically arranged figures. One featuring a pair of auctioneer's hammers: the logo, apparently of the Debating Union. All variations on the same institutional theme.

Bristol University.

Ben punched the air, almost upsetting his beer bottle. Then, just as quickly, the elation died. Did it really help that much? It didn't prove he went there; he might have borrowed the hoodie, or he might just have bought it because he liked it. People sported all sorts of things in the stuff they wore or carried; it didn't mean there was a connection. He himself had an England rugby jersey somewhere, a top he'd worn to watch the 2003 World Cup final but which he could no longer squeeze into. And he was no Jonny Wilkinson.

Still. It was something.

He opened the university's home page and found something unexpected: a search box for present and past students. He wasn't expecting that. Wasn't it all about data protection and passwords these days? Obviously not as far as searching a uni database was concerned. For the first time, he felt the wind was in his sails, only to be swiftly becalmed again when a search for Danny Croft revealed only a single result. It was a cancer newsletter that included a Danny Somebody and an address with Croft in it. He clicked on it and scrolled down anyway, just in case the kid he was after had changed his surname. A dead end. This Danny was a professor type, one of many academics shown in thumbnail alongside the various events they were attending. It was hardly surprising. The kid had mocked him about searching for that name.

He tried to remember what Zoe had said about Carly Fitzroy? Wasn't she a student of some sorts? Could the two of them have met at Bristol Uni? That avenue was also soon closed off; not even a single reference to her name.

Having no better idea, he clicked on Sports Clubs and Societies. There were over twenty headings, each of those containing their own cluster of sub-groups. There must have been hundreds all told.

Top of the list was Academic. That brought up another alphabet soup. The Actuarial Society, AeroSoc, something called AMP, Archaeology and Anthropology, and the Associate Membership Group. And that was just under the letter A.

There was nothing for it but to plough through. *Have you considered the actuarial profession or would like to learn more about it?* the first on the list asked. No pictures of any members, as he'd hoped. But there was a link to a Facebook group. That was all about images; maybe that would provide a lead? He needed a picture match. Easy to change your name, a lot harder to alter your appearance. And you didn't worry about doing that if you thought you couldn't be traced. That might just be the little fucker's Achilles' heel. If he *was* a Bristol student, it was just a matter of going through all the images connected with every department, every society, every club. Ben had nothing else to go on. And he had the time.

The Actuarial crew brought immediate disappointment. The Facebook link didn't work; it was a closed group. *Only members can see who's in it and what they post,* he read.

AeroSoc offered more encouragement. There were names of a long list of post holders, and this time he was granted access to its Facebook group. It was headed by a large group shot of the club's members at some formal gathering. Above their heads, the word AERO hovered, silver-coloured balloons appositely identifying the proceedings. Ben scanned the faces of the black tie-wearers for a smartened-up version of the scruffy kid who'd been in his house. Nothing. Not there, nor in the pictures of less dressy social events AeroSoc had held.

Ben rubbed his eyes and yawned. It was after midnight. If this was a wild goose chase, he needed to conduct it when he wasn't glazing over. He put the computer in sleep mode, hoping he'd be able to switch off himself as quickly. Two lousy groups down. Next up, when his eyes could focus, was AMP, whatever the hell that was.

79

Donna and Zbiggy went to bed a lot earlier than Ben, but both were still awake long after the latter lapsed into unconsciousness. Neither was sure whether the other had dropped off, neither wanting to ask the question. They were lying back to back, so any tell-tale blinking would have passed unnoticed. Physically, it was a narrow divide. Emotionally, the distance was a lot greater.

She'd told him. In an unplanned outpouring Donna had decided to come completely clean. They'd gone round in circles for ages on her theory about Rob concealing himself in the wardrobe, a theory that was neither provable nor disprovable by argument alone. There was no evidence that might come to light to sway things. Rob was the only person who could supply the truth, and there was no point asking him. Denial wouldn't make a jot of difference to her conviction, but it would leave the seed of doubt gnawing away inside Zbiggy.

And then, both to break the repetitious round and to rid herself of the last vestige of guilt, she'd blurted it out. She was pregnant. By Rob. From one of those two self-administered episodes. She wouldn't know which until she had a scan. Definitely not through intercourse, whatever he said.

Zbiggy had recoiled when she extended her hand towards him. These were meant to be the moments that deepened relationships, strengthened the bond. Donna realised it had been a fanciful hope that he would sweep her up in his arms on the news that she was carrying another man's baby. Right now they were functioning as individuals rather than a couple. All she could do was pray that the united front would return to give them a fighting chance of getting out the other side still together.

"Does he know?" he'd said flatly. "Have you told him?"

"No. I haven't told anyone."

"He's the father, isn't he? Shouldn't he know before me?"

They were wounding words, words that found their mark. Other men might have spat them with venom, but Zbiggy uttered them with a quiet despondency. He was defeated, broken.

It was Donna who provided the animus. "I want *you* to be the father, Zbiggy! I want to keep the baby and for us to be a family. It's what we've wanted for so long."

Finally, he bit. It was a provocation too far. "How can you ask that? You *can't* ask that, it's not fair."

"But you were happy enough to go with me and see that Phillips bloke. You bought into the idea of using a donor. What's the difference?"

"What's the difference? *What's the difference!* Don't be ridiculous! A stranger off the internet compared to one of our friends, someone we'd see every week? And all the lies that surrounded it? What else are you keeping from me?"

"Nothing! Nothing!"

She was shocked. The contempt loaded in that *Don't be ridiculous* comment was palpable. It was the meanest thing he'd ever said to her.

She got to her feet. "I've said what I wanted to say. I've told you what I want. It's up to you now."

She'd almost reached the door, feeling instinctively that it was best if she withdrew and let him mull it all over. His head was in his hands, and she wasn't expecting further comment, not even a goodnight. She got a lot more than she bargained for.

"Yeah? Up to me? And what if I said you should get rid of it?"

She turned to face him. This time it was her with the flat, calm statement contrasting with his naked aggression. "Don't think that hasn't crossed my mind. But I can't do it, Zbiggy. I won't. If you don't think you can live with that, maybe we'll need to call it a day."

80

Ben went straight back on the computer as soon as he'd rubbed the sleep from his eyes. He made himself coffee, resisting the urge to light up.

Whenever Zoe came back, she'd be able to tell. He'd tried it on before when she'd been away overnight with the kids, her sensitive nose always outgunning his attempts to mask the smell of stale cigarette smoke. He compensated by hitting the caffeine twice as hard.

He was getting a lot quicker at navigating the university website. One reason for that was the barriers that limited what he was able to see. He'd signed up as a visitor, which merely required him to submit an email and password. But he was still barred from accessing the inner workings of the clubs and societies, where pictures and profiles of the members lay, for all he knew. *Unfortunately your details don't match the criteria needed for joining the group.* If he'd seen that notice once, he'd seen it twenty times.

The Bar Society passed before his eyes. The Chinese Chess and Calligraphy Society. Bristol Against Plastic. Bollywood Dance. Nothing that meant anything to him until he came to The Clay Pigeon Shooting Club. He'd done that on a couple of stag dos, fancying himself as a bit of a sharpshooter. The Bristol Uni gun crew was the usual dead end, though. *Unfortunately your details don't match the criteria needed for joining the group.* But, like a lot of them, it offered a link to its Facebook page. Another group shot, this time lots of tweed and Barbour and flat caps instead of the formal wear of that Aero Club bash. No sign of Danny Croft – or the kid calling himself Danny Croft.

The search process was intense, requiring such concentration on his part that the phone made him jump. He grabbed it, hoping to see *Zoe calling*, only to be instantly deflated as he peered at the screen.

"Where are you?" said Zbiggy. "You coming to pick me up or what?"

Ben saw it was already quarter past eight.

"Bollocks! Soz, mate, lost track of time. Look, do you think you could finish up the deck job on your tod? There ain't that much to do. All this with Zoe ... I'm just trying to, you know, work stuff out."

There was gruff assent at the other end of the line. Only after the connection was broken did it occur to him that he'd forgotten to ask how things were between him and Donna. He'd do it later.

After showering and getting dressed, Ben grabbed another coffee and hit the computer again. More weird and wonderful groups, more blind alleys. It was mid-morning by the time he'd exhausted those clustered under the

Liberation umbrella. He hadn't lingered long over the Ginger Appreciation Society, set up in praise of redheads. Or the LGBT lot. The blokes in that group wouldn't have wanted a blowjob off the likes of Carly Fitzroy.

Next up was Media. He was almost halfway down the list now, which gave him a small shot in the arm. Still no word from Zoe.

He was surprised to find that the university had its own radio station. Plus a separate club to give wannabe DJs a grounding in production. And an in-house newspaper. Who knew?

Epigram had the famous Clifton suspension bridge as its logo. It had the usual blurb bigging itself up, but it differed from the others in not having a *Join Group* tab. That just saved him from reading for the umpteenth time, *Unfortunately your details don't match the criteria needed for joining the group.* There was no Facebook link, but there was a link to the paper's dedicated website. Ben clicked on the home page. Ignoring all the headers to do with content, he went straight to Meet the Team. That brought up half a dozen smiling faces: three boys, three girls. One of the males had high-swept fair hair, piercings and bumfluff. All the images were tight head shots, but Ben didn't need a wider angle to know that this gangly youth was probably wearing low-slung jeans.

Gotcha you little fucker, he breathed.

81

"Will you be staying for lunch?"

As invitations went, Pam Lester's lacked a scintilla of graciousness or warmth. She'd not hidden her vexation at Zoe's obvious dissembling the previous evening. "Tell me something I don't know," she'd said, after prising out of her daughter that she and Ben had had a row. "What about?"

Zoe's evasiveness left her with her own assumptions, which meant thinking the worst of her son-in-law. "Is it another woman? It is, isn't it?"

"I don't want to talk about. It's for us to sort out, it's none of your business."

"No, but you come here as a refuge, I see. It's all right when you *need* me."

"I *thought* you might be glad to spend some time with your grandchildren."

Pam watched Freddie and Tara through her kitchen window. She had no outdoor playthings, just a couple of boxes of toys in the spare bedroom. The children were hunched over in a conspiratorial huddle, Freddie poking something with a stick. Pam found them a lot more exhausting now that Freddie was pushing the boundaries and Tara was up and running. She was no longer used to the house being noisy or chaotic, and had to bite her lip regarding Zoe's overindulgence in matters of discipline. Their presence was beginning to grate. She'd be happy to wave them on their way. Little and often suited her as far as visits went, fitted with her disposition and lifestyle. And it didn't really need to be all that often.

"Lunch? Yes or no?"

"Yes, thanks. That would be great," said Zoe through a stuck-on smile.

The stand-off was interrupted by Freddie bursting through the back door, Tara following close behind.

"Look, Mummy! Look, Granny! We found a worm!"

He presented a stick with the soil-flecked creature looped over it.

"Wiggly worm!" said a delighted Tara.

"Ugh!" Pam made no effort to conceal her disgust.

"Wow, that's amazing," said Zoe. "Now pop it back where you found it. Worms like burrowing in the dark, damp soil. It wouldn't last long in here."

As Freddie turned round, his stick-carrying arm knocked against Tara and the worm fell to the floor. The children stared at it as it wriggled and coiled. Zoe was already stooping to rescue the situation when Pam bulldozed in, blasting the worm and surrounding area with bleach-rich cleaning fluid from a trigger gun, following on with a swab of kitchen roll.

"There. All done."

"Granny!" said Freddie. "You killed the worm!"

"Killed worm," echoed Tara.

"There was no need for that," Zoe scolded. "I was going to take it outside and clean up."

"Well, it's done now." She didn't add *my house, my rules*, but mother and daughter both knew that was the deal.

"Actually, we'll skip lunch. Come on, kids, let's get our things, we need to go home."

Pam said nothing, turning her back to wash her hands at the sink after depositing the balled-up kitchen roll in the swing bin. Ten minutes later, she was waving them off. Her equanimity had recovered now that they were going, and she'd hugged her grandchildren tenderly; her daughter less so.

"You two splitting up then?" was her parting shot to Zoe.

"Bye, Mum. Thanks for putting us up," was Zoe's.

She exhaled as Pam shrank in her wing mirror. Her phone, on the front seat beside her, pinged a message before she reached the first junction. *That would be great. Need a catch up. Free this aft.* She took in at a glance Donna's response to the text she'd sent just before setting off. *Heading home now. Sorry about yesterday. Must talk!!!!*

There was no reply yet to the other message she'd sent.

Back at lunchtime. Hope youve sorted somewhere to stay.

82

"I shouldn't have come," said Andrea. "It was a stupid idea to lay this on you when I've got to be at work." She looked at her watch. "God, is that the time? I have to go in five."

"It's a bigger decision than whether to have chips or jacket spud, that's for sure."

They both laughed.

"But I'm glad you came," said Drew. I'm glad you're asking the question. Trouble is, only you can provide the answer, you and Rob. It's easy for me, I've got no ties. Of course I want us to live together, get to know Beth properly. When and how that happens has got to be your call."

Andrea nodded. "Do you think Rob's got a point, though? About now being the wrong time?"

"I do," came the hesitant reply. "I'm just not sure there'll ever be a right time. You can always find a reason not to jump, my love."

"I suppose."

"He's bound to be feeling vulnerable now you've raised the issue. The question is, how much are his concerns to do with what's best for Beth, and how much are they about the impact it would have on him?"

Parked up fifty yards down the road, Rob watched them embrace on the doorstep. Andrea had no idea he'd fixed the settings on her iPhone, allowing him to pinpoint her location. She only used its basic functions and would never have noticed that it could be tracked. He liked it that way.

Why he'd made the detour, he wasn't sure. He could have gone straight to his viewing appointment and known just as well that she'd stopped off at Drew's before work. A ball bouncing on Cobham Street would have told him that. The only thing he would have missed was the doorstep hug. But after the conversations he and Andrea had had over the past twenty-four hours, he was feeling jumpy. She hadn't mentioned coming here that morning. Was it arranged after he'd left for work? Who had initiated it? Was that cow trying to unpick his argument, telling Andrea that Beth would cope just fine with the change?

As he anticipated, she didn't drive past him. Her car sped off in the opposite direction, for he knew, without using any monitoring device, the way she'd get from here to Sainsbury's. She was working at one; there was no scope for further diversion.

He watched Drew, or at least the back of her head, as she waited on the threshold until Andrea's car had disappeared from view. She gave a final wave that Andrea couldn't possibly have seen. Only then, and without casting a glance in his direction, did she step back inside and close the door.

He was going to have to fix Drew, just like he'd fixed Donna. Make the problem go away. He wasn't sure how yet, but he was fucked if he was going to stand by and be elbowed aside by that dyke.

He was about to head off for his appointment when his phone lit up. It was a message from Esther. *Hey stranger how about wining and dining a girl tonight?*

Esther Greaves. Yes, she might come in very useful. That could be two birds felled with one stone. Scenarios tumbled over one another in his head. It was just a matter of picking the one that most emphatically torpedoed any suggestion that his daughter would be coming to live in Cobham Street.

The lack of response brought forth a second message.

I'll make it worth your while.

There followed immediately a picture attachment. Esther Greaves on view from neck to midriff, open-bloused, the camera angled down her cleavage.

Rob grinned. Two birds with one stone. He punched in his reply. *Youre on.*

83

"Bollocks!" Ben hissed as he read the message. *Back at lunchtime. Hope youve sorted somewhere to stay.* He looked at his watch. Already gone half-eleven. Zoe obviously hadn't mellowed, having slept on it – the text made that all too clear. She was heading home because she and Pam had butted heads, as they always did if a visit extended beyond a few hours. Zoe was getting away from her mother, not rushing back to him.

Ten minutes later, he was firing up the van, and it was just gone midday when he pulled up outside Zbiggy and Donna's. There was no sign of the Clio, which he'd pretty much expected. If Zbiggy had wrapped things up at the deck site, he'd've rung to ask what to do next.

He was about to try Donna's number when the door opened. He grinned, pointing to his phone and then to her. She understood, smiling and beckoning him in.

"I've arranged to see Zoe later, just so you know," said Donna as she filled the kettle.

Ben nodded. "I'll make myself scarce if she's coming here, don't worry."

"I'm not going to take sides, and you can stay here for a bit while you … sort things out."

"Cheers. One bit of good news, at least."

"You'll be doing us a favour, actually. You can cut the atmosphere in this house with a knife at the moment."

"Peacemaker? Me? Not sure that's me strong suit, love."

"Referee, then."

Ben laughed, about to respond when his ring tone interrupted the conversation.

"All done, yeah? … another satisfied customer? …good, good … got the cheque, that's the main thing? … I'm at yours so shoot back here … you can leave your car and we can go back in the van for the gear … OK, see you in a min."

"Boy's on his way," he said after ending the call. "Now where's that ref's whistle?"

Donna seemed distracted, which he took to be anxiety over the next awkward exchange when Zbiggy returned, so he ploughed on. "Right pair, we are. Zoe's hacked off with me, Zbiggy's hacked off with you. Both of us innocent as the day is long. And –"

"I'm pregnant, Ben," Donna interjected. "I told Zbiggy last night. It's Rob's, but I didn't sleep with him like he said."

"Jeez." Ben whistled his shock.

"God's honest truth, I did it myself, using a syringe."

"I believe you, love, I told you that already. Never doubted it for a minute."

"Zbiggy doesn't. I know how Rob did it – how he saw what he saw. I'm sure of it, but Zbiggy's made his mind up and won't budge. He's so stubborn at times."

She began to cry, the next words squeezed out through the sobs. "We're finally having a baby after all this waiting, and now it looks like we might be splitting up."

She buried her face in her palms. Ben got up and rounded the table where they were sitting, resting an arm across her back.

"Hey, come on, it'll be OK. It'll work out for the best, you'll see. Even if I have to bang both your heads together."

Donna uncovered her face, but Ben could tell it had nothing to do with his reassurance or attempt at levity. Her eyes were darting maniacally.

"What is it? What's up?"

"Oh God, I've just thought! If Zbiggy won't have his name put on the birth certificate, then Rob could … could …"

"Could what? What are you on about?"

"I … I don't know. I read online that if your partner declares himself the father on the birth certificate, there's nothing anyone can do. If he doesn't … I don't how it stands. Oh, I wish I'd just used that horrible Phillips bloke's sperm."

Her head sank once more. Ben hadn't really taken it all in and could think of nothing to say. After a minute in this static pose, he began to feel awkward. Sliding his hand off her shoulder, he withdrew to the chair where his half-drunk mug of coffee gave him something to do with his hands. It was like a switch going on for Donna, who suddenly remembered that he had problems of his own, and she was being a poor hostess by monopolising the talk of marital strife.

"I'm sorry, Ben. You've got enough on your plate, you and Zoe. Is there anything you want me to tell her when I see her?"

Ben shrugged. "Much the same as you, love. Not guilty, but try telling *her* that. She's gone and binned the evidence that could've bailed me out."

He told Donna about the test he'd looked into doing on the soiled knickers, a test that wasn't now an option. Worse than that, the timing of his suggestion, just after the rubbish had been collected, had made him appear even more guilty in Zoe's eyes, if that were possible.

"I've sailed close to the wind over the years, Donna, and I know I'm not a perfect husband. But I'm being hung out to dry for summat I didn't do, I swear."

Donna studied him. The tortured expression, the pained voice, the discomfort emanating from the body language – all harmonised in a note of sincerity. They'd been friends long enough for her to know he was a storyteller, a bullshitter. But he was no actor. There was a big difference.

"I believe you," she said simply.

"You do? And what's more, I know who …"

He broke off when he heard the key rattle in the door. Zbiggy appeared, looking almost apologetic, as though it was Ben and Donna's house and he were the interloper intruding on a private conversation.

"All sorted," he said sheepishly, handing Ben the cheque already in his hand. "Shall we shoot back for the gear, then? I told Mrs Jacobs – "

"Mrs Jacobs can sit on the stuff for another half hour," said Ben. "You come and park yourself; we've got things to talk about."

84

"How was she? Your mum?"

Zoe shot Donna a raised-eyebrow, rolling-eyed look. "The same."

"Come on, she's not that bad!"

"Oh, yes she is. Couldn't get away quick enough."

Zoe was pushing Tara on the swings, responding to the *higher, Mummy, higher* shouts with an extra shove while keeping an eye on Freddie as he explored the ramps, walkways and tunnels of the climbing frame.

"Speaking of annoying family members," she went on, "Ben's at yours, I take it."

Donna nodded. "He's well cut up."

"Good."

"Says he knows who stitched him up. I believe him."

"You're a softer touch than me, he knows that."

Donna gave a hollow laugh. "Dunno about that. At the moment, Zbiggy thinks I'm a scheming liar who sleeps around. And gets herself pregnant."

Zoe turned to have the statement confirmed by eye contact, so dumbfounded that she missed Tara's backswing and the seat struck her a glancing blow. "*What did you say!?*"

Donna went through it all again. Her reasons for choosing Rob, the two insemination episodes, him turning nasty when he found out the truth and she tried to call it off, how he tried to blackmail her into having sex, the confrontation, the punch. And about getting inside the Allens' house.

"You broke in?"

"Hardly breaking in when you've got a key."

"Even so."

"I was desperate, Zoe. My marriage is on the line."

"Snap."

It started to spit with rain, darkening clouds suggesting it was a prelude to a lot worse. Zoe ran to haul Freddie from the bowels of the climbing frame, while Donna lifted Tara out of the swing seat and into her pushchair. After a dash to the Tiguan, Zoe suggested they go for tea at Parry's, a child-friendly cafe that had a soft play area to keep the kids entertained. Having onboard drinks bottles for them, she ordered a pot of tea for two and a couple of Belgian buns from the counter.

"Not sure I've got room for that," said Donna.

"There's always room for cake, especially when you're expecting. Quick, while the gannets are away. Far too near tea-time for them to be eating."

The children's antennae homed in on them before they'd finished, Zoe breaking off part of her iced bun to assuage Freddie, Donna doing likewise for Tara after being given the green light to do so. Zoe shooed them away while they were still chewing.

"You've got all this to come."

"Not if Zbiggy had his way," Donna replied. Lowering her voice, she added, "He suggested I have an ..." She couldn't articulate the word. "A termination."

"Christ. Are you considering it?"

"No. Well, maybe for a fraction of a second, so I wouldn't have to tell Zbiggy. But no. I'm having this baby, whatever he decides."

"Good on you. Whatever sex it is, I've got plenty of gear to keep you going for ages."

"Ha! Thanks, I'll hold you to that. I'll need all the help I can get if I end up a poor single mother."

Zoe pushed at Donna's crossed leg, her hand sliding up to feather her tummy. "Get away with you. It won't come to that."

Both left the hopeful assertion hanging. They finished their buns, and Zoe peered into the teapot to see what was left.

"You have that," said Donna. "I'm watching the caffeine."

"Everything by the book, eh?" said Zoe, as she squeezed out the dregs.

"I might have a lot of spare time to read all those books, too. If Zbiggy packs his bags." She tried to smile, catching a tear as it formed in the corner of her eye.

Zoe squeezed her hand. "What about Rob? What will you do when you start showing?"

Donna related what she'd read about being named on the birth certificate, expressing her fears over what would happen if Zbiggy refused to accept being the child's legal father.

"That's way over my head, Donna. You need to get legal advice."

"I know, and I will. But even if Zbiggy comes round and it's all legal and above board, Rob would still be there, wouldn't he? Like a dirty great black cloud hanging over us. How could we live in the same town, knowing we could bump into him round any corner? It'd be like walking on eggshells. And just because it's all tied up legally, it wouldn't stop him spilling the beans when the kid was older, would it? A word in his or her ear. Sow the seeds of doubt. *If you don't believe me, have a blood test and let's see who's telling the truth.* What's to stop him?

Zoe had no answer, draining her cup to cover the hiatus. Suddenly, she brightened. "But he doesn't know yet, does he? That's your advantage. It won't last long, but while it's there it's something you can use."

"Funny," said Donna. "Ben said exactly the same thing just before I came to see you. About Rob and the baby, and about the person who sent that stuff to you through the post. A right pair of scumbags, he called them, and they're both in the dark. Ben said they both needed fixing good and proper."

85

Dad. Hey sweetie!!! How r u??? Got a late work meeting tonight so wont make it home. Mum will have to crack HW whip for once! Be good. See you tomorrow. Love you tons!! xxx

Beth. I bet youll be drinking BEER!!!! YUK!! Oh and no maths tonite hooray just had to find stuff out about mary queen of scots shes a tudor queen. love you more!!! xxx

Rob. Staying at a friends tonight. Probably head straight to work tomo. Texted Bethalready, shes fine. See ya! x

Andrea. Is this a new "friend" or one of the old ones!!! Yeah thats no prob. Remember im at Drews on Sat – fairs fair!!! x

Four hours had passed since Rob had sent the two texts and received the corresponding replies. He and Esther were still on their first drink at the wine bar when he popped the question. "Look, I know this is going to sound calculating and presumptuous, but I really could do with knowing the answer now. Do you want to get a room later?"

She'd spluttered mid-mouthful, but it was just admiration at the cheek of it rather than taking offence. "And they say romance is dead."

"Sorry. Practicalities and all that. If I'm staying out, just wanted to message my daughter, say goodnight and all that."

"And your wife?"

"I'll drop her a line too – I'm a polite kinda guy, you know. Not that she'll be fussed."

"Weird set-up."

Rob waved his phone at her. "Is that a yes?"

Esther drained her Pinot Grigio. "Get me another one of these and I might be tempted."

They'd had two more, then a sit-down Chinese meal at a place where the staff had been glad of the walk-in trade on a slow midweek night. Rob opted for Tsing Tao beer as he ploughed his way through the all-you-can-eat buffet: a cornucopia of chicken and sweetcorn soup, king prawn toast, pancake rolls, sweet and sour, curry, fried rice and noodles. Esther matched him stride for stride, hesitating only over the drinks menu. "Don't know if I'd be better off sticking to the vino. Perils of mixing it and all that."

"If it gets you pissed quicker, definitely go for the beer," grinned Rob.

"I should warn you I pass out quickly when I reach my limit. And beer after wine lowers that limit a lot."

"On second thoughts, maybe stick to wine, then!"

She couldn't resist the twinkle in his eye or the cheeky laugh. The subtext, which could have made her run for the hills uttered by someone else, drew her in. *I want you conscious*, it said, *for the fun and games I've got in mind.* She'd already decided she wanted exactly the same. A night on the razz, away from the family nest, an opportunity to get laid. There had been not a hint of carnal pleasure the entire summer, stuck out in the remote, godforsaken French countryside. In fact, the last time she'd got wet – through male intervention, at least – was with Rob himself, that night just before she left the country and headed for the Vendée. Four months on, she could still recall his practised fingers sliding up her skirt in the car, unbidden and unbounded. The promise of that night would be realised this evening.

Esther didn't know if she was buying everything he was telling her about the state of his marriage. But he'd made no attempt to shield his phone when he'd texted his wife, even waving the reply under her nose. It obviously got the wife's blessing, so there was no need to feel a home-wrecker's guilt. Everybody knew the score. Everybody was happy with it. Just a bit of fun.

She'd teased him about the choice of a Premier Inn. "Is that the best you can do? What kind of girl do you think I am?"

"If it's good enough for Lenny Henry …"

Only then did she finally text her own mother, saying she was staying at a mate's. A solicitous reply came straight back, well-meaning but suffocating. She was glad not to have her mum flapping and fussing over her for one night and one morning, counting the days till she could afford to move out again. Part of the long-winded text had asked if she wanted some overnight things brought round – toothbrush, nightie, clean underwear. *You've probably had a drink, it's no trouble. Just send the address …*

Esther's eyes had struggled to focus, catching enough of the gist to send a peremptory refusal. *I can borrow what I need ta.* The drink was starting to affect her. The flaw in the plan to stick to white wine was that she'd received precious little help with seeing off the bottle. She'd lay off now. Nicely squiffy, relaxed enough to enjoy what this good-looking hunk had to offer. There didn't need to be a second instalment. *Carpe diem.*

They were lying there now, both on their backs, as sated by the sexual banquet as their stomachs had been by the Chinese fare. Esther left a leg hooked between his, while the back of Rob's hand had come to rest on her midriff.

"Well, thanks for showing me round," said Esther. "I'll let you know if I decide to put an offer in."

Rob roared, brought back from the brink of post-coital sleep. "All part of the service."

He was going to leave it till the morning, but as she'd brought him round, and he was suddenly feeling quite alert, he decided to strike.

"Can I ask you a favour?" he said, rolling onto his side to face her, propping himself up on his elbow.

"Naughty boy, you're insatiable. Give me half an hour, I just need a little – "

"I'm all spent in that department, love. No, it was about my missus. Or rather, her lady friend."

"What about her?"

Rob weighed his words. "Frankly, I don't like the woman. She can be a nasty piece of work. All sweetness and light when Andrea's around, but I've seen the other side."

Esther rolled onto her side, too, drawing the duvet up to her chin. "You can spoon if you want to."

"The thing is," said Rob, ignoring the offer, "it's Beth I'm concerned about. Andrea's talking about moving in with her, and I'm not happy about Beth being around the woman for any length of time. 'Course, if I broach the subject, Andrea thinks I'm biased against her, that I've got an *agenda*." He spat the word out like a popped cork.

"Familes, eh?" Esther muttered sleepily.

Rob drew himself in to her contours, his hand falling naturally across her breasts. *Don't nod off yet, you silly cow.*

"Mmmm, that's nice. Sleepy time."

"So I was thinking, she'd more likely believe it if it came from someone else. You could say you were an ex of this lady friend, this Drew woman …"

"*Me?*"

"… and that she was abusive, or nicked money off you, or – "

"Rob," Esther broke in, turning her head so she could just see him in her peripheral vision. "I don't think we're on the same page here. I came out tonight to have some nice food, a few drinks and decent sex. I've had all three, thanks. Maybe we'll do it again, maybe we won't. But if you think on the back of this I'm going to get involved in your weird ménage, if you think I'm going to pretend to be some miffed lesbian old flame so you can score a few points, you're badly mistaken. Now I need to get some sleep. If you wake up in the middle of the night and want to go again, give me a nudge and I may well be up for that. If not, see you in the morning."

86

Dear Mr Shields,

I was born and raised in Bristol. I wandered if you'd be interested in some info for your paper on what it was like growing up there in the 80s. It was a very different place back then I can tell you, no Ikea for a start. Long before your time I bet. I hung out with Banksy a lot way before he got famous. Nice bloke.

Let me know if your interested and fancy meeting up. I'm sure your readers would find it interesting.

Cheers

Zbiggy Kuzminski

Ben reread the email and gave a smug smile. That would get a bite, he thought. The little fucker wouldn't be able to resist the Banksy connection. That was inspired, if he didn't say so himself.

He could count the number of times he'd been to Bristol on one hand. That very same Ikea store with Zoe twice, the second to confirm the first was as bad as he thought. She'd been back without him since he put his foot down, sometimes on her own, sometimes with Donna. *I'll stay and look after the kids. Don't want to drag them round there, they'll be bored stiff.* Nor was he remotely tempted to give it another go now they'd opened a shop in Exeter, which was a lot closer. He'd also been to a gig at Colston Hall, though he couldn't recall who it was he saw. As for Banksy, all he knew was he came from the Bristol area, and that there was a print of the girl with a balloon in their downstairs bog – Zoe's choice, obviously.

"There. Whaddya reckon?"

He leaned back in the computer chair to allow Zbiggy and Donna a better view.

"Still can't see how it's gonna help. He'll suss you in no time."

Ben rolled his eyes. "I ain't gonna meet the little …" He checked the expletive for Donna's sake. "Ain't gonna meet the toe rag. Just wanna find out a bit more about him, that's all. Get an edge."

"You mean you're going to fight him, don't you?" said Donna tersely. "Get him down some dark alley, and – "

"Don't be daft," Ben cut in. "He's the only proof I've got to show Zoe I was being straight up. The sooner I can get to him, the sooner I'll be back in me own bed."

"Well, I don't like it. I don't want anything to do with it."

Nothing more was said as she grabbed her coat and bag, but she turned at the front door, not to say goodbye but to deliver a parting shot. "That email's got your name on it, Zbiggy. It's your funeral." The letterbox rang out as she slammed the door behind her. Zbiggy watched ruefully as the Clio pulled away in over-revved first gear.

"Don't worry about her, mate," said Ben, whose eyes had remained on the screen. "Everything'll be back to normal once we fix this problem with Rob. And *this*," – he swept his hand ostentatiously across the screen – "will help do that. Trust me."

"Will it? That's all I want."

Ben's finger hovered over the Send button. "I'm going for it."

Zbiggy nodded, though his whole demeanour suggested he knew it was a big mistake.

87

Rob beat Andrea home by fifteen minutes. It was 8.40 when he walked through the door, slap in the middle of the school run. He'd showered at the Premier Inn, up and about long before Esther stirred herself.

"What time do we have to vacate?" she'd mumbled, her face buried in the pillow.

"Dunno. Ten, I suppose. But I'm off now. Some of us have to work."

"How can you be so … *awake*?"

"I'll call you."

Then again, maybe I won't if you're gonna be so unreasonable about a simple request.

Esther couldn't blame him for lack of sleep. He'd woken around four o'clock, but he hadn't slid over to her; he hadn't cupped a breast or shoved a stiff dick in the small of her back. No. He'd been turning her rejection over, weighing the chances of her being talked round and deciding they were negligible. That took him down alternative tracks, and by five-thirty, one of those stood head and shoulders above the others. He'd dozed for the next couple of hours, then sprung out of bed to set the wheels in motion.

"Didn't expect to see you this morning?" said Andrea. "Thought you were going straight to the office?"

He was straightening his tie in the hallway mirror when she entered.

"I had time, so just popped back for a clean shirt and that."

"I see," said Andrea, with a knowing smile. "Had fun, did we?"

"A gentleman never tells."

"I know. That's why I'm asking you."

Her voice trailed off as she went into the kitchen. Rob heard the kettle being filled.

"You had breakfast? Do you want anything?"

"No, thanks. You're working at eleven, aren't you?"

"Mmm. Beth's going to Livvy's for tea. I'll pick her up from there, the timing will be about right."

"OK. Good."

He coughed to mask the sound of him picking up her bunch of keys. His own was lying just next to them, so a jingling noise was hardly suspicious.

Closing the door of the hallway cloakroom behind him, he soon lighted on what he was looking for. Andrea had showed it off to him a few months back, unable to contain herself as she had so few outlets to reveal how the relationship with Drew was developing. *Look, she's given me a key, so I can let myself in if she's not there.* It stood out like a beacon, the shiniest key on the ring.

He slipped it off, pocketing it as he opened the door. He was ready if she'd been there to confront him. *What a dummy, picked up yours by mistake.* But she wasn't there. He could hear a teaspoon rattling in a cup.

"Right, I'm off. See you later."

"Yeah, see you. Have a good day."

It was a calculated risk. She hadn't mentioned going to Drew's before work. Then again, she hadn't the other day, either, and he'd watched the two of them embrace on Drew's doorstep. Still, even if she was planning to drop round there before work and hadn't bothered to mention it, Drew would have had to be home. She wouldn't be needing her key, and wouldn't be wondering why it was missing.

Rather than head for town, where he couldn't park close to any of the places that did key cutting, he headed for Andrea's place of work. Sainsbury's had a Timpson's concession next to it, and, two hours before Andrea was due there, he was the shop's first customer of the day. Four quid bought him gleaming access to his wife's lover's house.

He was on his mobile as he hurried into the supermarket afterwards. *Running just a bit late. I'll be in soon.* He was the assistant boss, so it was no big deal. Five minutes later, he was back in his car with a coffee-to-go. Black, just to make it look good. He opened the door and tipped half of the scalding liquid away, topping it up from a water bottle lying on the seat. He splashed some of the cooled coffee down his front, feeling it seep through his shirt and dampen his skin.

"Would you credit it?" he announced with a convincing note of irritation as he barged through the front door. He found Andrea where he'd left her, her own coffee cup now empty, her iPad open.

"Had only been there two minutes," he said, opening his jacket and showing her the stain.

"You mucky pup! That shirt must've set some kind of record."

"What's best for coffee stains?"

"Come on, give it here."

He took off his jacket, loosened his tie enough to slip it over his head and peeled off the shirt. While Andrea rummaged through the under-sink cupboard for any product that might help, Rob bounded up the stairs two at a time. It took less than a minute to put on yet another fresh shirt and replace the key on the ring; the ring he'd palmed when he dropped his own bunch on the hall table.

"I found an old bottle of stain remover," said Andrea as she fixed his tie for him. "I think I should be able to save it."

"Cheers," said Rob. "You're a star."

88

Donna saw him; he didn't see her. She felt her heart rate quicken as their cars crossed. All she could do was tuck up as close as possible to the van in front as they awaited their single-file turn in a road where slaloming through the parked vehicles was the norm. Had Rob glanced to his right to acknowledge those who'd given way, he would surely have spotted her. But there was no cheery wave of thanks, not to the van driver or her. He ploughed straight through at a fair lick, though not so fast that Donna couldn't make out the smirk on his face. Had that been his expression when he hid himself in the wardrobe, watching her spread her legs? A leery smirk?

She hadn't considered he might still be at home at this time. Five minutes earlier, and she could have bumped straight into him on the doorstep. Hanging around to watch Ben two-finger typing his email, and warning Zbiggy not to put his name to it, had saved her from that awkward confrontation, even if it had achieved nothing else.

"Oh! Hi."

Andrea forced a thin smile to go with a cool greeting that showed exactly where her sympathies lay.

"Hi. I wondered if we could talk?"

"I was just getting ready for work," she lied.

Donna guessed that her friend wasn't too pressed for time, that she was being fobbed off. She knew what chasing round to get out of the door looked like, and this wasn't it. "Five minutes?"

Andrea nodded in resigned fashion and retreated inside, leaving Donna to close the door. The usual hug was glaring in its absence.

"I haven't come to make trouble."

"That's nice," said Andrea witheringly. She was standing with her back against the oven, close to where Rob had had his head rocked back by Zbiggy's punch. She didn't invite Donna to sit down.

"About the other night. It's put a wedge between me and Zbiggy."

"It's put a bruise on Rob's face. He could have broken his jaw."

"I know, and I'm sorry about that. Zbiggy shouldn't have lost it the way he did."

"But he's not here to apologise himself, is he? Did he send you to do it?"

"We're barely speaking, Andrea. He lashed out because he was defending me. Then, after Rob said what he did, Zbiggy … doesn't trust me. I'm worried he's lost faith in us, that we'll end up separating."

"Whose fault's that?"

Donna bit her lip. It was every bit as tough as she'd anticipated and, as someone who hated confrontation, she now just wanted to say her piece and leave.

"Of course, I blame myself. I shouldn't have approached Rob for help –"

" – approached my husband for sexual favours before you even knew I was gay, I think that's what you mean, isn't it?"

"*Sexual favours?* It was nothing like that. I wanted a baby, Andrea, that's all. Just like you. Just like Zoe. That's my only crime, if you want to see it that way."

"Seems to me – "

"No, please let me finish, then I'll go. It was stupid and naive to think I could get pregnant by Rob and for it not to come out. Guilty as charged on that one. But I swear he only provided semen, as requested. There was no funny business."

She hadn't decided, when she walked through the door, whether to mention her clandestine visit. Instinctively she knew it was a bad call. Had Andrea shown any inclination to believe her, she might have risked it. Not now.

"I've been racking my brain to think how Rob could have known about … you know what. All I can think is that he was here when I did it the second time. Here. Upstairs. That he left the pot of semen for me, as he said he would. But didn't leave himself."

"*What!* You're accusing him of *spying* on you now? You've had all week and that's the best you can come up with? I think you'd better go."

She brushed past Donna, avoiding physical contact but making it clear she expected her to follow.

"I used your spare bedroom, which he prepared for me. He led me to it and must have been there the whole time, in a cupboard or something. It's the only thing that makes sense. Can you at least look to see if it's possible?"

Please, Andrea, go and check the cracks in that ill-fitting wardrobe door, see what's on view when the key's removed.

"No, I can't. It's the most absurd thing I ever heard. For your information – not that it's any of your business – Rob stayed out last night with some latest flirtation or other. There's been quite a few. He tells me about them, sometimes in a fair bit of detail. It's not only with my blessing, I encourage him to do it. Why shouldn't he, when I can't be the woman he wants? He's got to look to the future. But here's the point: Rob does not have any trouble attracting women. The opposite, more like. And you want me to believe he's some kind of Peeping Tom? In his own house?"

They were at the door now. Andrea wrenched it open and stood back to let Donna pass.

"I know it sounds crazy, but it's the only explanation that fits."

"Rob's shown himself to be a lot more honest than you, Donna. So I'll believe what he says, what makes perfect sense to me. Now I'd like you to leave."

As the letterbox rattled with her on the outside, it occurred to Donna that she hadn't got as far as telling Andrea about the pregnancy. Had the news reached her, via Zoe perhaps? And would she be even angrier when she found out?

89

Hi Zbiggy.

Many thanks for your email. It sounds like you have the kind of personal experience of this great city that would make an interesting article. Fancy you knowing the elusive Banksy!!! You weren't a student here, though, I take it? That would have been a bonus but never mind. Whereabouts are you? Let me know where and when would suit you and maybe we could have a chat – preferably over a beer!!

Regards,
Perry Shields
ps. when I'm not on campus, I'm living in the Clifton area at the moment, if that helps.

Zbiggy blinked at the message. It felt weird, seeing it addressed to him but talking about stuff he knew nothing about. And didn't want to. The only thing that struck a chord was the Clifton reference. The bloke must live not far from the suspension bridge. Zbiggy liked watching pro-grammes about famous civil-engineering projects – better than subtitled

Scandinavian thrillers, truth be told – whether it was Brunel, the Pyramids or the cutting-edge stuff going on in London. Donna said she quite fancied dinner at The Shard, but hadn't shared his enthusiasm during the documentary about Crossrail, when they said the tunnel was dug inches away from the foundations of the ground-level buildings.

He waited until Ben had finished smoothing things over with Mrs Jacobs before showing him the screen. She'd been put out by the fact that the equipment had been left overnight when she'd been specifically told it was to have been collected the previous day.

"Ah," he heard Ben say as he lugged the gear into the van. "We had a bit of an emergency on. On our way back here yesterday aft, we were, when we got a call from one of our regular customers that they'd had a burst pipe."

"That's hardly anything to do with me," said Mrs Jacobs sniffily.

"Very true, Mrs J. Only she's a young single mum, struggling on, you know. Didn't like to think of her and her two kiddies wading knee-deep. Said to her, I did, *you know you've got Mrs Jacobs to thank? We should be there by rights, but I'm sure she'd understand, in the circs. Diamond of a woman that she is.*"

Mrs Jacobs sniffed a little less. "It would have been nice if you'd let me know."

"Thought we had, love. Told Zbiggy here to ring you but the great lummox forgot. Trust me to get stuck with the one Polish builder who's a bit light up top."

They drove away, leaving Mrs Jacobs gladdened by the good turn she'd inadvertently done.

"It's bad enough you giving her all that bullshit without making me look an idiot," said Zbiggy.

"Never mind that. The old girl's all sweet about it, that's the main thing. Who cares if she thinks you're a dozy twat?"

Ben clapped him on his tree-trunk leg, trying and failing to get him to share in the laughter.

"Where we off now, then?"

"Back to yours, mate. I need to reply to little Perry here. The bastard's gonna regret fucking with me."

90

Rob managed to park in just about the same spot from where he'd watched Andrea embrace her lover. The visit Andrea had failed to mention. The visit that may well have run along the lines of *Rob reckons it's a bad time for me and Beth to move in with you. What do you think?* He couldn't take the chance that it hadn't gone that way.

He'd rearranged a viewing for a vacant property to the end of the day. The client said that actually worked better for him, and it was easy enough for Rob to tack it on his way home. The freed-up space, plus the lunch break, meant he had the best part of a two-hour window. There was no rush. He'd been watching the place for ten minutes already, and it looked graveyard-quiet. That didn't mean she wasn't in there, of course. She definitely had some kind of white estate – he remembered that. Not the make, but he was sure of the colour. There was no white vehicle in sight.

He weighed the newly cut key in his palm. Her car could have been at the garage or something. But the odds were that she was out on some work appointment. Out with all her mobile hairdressing paraphernalia. The question was, was it some time-consuming cut-and-colour job, with bits of tin foil stuck on sheaves of hair? Or was it a short back and sides, a quick in-and-out job? Maybe it was both, for Andrea told him Drew sometimes did whole families at a time: mum, dad and kids all taking their turn. Or perhaps someone was getting married today, for she did weddings, too. Friday nuptials with lots of bridesmaids; now that would take ages.

Just as he'd done when he'd slipped into the downstairs toilet with Andrea's set of keys, he had his cover story ready in place. If she was home, if her car was out of the picture for some reason, then he'd bluff his way through a chat about her plans for the future. He was the concerned dad, after all. What could have been more understandable than wanting to get the measure of someone who might be having his kid under her roof? *In loco* fucking *parentis*.

But there was no answer when he rang the bell. He left it till long after it was obvious nobody was in before slipping the key into the lock. Were there eyes boring into his back? It was a chance he had to take. Resisting the urge to do a furtive sweep of the street and the houses opposite, he breezed inside as if he owned the place.

Andrea had described aspects of Drew's place, passing conversation that had gone in one ear and out the other. Some room or other had had its ancient woodchip stripped. Some shabby-chic item picked up at a boot sale and revamped. White noise.

Drew was clearly a fan of vintage. Floral patterns, turned furniture legs and heavy materials abounded. There was a patchwork sofa that looked like a DIY job. Sanded floors that hadn't been varnished to within an inch of their life. Some of the stuff looked like it had been rescued from a skip. Laura Ashley knock-off.

Rob cast his eyes over the downstairs space: two separate reception rooms and a kitchen that looked out on a courtyard garden. Nothing there.

The boldly striped stair runner softened his footfall as he climbed to first-floor level. There were four panelled doors, all gnarled and chipped. He ignored all of them, for the generous landing accommodated what he was looking for. An ancient school desk, complete with ink-well, employed as a computer station.

A keystroke roused it from its slumber. As he surmised, why bother shutting down and password-protecting a computer when you lived alone? Opening the browser, he brought up the search history. He took none of the names in. It was just a list of websites, a list he captured on his phone before clearing it. Drew's digital past obliterated. Sort of.

Now came the laborious part. He did enough keyboard work as part of his job to make it reasonably speedy. Soon the screen looked exactly as it had before.

With one big, lurking exception.

91

Send it now

Ben looked at his watch. Quarter to six. He'd been there twenty minutes already, tucked away in a corner, cap pulled low over his brow, collar up, newspaper splayed out in front of him as a second line of defence. It was probably overkill, but if it was this little fucker who photographed him with Carly Fitzroy – the snotty-nosed kid who'd just walked through the glazed door – then it made sense to be unobtrusive. The fly on the wall, seeing everything while remaining unseen. The setter of the fly-trap.

Gordano Services was heaving; that helped too. The place was as rammed as the M5 had been, predictably enough for a Friday afternoon. Traffic had slowed to a crawl around Tiverton, then begun flowing again for no apparent reason. The concertina effect, presumably. Someone hits a brake light, and two miles further back, chaos ensues. Action and magnified reaction. That was a simulacrum of what was happening here, now, in Gordano Services Welcome Break. The little fucker and that bitch of his had started it. Now there were going to be major consequences. Except in this case, he was going to be the one at the sharp end, not sailing off blithely into the distance.

The timing had to be perfectly choreographed. Not that that was difficult, seeing as Ben himself had overseen the writing of the emails before he'd left. The first one:

Dear Mr Shields
I'm glad you think my story might be of interest. I'm not local anymore. I moved away from Bristol a long time back but funnily enough I'm heading past on the M5 this afternoon. How about meeting up at the services? Say 6 o'clock at Gordano Services would that suit?
Cheers
Zbiggy Kuzminski

The reply had been nigh-on instantaneous.

Dear Zbiggy
Yes I could make that. I have something on later in the evening but six till seven, or till whenever you have to get away, works for me. Gordano cafeteria at six, then. Shame about the beer … coffee and snacks are on me!
Cheers
Perry

And now it was time for the other message Ben had composed before setting off. The one he'd dinned it into Zbiggy over and over to make sure there was no fuck-up. *So you're sure what you're doing? You wait for my text, then send this straightaway. Got that?*

Me again. Bad news I'm afraid. Only gone and broken down. Waiting for the RAC. It's gonna be too late to stop off by the time they get here and fix it. Hope you haven't set off yet, or at least not gone too far. Can we do it some other time.

A minute after he'd told Zbiggy to send it, Ben could see the effect of the message. For there he was, the gangly youth with low-slung jeans and high-swept fair hair. The kid with piercings and bumfluff. Looking well pissed off. Getting up now, his chair scraping noisily across the tiled floor. He hadn't bought a drink, so there was nothing to finish, nothing to keep him.

Ben kept well back, loitering behind an arcade machine while the kid dived into the toilets. The latter's phone was in his hand when he went in, still there when he emerged. Had he been ranting while having a piss? *Would you believe it! Trailed all the way out to the M5 to do an interview and it's a no-show. Aàaaggghhh!! I need a pint!!!*

Whether it had anything to do with messages sent or received, the kid quickened his step out in the car park. Ben followed suit, keeping him in view as he gunned the Tiguan, which he'd purposefully left in prime position close to the building's entrance. In a slow dance, he brought the VW down the parallel thoroughfare, then skirted round to complete what would have been a full three-sixty had he continued. The spaces were more plentiful here, and he was able to pull in lengthways on, spanning three bays. He watched as the kid got into a blue Corsa, ready to follow whichever way he turned, either with the arrows or against them.

They were soon heading along the A369. Ben didn't bother keeping a vehicle between him and the Corsa. The dumbass would never twig. Within minutes he saw the suspension-bridge towers rising out of the gloom. Zbiggy had been banging on about how it was built after watching a documentary a few months back. Endless facts and figures that bored him rigid. One detail he didn't mention was the quid toll for getting across the bastard thing. The Corsa was well on its way while he was still rummaging in his pocket, eventually forced to shell out a two-pound coin, which was happily accepted without giving change.

He knew it couldn't be too much further, as the kid had said he lived in Clifton. And, sure enough, the Corsa pulled up not long after the towers disappeared from the rear mirror. Ben left it five minutes before getting out of the Tiguan to establish his bearings. Manilla Road. Substantial properties on either side, terraces on four levels with modern windows slapped incongruously into ornate bays. Complex rooflines with some natty woodworking on the bargeboards.

He sidled up to the door into which the kid had disappeared, relieved to see his name: *Flat 1 Perry Shields*. It was good to have it confirmed that this was his place, that he hadn't stopped off at a mate's who also happened to live in Clifton. It would have been an arse pain to have had to hang around, waiting for the kid to go to his own home.

Back behind the wheel, Ben punched his address into the satnav, for he was in a one-way system and couldn't retrace his steps. The assistance wasn't needed for long, as he was soon approaching the bridge once more. This time he found a pound coin in the well by the gear lever.

More importantly, he'd found out where Perry fucking Shields lived.

92

"You nailed that, princess! Well done, you!"

Rob held up his palm, which Beth, more self-consciously than usual, met with her own in a discreet high five.

"Super proud of you," beamed Andrea, confining herself to an affectionate hand on her daughter's back. She was sensitive to the fact that Beth was becoming far more socially aware and body conscious. She'd preened herself in front of the mirror when trying on her new leotard, studying the fit, seeing if it was an image she'd feel comfortable sharing with her friends.

"Was it all right? Really? You're not just saying it?"

"It was dead good," said Rob. "Perfect ten from me. You'll breeze the exam."

"It's tap I'm more worried about, "Beth replied. "I can't do the shuffle steps."

"Just do your best, love. And don't *worry*! It's meant to be *fun!*"

"That's easy for you to say, Mum. You didn't do dance when you were little."

"Because I had two left feet," Andrea replied. It wasn't the time or place to tell Beth the truth, about how she'd hated being dolled up in girly clothes, feeling alienated from an early age by her disregard for *My Little Pony, Polly Pocket,* pointe shoes – just about all the default interests of her primary-school peer group.

Beth skipped off to change in the hall's anteroom, swallowed up in a huddle of girls animatedly chattering, gesticulating and reprising moves that they'd either aced or fluffed.

"I hope she passes," said Andrea, the doubt evident in her voice. "What with SATS and everything, the pressures on kids these days."

Rob squeezed her arm. "She'll be fine. And she can always take it again, if the worst happens."

"Hope it doesn't come to that. The costume was thirty quid. With class and exam fees, you almost need a second mortgage. God knows how people with two or three kids manage."

"If it's a second mortgage you're after, I can recommend an independent financial advisor."

Andrea laughed. Yet she knew there was a serious point behind the throwaway comment. Moving in with Drew would relieve the financial pressure, make the little luxuries a lot more affordable. She really ought to think about broaching the subject again. If Rob could buy her out, that would be the best of all worlds: Beth having the comfort of her old homestead when she visited, and a nice nest egg for Andrea herself. She wondered if the money could be used to set up a salon for Drew. Maybe she'd mention it in passing that evening. Any idea, though, was predicated on her making the decision to jump, ending the unsatisfactory clandestine arrangement. Rob and Drew were in strange alliance over that one, neither convinced that now was a good time. But, if not now, when?

"Any plans for later?" she asked. "You and Beth?"

Rob shook his head. "Maybe grab a Domino's? Or I'll see if she wants to go out. I just hope it's not the *Billy* sodding *Elliot* DVD again, or I swear I won't be responsible for my actions."

Andrea laughed again. He'd always amused her. Once they made the decision to split, it would let him commit to someone instead of the endless round of one-offs and flings. He'd be a great catch for the right woman. To think Donna had had the cheek to come to her door and accuse Rob of … She was still angry about that. Hadn't mentioned it to Rob. If that was the end of her and Donna's friendship, tough.

"What about you? What time are you out?"

Before she could answer, Andrea's phone pinged. "Look at that," she said, showing him the screen. "Right on cue."

Any idea when u might land? Come hungry Im going to COOK!!!! Oh and any thoughts about family plans for Crimbo? Wd be nice to get away for a night (or 2!!??) if OK with Rob. C U l8r. x

93

Ben was dismayed when Zoe opened the door to him before he had the chance to use his key; dismayed to see that she already had her coat on. It was like taking over a watch, next turn of duty, with just a passing nod between the person coming on shift and the one clocking off. Businesslike. Unfeeling. Still no sign of a thaw.

"Daddy!"

Freddie and Tara flew past their mother, attaching themselves to a leg each before Ben swept them up in his arms.

"Are you still building the giant house?" Freddie asked, wide-eyed. "Mummy says it's going to take a long time to finish."

"This long," said Tara, stretching her arms out wide.

"Is that what mummy said? Well, in that case it's going to be a very big house, big enough for a giant to live in. Shall we draw it, then you can decide who's going to live there."

He lowered them to the floor, Tara squealing excitedly as her brother pretended to be a giant coming to get her.

"Don't rush off on my account," said Ben. "I thought we could talk."

"I've got shopping to do. I might have done it last night – if I'd had the car."

"Yeah, sorry about that. I, er, went to find the person, you know, the one who set me up."

"Yes?" said Zoe unenthusiastically.

"Yes. I couldn't talk to him. Not then. But tomorrow I'm gonna have it out with him, get him to back up what I've been telling you all along. I just want things to get back to normal, love."

Tara, still squealing with delight, reappeared, weaving between his and Zoe's legs, pursued by her brother.

"I dunno, Ben," said Zoe as the kids scooted off again.

"Ask Donna. *She* believes me."

"I daresay she does. She's more trusting than me. The truth is, it's a long time since I thought the sun shone out of your arse."

"Mummy, Mummy, you said a naughty word!" said Freddie, who caught the last of the exchange on another lap round the parental obstacle course, this time with Tara as pursuer.

"Bottom, darling. Mummy meant to say bottom."

"You just wait till tomorrow," said Ben. "I'll have the proof; you see if I don't."

She closed the door behind her, merely telling him she'd be a couple of hours as a parting shot. Ben kicked his shoes off, then, remembering something, followed her outside barefoot.

"I could do with having the car again tomorrow. Not sure the van would make it up the motorway. Around tea-time. Is that all right?"

94

The Clio sped past Aldi, thereby precluding the possibility of Zbiggy bumping into Zoe. It also went by the Sainsbury's turning, for he had no idea whether Andrea was on shift and wasn't in the mood for a public face-off with her. Nor did he want to return home too quickly. For Ben had gone out early, leaving him and Donna dancing awkwardly around one another in yet another bout of stilted banalities. So he'd offered to do a supermarket run, making a list as Donna worked her way through the cupboards. *Laughing Cow cheese, biggest pack you can find … yogurts … bananas … French stick …washing-up liquid … we're nearly out of shower gel, so if you can get some Dove for me, and whatever you want …* And so it went on. A dance of practicalities, skirting round the central issue.

The Tesco at Newton Abbot was a lot further, adding a good forty minutes on to the journey. Ordinarily, that would have piled on the drudgery. But this wasn't an ordinary week, and he relished the heavy traffic, which slowed to a crawl as shoppers and the punters heading for the the racecourse converged along the same approach roads. Forty minutes could well be spun out to a welcome hour.

The car park was heaving. While a couple of vehicles tracked shoppers returning to their vehicles, hoping to bag a prime spot near the entrance, Zbiggy squeezed past and pulled up at the far end, near the recycling bins where spaces were at less of a premium. As he walked back to the store, he fell in step behind a young couple. Even from an oblique perspective – the occasional profile view occasioned by a sideways glance – he could tell they were probably in their early twenties. Over ten years younger than him, yet here they were, already clutching an infant son. More specifically, the guy was clutching and jiggling, the girl joining in with the cooing and pointing and showing and talking.

He shadowed them round the aisles, even through the tinned goods section which he knew he could have bypassed. It was as though he were hypnotised by the interactions, between each adult and the child and between the couple. The little boy was strapped into the trolley now, freeing up the guy's hands, which regularly found the girl's apart from when one or the other pulled away to grab an item off a shelf.

Zbiggy was hypnotised. And envious.

There was no logic to it. He'd witnessed young parents delighting in their kids a million and one times, both with Donna and on his own. There was no reason why this time it should have been different. But some switch was thrown, some synaptic connection made or unmade, and he suddenly saw the bigger picture. The end result, not the process. Whatever Donna had done, it was an act of desperation, not betrayal. He saw that now.

Even as he hurried through the self-checkout – having forgotten the yogurts – he hadn't lost sight of the difficulties that lay ahead. They would have to move, that was a given. Then again, maybe a fresh start to his working life, without Ben, might not be a bad thing. No more cracks about Polish builders, for one thing. He could strike out on his own, a one-man band doing smaller jobs. Or even take on an apprentice, whom he'd not use as the butt of jokes, like Ben did.

The snarl-ups that hadn't bothered him on the way left him exasperated on the homeward journey. He threw up his hands when a woman began crossing at lights after they'd changed against her. He took out his phone, considering whether to call Donna. Dead as a doornail; in all the head-swirling turmoil he'd forgotten to put it on charge. No matter. For the best, in fact. He wanted to hug her, tell her what an idiot he'd been, assure her that everything would work out brilliantly. They would be amazing parents to an amazing child. The conception details were incidental compared to the nurturing he or she would receive.

He left the shopping on the front seat when he reached home. Unloading from this personalised matchbox could wait. Rosie's days were numbered, thank God. He was wearing a puffer jacket, which seemed to leave him filling the entire cabin, like an airbag that had gone off. The countdown was on, both to fatherhood and ownership of a nice roomy estate or 4x4.

He stubbed his toe and almost fell over the threshold. "I'm sorry, love. I've been a total idiot. You …"

Donna was sitting on the bottom stair, hands clasped around drawn-up knees. "I've been trying to call you," she said in lifeless monotone.

"My phone's … what is it? What's the matter?"

"It's gone, Zbiggy. The baby's gone," she sobbed. "So little blood. But enough. Enough to put an end to it. *My baby!*"

Her head slumped forward and she began to howl. Zbiggy remained motionless for a moment, then sank to his knees in front of her. He couldn't summon any words, so he placed his hand on hers. Just like the supermarket couple, fingers and palms seeking each other out, touch making its own heartfelt statement, rendering words unnecessary. But when his skin met hers, she recoiled. She withdrew her hands, as if they'd touched a hot pan, and drew her knees in even tighter.

"It doesn't matter who the father is now, does it?" she wailed. "*Are you happy?*"

95

Ben was as ill-tempered behind the wheel as Zbiggy had been, and more demonstratively so. He'd blared his horn at a car that dawdled at some traffic lights, preventing both of them from getting through before they turned red. Only then did he notice the P plate, not that it made him feel guilty or prompted him to make a gesture of contrition.

Zoe had been as offhand when she came back from the shops as when she'd left. No niceties. No attempt at conversation. No offer to stay for lunch. Every indication that now he'd had some time with the kids, he ought to be on his way.

"What? Back to work on this big castle you've told them I'm building?"

The words were out before he knew it. He regretted the snarky comment immediately.

"If you like," said Zoe as she busied herself emptying the shopping bags. "I had to tell them something."

"You could just tell them I'll be back later, in time for bath and bed. If you wanted to."

"That's the thing, Ben. I don't want. Not just now, anyway."

He noticed that the Clio was halfway up the kerb. It wasn't like that before. Either Zbiggy or Donna had been out and back again in the time he'd been away. If they were both in, what was the mood going to be like this time? Did another afternoon of peacemaking lie ahead? Another round of piggy-in-the-middle? They were mates but, Jesus, this situation was beginning to grate on him. Maybe he could get Donna to go and see Zoe again, have another go at smoothing things over. He could drag Zbiggy out for a game of snooker and a few beers. Anything to make the next twenty-four hours pass, before he could beat the truth out of this Shields kid.

They'd given him a key, but just as he was about to slip it into the lock, the door opened. Zbiggy filled the frame, blocking all but the tiniest glimpse of the interior.

"Not now, mate. Not a good time. Do us a favour, will you?"

He jerked his head slightly, a nod that said *trouble indoors*; a sign that Ben was interrupting something.

"Come on, I'll cheer you two up, bang yer heads together if needs be." Ben made as if to push past, expecting Zbiggy to yield .

"I said not now. Please. Just bugger off for a bit, will you?"

"Blimey!" said Ben, taken aback by the stiff rebuff. "All right, keep yer hair on. I'll … I'll … leave you to it, then."

The door clicked shut, the spare key still in the lock. Ben pocketed it and returned to the van, his plan for an afternoon's entertainment, while Donna mediated on his behalf, falling at the first fence. The pub was still an option, though. He could message Zbiggy later, maybe get him to come and join him for one, then drive them both home. Donna could go round to see Zoe later, when the kids were in bed. Yes, that might be a better plan.

As was usual with Ben, choices were always liable to be jettisoned if an even more enticing opportunity presented itself. One did just that when he found himself on the road adjacent to Julia Hennessey's place. A repeat performance. Why not? He could still text Donna and ask her if she'd go round to see Zoe. So all he was missing was the beer and Zbiggy's long, miserable face. Julia Hennessey, by contrast, would have a nice drop of red in, and be a lot more welcoming. Soft bed. Accommodating thighs. After all, he'd ignored that turkey neck once and enjoyed himself. He could do it again.

"Hello, Ben."

"Hey, Mrs H, how's tricks? I was just in the neighbourhood and thought, you know what? I'll drop by and see how that concrete floor's curing at Mrs H's. Never mind that it's a Saturday, all part of the service."

For the second time in less than an hour, he found a human barrier across a threshold. Julia Hennessey did not cut such an imposing figure, yet presented just as formidable an obstacle.

"Now's not a good time."

The same words Zbiggy had used.

"Maybe you could give me a ring next week? To come and look at the floor, I mean."

"But I'm here now. Seems a shame, and it'll only take a minute."

He edged forward, grinning and giving her his best boyish wink. He fully expected the defence to tumble, her legs to spread. But she showed no intention of stepping aside or inviting him in.

"Look, Ben. The other day was ... what it was. I'm too long in the tooth to regret it. But it was a one-off, understand? Whether you're back with your wife or not, it makes no difference. I'm flattered you might want to spend some time with an old bird like me. Or maybe you don't, maybe you see it as a perk of the job. Whatever. Let's both put it down to experience."

She was already closing the door on him.

"Oh, and maybe it would be best if you send Zbiggy round to look at the orangery floor. I've chosen some nice tiles. Maybe he can fit them for me?"

96

"I've brought red and white. I wasn't sure what you were cooking, so I got both. Taste the Difference range, I'll have you know, none of the cheap rubbish."

Andrea had let herself in, as she usually did, announcing her presence by revealing the contents of the carrier bag she was holding. The bottles clinked as she set it down to slip off her coat.

"Hellooo! You upstairs?"

She stood at the foot of the flight, peering up and listening. The power shower had a noisy motor; you couldn't hear a thing when that was running. But, no. No sound of running water. It was strangely quiet. No cooking aroma wafting through the place, either. She'd beaten Drew home before, and even without checking every room, it just felt like an empty house. If Drew had popped out, she'd done so on foot – her car was still there. But if that had been the case, and she knew it would have been around the time Andrea was due to arrive, she would have rung or texted. That was her way. *Running late. Pour yourself a glass – just a large one for me!! Back in a jiff. x Not make yourself at home.* They were long past that, but they weren't beyond the common courtesies.

Already Andrea was feeling apprehensive. The police didn't worry about missing persons until twenty-four hours had passed – that was a staple of TV crime dramas. But that was broad brush; it didn't take personal disposition into account. Some people went AWOL and you knew they'd turn up in their own sweet time. Drew wasn't one of those. The twenty seconds that had elapsed since she'd opened the door was enough to give her a queasy feeling that something was amiss.

"Oh! There you are!"

Drew was in the lounge, perched uncomfortably on the edge of her patchwork sofa. The window blind's wooden louvre slats were almost closed, shutting out what little autumnal light was available on a gloomy evening. No lamps had been switched on, so Andrea couldn't read the expression on her lover's face; just that the face had turned to look at her.

"What are you doing, sitting here in the dark? I thought you were out."

Andrea sat down beside her, mirroring her lover's body position and extending an arm round her shoulder. Drew squeezed Andrea's hand and cast her a thin smile. The latter's eyes were already becoming accustomed to the light and, in any case, from the short distance they were apart there was no mistaking the expression. What was it? Anxiety? Panic? Fear? Heartbreak?

"What's wrong? What is it?"

They held each other's gaze for several seconds, Drew finally turning her face to the floor when she could sustain it no longer.

"Come with me," she said. "I need to show you something."

Andrea followed, perplexed, as Drew led the way upstairs. The bench seat for the school desk could just about accommodate two, if they were cosily conjoined, each happy to have a buttock cheek in free air. They'd sat like that on many occasions, searching out some off-the-beaten-track eaterie or places that would make a nice day out. But this time Drew stationed herself centrally on the bench, Andrea instinctively understanding that she was meant to stand over and watch.

"I'd just come out of the shower an hour ago, and thought I'd have a search to see what mini-break deals were around over Christmas. I know you haven't said how you might be fixed, but I thought, no harm in looking."

"And? Come on, Drew, you're spooking me."

"And this is what came up when I Googled."

Andrea stared at the screen as Drew tapped two keys: c h

"Nothing very festive about that, is there?"

Andrea shook her head uncomprehendingly. "I don't understand. I'm not very good with computers. What does it mean?"

"It means," said Drew, "that there's been a search for child pornography. On this computer."

Andrea recoiled, as if the two words were a digital contagion that could infect her. Then the import of what Drew had said hit home, the accusatory tone.

"You think I …?"

Drew, an instant behind her lover, realised how her words had come across. "No, no! No, my love, never. Not for a minute." She stretched out a hand, Andrea allowing herself to be gently shepherded back. Only now did Andrea make room on the bench seat. "Come and sit."

Andrea did so dumbly. The shock had worn off, and she even allowed herself to stare at the search box.

"Is it a bug, then? One of those virus thingies?"

"No, Andrea. I wish it was that simple. Get a man in, clean the hard drive up. But …" She faltered, first to blink once again as they stared into each other's eyes.

"But what?"

Drew inhaled deeply. "OK, I'm just going to say this. It might mean something, it might mean nothing. But you've a right to know. When I got back from work yesterday, I had a conversation with Mrs Macy."

"Who's Mrs Macy?"

"She lives across the road. She's a widow. And our local curtain twitcher. Getting on a bit but sharp as a tack. She asked me about my gentleman caller, someone who came to the door around lunchtime. She watched him, she said. He looked shifty – that was her word. I checked inside for a leaflet or something, but there was nothing. It wasn't a delivery. Mrs Macy said he didn't go up to any other doors, as far as she could see. Just mine.

"She got distracted. Something about her cat knocking an ornament over. When she looked again, he was nowhere in sight.

"I went round checking everything. Not that there was any sign of a break-in. Just for peace of mind. There was nothing out of place that I could see, nothing missing, and I assumed she was just being her nosey old self. Until this came up."

She pointed to the screen.

"I don't understand any of this," said Andrea. "What does it mean?"

"That's all I've been thinking about for the past hour. Why would anyone want to have child pornography show up in my search history?" It was said knowingly, in the hope that the dots would be joined without her having to guide the hand.

"Wait a minute. So you're saying this person – this man – somehow got into your house, didn't steal anything, just used your computer?"

Drew nodded. "Think how bad it would look for me if, say, I was going to bring a child under my roof and Social Services found out about it.

"But that's crazy, you're not going to …"

Drew could see the fog clearing, the same obscuring mist she'd penetrated herself half an hour before. She clutched Andrea's hand tighter as she delivered the next blow.

"Mrs Macy didn't get too good a look at the man. Mostly from the back. But he was tall – easily as tall as her Billy, she said, and he's a strapping six-footer. Dark blue suit. Curly brown hair. And one of those short beards, she said – a bit like George Michael used to have."

97

The van journey up the motorway was even more torturous than Ben had anticipated. The engine had coughed and spluttered and struggled, and it started jumping out of second gear. What was manageable for short-hop work purposes was anything but for the open road. He'd been forced to crawl along the inside lane, watching as everything – a Smart car and small-engined motorcycle included – sped past. But he was there now. The M5 behind him; another pound coin contributed to the Clifton bridge toll kitty; a grimy van window framing the view of Manilla Road, its patchwork of lit windows rising up on both sides as the multi-storeyed houses responded to the gathering gloom.

The ground-floor flat of the property Perry Shields had entered was not one of them. At least, not the street-facing window. That didn't necessarily mean anything, of course. Maybe it was a bedroom, and Shields was ensconced further back. Having a bath. Taking a dump. Reading the paper in some rear sitting room. Maybe his *own* paper.

Ben's eyes ran up the edifice. The third-floor light was on; that was it. That, and some of the others illuminating Manilla Road, would be going out soon, for it was nearly seven o'clock: time to hit the town. Or maybe left on, to try and kid any opportunist burglar that the place was occupied. Lights really told you very little.

He began to wonder if the change of plan was a good idea. He'd set off in a foul mood, pissed off by Zoe, then Zbiggy, and finally by Julia Hennessey. That was the final straw, being turned down by that old hag. As if she was going to get a better offer on a Saturday night. Before he'd known it, he'd been chugging up the motorway, the van's constant complaining doing nothing to improve his temper.

Saturday? Sunday? Did it really matter so much? He'd reasoned that a forty-eight-hour gap from the missed appointment would be a safer bet. Why would anyone connect a cancelled meeting on a Friday with … with what? Well, that depended on how cooperative Perry fucking Shields was. If he fessed up, returned Ben's money like a good little boy and provided evidence to square things with Zoe, maybe, maybe, he'd let him off with a good slap. Just let the little fucker try and report him to the police. *Yes, officer, him and his bitch accomplice screwed me over. Never mind his split lip, you ought to do him for blackmail and extortion. Of course I'd have liked to get my hands on him, dead right I would. But both of them did a runner, disappeared off the face of the earth – check the phone if you don't believe me. I don't even think they gave their right names, so how would I know where to find him? This happened in Bristol, on Saturday night, you say? Well, there you go, then. I was with my mate Zbiggy all evening …*

Ben turned his dead phone over in his palm. He'd meant to arrange the alibi before he left, before the original Sunday plan was put into effect. That was a slip-up, and he couldn't call or text now.

Why was your phone off between five-thirty and ten on the night in question, Mr Fuller?

219

Was it? Battery must've died. Like I said, I was having a few beers with me mate, can't say I noticed.

He'd just have to sort it with Zbiggy later. And Donna, if necessary.

This was all worst-case scenario anyway. A scumbag like Shields wouldn't report it. He'd tried a scam, found he'd bitten off more than he could chew and got a slap for his trouble. It went with the territory. He'd take it, lick his wounds and make sure of an easier target next time.

He almost missed it as his mind wandered through all the possible outcomes. The light in the ground-floor flat flicked on and off in quick succession. If it was indeed a bedroom, someone might have been grabbing a coat or scarf. Something ready to hand. Was he going out? Was anyone else there with him? Better if Shields didn't have his own witness to even things up. Though even if that were the case, and the flatmate or visitor tried to call the police, Shields would probably tell them not to. Take his medicine and not have his own racket exposed.

Once out of the van, Ben strode purposefully up to the door. People were more likely to recall suspicious loitering, if it came to it. He looked at the names next to the four bells. Flat four, presumably the unlit top flat, was occupied by a Dave Robertson. Unless he was Perry Shields' visitor, he'd do very nicely.

He rang the bell at the top of the column, a gloved hand leaving no record.

"Got a parcel here for Dave Robertson, flat four. He's not in; can I leave it with you?"

He pulled the same trick as when he'd been to the flat Carly had rented, except this time there was no need for a ham-fisted, unconvincing attempt to actually present an item for delivery. No bottle-trap for Perry Shields.

Just a trap.

"For Dave? Yeah, no problem. Hang on a sec."

The intercom clicked. Wherever Dave Robertson was, it wasn't in flat one. So far, so good. Now it was just a matter of seeing if Shields had anyone with him. If not, it was a home run.

As soon as the door opened a crack, Ben put his shoulder to it. Zbiggy could probably have taken it right off its hinges. He couldn't summon that strength, but he knew he was a lot beefier than Shields, and he had the element of surprise in his favour.

"*What the fuck!*"

In the dim light of a sub-strength, unshaded eco-bulb, Ben saw Perry Shields rocked to his haunches, prevented from being laid out as he crashed against the newel post. After calmly closing the door behind him, Ben took in a scene where the choice was binary: up the stairs on his right, or along the hallway to the left, where a rectangular pool of light illuminated flat one's entrance.

Ben grabbed Shields' neck – part polo-shirt collar, part skin – and dragged him across the sticky, squared lino. A foot kicked out, adding another mark to the grubby wainscoting. At the threshold, Shields almost wriggled free as Ben stretched out a hand to shut the panelled door. But once the view of the hallway was closed off, Ben clamped his right arm in a V-shape noose around Shields' neck, rendering escape attempts redundant. The latter gasped and grasped at the powerful forearm crushing his windpipe, trying vainly to dislodge it.

Now Shields was assaulted on a second front, Ben swiping open-handed with his left, the blow finding its mark in a static cheek.

"Shut the fuck *up!*"

He took in a long, narrow room divided by an arch. To his left, in front of the darkened window he'd observed from the van, there was a double bed, with a Foo Fighters poster in place of a headboard. There was a tubular hanging rail on castors, the kind used in theatrical circles or as a stopgap wardrobe when people moved house. Here it looked like the permanent home for the occupant's stuff. No place for the footwear, which was piled up underneath, unpaired.

On this side of the arch, a low-wattage lamp and computer screen illuminated a work-station and an acoustic guitar on a stand next to it. The light dissipated to nothing within a few feet. No wonder it hadn't registered with Ben from the street. The room was brighter now, for above their heads was a paper-globe ceiling light. Ben spotted the switch immediately, next to the door jamb. In flicking it off, he'd returned the large through-room, with its dual pinprick light source, to its former murky state.

"Anyone else here?"

There was only one other door, over on the right-hand wall. Presumably a kitchen and bathroom completed the layout of the long, narrow flat. Ben's eyes rested on that half-ajar opening, concluding that the kerfuffle would have brought anyone out there to investigate. Shields confirmed it with a minuscule shaking of his head, all he could manage.

"Good. Now we're getting somewhere."

He dragged Shields over to the plastic swivel chair where he must have been sitting before answering the door, maintaining his grip as he pulled his victim down onto it. Now Ben had him pinned from behind, bending to bring his mouth close to Shields' ear.

"So. Here we are. I come into your place uninvited, just like you came into mine. Seems fair, don't you think?"

He whacked Shields again with his free hand, this time a more vicious short-arm punch to the temple.

"Except it's not quite fair, is it? We ain't even, you and me, not by a long chalk. But we will be before I leave, I promise you that, sonny."

He accentuated the word promise with yet another punch.

"I'm gonna take my hand away now, and you're gonna sit there. If you don't, I'll kick the shit out of you. I'll do a lot worse to you than you ever did to Carly, trust me. We ain't talking a little bruise, got it?"

This time a microscopic nod, eyes blinking in affirmation.

"There you go," said Ben, releasing his hold but planting a constraining hand on each of Shields' shoulders. He allowed the latter to slump forward and suck in some air. The respite was brief, Ben suddenly forcing the chair round in a one-eighty that left the two eyeball to eyeball. He smiled at the look of dread fear on Shields' face.

"You see, Perry, you fucked with the wrong person. You're wondering how I found you, aren't you? It wasn't through Carly, in case you were wondering. Nope. You might go to a fancy university, sonny, but you ain't smart enough to put one over on me. Anyway, down to business, I ain't got all night. Let's sort the money first. Two hundred quid, plus petrol money, plus inconvenience, plus VAT – don't forget the VAT. Oh, fuck it, I'm gonna be generous and call it four hundred. That's the kind of bloke I am."

"I don't have four hundred quid," Shields spluttered, cowering as Ben feinted to strike him again. "Think I'd have that kind of cash lying around?"

"No. I suppose not."

"I think three hundred is the cashpoint limit. I could do that."

"Could you now? Sorry, sonny, that ain't gonna fly. We ain't going out on no cashpoint hunt. How much have you got here, in readies?"

"Dunno exactly. Twenty quid?"

"*Twenty fucking quid!* You really are determined to wind me up, aren't you? I've spent nearly that much getting over that fucking bridge."

Ben dug his nails into his scalp, trying to massage life into an ill-thought-out plan he felt was starting to unravel. He decided on a change of tack, a change whose flaw immediately presented itself. Taking his phone from pocket, he hovered over the powering-up button. That would give away his location, screw any alibi. But he needed it on to record the confession, to straighten things out with Zoe. Mentally cursing himself for not bringing his camera, he turned the phone on. But all was not lost. The lack of an alibi wouldn't matter, because the scared-shitless little fucker wouldn't report it. Ben had plenty of evidence to back up the extortion scam. Footage of him and his bitch girlfriend in their house, for one thing. Then there was the woman and bloke he'd spoken to at the Airbnb place; they'd remember him. The police would be able to find out who stayed there that night. The money Ben withdrew to pay them off would show up. Shields could get done for far worse than a little slap, and once they traced Carly, she could add her own injuries to the charge sheet.

All these thoughts, random and fragmentary, flashed through Ben's mind as the stand-off ticked round to the minute mark.

"Right," he said, holding the phone out in front of him to bring the impasse to an end, "you're gonna watch this little birdie and say how you and Carly tried to shaft me. About the money. Everything. But, right up top make it crystal clear that I didn't fuck her. That it was all set up to look like that. Do a good job, then, once we find a way of you paying me back what you owe, I'll be on my way. Now – "

In the fraction of a second that his focus turned to the phone to hit the record button, Shields barged headlong at him, fists flailing. The insurrection was over almost before it started. Ben was rocked back on his heels, dropping his phone. But the action brought an immediate reaction. Ben swung from his hip with his right fist, the energy gained from the long arc concentrated in a crashing blow to Shields' cheek. The guitar offered no cushioning, a cacophonous assortment of notes echoing as he collapsed on top of it. Ben stood over him, ready to dish out more punishment. But even before the instrument's vibrations had ceased, it was clear that Perry Shields was finished. He gave out a low moan, a note of his own that didn't change when Ben landed a meaty kick to his stomach.

"I told you not to fuck with me!"

But he knew it was a hollow triumph. A mission a lousy one-third accomplished. He had nothing to show Zoe, and no money; just the satisfaction of doling out a bit of retribution.

The kid's wallet was on the table, next to the mouse. Ben opened it, ignoring the cards and pulling out the two notes it contained. A twenty and a ten.

"You lying little toe-rag," he said, his boot finding its mark once again as he pocketed the money.

A cursory glance round the place told him that he'd already seen its most valuable contents. The Samsung phone looked to be the biggest, most portable prize. But it was too risky to take that, or the laptop that had now lapsed into sleep mode. The latter must have doubled as a telly, for there was no sign of one – not that they fetched much second-hand. The guitar was probably the only other thing worth a few quid, but that was no good either. Too bulky, too memorable for curious eyes. Plus the decent ones had serial numbers; he knew that much. And anyway, it must have been damaged when Shields fell on top of it. Not worth pushing the groaning carcase off the instrument to check.

He cast a desultory glance into the kitchenette and bathroom, both rooms fulfilling their brief without a care for aesthetic value. The kitchen cupboards and drawers were woodgrain effect, no two lying in the same plane. The stainless-steel sink, which would have sounded good on a landlord's inventory, was no modern, chic iteration, but a tatty throwback to the 1980s. The bathroom tiling told a similar story: job-lot white, small-squared with grout that was discoloured at best, mouldy at worst. The toilet cistern was plastic, barely wide enough to sit the bog roll on top.

Shields hadn't moved. He was still letting out the same pained moan in time with every exhaled breath. Ben stood over him, delivering one last kick to vent his frustration before leaving. Well out of pocket. Nothing to bail him out with Zoe.

He was about to close the door behind him when he remembered his phone. That would have been the icing on the cake, leaving that there. He picked it up off the floor, his relief at remembering it evaporating at the sight of a spider's web crack in the screen.

"*Bollocks!*" he breathed.

98

What time u back?? B got her extra dance class at 11 remember x

"As if I'd forget! She's *my* daughter!"
Andrea threw the phone down on the duvet, then picked it up to show Drew, answering her enquiring look.

"Oh."

"Oh, indeed!"

Drew placed her hand on Andrea's shoulder. She'd slept fitfully, and could tell that Andrea may have fared even worse. An evening that had promised so much had seen her look on helplessly as Andrea went through the emotional wringer, battered by waves of incredulity and denial, anger and revulsion. Drew had advised her against returning home there and then, all guns blazing. There was Beth to think of, for one thing. And the evidence wasn't hard enough to start throwing allegations around. Not that she believed that for a minute. She had no doubts. It was him. But she felt it incumbent on her to take the charitable view, to act as counterweight to Andrea's conviction.

"What are you going to do?"

Andrea punched in her response, jabbing at the screen. "I'm going to get the proof. And when I do ..."

"*If* you do."

"... then I hope you'll be up for taking in two strays."

She showed Drew the screen again.

You go on if im not back by quarter to. ill follow.

"No kiss?"

"I've shared those far too long. They'll only be for you from now on, even if it's just a cross on a page."

By 10.40, Andrea had her house in distant but clear view. She'd turned down Drew's offer to accompany her. This was something she had to do on her own, and the fact that Drew had acquiesced immediately showed that she thought so too, really.

Andrea was stationed a good seventy yards away. Rob would get no closer, for she knew the route he'd take to the dance hall. Even if he needed to divert to get petrol, the nearest filling station was in the same direction. She was safe. She tried to put to the back of her mind the fact that Beth was being ferried by him. He wouldn't harm her, of course he wouldn't. But when it was all out in the open, his days of taxiing her daughter around were over.

It was nearly quarter to eleven now. *Come on, Rob, you'll be late.*

Right on cue, there they were. Beth in an anorak over her costume, Rob in jeans and jumper. She tapped out a message, just able to make Beth out in the passenger seat window as she lowered her head to read it five seconds later.

On way home my darling – traffic horrid! C u there xxx

99

Ben declined the offer of breakfast, telling Donna he'd grab something later, when he was out. He didn't add back *at my own gaff, if I've got anything to do with it.*

He put the kettle on to make himself an instant coffee, staring at his two hosts as it rumbled into life. Sullen. Not talking. Not even making eye contact. Zbiggy finishing off some toast, Donna swiping desultorily on her phone. He was glad he'd stopped off at a pub on the way back from Bristol if that's what he'd have come home to the previous night. As it was, they'd gone to bed by the time he returned. No flicker of light under their door. Not a murmur.

"Coffee, anyone? Tea?"

No takers, as he expected.

"Right," said Ben, banging his mug on the worktop after taking a large gulp. "Listen up, you two."

He was glad that he'd used his phone at Shields' flat now. For it meant he didn't have to embroil Zbiggy and Donna in some convoluted alibi story. That was the last thing they needed, and he was safe enough anyway. Perry Shields wouldn't talk; he had too much to lose. Minor assault v extortion – let's see who wins *that* one.

"You're my best buddies," he went on, "and this is getting past a joke. I've sorted my little problem out, and I'll soon be back home, out of your hair."

"What do you mean?" said Zbiggy.

"Never you mind. It's sorted, that's the main thing. Now you two need to get back on track. And that means you," he added, eyeballing Zbiggy, "need to stop acting like a dickhead. Why you don't believe Donna is beyond me, mate. She's a saint and you're being a dozy twat."

"Oy!"

"Fancy taking Rob Allen's side when she's told you what happened. In my book that makes you a *thick* dozy twat!"

Zbiggy opened his mouth to come back at him but was beaten to the punch.

"Shut up! Both of you!" Donna sprang to her feet, angry and tearful in equal measure.

Zbiggy closed his mouth and visibly shrank.

"Sorry, love," said Ben. "But it had to be said. And that Rob needs fixing good and proper for stirring it up between you two."

As well as being relieved at not having ensnared them in a cover story, Ben was also glad that he hadn't shot his mouth off over the vague notion he'd entertained to give Perry Shields his comeuppance and pin the blame on Rob Allen. It saved him from having to admit failure, raising expectations and not seeing it through.

Donna, regaining some composure, ignored Zbiggy as she brushed against the back of his chair. Reaching the door, she turned to Ben.

"It doesn't matter about Rob now. I know what he did, that's enough. He" – she jerked her head in Zbiggy's direction – "didn't choose to believe me. And now there's no baby anyway. That's right, Ben. Gone. Flushed away. I knew I had a childless marriage. Now I haven't even got a marriage worth the name."

100

Izzy Chalmers hadn't asked her mother if Beth could come back to their house after class. She hadn't enquired if Beth could come and practise the ballet exercises ahead of next week's exam. Hadn't suggested a lunchtime play date. The request had come from Andrea, who sidled up to Samantha Chalmers when she crept into the hall late. "*Sam, I know it's a cheek and short notice, but is there any chance Beth could come back to yours for a bit afterwards? I wouldn't ask but it's a bit of an emergency.*"

Sam had duly asked Izzy if she'd like Beth to come for lunch, and Izzy had excitedly made the offer. Beth, equally animatedly, was desperate to go. By the time it reached Rob's ears, the arrangement appeared to come in the more natural order: a child initiating the request, a parent granting it when confronted with two pleading faces. *All right. As long as it's OK with Beth's parents.*

"Loose end, then," said Rob as they waved Beth off in Sam Chalmers' car. "Last one home makes dinner?"

"No, let's go to a pub. I could do with a drink."

He didn't need any persuading. By the time Beth had got to sleep the previous night, he'd only had a single bottle of Budweiser. And he'd relented over *Billy Elliot* for the umpteenth time.

"Sure. Anywhere particular?"

"You lead, I'll follow."

They got into their cars, Andrea sitting on her husband's tail as he led the way to a nearby Beefeater. It didn't matter to her. Any public space was fine for what she had to say.

"I thought here in case you fancied a carvery," said Rob as Andrea pulled up next to him. "Shall I check if we can eat? Car park doesn't seem busy, we might be in luck."

"Your luck," Andrea shot back icily, "has run out."

"Eh? What's that supposed to mean?"

She left him standing there, and by the time he'd followed her into the bar, she'd already targeted a vacant alcove table. She was doing the leading now.

"I'll get us a drink. Then maybe you can explain what that crack was all about."

"Sit down, Rob. We both won't be staying, anyway."

"Eh?"

For a moment he was thrown, trying to assess the situation. Then Andrea produced a Ziploc bag; in it lay a shiny new Yale key, hermetically sealed. She waved it at him metronome-style, like a hypnotist trying to scramble someone's brain.

Rob sank into the bench seat opposite, transfixed. "What's that?"

"You should know, Rob. I got it from your suit pocket. Your blue suit. The one you wore on Friday."

"Ah!" he said, unconvincingly nonchalant. "*That* key. It's for the office storeroom. Just had it cut, must put it on my ring."

He made to grab it, but Andrea was too quick, the damning metallic evidence disappearing under her coat.

"We both know what door this key fits, Rob. You were seen. Described in accurate detail going into the house. But just to make absolutely sure, so that there was no room for mistake, I went round to try it in the lock. Fancy this key —" she brandished it again fleetingly "— fitting your storeroom *and* Drew's front door. What are the chances of that?"

He gave a strained laugh, offering her both clenched fists drawn close together, ready to accept a pair of imaginary handcuffs. "What can I say? You got me. And you know why I did it, don't you? Because I didn't want *her* taking my place. I didn't want Beth living with mummy and mummy's *lady friend*. And I didn't want to be tossed weekend-visit crumbs while you three play happy families."

"How *dare* you!" flashed Andrea. "I've bent over backwards to make our relationship work. I was straight with you —"

"Unfortunate turn of phrase, in the circumstances."

"That's just ... *pathetic*. And unfair. I might have lied to myself all those years, but I never lied to you. I encouraged you to look elsewhere. I wanted you to find somebody else. Don't you lay a guilt trip on me, not when you've tried to make Drew out to be some kind of *child molester*!"

She hissed the final two words, quietly enough so that the accusation didn't travel beyond the confines of the booth, but no less venomous for that.

Rob shrugged. "So. Where do we go from here?"

"You're going home. To pack your stuff. Anything you can't take can be sent on."

Rob leaned forward. "Now you wait a *fucking* minute. Beth might not be mine, not legally. But the house is in both our names. I'm not going anywhere. Up to you if you want to go and shack up with that *dyke*."

Andrea nodded, as if mentally counting off the insults. *Is that it? Is that all you've got?* her body language screamed.

"We both know where we stand, then. But think about this. I'm going back to Drew's now, and picking Beth up at half three. If you're there when I get back, two things will happen. One, I'll be taking Beth to introduce her to mummy's new partner. Wouldn't be my choice to do it that way, but I will if pushed. And, two, I'll call the police, get their experts to look at Drew's computer. I doubt it will take them long to work out what you did, and when. Then they can interview the neighbour who saw you go into the house. And the clients Drew was seeing that day – she had a full list and didn't get home till six. Were you careful about getting fingerprints on it?" She brandished the plastic bag once again. "Even in the shop where you had it cut? Doesn't matter. There can't be that many places to check round here. Everywhere has CCTV these days.

"I'm not even sure what the charges will be, but you can bet they'll be serious. Prison, I shouldn't wonder. Cut off completely from Beth, I'll make sure of that. I'll apply for a restraining order when you get out. But if you do what I say, there'll be no police, you'll get your share of the house money when it's sold. And if I can ever get over what a devious bastard you are, you may *just* get to keep some kind of relationship with Beth – for her sake, not yours."

Rob let his hands fall to the table. He stared at them, as if imagining them bound by real cuffs in cold steel. The bravado was gone. No hint of chutzpah. No sign of a smart comeback. He slumped in his seat, defeated.

"That's settled, then," said Andrea, rising to her feet. "I'll leave you to enjoy your carvery."

She turned her back on him, heading for the door. Then she checked herself and swivelled. He hadn't moved.

"By the way," she said, leaning over him in a way that might have looked touchingly intimate from across the room, "I didn't try the key in Drew's lock. I would have missed half of Beth's dance class."

101

Ben decided not to mention the fact that Donna had lost the baby. Zoe had been a bit more welcoming today, reduced to howls of laughter when he'd made sure he splatted himself over and over again playing Pie Face with the kids. He felt this was a propitious moment, one that would be lost if Zoe found out her best friend had miscarried. There was time enough for that news to filter through.

Freddie and Tara were out in the garden now, shooed outside by Zoe to get some fresh air.

"Be careful, you two," Ben called through the window as they bounded on the trampoline, holding hands. "My turn in a minute."

He glanced at Zoe, checking to see if he'd overstepped the mark. She said nothing, suggesting he was safe for those sixty seconds at least. It was time to use them, squeeze every ounce of credibility from that short window. Ben pulled out his phone, knowing the evidence he was about to present was flimsy, a lot less persuasive than he'd hoped.

"I went to see him. Yesterday. In Bristol."

"Who?"

He bit his lip to hide his exasperation. "The kid I've been telling you about. The one who was beating Carly up. The one who tried to blackmail me. Shields, he's called. Perry Shields. Look."

He cued up the video clip on his phone, letting her see Shields' static face through the spider's web crack before pressing the play button.

"It goes all dark in a sec and you just get the audio, 'cos he had a pop at me instead of fessing up, and I dropped the phone. That's how the screen got broken."

The file played on, Ben providing a running commentary.

"That's him falling over his guitar."

He heard the muffled sound of his boot going into Shields' gut, but decided to let that pass without explanation.

I told you not to fuck with me.

Zoe shot him a disapproving look.

"Yeah, I know. What can I say, I was angry. I had every right to be after what that kid's done to me. To us."

Zoe strained to hear the rest of the clip. There was a faint slapping sound, which he identified as him disgustedly throwing Shields' wallet down on the computer table – after removing the thirty quid.

You lying little toe-rag.

He left that hanging as a general indictment of Shields' honesty, not a reference to the kid's attempt to pull a fast one over how much he had in his wallet.

"It goes quiet for a bit now. I had a quick look round the place, just to see if there was anything else to prove he was trying to stitch me up."

"And was there?"

Ben imagined his movements as the clip played out. Putting his head round the door of the kitchenette and bathroom. The woodgrain-effect cupboards, the manky stainless-steel sink, the cheap tiling, the mouldy grout, the plastic toilet cistern barely wide enough to sit a bog roll on top.

"No," he said sheepishly.

The frozen image moved at last.

"That's me picking it up off the floor. That's it. I left then."

Come on, Daddy! Come and bounce with us!

Zoe couldn't hide her disappointment. She'd hated the last few days, hated having to scuttle up to her mother's and endure twenty-four hours of needling. How wonderful Mattie was, how amazing his partner was. It was one thing for her to snipe at Ben, but she bristled when her mother got going on the subject. She wanted him back, and had so hoped that the video would eradicate the memory of those pictures and soiled knickers.

"What am I supposed to make of that?" she shrugged. "It's a picture of a young kid."

"The kid who was here in our house, love, when he had no right to be. In thick with that Carly. Using her as bait to make it look like I …"

He left the rest unsaid.

"I don't hear any confession, Ben. All I hear is you, and him crying out, presumably when you hit him. What does it prove?"

"I know it's not what I wanted to get out of him, but he doesn't deny it, does he? And the fact that he had a go at me. If he was innocent, why would he fight like that?"

"How about because you'd broken into his house and were threatening him? That would spook most people."

Ben stared at his feet. She was right. What he'd recorded proved nothing. The bluff had failed.

"I could take you there, love," he mumbled. "Right now. Manilla Road, just over the Clifton Bridge. You could see for yourself. Ask him."

His voice betrayed him. He knew what the answer would be, the tone of the offer anticipating the negative.

Daddy! Daddy!

"Why don't you go out and play with them," said Zoe. "Ten minutes. Then I think you should go."

102

Andrea waved at Drew through her car window. She gave a smile and a nod, broad-brush reassurance before going inside and providing the fine detail. Drew didn't always hear her car pull up, Andrea guessing that she'd spent long anxious minutes at the window, waiting for news of how the confrontation had gone; desperate to know if the poison infecting her computer had been drawn.

She didn't get out. The journey home – yes, she was already beginning to think of it in those terms – had thrown up a mass of tumbling thoughts. Beth front and centre, naturally. How to manage the change, how to maintain stability when the only props she'd known were sinking in soft ground. What to do if Rob brazened it out, defying her to bring the police to the door to investigate the only father Beth had known. Would she be able to see the man Beth adored put away? What damage might it do to carry that out, and then bring a new partner into her life? *Mummy and mummy's friend*. What if Beth hated Drew, either on a personal level or just because she saw her as the architect of her misery? The wicked stepmother role, exacerbated by the perception that she'd hurt her poor dad. *I know you're upset and finding this all very difficult, but Daddy left a nasty message on Drew's computer*. How far could she go along that line?

Then there was the evidence itself. Was it as solid as she'd made out? The police would only have her word that she found the key in Rob's suit pocket. If it bore no fingerprints, if there was no shop CCTV, if Drew's neighbour couldn't identify him in a line-up of curly-headed six-footers with George Michael-style stubble – and you could bet any defence counsel worth their salt would go to town on that – was a conviction guaranteed? They could easily clear Drew. The timings and her work diary would do that. Conversely, Rob would have no alibi. And a giant motive. Who else would gain from leaving such an insidious calling card on Drew's hard drive? But was it enough? Andrea had a nagging feeling that it could be one of those cases where everyone was sure what had happened, but the person in the dock got off scot-free. Like they say, what you know and what you can prove are two different things.

It was all too much. One step at a time. And the smallest of those bridges could be crossed right now, with a few taps of her phone keyboard.

Sorry abt Friday. Think you were right abt Rob – not the man I thought he was. Will explain later. Wish Zbiggy had punched him harder!!! x

She pressed Send, hoping that it would smooth things over between her and Donna.

103

The Clio was gleaming. That was scarcely a surprise, given that it hadn't been particularly dirty when Zbiggy attacked it with a bucket and sponge. *White paintwork doesn't half show the muck.* He'd muttered something of the sort as an indirect announcement to Donna of where he'd be for the next half hour. She'd said nothing.

Thirty minutes had turned into forty-five as he went over the bodywork again and again. He'd got a brush right under the wheel arches, and put a mirror-like sheen back on the cover trims. He'd spent a lot longer than needed with the gun-hose on the final rinse, when normally he'd have been conscious of the water meter ticking over more than was necessary. Numbers on a dial. That's where it had started for him. When he'd logged the mileage and knew Donna hadn't been to meet with Michael Phillips.

But nothing was normal at the moment. He didn't know what else to say to her, and couldn't bear the contempt that was all too clear in her voice and demeanour. So he'd bailed out, removed himself from the picture. If the marriage was tarnished, at least he could make Rosie sparkle.

He was looking forward to Ben coming back. All the insults, the barbs and the swearing – with him as the butt – were better than this silent dance he and Donna were engaged in. *I'm making coffee. You want one?* That was her last comment, uttered when he was filling his first bucket. An offer that sounded like a threat. Donna no longer worried about caffeine intake.

Zbiggy studied the car's exterior. It wasn't going to get any better, clean enough now to show up all the scratches and chips the surface grime obscured. The inside, though; that was another matter. That needed a good vacuuming and clear-out. More to the point, it would kill another half hour.

He didn't get the chance for another muttered statement of intent. No time to announce that he was *just going to give the inside a tidy-up* as he reached for the vacuum cleaner. For Donna appeared in the doorway, coat on, phone in hand, stony-faced.

"Are you finished? I need the car."

"Er, yes. All done. I was going to do the inside, but …" He let the sentence trail off. "Are you going to be long?"

Only a handbag. Not a suitcase, he noted.

"I just got this," said Donna, ignoring the question.

She held the screen up for him to read Andrea's message.

"By my reckoning, that just leaves my own husband who doesn't believe me."

He stared at Andrea's finger-pointing text, words that impacted him no less than Rob.

"I do believe you," he mumbled weakly.

"No, you don't, Zbiggy. You changed your mind about accepting the baby, not about how it was conceived. There's a big difference. Not that it matters now."

"Is it Andrea you're going round to see?"

For the second time, she ignored the question. The car pulled away, leaving Zbiggy with an empty bucket, a sponge and a hose with a coil memory that made it a bitch to use.

104

Rob made two attempts to call, not bothering to leave a message on either occasion when she didn't pick up. He wanted to speak to her; the direct approach offered a better chance of success. But in the end he had no option, forced to tap out his own partial version of events, an account that couldn't be gainsaid.

After driving round for a while, he'd gone back to the same Beefeater. It was thinning out by then, the alcove he'd bagged with Andrea one of the few still occupied. He'd had the carvery he'd expected to have with her two hours earlier. Maybe he'd got the dregs of the lunchtime offering, the sorriest roast spuds and driest cuts of meat, for its only recommendation had been a means of filling his stomach. The meal was lying heavy as he weighed the words, searching to strike the right note.

Hey what are u up to?? Fancy meeting up? Just left her for good. U were right … weird set up, Im well shot. Dunno why I stuck it so long. Time to celebrate, wanna join me???

Yes, that would do nicely. He'd left the marriage on his terms. He was free now to pursue other options – options which might include her, if she was up for it. There was no chance of that happening, of course. Esther Greaves was presentable enough, decently indecent in the sack. But definitely short-term filler material, which was just what he needed right now. Pity she didn't have her own place; that would've been worth an extra brownie point. Living with parents meant he had to dock her one. Still, another night round at Lenny Henry's gaff wasn't the worst outcome. Take stock tomorrow.

The reply arrived suspiciously quickly. After two missed calls, suddenly she was available. Was it a coincidence? Or had she not wanted to speak to him? Her text left both options open.

Sorry no can do. Off to LONDON!!!! tomorrow so lots to do. Mate sorted an interview with a PR firm … wish me luck!!! Glad youve split tho. Both of us moving on!! Exciting!!

He deleted it, not just the message but the thread. Removed her from his Contacts. It was probably for the best. He'd have been in the same boat tomorrow morning. It would have just bought him one more night of Premier Inn passion.

His eye turned to the next one on the list. Grace. He reminded himself of how that had been left. *Enjoyed the other night. Sorry about how it ended. Youre just too sexy I guess! Hope we can do it again.* He tried to remember what she'd said about her living arrangements. Not with parents, he was pretty sure. Was that worth a punt? He reread her last message. *Not crazy or a prude, just need a bit more time. Anyway, if you haven't forgotten me and want to give it another go, let me know. x*

He noted the kiss. She'd been there for the taking, crawling back after realising her mistake.

If only he'd ignored that plea, he might have left himself some wriggle room. He could have said he'd been mega-busy. Or that he'd met someone else in the gap she created, claiming it wasn't right to message her when something else had been started. Something that hadn't worked out. So if she was still at a loose end …?

But he hadn't taken that sensible route. He hadn't been able to resist the sideswipe after he'd hooked up with Esther, and with Donna also in his sights.

You missed the boat love. Ive moved on to a hot blonde wholl be a lot more willing. Your loss.

He frowned at the screen. If he received something like that, there was no going back. Then again, maybe she was more forgiving, less proud. More desperate. Fuck it, he thought. Nothing ventured, nothing gained.

Hey Grace! How r u? U caught me at a bad time when I sent that last text. Total dick, sorry. If you want I can make it up to you. How about dinner? Tonight any good?

Nothing for ten minutes. No swift knockback, like Esther. It was marked as Read, too, so she'd definitely seen it. He was still wondering if the delay was a good sign, whether she was turning the idea over, as he got into his car. Now the text notification sounded, and he was quietly confident as he opened it up.

This is Grace's sister. She's more polite than me so I'll say it. You're a lowlife wanker. Fuck off and don't use this number again or I'll report you.

105

Ben was glad to get back to work. It was starting to get to him, this fall-out with Zoe. Seeing the kids less often than a lodger would. Watching their eager faces as they asked him how tall the giant house mummy said he was building had got so far. Having to play along with the charade. *Not very tall yet, but it'll be bigger than Jack's Beanstalk by the time I've finished.*

The giant house was actually a modest three-bed semi. An untrammelled cheese plant would have monopolised the space, never mind a mythical beanstalk. He'd rung Mrs Peters late Sunday afternoon, telling her he'd freed up space in the schedule to get started on the kitchen refit. *I know it's short notice, Mrs P, but we've had a few emergencies to deal with. Burst pipes, collapsed walls, you name it. Fixing other people's cock-ups. You don't wanna know, trust me. But I've told everyone, that's it, no more, I'm clearing the decks 'cos Mrs P needs her new kitchen fitted.*

She'd faltered initially, thrown by having less than twenty-four hours notice. But then Ben had a real result. She'd discussed it with her old man, and not only had they given him the green light, they'd arranged to stay at her sister's for a couple of days. He could rip out the crappy old units without having to think about leaving them with temporary cooking facilities. He could put the radio on loud, brew up when he liked and work his way through the packet of Bourbon creams Mrs Peters had left out for him. Trusting pair of old souls, they were. Not that they had anything worth nicking.

It was all cheapo off-the-shelf stuff from B and Q, less than a grand's worth including oven, hob and sink. Double that, fitted. Decent profit for a couple of days' graft.

He'd dispatched Zbiggy to Julia Hennessey's. That was the result of a curter Sunday afternoon phone call. *Gonna send Zbiggy round in the morning to make a start on your floor tiles OK?* As Zbiggy was going to need materials first, he'd dropped Ben off and taken the van. After another sour evening, alleviated only when he'd dragged Zbiggy out for a pint, he was glad of some time on his tod. Time to ponder his next move as he gutted the kitchen. He couldn't see past another confrontation with Perry Shields, preferably with Zoe along for the ride if it could be managed. On his own if not. And this time he'd make sure he had a watertight get-out-of-jail card to show his missus.

He wondered what the kid had been doing since Saturday. Not reporting him, that much was obvious. Ben was bang on the money with that prediction. Licking his wounds, probably. Wondering how he'd been tracked down to his scabby flat. Regretting not picking on an easier target.

He'd made good progress by eleven o'clock, even allowing for stacking the old units semi-neatly instead of chucking them in a skip. One vanload down the tip would probably cover it; a useful saving to keep the bottom line healthy. He'd need to liaise with Zbiggy over who needed the wheels when. Work out how best to combine the two jobs in terms of transport, to save on juice and try and keep the bloody thing going for a bit longer by curbing the mileage.

When the phone went, he fully expected it to be Zbiggy checking in. Turning down his site radio, he blinked at the screen. *Zoe calling.*

"Yes, love?"

"You need to come home. Right now."

The line went dead. It was a rerun of the summons he'd received after she'd got the photos and knickers in the post. Pretty much word for word. The same portentous tone, which didn't suggest she wanted to discuss a reconciliation. One of the kids could have had an accident, but he instinctively knew that wasn't the case. As he punched in the short cut to call Zbiggy, Ben had a sinking feeling that Shields had got in some kind of retaliation. He cursed himself for not thinking about that. He'd only factored in the possibility of Shields going after an assault charge, an eventuality quickly dismissed. He hadn't considered he might hit back off his own bat; no police involved. They were adversaries who both knew where the other lived. Except he had a wife and kids, and that made him uncomfortable.

Zbiggy was in Wickes, on the other side of town with a flatbed trolley piled high with tiles and cement. He said Julia Hennessey had done a recce there and chosen the ones she wanted, which were on special offer. She'd sent him off to pick them up, even worked out how many packs he'd need. She'd been a bit off with him, he said, not her usual chatty self.

"Bollocks!" Ben breathed, cutting him off short and ending the call. Two minutes later, he'd locked up and was sitting on one of the old cabinets, drawing heavily on a fag as he waited for the taxi to arrive. He knew another shitstorm awaited him at home. He just couldn't fathom what form it would take.

106

"Donna! Hi."

"Is it a bad time? I swung by yesterday afternoon but think everyone was out."

"No, not at all. Come in. I'm glad you're here."

It was a scene that had been replayed countless times. A casual visit, a smiley welcome, coffee or wine to lubricate a gossipy catch-up, depending on time of day. But this occasion was different. As soon as the door closed, the two women fell into an embrace. Neither initiated it, neither was the respondent. It was perfectly mutual, both tacitly understanding that it was the right thing to do. They'd hugged many times before in greeting or bidding goodbye. This was different. A hug of reconciliation, a wordless recognition of the lack of judgment they'd each shown.

"I shouldn't have gone behind your back and asked Rob to be a donor."

"And I should have believed your version of what happened. I said some terrible things."

Both shed tears. Donna searched for a tissue, Andrea pre-empting her by offering her the box from the console table, before taking one herself. They broke into relief-driven laughter, which redoubled when Andrea checked herself in the hall mirror and noted that her make-up had gone to ratshit. "Yours always looks perfect, of course," she added, wheeling Donna round so that both could see their reflections.

They swapped stories of what had happened since their tetchy meeting on Friday. Donna described the elation of finding she was pregnant, joy that been cut so short. She consoled Andrea, whose hand had shot to her mouth in shocked concern that she might have been partly responsible for the miscarriage.

"Those things I said. Imagine what they must have done to your blood pressure! That might have …"

Donna shushed her, even though those selfsame thoughts had crossed her own mind.

Then it was Andrea's turn, Donna's jaw dropping as she took in an abbreviated version of how Rob had tried to sabotage things with Drew.

"I can't say for sure whether he did what you said he did, here in our spare room," said Andrea. "But when you can sink as low as that, who knows?"

"Where is he now?"

Andrea shrugged. "At work, I assume. Looking at the accommodation on his books, I hope. I don't know where he spent last night. And I don't want to."

"God, what a mess," said Donna dispiritedly. "All round."

Andrea grabbed her arm. "We aren't in the same boat, you and me. I was always going to move on, it was just a matter of the timing. He's done me a favour in that respect. But you … you and Zbiggy need to patch things up. Don't let this break you two. You're the most forever couple I know."

"But he didn't believe me when I needed him, Andrea."

Zbiggy's brutal words returned to her. *He's the father, isn't he? Shouldn't he know before me? What if I said you should get rid of it?"*

In their own way, those comments were as startlingly revelatory as anything Andrea had said about Rob. Zbiggy hadn't broken into someone's house and planted a malicious internet search, yet his cruel words had rocked her to the core. Made worse by the fact that his wish had been granted so soon afterwards. Unmitigated by his belated retraction, uttered when the blood in her underwear had already carried the nascent life away.

"I'm not sure there's any way back," she said.

107

There was no reconciliatory hug in the Fullers' hallway. Ben opened the door to find Zoe on the other side, but her expression gave away that this was no eager demonstration of uxorial affection. Her hands rubbed against each other, like a doctor scrubbing up. Occasionally the fingers of her right halted on her wedding ring, spinning it round.

"What's up, love? Kids all right?"

Zoe nodded. "Freddie's at nursery, Tara's asleep."

Ben's eyes automatically drifted up the stairs. "So?"

"You haven't heard the news?"

"I've been working, haven't I? Had the radio on, just music. What news?"

"About the boy in Bristol who's been found dead."

He didn't react, he didn't flinch. An anonymous death in a big city. So what? And yet, and yet. Why was Zoe looking drained; terrified, even?

"Tell me you're not putting two and two together and making seven."

"The police aren't releasing any information …"

"There you are, then."

"… except that it's in the Clifton area. Manilla Road."

He blanched. Had he told her the address? He couldn't remember. But then his composure returned. He'd given Shields a tap, left him spluttering. He'd whacked Zbiggy a lot harder in jest.

"It's a coincidence, love."

"They're asking for anyone who was in the area from Saturday afternoon on to come forward."

He brushed past her, going to the kitchen tap and filling a mug with water. "This is crazy, you know that? I barely touched the kid. Besides, that road had loads of houses, loads of flats."

He tried to recall the name of the top-floor occupant, the one whose name he'd used to lure Shields to the door. He couldn't remember it, or the names of those who lived in the other two flats.

Zoe had followed him into the kitchen. She picked up her iPad from the dining table and handed it to him, open at the screen grab she'd taken minutes before. He read:

A police investigation has been launched following the discovery of a man's body in the Clifton area of Bristol. The death is being treated as suspicious, and a cordon has been put in place in Manilla Road. Forensics investigators are at the scene. A spokesperson for Avon and Somerset Constabulary said police had been alerted yesterday evening, when the victim failed to attend a family gathering. He has not been named, but is believed to be a student at Bristol University. Police are appealing for witnesses.
More to follow.

"It can't be him, Zoe. It just can't. I told you, I hardly touched the kid. You heard it on the phone, it was barely a scuffle."

She held up her own phone. "It *is* him, Ben. Police aren't naming him, but it's all over Twitter. Look! Different sources all saying the same thing. It's Perry Shields."

108

"I like Drew. She's nice."

Andrea tried to hide the long exhalation of relief as she pulled away at the lights. They'd only gone a few hundred yards, agonising seconds ticking by, before Beth delivered her verdict on the visit. Andrea had found it hard to rein herself in, wanting to ask the question as soon as they were buckling up. *Well? What do you think of her?* But she stayed her hand, knowing that it was better to let it come from her daughter. She'd almost reached the point of thinking it was going to be a non-committal draw: neither positive nor negative, which she felt was OK, something to build on. Finally, Beth had piped up, a casual, unprompted approval rating that gladdened her mother's heart.

She'd kept it low key, telling Beth they were calling in to see one of mum's old friends on the way back from school. Drew had been in a flap over the short-order visit.

"*Today?* That's a rotten idea. The place is a tip, I've got four appointments and the cupboards are bare. You choose your moments!"

"We'll just pop in for a drink and a biscuit. I'll even bring Jaffa Cakes; Beth likes those."

Once Drew was able to reschedule her three o'clock, she could see that it made sense. She'd wanted to meet Beth for a long while, knowing it was a watershed moment in her and Andrea's relationship. The only difference a week's notice would have made was to extend the period in which she repeatedly chewed over the big question: *Will she like me?*

"She is funny," said Andrea. "And a lot better at doing hair than me. Then again, it is her job. Maybe she can do yours sometime?"

Beth nodded matter-of-factly. "We spoke about it. She said she'd do my French plaits before the dance exam."

"Did she now? That's nice of her."

She beamed inside. The offer must have been made when she'd absented herself to go to the loo, a move that had created panicked eye contact on Drew's part, a reassuring blink on hers.

Andrea decided to leave it at that. The visit had gone as well as she could have hoped. It was all about small steps.

"Do you ever think about your real dad?"

She blurted it out, a stray thought that was on her tongue before she realised it. The early upheaval that Beth was oblivious of, a biological fact that had been offered up and parked in some remote part of her daughter's brain.

"Huh? Dad's my real dad."

"Yeah. Of course he is."

No, it wasn't going to be easy. There was a long road to travel between Jaffa Cakes, juice and French plaits, and having Drew as the live-in adult, Rob the marginalised, appointment-based parent.

Small steps.

109

The official news feeds had finally confirmed what social media had been circulating for many hours. *The victim has been named as Perry Shields, a 20-year-old student at Bristol University.* Ben absorbed it in a trance-like state, shaking his head at every replaying of the events of Saturday night. Zoe took Tara with her to pick Freddie up from nursery, when it would have been easier to leave her at home.

"You'll be all right, won't you? I won't be long."

The children seized on having their dad home at tea-time, Zoe telling them he was feeling poorly and couldn't join in any games.

"Poor daddy. Does your tummy hurt?" Freddie asked.

"I kiss it better," said Tara, mimicking what she'd heard grown-ups say to her.

Zoe fed and watered them, fish fingers, chips and peas making for easy prep and almost guaranteeing there was no mealtime battle. She bathed them early, and broke her rule by allowing them screen time in their pyjamas. Peppa Pig and milk allowed her to check her phone properly again.

Ben hadn't moved. The strong tea she'd made two hours earlier lay untouched.

"Christ!"

Where the other domestic sounds and kiddie hubbub had failed to penetrate, this monosyllabic utterance from Zoe snapped him into a state of heightened alertness.

"What? What is it?"

"Shit!" she breathed. "They're saying he was a haemophiliac. That if he was attacked and started bleeding ..."

Ben's state of denial surfaced once again. "No," he said, shaking his head violently. "It can't be. He'd have said. And there was no blood anyway. It was just … *a bit of a scuffle.*"

Before she could reply, Ben's phone signalled a new message. He glanced at the screen but didn't pick it up.

"Donna. Wanting to know if I'm coming back for dinner."

Zoe replied off her own phone. She'd have sent him packing by now, in the normal course of events. But she couldn't do it now.

Ben's here. He'll be staying tonight.

Then the swift reply:

Glad you two have made up! xxx

We haven't, Donna. Not by a long chalk. Just need to get through today, then see what tomorrow brings.

She put the kids to bed, promising daddy would come and tuck them in if they were good. She'd barely reached the foot of the stairs when Freddie's voice sang out, "We're being good!"

"Very good," chimed Tara.

"Can you go up and see them?" said Zoe. "I promised you would."

Ben jumped up, the lassitude suddenly lifted at the request. But instead of passing her, he enveloped her in his arms.

"I've been thinking. If he's dead, it doesn't matter that my phone was on."

"Eh? What are you talking about?"

"Don't you see? There's nothing to connect me and him. He made sure I couldn't find him. That works in my favour now. We just need to sit tight, keep calm till it blows over. It was an accident, Zoe, I swear. He didn't deserve to die, but he was a blackmailer and a thug, don't forget that. You didn't see Carly's bruises like I did."

Zoe pulled free, wrestling with the implications of what he'd said.

Planting a foot on the first stair, Ben turned to her. "If we hold our nerve, love, I'm in the clear.

"Trust me."

110

I want to tell you about Perry. Perry Shields. The Manilla Road investigation. I can help you. I can tell you who was involved and why. I can't tell you how it happened and when, but those are the things you already know, I guess. I can fill in the blanks. I can tell you who's responsible. Me, that's who. I can also tell you who attacked Perry. There's a big difference between those two things. There are twin culprits for Perry's death, you could say. You'll only be interested in one, but there are definitely two.

My grandad died in August. That's not really where it started, but I have to pick a point and that's the one I'm choosing. Pancreatic cancer. He was seventy-six – not much of an age these days. But compared to other stuff that's happened in our family, he came out of it OK. Well out of it on 10 August. At peace, isn't that what everybody says?

I wasn't. At peace, that is. The truth is, I was already struggling. Bulimia, anorexia, booze, pills, self-harming – you name it. I had problems with them all over the years. Maybe others would have coped better. Maybe I'm just the type that can't.

I'd already half-decided not to go back for my third year at Bristol, and after grandad died, that sealed the deal. Because he left me something – something that turned everything upside down.

I need to tell you about my sister. Chloe. My big sister. She died when I was nine. 2007. She was really unhappy, mum told me, and decided to go up to heaven early. You know the kind of thing. Later, she told me how Chloe had taken pills. I must have been around fourteen, already going off the rails. She probably told me about Chloe as a warning. No harps or angels anymore. All talk of heaven gone.

I didn't have a dad. He'd bailed on us early, no idea where. I don't remember him. Chloe had a different dad. He'd left too, remarried and was living somewhere in Yorkshire. She rarely saw him once he had a new family. So it was the three of us for a long time – me, my half-sister and mum. Just the two of us after Chloe died.

Then I found myself on my own. All the while mum was lecturing me about substance abuse and stuff, she was drinking herself to death on the quiet. Looking back, I don't blame her. Two lousy relationships, two kids, her first born dead and the other one making her life hell. Who can blame her for self-medicating? Vanessa Price. Look her up.

I went to live with my grandad – my mum's dad – and had an OK time when I was in sixth form. The most stable I'd been in a long while. It suited both of us. He was a widower and glad of the company. I had plenty of freedom to do what I wanted.

Uni was more of a struggle. I found it hard to adjust, struggled to fit in. Then grandad died. He was in a hospice by then so I'd already come to terms with it. All they were talking about was palliative care, and I didn't mind that he just drifted off. I didn't feel cheated, even though I missed him that last day by a matter of minutes. That's because I made sure I said my goodbyes on every visit as though it was the last.

I think he knew his time was nearly up. The envelope he left me hadn't been there the day before. I like to think he put it out for me with his last ounce of strength, then slipped away like a boat leaving harbour. There are worse ways to go.

Sorry if this is going on too much. Probably needs editing down. My teachers and uni tutors always said as much: content fine, full of good ideas but lacking in structure. Still. No one's marking this though, are they, so who cares? It's my story and I'll tell it the way I see it, the way I remember it. I want to get it all down in one go, no second draft.

The package contained a note from grandad and a sealed envelope with a letter from mum. I burned both, so I can't give you the first-hand evidence, I'm afraid. Bear with me, though, I can back this up. Corroborated, as you'd say.

Grandad's note had a lot of gushy stuff, sorry that he wasn't going to be around to see me grow into "a fine woman" (that's a direct quote!!) – maybe even walk me down the aisle. (Ha! Fat chance.)

He said mum had given him the letter when her own health was failing. She died in 2013, so some time before that. It was for me, but she said he wasn't to pass it on until my own life was on an even keel. Mature enough to handle it. That isn't a quote, but it's the gist. How much he knew about what was in the letter, I don't know. My guess is that he realised whatever it said would shock or disturb or mess me up in some way, so he just kept putting it off. If I was having a bad time – and there were plenty of those – he wouldn't have wanted to add to the troubles. And if I was in a better place, he wouldn't have wanted to drag me down. That's my feeling anyway. I don't blame him. So he waited and waited until he had no choice.

It's easier if I just show you mum's letter. Yes, I burned the original like I said, but unlike grandad's note to me, I kept a copy of hers. And of Chloe's. Yes, she left a message when she died. You can't read one without the other. It'll all make sense.

Why did I destroy them? I suppose I didn't want any other hands touching the actual paper either of them had used. Once I read them and copied them it felt like the right thing to do. I hope they don't get shared beyond anyone who needs to know, but that's a chance I have to take. At least it's only their words, not their scent or DNA or anything. I wouldn't have liked that.

111

Darling Em,
I don't know when you'll be reading this. In your 20s maybe? Or 30s? Working in some high-powered job after graduating as a star student? Married with children of your own? If it's the latter I hope you choose better than I did!! Then again, your dad and Chloe's gave me you two, the best daughters anyone could have, so I can't be too hard on them. And I'm sure I had faults that contributed to the failure of those relationships (but let's not make a list of THOSE, right???!!!)

You've had such a tough time, I hate to think I'm adding to it with my problems. But there's no getting away from it. The die's cast, as they say. There was a time when a liver transplant might have done the trick, but I think we're well past that. How much of it was the addiction and how much was not really wanting to give alcohol up, to get better, I really don't know. For me the world looked a lot better through a fog of booze. Yes, I can hear you telling me off for being a hypocrite, for moaning at you when you threw up on cheap cider when you were 13. Remember those rows!!! Don't forget the old "Do as I say, not as I do" defence, which I'm sure you'll use often enough when you have kids of your own.

I don't think I'll be around much longer. They aren't saying as much but I feel like I'm on my last legs. Of course, I hate the thought of leaving you, not sticking around to see you blossom. But it won't be long before you're off to uni, making your way in the big wide world. You'll have grandad. I've already spoken to him about what'll happen after I'm gone. I hope you'll go and live with him, at least till you're eighteen. It makes so much sense all round (and anyway, Social Services ain't gonna let a 15- or 16-year-old do their own thing so you can scotch any ideas about living alone and having endless takeaway pizza parties!) I've told him to sell the house and bank whatever's left after the mortgage is paid off. It won't be a fortune but should be a nest egg to get you through university without having to do some crappy job, plus enough to put a decent deposit on a place of your own when the time comes. You'll inherit grandad's house one day too, but that's just a secondary reason to keep well in with him!!! I know he'll always be there to give you good advice when you need it. I wish I'd taken it more often myself!

You'll do just fine, I know it. You've come through so much, a lot more than any child ought to endure. It's been a helluva battle but you've survived. You're stronger than me.

I can't go without filling in the blanks about Chloe. You two were so close, it wouldn't be fair. If there'd been a couple of years age difference you'd probably have fought like cat and dog. I never planned for a nine year gap between kids by two different blokes, but that part worked out amazingly. Chloe doted on you from the day you were born, and I know what she meant to you.

I suppose 16 wasn't particularly young for a girl to want to spread her wings. After all, I had her when I was not much older. I knew she'd met a boy but she got very cagey whenever I asked about him. I asked her to bring him for tea but she dodged that one, said it was nothing serious.

Then her mood changed. She was miserable and sullen. He'd obviously finished with her and she was licking her wounds. First heartbreak! When I tried to cheer her up she bit my head off, so I left her to get through it on her own. We all deal with emotional stuff in different ways, right? I thought she just needed to wallow for a bit rather than talk about it. Or maybe talk about it with Hannah and Josie, her two best mates – not with me. Nothing wrong with that. I couldn't very well check with those girls, could I? It would have got back to Chloe and made me look like I was sneaking round behind her back. Obviously I wish I'd done that now. Had a blazing row about being an interfering old witch! Better that than losing her. I'll regret it to my last breath.

Then it was too late. 19 March 2007. It was a Monday. A normal kind of day. School for you. I was working at the surgery, dealing with appointments for people with all their different ailments when my own daughter was ending her life. Helping others instead of her. That still hurts a lot.

Chloe had gone to school as normal. GCSE revision would concentrate her mind, so I thought. Help her forget about the boy, so I thought. But that day she slipped out of school at lunchtime and came home without telling anyone. Hannah and Josie had no idea. I think she chose it because she knew you had gym club after school. She wouldn't have wanted you to see.

Remember the stories I told you about Chloe being really sad and wanting to go up to heaven early? The reality was a fistful of paracetamol, as you know. I was told deaths from paracetamol overdose are rare, they have antidotes that work long after the pills have been taken. Chloe was one of the unlucky ones.

I know what you're thinking. That she knew she'd be saved, that it was a desperate cry from a sad young woman. I don't think so, as you'll see in a minute. Not that it makes it any easier to bear.

I found her. She was in the kitchen, lying unconscious with her head resting on the open oven door. I lay her down flat, tried to remember about recovery positions and CPR while waiting for the ambulance to arrive. There's me, working in a doctors surgery and hopeless when it came to first aid. The medical people never said as much, but I've often wondered if she'd've pulled through if I'd made her vomit. I wasn't thinking straight. Maybe it was because of the way she was propped up. That and the note she left.

I didn't show it to the police. I didn't want her final words to become public knowledge. They were sacred. In any case, it wouldn't have helped.

I want you to see them, though. Grandad must have decided you're strong enough to know everything, otherwise you wouldn't be reading this. I'm going to break off now while you see what your sister wrote that terrible, terrible day.

x

112

Dear Mum (and Em when you're a bit older!!)

I'll be gone by the time you read this. I know you'll be sad (there'll be BIG trouble if you aren't!!!) … but it's just got all too much for me. It's like carrying round a lead weight on my shoulders. Which is a rotten cliched simile (and probably one of the (many) reasons I would've failed English this summer!!) because I'm actually only carrying an extra few ounces. I don't want those ounces to grow into pounds, not now.

That's going to make you angry as well as sad, robbing you of your first grandchild. I'm so sorry.

What a family we are. You never had much luck. Now me. At least you got to the altar twice … I got dumped. Let's hope Em can break the curse, find herself a nice guy when she's older and maybe give you a few grandkids!!! Kiss my beautiful, amazing little sister for me.

Lots of love,
Chloe
xxxxx

Fever 103°
I'm going up to Paradise

113

I never knew about the pregnancy. Where was my feminine/maternal intuition when I needed it? If I HAD guessed, talked all the options through with her, would it have made a difference? I don't know. Hannah and Josie said they didn't have a clue either so she did a good job of bottling it up unfortunately.

The police, the coroner, they didn't take too long over it. Pregnant teen, no boyfriend on the scene, exams coming up. Stress. Overload. Even without seeing Chloe's note (I wasn't sure if they completely believed me about her not leaving one) you could tell it was a story they'd heard before. The lack of a note did mean they returned a narrative verdict rather than suicide – that was a technicality, they told me. What difference did it make how they categorised it? I had you to think of and just wanted it to be over. Chloe had told me – us – how it got to that point and, hard as it was, I had to accept it.

They asked me about the father. I told them I had no idea, except that the relationship had broken down. What was the point of finding him? What good would it have done? She was sixteen so it was just the right side of legal. How could anyone prove the circumstances one way or the other? The boy could have plied her with drink and taken advantage of her. She might have told him she was on the Pill when she wasn't. Obviously that wouldn't have been true but that's beside the point. It would have been claim and counterclaim. I had a horrible vision of the boy's lawyer dragging Chloe's name through the mud. What if he'd been 15? Underage? A lot of nasty stuff might have reached your tender ears sooner or later. Imagine if the boy said he told Chloe he wanted her to keep the child and she got rid of it to spite him? I KNOW it wasn't like that. I'm sure the obvious was the truth – he got her pregnant and abandoned her, not caring a jot. But think of the horrible things that might have been suggested if it had all become public She'd lost her life, I couldn't bear the thought of her memory being stained too.

I'm not sure if the police ever spoke to him. It would have been easy enough for them to find him. She switched off her phone that day and threw it away somewhere. It was never found as far as I know. But they could have looked up the records, the calls, the transcripts of texts. I told them flat I didn't want to see any of that.

It was a bit odd how she signed off, don't you think? The overdose killed her. No one said anything about a fever. 103 is burning up, and that's not how she was when I found her. I dug round the issue as much as I could but I was limited by being determined to keep her last words private.

As for going to paradise, I'm glad she went thinking there was a better place. I thought she was like me, strictly births, marriages and funerals when it came to churchgoing. She never said anything to me about religious belief, finding God or whatever. Then again, they do say even diehard atheists often say a prayer when they know their time's nearly up. Hedging their bets … I can't say I won't do the same!! Anyway, we'll never know now, but if she went feeling comforted, that gives me comfort too. And you, I hope.

Well, my darling, I've rambled on long enough so I'll finish now. I hope *grandad lives to a ripe old age and you don't get to see this letter for many a long year. In case you haven't already, make the most of life, grab every opportunity, don't waste time on regrets. Be happy. Be amazing. Most of all, be your wonderful self!!!*

Love, Mum xxx

114

So there they are, my mum and my sister. Whatever sense of them you get through those letters, they were ten times more brilliant in real life. Chloe telling us there'd be trouble if we didn't do the whole grief thing – that was so her. And trust Mum to get a dig in about that cider binge. She played hell with me over that alright.

Can you see what she missed? Mum, I mean? It's not really a surprise. She never liked school, she said. Left as soon as she could, got a job in a shoe shop and took up with Chloe's dad. Regretted it later, of course, which is why she wanted us to make the most of our education. Always said she'd do a uni course one day as a mature student. Once we'd flown the nest, she reckoned she'd go off and be a mother hen on some campus. Never happened of course.

There was no fever. Chloe wasn't running a temperature. 103 degrees is the title of a Sylvia Plath poem. Mum wouldn't have known that. Wouldn't have known that Plath wrote it just before she gassed herself in 1963. Her husband, the poet Ted Hughes (surely you've heard of HIM!), had left her for another woman. She wasn't pregnant like Chloe was but she did have two young kids. She taped up the door so the gas couldn't escape into the room where the children were. Don't you see? Chloe was replicating the scene, except we had an electric oven so that bit was just for show. The poem ends with Plath describing an ascent to paradise. I've no idea whether Chloe had "found God" or any of that stuff. I doubt it. I think it just fitted her big dramatic exit neatly, though she might have realised that it would make things a bit easier on mum. Win-win.

I couldn't leave it like that. I understand why mum did, when it was all so raw and she had me to think about. It was easier for me. I had time. Money wasn't an issue. And I had a lot more hate in my heart than her. All the ingredients to put things right.

It wasn't hard to find him. Talk to Josie Hudson, she'll fill you in. She lives up Crediton way. She and Hannah – Chloe's other closest friend – didn't tell mum the full story. For instance, that the "boy" was actually twenty-four. They knew he was called Ben, and had even seen him from a distance when he picked her up from school. Josie said Chloe had been more distant with her friends since that Christmas. Not a change for the better either because she got full of herself, forever making comments about everyone at school being immature. Not like her precious Ben.

And she did tell them about the pregnancy. Told them before him. She was excited, full of it. Study was going on hold while she set up home and became a mother. She just had to pick the right time to tell her mum, Josie remembers her saying.

Then it all went wrong. She told him, thinking he'd be as pleased as she was. He said he didn't want to be a father, and as far as he was concerned the relationship was done anyway. He told her to get an abortion, which was best for her. Who'd want to be tied down with a kid at seventeen? Said he'd help pay for her to get rid of it. Like he was doing her some great favour.

This was just before Chloe died. Maybe the Friday before, Josie said, but she couldn't be sure.

I didn't bother tracking Hannah down. Josie hadn't seen her for years, but I was pretty sure she wouldn't have been able to add anything extra. I started going through Chloe's stuff instead. Mum had done what a lot of people do, left her things untouched for ages like a shrine, then suddenly boxed it all up in a whirlwind one weekend, except for the clothes, which she took to a charity shop. Those boxes eventually went to grandad's – my house now – and I trawled through old family photos, things she'd made at primary school, favourite toys ... Sorry, rambling again. Cut to the chase. Fast forward to her fifth-form exercise books. Random scribbling in the back of one of them. A name repeated over and over. Chloe Fuller. Chloe Fuller Chloe Fuller. Chloe Fuller.

My sister, practising what she expected would be her signature one day soon.

115

24+11 = current age. Full name. Facebook. I soon had Ben Fuller in my sights. I had no real plan at that point, just hung around getting a feel of things. Pretty wife. Two young children. Those three were all innocent, but so was the nephew or niece I might have had. Those three deserved better than Ben Fuller. They had a right to know.

I followed him to work a couple of times, him and his builder mate. Then I followed her one day when she was out with the kids. On the spur of the moment I snatched a doll from the pram rack when she was distracted, giving it back as though it had fallen off accidentally. We got talking. Had coffee. I got on well with her – she's called Zoe – and made a fuss of the children. That part was all genuine. In other circumstances we might have become mates.

I introduced myself as Carly Fitzroy. That was the only thing I did plan. Carly just because I liked the name. Fitzroy because that was the road where Sylvia Plath was living when she killed herself. My own little poetic flourish, you could say.

Zoe offered me a babysitting job. A way in. Better than I could have expected. But I still had no idea what I was going to do.

Then I met him, while they were getting ready to go out. Loud. Full of himself. Full of shit. Shirt tight on the chest, unbuttoned at the neck, flapping over his paunch. Dirty fingernails. Undressing me with his eyes. Made my skin crawl. They were paying me six quid an hour, extra past midnight. I was going to make him pay a lot more than that.

It was almost as though they were trying to make it easy for me.

English and drama are my thing, so I spotted the camera they used to spy on me almost immediately. Not one of the pro-level ones Perry and I used in the studio (he was on the same course as me, did I mention that?) – just a shitty cheap recorder. Then, just like with the doll, I took a gamble. A calculated risk, because over coffee when I first met Zoe, she said something about being hopeless with tech. I showed her on her iPhone where all her passwords were saved and explained about tethering. Easy stuff she didn't know. So I guessed he was in charge of setting up the camera, keeping watch on the new babysitter to see if she was up to scratch. Of course, they might have reviewed the footage together, or he could've cued it up for her. Like I say, it was a gamble. If it hadn't paid off, if they'd told me to piss off after watching it, I'd have just found another way. Crashed my car into his. Maybe even run him over, who knows?

But I didn't need to consider that. Plan A – yes, a plan was taking shape now – had a good start. I gave the lecherous bastard a floor show. My drama teacher would have been proud. Right up there with Meg Ryan in When Harry Met Sally, *if you get the drift. I pretended to get a FaceTime call from my boyfriend and was performing for him. But all the while it was for Ben Fuller's benefit. If I'd been a bit younger they'd have called it jailbait. I liked the jail bit.*

I waited. No call. No irate Zoe on the phone telling me how disappointed she was, how I'd abused her trust. She hadn't seen it. On to round two, upping the stakes.

Perry didn't want to do it. I talked him round. We'd been dating for a year until I ended it in early summer. I knew he wanted us to get back together and I used that. I used it shamelessly. Come and play this walk-on role, I said, and we'll see. Dangled a carrot I never should have.

He played the part of Danny Croft, Carly Fitzroy's smug, superior boyfriend who pops round to see his girlfriend when she's babysitting. It was like a bad porn film. But I was convincing again when I pretended to give him oral with my back to the camera. Plenty to titillate Ben Fuller.

The grand finale had Perry – Danny – "noticing" that the camera was on. Cue big kerfuffle, searching for the off switch etc. Anyone watching the footage back now knew that we knew. Who was going to blink first? Me the embarrassed student or him the pervy voyeur?

Zoe was as chatty and cheerful as ever the next time she booked me. She clearly didn't have a clue. As soon as I saw him I guessed he'd seen it. His body language was different, he struggled to make eye contact with me.

I was always one step ahead of him. Booked a room that night in an apartment block. Surprise surprise, he offered me a lift home!! I suggested a nice little clear-the-air chat and he couldn't get through the door quick enough. So not only a perve but a dumbass too. Because that confirmed he'd watched the show. Seen two free performances and forgot to mention it to poor old Zoe. What an idiot! He could have played innocent, said it had been recorded over, that they would only have reviewed the footage if some incident had occurred. Instead he squirmed. And I reeled him in easy as you like.

I made Danny Croft out to be the bad guy. A controlling boyfriend who slapped me around. I had the bruises to show for it. Now that was particularly good make-up, a few tricks of the trade I'd learned on the course. Throw in some tears and it really was another Oscar-worthy performance if I don't say so myself.

I let him comfort me. I knew exactly what kind of embrace would look best on camera. Best for me, worst for him. My equipment was better than his, and better hidden. And I know all about camera angles. The pics I got from it were even better than I expected.

He thought it was all about the money. That I was a little wallflower accomplice in a blackmail sting. He agreed to pay 200 quid to make it all go away. You'll be able to find that cash withdrawal in his account. Handing the money over was another nice photo opportunity. Perry did the honours. He was still dead against it, but he did it for me, for the chance of us getting back together again. That was his last involvement, taking photos through that cafe window of Ben Fuller paying us off to stop Zoe finding out about his nasty little video habit. You'll see I've left copies out for you, and of the shots taken in the apartment.

I sent Ben those photos. "Danny made me do it" – that was the line. I texted him an impressive piccy of my bashed up face and said I was going far away, leaving Danny as he'd suggested. All I did was switch to another pay-as-you-go phone. Easy.

"Danny" told him the price had gone up to ten grand. I confess I went all dramatic again at this point, this time behind the camera. I photographed him putting the money in a bin in the local park. An envelope anyway. Just as well I wasn't after his cash because he tried to pull a fast one. It was obvious he would, but I did quite like the thought of him binning a small fortune before I sent Zoe the evidence, stuff to wreck that bastard's marriage.

I got a bit carried away by including a pair of my knickers with the pictures. The drama student coming out again, I'm afraid. That was stupid, a big mistake. It wouldn't have taken a Nobel Prize-winning chemist to find the grungy deposits on them were just flour and water. And if Zoe realised that bit was fake, she might have believed him that the whole thing was a set-up. I don't know what happened to those pants but somehow I got away with that error.

That should have been the end of it. She kicked him out, I spotted that. No less than the scumbag deserved.

And then I found out Perry was dead.

116

I saw him on Friday night. He invited me round to the flat. Cooked pasta. We drank a lot, and I'm sure he was hoping I'd stay over. I didn't. It wasn't that I didn't love him, which made it hard for him to understand. It was about me shutting people out when they got too close. I've had counselling. They say I have abandonment issues. My dad, my sister, my mum and now my grandad. All gone under different circumstances. I don't know if it's mumbo-jumbo or if there's something in it, but I have to admit it has a ring of truth. Get rid of people before they leave you.

That's a side issue. Perry's clever enough to know the score and we didn't talk about any of this on Friday. We did talk about an appointment he had that was never kept. Earlier that evening he was meant to meet someone at the motorway services, someone he was going to interview for the uni magazine he edited. It sounded a bit weird from the get-go, especially the bit about Banksy (the artist – you must have heard of HIM!!). The person who contacted Perry said he used to hang out with him when they were kids growing up in Bristol. Perry thought it was going to be some great scoop, disappointed when the guy said he'd broken down and had to cancel. I just thought the whole thing was strange. I mean, did you see that stunt Banksy just pulled, shredding one of his pieces while it was actually being auctioned? Genius or what? He goes to great lengths to keep his identity secret, yet this guy who contacted Perry out of the blue was going to give him the inside track on the young artist? When he could have flogged the story to a major for big bucks? Really?

Perry was more trusting. He just thought it was an old Bristolian wanting to share his memories of growing up in the city. Knowing the young Banksy was just part of a bigger picture.

I should have made more of it. It wasn't until I heard he was dead that I replayed that last conversation. Don't police investigating a crime ask if anything unusual had happened recently? Well that was unusual in my book.

So I followed it up. Perry had shown me the guy's messages and I remembered his name. Zbiggy Kuzminski. Not many of them on Facebook, not this side of Warsaw anyway. I recognised him straightaway. Ben Fuller's builder mate. There's loads of pictures of him and a woman I assume is his partner with Fuller and Zoe.

There's no coincidence here. I have no idea how Ben Fuller traced Perry. But he did. And he used this Polish mate of his to draw Perry out, then one or other or both of them did whatever they did at his flat. The bit you already know.

There's a rumour going round social media that the cut end of one of Perry's guitar strings punctured a blood vessel in his neck when he was knocked to the floor. And that he had internal bleeding too, from being punched or kicked. I suppose whoever defends Fuller will make a lot of the fact that he couldn't have known Perry was a haemophiliac. That it was a terrible accident. I can't bear the thought of him getting away with it, not again. He's got the blood of three people on his hands. Four if you include my mum, which I do. I'm counting on you to see justice done.

Emily Price
25 October 2018

117

She hadn't expected to fall in love with Topsham, not as they sailed under the grim M5 portal with an Aldi acting as gatekeeper; not as they passed rows of unprepossessing new-build clones thrown up by major developers in a pincer assault on the eyes from either side of the road. Reading her unimpressed thoughts that day, Perry had told Emily not to rush to judgment, to wait until the place had fully revealed itself to her. It wasn't far off a metaphor for their relationship, for he'd been glad that she'd given him the benefit of the doubt after a clunky first date, when he'd been too nervous to shine.

Emily parked her car just before the streets began to narrow, where the charm offensive began in earnest. She savoured every step as the road drew her past the quaint, characterful buildings that were now like old friends;

past the small independent shops that bucked the carbon-copy high-street trend. Past the red-brick properties that cohabited harmoniously with renders of pink and blue and cream. Past the burst of Tudor black-and-white, past a portico and railing-fronted house that wouldn't have looked out of place in Downing Street. Past the two beautiful churches that stood a stone's throw apart. She'd never had any desire to go inside either, and had as little use for the old red telephone boxes the place boasted. But she was glad they were there. Even the charity shops and Co-op had a grand elegance about them, and Emily was easily able to forgive the place its Shauls bakery.

On and on she went. And, like a clever magician, the town saved a *ta-da* revelation for the big finale: the Exe lapping at its flank; a trick that lost none of its power to impress no matter how many times it was performed.

Perry had brought her here not long after they'd become an item. He'd grown up in Dawlish, and knew the county's jewels a lot better than her. A suitor out to impress. After hours of mooching and exploring, during which time she'd announced she could see herself having Clara Place as an address, he'd taken her to a wonderful little Italian restaurant, where they'd blown out on bruschetta and linguine. Then they'd rounded off the evening with a last drink at the nearby waterfront pub. They'd lingered at the outside table long after the dropping temperature had pushed all but a boisterous group of youths indoors; long after their glasses were empty, drinking in each other and the glorious sweep of the estuary panorama.

"I did think about blowing the budget and booking a room," he'd said.

"Looking at the house prices in those estate agent's windows, that would probably be our only chance of a sleepover here," she'd replied.

He'd laughed at that. A joke about affordability, he noted, not an outright dismissal of his convoluted way of seeing if she was ready to sleep with him.

"I think I'll use the profits from directing my first smash-hit feature film to buy a place here. In fact, I might even set it here. I mean, you've got all the du Maurier stuff down in Cornwall, *The French Lieutenant's Woman* up the road the other way in Lyme Regis. What do you think?"

"OK, but I think a car chase would be out, unless it's all in first gear."

He'd roared at that.

"You'd be the leading lady, obviously. They haven't had any star actresses round here since Vivien Leigh so they must be ready for some new talent."

"Well I *de-clare!*" she'd said Southern belle-style, for the umpteenth time since seeing the *Gone With the Wind* star's memorabilia at the local museum.

"Thanks for coming," Perry had deadpanned. "We'll let you know."

It was dark now. She'd shied away from all the artificial pools of light, keeping to the shadows, altering course if she saw another person approaching. She would have liked to drink a final gin and tonic at that same table she and Perry had first occupied, just over a year before. But, no. She didn't want staff or patrons recalling her presence. She didn't want to feed the gossipmongers or those left wondering if they could have saved her. Not that anyone would have had anything to feel guilty about, but there's always an element of *if only I'd known* ...; a hypothetical that bore down on her with a weight that was utterly insupportable.

Skirting the pub, passing the forest of masts in the boatyard, she reached the secluded pathway that was her destination. Hesitating as a dog walker came into view, she installed herself on one of the benches overlooking the river front, pulling out her phone to feign a call. He'd remember her, for he'd had to rein in the pug as it trotted over to sniff at her legs. It wouldn't take the police long to realise Emily Price made no call, left no last message to the world.

Through the gloom she could see her bench had a memorial plate and a small plant pot containing some kind of heather lashed to the side of the frame. Someone had enjoyed this view in life and had it marked in death. If she hadn't pushed Perry away, if he'd become a successful filmmaker, if they'd lived here happily for fifty years, then maybe the surviving partner in the relationship might have made this same kind of romantic gesture. But she'd rejected him, only to draw him back after her grandad left her that shattering bequest. Used him; there was no other way of putting it. Nothing could dispel the image of him taking those fatal blows from Ben Fuller, refusing to sacrifice her in order to save himself.

She'd collected the stones earlier, maintaining the casual look of a beachcomber as she popped them in her tote bag. If anyone noticed that there was no driftwood or pretty shells, that the theme of the treasure trove seemed to be weight and bulk, no one mentioned it. With an absorbent woollen coat, she wasn't entirely sure if they were absolutely necessary. Still, Perry would have appreciated the theatricality. Chloe, pregnant and abandoned, had presented a Sylvia Plath tableau at her death. She was choosing Virginia Woolf, who had lost a beloved sibling and her mother early in life, suffering repeated bouts of mental infirmity before wading into the River Ouse in 1941. Emily had gone further, leading a doting former lover to his death. Woolf 2.0. Maybe no one would get the reference, make the connection, but it didn't matter. There was no one left that she cared about.

Before her lay the stone slipway. It must have launched countless journeys, and now it was going to end hers. Leaving her bag on the bench, she hurried down the slope, stones chinking in her weighted pockets, not breaking her stride as she allowed the cold dark water to consume her.